THE ULTIMATUM

BY THE SAME AUTHOR

Hush
Hunted
Shiver
Sleepwalker
Justice
Shattered
Pursuit
Guilty
Obsession
Vanished
Bait

The Charlotte Stone Series

The Last Time I Saw Her
Her Last Whisper
The Last Kiss Goodbye
The Last Victim

KAREN ROBARDS

THE
ULTIMATUM

HODDER &
STOUGHTON

First published in Great Britain in 2017 by Hodder & Stoughton
An Hachette UK company

1

Copyright © Karen Robards 2017

A CIP catalogue record for this title is available from the British Library

Hardback ISBN 978 1 473 64733 6
Trade Paperback ISBN 978 1 473 64734 3
Ebook ISBN 978 1 473 64735 0

Printed and bound by Clays Ltd, St Ives plc

Hodder & Stoughton policy is to use papers that are natural, renewable and
recyclable products and made from wood grown in sustainable forests. The logging
and manufacturing processes are expected to conform to the environmental
regulations of the country of origin.

Hodder & Stoughton Ltd
Carmelite House
50 Victoria Embankment
London EC4Y 0DZ

www.hodder.co.uk

The Ultimatum is dedicated to my husband, Doug,
and my sons, Peter, Christopher and Jack, with love.

1

It was a small, one-story house nestled all by its lonesome on the shore of Lake Michigan, some fifteen minutes outside the sleepy little town of Port Washington, Wisconsin. Turned silvery gray by natural weathering, its cedar shingle walls blended well with the towering line of shaggy hemlocks that all but hid it from the narrow road that passed in front on the way down to the lake. Had it not been for the muted light glowing through one of the back windows—a bedroom, he guessed—John Kemp might well have overlooked the house in the darkness of the overcast, moonless night. Approaching the house on foot, backpack riding high between his shoulder blades, his hands buried deep in the pockets of his black Polartec jacket to combat the late-October chill, he listened to the wind whistling through the trees, smelled the slightly brackish scent of the lake and observed the acres of woods stretching into the distance with satisfaction.

The isolated setting couldn't have been more ideal.

He was there to kill everyone who lived in the house.

In the house's sparsely furnished back bedroom, four-year-old Beth McAlister lay snuggled up in her bed next to her mother, Issa, stubbornly resisting sleep. She was too excited, too nervous. Too happy/sad/scared. First thing in the morning they were moving. Her suitcase was all packed and waiting with her mother's by the front door. Her father was on his way to get them. He would arrive sometime during the night. Which was where the happy part came in: she really wanted to see her dad.

When he was around, things were better. Her mother was happier. Beth didn't feel afraid.

"'...she said, I did it all by myself. So...'" Dressed like Beth in flannel jammies, propped up on pillows against the headboard with a pile of covers pooled around her waist, Issa sounded tired as she read aloud from one of the stack of books Beth had kept out. The books were her favorites, and they would be packed away at the last possible minute along with Mousie, Beth's stuffed kitten, which crouched now beside the pillow on which her head rested. Beth badly wanted a real kitten, but they never stayed in one place long enough. Her mother always said, *One day.* One day they wouldn't have to move anymore, one day her dad would live with them full-time, one day—well, lots of things would happen one day.

Beth wished *one day* would hurry up and come.

She heard something—a faint crunch like a footstep on gravel—and looked away from the pictures in the book, past the lamp that cast a circle of light across the bed, toward where the plain white shade was pulled down over the window to block out the night. There was a gravel path out back that led from the patio to the lake. It went past her bedroom, and it crunched whenever anyone walked on it. Which it sounded like someone just had.

She sat bolt upright in bed, smiling.

"Daddy's here!"

"No!" Issa had stopped reading to look at the window, too. Now she sat up and dropped the book and grabbed Beth's arm when Beth would have scrambled out of bed to peek outside. "Don't do that. Stay here."

The look on her mother's face scared her.

Her voice dropped to a whisper. "Mommy, what?"

"I don't think it's Daddy. Daddy would come in the car." Whispering, too, Issa grabbed her cell phone off the nightstand. She started punching in numbers even as she flung her legs over the side of the bed and stood up. "No. Oh, no. There's no signal."

That was bad, Beth knew. The harsh note of fear in her mother's voice made her heart start to pound. Before Beth could say anything else, Issa turned, grabbed her up off the bed and carried her out of the bedroom. Her mother never carried her anymore—Issa said she was too big. Issa was small and slender, with straight black hair and brown eyes, while Beth was blonde and blue-eyed, tall for her age and sturdy.

"Who is it? Who do you think's out there?" Terrified now, Beth wrapped her arms around her mother's neck and hung on.

"Shh! It's going to be all right. Remember the hiding game?" Hampered by Beth's weight, Issa half walked and half ran down the dark hall past the only bathroom. She turned into the laundry room, her bare feet making quick slapping sounds on the linoleum. She didn't turn on the light.

Beth buried her face in her mother's neck. Issa smelled of vanilla and soap.

"I don't want to play." Her voice came out all squeaky because her throat was tight.

"You have to. We have to."

Built into the wall on the other side of the washer and dryer was a big metal cabinet where they kept detergent and stuff. Issa dropped Beth's feet to the cold floor as she yanked the cabinet open, then crouched down to sweep a bucket and some cleaning supplies to one side.

"Get in." Issa's face showed white through the darkness as she turned back to her daughter.

"Mommy, no!"

"Get in."

That was Issa's I-really-mean-it voice. Beth crawled into the cabinet. It was metal and crowded with all the things her mother used to clean with, but the cleared-off spot was big enough for her to sit in. She did, with her back pressed against the cabinet's side and her knees drawn up to her chin. Swallowing hard, she looked out at her mother.

"Please don't leave me." Beth knew she was probably whining, which her mother hated, but she couldn't help it. The cabinet was dark and cold and smelly inside, and she was really, really afraid.

"It won't be for long." Her mother's eyes were enormous shadowy pools in the darkness. Beth made a little whimpering sound, and Issa reached in to stroke her long, loose hair back, tuck it behind her ear. Her hand felt cold as ice. "We're going to play the hiding game just like we practiced. Remember? You stay in here and be as quiet as a mouse until I come and get you."

Beth could feel the tremor in her mother's fingers. She grabbed Issa's hand, held on tight. They *had* practiced, everywhere they'd lived for as long as Beth could remember, with herself huddled up in what Issa called a safe spot and being as still as she could be until Issa came for her and ended the game. But this was different. This was for real. This made her stomach feel sick.

"I'm scared," she whispered. "You get in the cabinet, too."

"Baby, I can't. I have to...go do something."

A muffled, metallic-sounding thud from the front of the house made them both jump. For a moment they stared in the direction of the sound. Then Issa yanked her hand free of Beth's grip and stood up.

"Mommy—" Frantic at the idea of being left, Beth started to crawl out of the cabinet. Issa shoved her back inside with both

hands. Beth looked at her in wide-eyed surprise. Her mother was never rough with her.

"You sit your bottom down and stay in there." Issa was whispering, but her voice was fierce. Her eyes bored into Beth's through the gloom. She pointed a warning finger at her daughter. "Don't you dare make one sound. You hear me? Not *one* *sound*. And don't you come out. I mean it."

Beth's lips trembled as she shrank back and sat.

"Good girl." Issa stood and went up on tiptoe to reach for something on the shelf above the cabinet. For a second Beth could only see her mother's lower half, her blue-flowered pajama bottoms and bare feet. Beth knew what Issa was after: the big shotgun her dad had stashed up there and warned her never to touch. When Issa sank back down and the shotgun came into view, Beth couldn't breathe.

"I'll be back as soon as I can," Issa leaned over to tell her and closed the cabinet door.

It was instantly dark, so dark Beth couldn't see anything. The quick pad of her mother's feet walking away told her that she was alone. She shivered, with cold and with fear, hugged her legs and felt tears sting her eyes. She wanted to cry, but she didn't. Crying made noise, and she was afraid to make noise. She opened her mouth over her knee, bit down. The fuzzy pajamas tasted weird and felt bad against her tongue, but it kept her from crying.

She knew what was happening: The Shadow had found them. She'd known about the Shadow for as long as she could remember. The Shadow was why they kept moving to different houses, different towns. The Shadow was why her mother drew the curtains tight every night as soon as it started to get dark. The Shadow was why they left whatever place they were living in only to go to the grocery, or the doctor, or, every once in a great while, to church.

The Shadow was always out there somewhere, hunting them, wanting to hurt them.

Now it had found them. It was here.

Beth hunched her shoulders, trembling.

"Who are you? What do you want?" Issa shouted. She sounded like she was still in the hall. Her voice was shrill with fear.

Beth pressed her mouth so hard against her knee that she could feel her teeth sinking into her skin. It hurt. She didn't care.

Bang.

Beth jumped. She knew that sound: it was the shotgun. Her mother had pulled the trigger. She'd heard it before, when her dad had taken her and Mommy out to a big empty field and shown Mommy how to use the shotgun.

"All you have to do is point and shoot," her dad had said. "This thing'll take out a moose. And you can't miss."

And her mother had pulled the trigger, and the big gun had made that sound.

Now, inside the house, Issa screamed, jarring Beth into jumping again and then squeezing her eyes tight shut. The sound tore through the air, through the metal cabinet, through Beth's heart and soul, before being abruptly cut off. Beth was so scared she felt dizzy. She bit down hard on her knee and hugged her legs and rocked back and forth. Tears streamed down her face.

Mommy.

For a long moment she strained to hear through the darkness.

"Beth." It was a man's voice, soft and kind of gentle, calling her. Her eyes popped open. She stretched them wide, but she still couldn't see anything, not even her own hands or legs or feet. Just dark. "Be-eth."

Beth froze. *He was in the house.* Every tiny hair on her body stood upright. Her heart beat so hard it felt like a hammer knocking inside her chest.

The Shadow. That was who was in her house. She knew it, she could feel it. The Shadow was a man, and he had found them at last.

Her insides twisted. Her mouth was all sour, like fear had a taste.

"It's okay, sweetheart. You can come out now." The voice sounded closer. The Shadow was walking down the hall toward her. She could hear his footsteps, hear the barely there rustle of cloth.

Mommy. Where are you, Mommy?

"Beth," he called. "Beth, come on out."

If her mother was still out there with the shotgun, the Shadow wouldn't be walking down the hall.

Mommy—

More tears rolled down her cheeks. Her nose was running, but she didn't dare sniff. Lifting her head, she wiped her nose on her sleeve instead.

"Your dad sent me." The Shadow was outside the door to the laundry room. His voice sounded so close that she shrank back against the wall behind her and tightened her grip on her legs. Her breathing stopped. She trembled so hard she was afraid of making the cabinet rattle. "I'm here to take you and your mom to him. Come on, honey, we don't have much time."

Staying as still as she could, Beth stared blindly into the darkness. Her eyes streamed tears. Her nose ran some more. She wanted to go to her dad. She wanted it so much. But—

Mommy knew she was in the cabinet. Mommy would come and get her if she wanted her. The Shadow was trying to trick her.

Be quiet. Don't come out. She could almost hear her mother warning her. Shaking, she squeezed her eyes shut and tried not to breathe.

"Beth." The Shadow didn't sound so nice now. He was farther away—she could hear his footsteps moving toward her bedroom. "No more games. Come out right now. Your dad's waiting for us."

There was a rattle from her bedroom. She knew that sound: it was her closet door. When it slid open, it made a sound like that. He was looking in the closet, searching for her. He would check under the bed—

Cold little prickles of sweat popped out on her forehead. Mommy—he'd done something bad to Mommy or she would be talking and making sounds. If he found her, Beth, he would do something bad to her, too.

Should she try to run or—

"Beth, if you don't come out right now, you're going to be in big trouble. You don't want to be in big trouble, do you?" He was next door, in the bathroom. If she was going to run, she needed to go *now*. Or was it already too late? She heard him open the closet, pull the shower curtain aside, open the cabinet under the sink. If she moved, if she ran, would he hear her, too?

The laundry room was next. She was crying full-on now, muffling the sounds with her hands pressed over her mouth. Her chest heaved. Her leg muscles were so tight they ached. She wanted to burst out of the cabinet and run as fast as she could toward the front door as badly as she had ever wanted to do anything.

She pictured the long, narrow hall, the heavy, black-painted door at the far end of the living room. She would have to reach that door, pull it open, push out through the screen door that sometimes got stuck—

The Shadow was a grown man. He was faster. He would catch her.

She could hear him leaving the bathroom, walking toward the laundry room. Butterflies were inside her stomach. She felt freezing cold.

Mommy, what do I do?

Beth tried to pray, but the only prayer she could think of was *Now I lay me down to sleep* and that was no help.

"Beth." He was right outside the laundry room door. He sounded mad. The laundry room light came on. Inside, the cabinet was no longer pitch-black. Petrified, she realized that she could see the bucket and the cleaning stuff and the lines of brighter light around the door. When he opened the door, he would be able to see *her*. "I'm not going to—"

A cell phone rang. His cell phone, she knew because he answered it. "Yeah."

He was close, so close. She'd missed her chance to even try to run. There was only one way out of the laundry room, and he was standing right there in the doorway. When he quit talking on the phone, he would search the laundry room, look in the cabinet. Even though she knew he would see her the instant he opened the door, she pressed back against the metal wall, trying to be as small as possible, trying to disappear. Her heart pounded so loud that it sounded like a drum beating in her ears.

"I'm wrapping up now," he said into the phone. "Thanks for the heads-up."

He was walking again. Beth could hear him. He was heading away from the laundry room, down the hall, toward the living room and the front door.

"Bye, Beth," he called as he left.

He didn't look in the cabinet. He didn't find me.

He'd left the laundry room light on. She could see all the cleaning supplies, the lines of light around the cabinet door.

She heard the front door open and close.

She stayed where she was, frozen, listening.

Was it a trick? It might be a trick. He might still be in the house somewhere waiting for her to come out.

She didn't know what to do. She wanted to crawl out of the cabinet and run away just as fast as she could. She also wanted to stay right where she was, still as a rabbit when a dog was nearby.

Mommy. I have to find Mommy.

Taking a deep, ragged breath, she crawled to the cabinet door and pushed.

Boom.

The sound was so enormous that it knocked her backward, knocked the door closed behind her, shook the cabinet. It swept over and around her, expanding through the air and snatching her breath away and blowing out her ears.

A split second later the force behind what made the noise smashed into the cabinet, into *her*, like a giant wave. It grabbed the cabinet up and blew it skyward, higher than the clouds, it felt like, tumbling her around inside it like a sock in a washing machine and tumbling the cabinet end over end, too. There was a blast of scorching heat, an explosion of orange light and a terrible burning smell.

Screaming, she was knocked against the hard metal walls until at last the cabinet slammed into something solid and fell to earth, crushed like a soda can by the hand of a giant.

Beth never even knew when she hit the ground. For her, the world had already gone black.

Crouched on the side of a hill overlooking the destroyed house, Kemp surveyed the inferno he'd created with clinical detachment. He was almost finished: the people inside the house were dead. The job had been more trouble than he'd anticipated. The frightened, submissive woman he'd been expecting to encounter had fired at him with a shotgun, and if he hadn't jumped back, the night might have gone very wrong right there. As it had happened, though, he *had* jumped in time and she hadn't been combat savvy enough to take cover immediately after discharging her weapon. He'd been able to take her out with a silenced .44 round to the forehead while she was still holding her gun, so the whole thing had worked out. He wasn't all that sorry he hadn't found the kid. Shooting little girls wasn't really his thing, and blowing the house up with her in it had worked just as well.

He was facing what was left of the house now from maybe sixty yards away. The fierce orange glow of the leaping flames lit up the whole area, including the wooded hillside he was on. The heat actually felt good on this cold night. He'd been careful to choose a spot in the shadow of some tall pines so that no matter how bright the blaze got he wouldn't be seen. He took a minute out of the process of setting up to admire the giant bonfire that was hungrily consuming what little remained of the house's charred frame. He savored the fire's savage crackling, the sparks shooting upward of fifty feet high, the burnt-plastic smell of the C-4 he'd used.

Most of all he savored the sight of the headlights on the narrow road out front as they raced toward the destroyed house.

Just as his caller had advised him, the man of the house was on his way home.

Mason Thayer's eyes would be glued to the flames, his thoughts centered on the fate of his sweet little family, his training and instinct and reflexes subordinated to terror and grief.

The car reached the house and braked so hard it fishtailed. Kemp felt a surge of satisfaction. He'd come up with a way to take out the man everyone said was too dangerous to take on.

The wages of sin, he mentally taunted his target. Dropping down on one knee, he raised the sniper rifle to his shoulder, trained its sight on a spot about two feet above the top of the driver's door and waited.

The wait was only a few seconds. The door shot open and a man, tall and lean against the flames, leaped out.

Kemp smiled as he blew Thayer's head off.

Mission accomplished: he'd killed everyone who lived in the house.

2

There's a saying among grifters: if you're playing cards and you don't know who the sucker at the table is, it's you.

Bianca St. Ives was struck too late by those wise words as she fled up the ancient stone steps in the dark, dank, crooked stairwell as though her life depended on it—which it did. Her heart galloped from her headlong race to escape before what gave every sign of being a trap snapped shut around her. Her head spun from the horrifying discovery, made exactly two minutes, twenty-six seconds before, that she and the quartet of world–class criminals she was attempting to commit the robbery of a lifetime with were quite possibly the suckers at this particular table.

I'm not going down like this. The mere thought of it sent what felt like an icy finger sliding along her spine. Shimmying open the lock on the heavy metal security door at the top of Bahrain's Gudaibiya Palace's cellar stairs with a practiced jiggle of the pick she carried, she reached through the deliberately provocative slit in her tulle-over-silk skirt to clip the pick back into place high on her thigh. Then she pulled the door open, cast a quick look around and stepped out of the gray gloom of the stairwell into the dimly lit hallway.

The musty smell was replaced by the scents of roasting meat

and heavy spice. Of course. The large industrial kitchen was located directly to her left, on the other side of the wall.

No one around. Twitching the nuisance-y train of her shoulder-baring black evening gown out of the way, she carefully eased the door shut. Then she started walking, fast, but not so fast that it would raise suspicions if somebody happened to catch a glimpse of her. Given the high-profile nature of the black-tie event she was attempting to rejoin, and the proliferation of security guards as well as nearly undetectable surveillance cameras, it was impossible to be completely certain that there were no watchers in this staff-only area no matter how careful she was. The rapid *click click* of her elegant stilettos on the marble floor made her wince. The sound seemed preternaturally loud in the high-ceilinged, narrow space, but what could she do? Tiptoeing was a nonstarter.

As in everything in life, projecting confidence was the key to success.

Even while running for her life. No, *especially* while running for her life.

She was still finding it almost impossible to wrap her head around what had happened: the two hundred million in cash their crackerjack gang had joined forces to steal was already gone when she got the vault open. One disbelieving glance inside the steel-walled underground chamber and it had become staggeringly obvious that they had a disaster on their hands: the vault was empty. The mountain of bright orange money bags, each of which held one hundred thousand dollars in untraceable US dollars, that had been inside it as recently as six hours prior, was simply not there anymore.

Could anybody say *holy freaking screwup?*

Thump. The sound heralded the sudden opening of a swinging door a few yards in front of her. It was all she could do not to jump with alarm as a man unexpectedly emerged from the kitchen. He checked at the sight of her.

"Kya main aapki madat kar sakta hun?" he said as the door swung shut behind him.

Bianca just managed to keep walking toward him as her brain automatically adjusted to the language, which was one she was semifluent in. *Can I help you?* was what he'd asked her, in Urdu. Okay, not exactly threatening despite the frowning look he was giving her. Short and compact, he wore traditional Arab garb. His long, grizzled beard was bound into a neat spike with rubber bands. From his language, which was not that of the Bahraini upper class, and the fact that he was there in the restricted area where outsiders were absolutely not permitted, she concluded that he was most probably part of the regular palace security staff.

Thank God he didn't catch me coming through the door from the cellars, she thought even as she shook her head as though she didn't understand. Urdu was not a language that her alter ego would be expected to know. Doing her best to look both apologetic and clueless, she said in English, "I'm looking for the ladies' room."

Fortunately for her, men rarely suspected attractive young women of anything nefarious. His eyes slid over her once more, this time with barely veiled appreciation. Then he gestured toward the gilded, arched double doors that had been her goal all along. "Go back into the ballroom. There is a ladies' restroom along this wall to the right."

This time he spoke in English, too.

"Thank you."

Giving him a drippingly sweet smile, she glided past him and slipped back into the packed ballroom, trying not to look as agitated as she felt.

They must have known we were coming. That terrifying thought snaked through her head as she inserted herself into the crowd of laughing, chatting partygoers and started making her way toward her chosen exit at the far end of the room. Her stomach churned with the force of it. It opened up so many harrowing possibilities that her blood ran cold.

The plan had been to take the money, replace it with identical bags filled with counterfeit bills and close up the vault again so no one was aware that a robbery had occurred. Her role had been to get herself invited to the ball that was taking place in this, the palace above the hidden vault, obtain by whatever means worked (she'd used a combination of charm, sex appeal, carefully researched knowledge of the mark, sleight of hand and good old-fashioned double-sided tape) the key, the code and the fingerprint necessary to access the vault, and open it. She had done so, and would have returned to the ballroom at that point to deflect any possible suspicion from herself while the others carried off the cash, but the entire carefully thought-out plan had crashed and burned as soon as she'd beheld the empty vault.

For a terrible moment she'd been immobilized. Then every instinct she possessed started screaming, *Get out*. One of the rules that had been relentlessly drilled into her head over the course of years of training was *Don't be a hero*. Which, as she had learned the hard way, meant save yourself first, and at the expense of everybody else if necessary.

She was now on her way to safety. She had the cover of the conversation and noise and activity in the ballroom to mask what she was doing. It wouldn't slow her down; it posed no additional risk. That being the case, she seized the opportunity to alert her confederates that the night had just gone horribly wrong.

"They're out of shrimp." It was all she could do not to scream that prearranged signal to abort the robbery into the burner phone that was her emergency means of communicating with her father, Richard St. Ives. Though right now, as head of their team and the operation's mastermind, he was using the false identity of Kenneth Rapp. What he'd been expecting to hear, what she would have said once she'd gotten the vault open if everything had gone according to plan, was "The champagne's Krug, and it's divine." The code was necessary because surveillance was unpredictable. Even in the absence of cameras, remote scanners or other types of listening devices were often able to pick up conversations at a considerable distance. Thus once an operation started, they communicated only when absolutely necessary, and they never, ever said anything during a job that could alert authorities or anyone else who might be listening to what was going down.

"What did you say?" Richard's deep, cultured voice was sharp with shock.

"They're out of shrimp," she repeated. Clouds of expensive perfume, released as she nudged her way past pockets of chatting guests, made the air seem thick. She was having trouble finding enough breath to get the words out. *"They are out of shrimp."*

"I understand." Richard disconnected abruptly: message received.

The specially configured burner phone now became a liability. Bianca felt like a kid playing hot potato as she looked down at it clutched in her hand. She pushed a button to wipe its memory. Unfortunately, there was no convenient trash can or other place in which to dispose of it in sight. Dropping it back into her evening bag to be dealt with later occurred to her, but that created a loose end that might come back to bite her. It was always possible that, even turned off and wiped, the thing could still be emitting a signal that might allow someone to track her.

Next order of business: find somewhere to ditch the damned phone.

Turned out that under the circumstances the best place to dispose of it was in the pocket of a tux, she concluded as she threaded her way through more layers of densely packed guests.

Brushing past the elderly gentleman whose jacket she'd targeted, Bianca neatly deposited the phone in his pocket. The man kept right on talking without feeling a thing. No surprise. She was *really* good at— She nearly stopped dead. She nearly gasped.

He was there.

Her father's sworn enemy stood almost directly in front of her, his head turned a little away as he said something to a beautifully dressed woman on his left. Bianca's throat went tight as her eyes fixed on the hawk-like nose, the heavy bone structure of the face, the thin mouth and narrow dark eyes beneath bushy gray brows, the thinning dark hair, the swarthy, pockmarked skin. It *was* Laurent Durand—there was no mistake. He was close to her father's age of sixty-four, but while Richard was tall and elegant, the ultimate silver fox, Durand with his burly body and dour expression looked like the gendarme he'd once been, even in a tux.

Her heart stuttered before ramping up to a thick, slamming rhythm. That she managed to keep moving and let her gaze slide past him as if he was of no more consequence to her than any other guest was solely due to a lifetime's worth of practice in keeping her cool. The sight of the French Interpol agent, champagne flute in hand as he made himself at home among the black-tie crowd, was a blow almost as stunning as the empty vault had been.

Careful not to look at him again, she altered her path to give him a wide berth while at the same time picking up her pace. On autopilot now as she hurried toward the exit, Bianca was still in the process of officially if silently freaking out at Durand's presence when it hit her with all the force of a baseball bat to the head. *Holy hell, we've been played.*

Whatever had happened to the money, whoever had it now, she and her team had been set up to take the fall.

It was the only thing that made sense.

Durand had been trying to catch her master-thief father in the act for as long as she could remember. Under the nom de guerre Traveler, apparently bestowed on him because no one in authority was quite sure of exactly who he really was, Richard was a legend in the circles of those elite criminal and law enforcement entities who knew he existed, who followed his crimes, who admired and/or hunted him. He was on every major most-wanted list in the world, including several that ordinary people had no idea even existed. He assumed a different identity for each job, and the list of his aliases was long. He was credited with some of the biggest robberies, cons, swindles, etc., of the past twenty years, many of which he'd actually been responsible for. He'd never been formally charged with a crime, never even been arrested, yet his reputation was such that he was automatically a suspect in any big, well-planned, successful operation that went down.

Exactly when and how he'd become Durand's Holy Grail Bianca didn't know, but that was what he was. She'd been taught to fear him like a mouse does a cat.

Durand was there, and the money was not.

It can't be a coincidence.

She could only conclude that Durand had somehow become aware of tonight's intended robbery and was there to oversee what he was expecting to be the takedown of his career. His men might very well be closing in on her *now*.

The thought made Bianca's palms sweat. Her breathing quickened. Her skin prickled, as if predatory eyes were suddenly boring into her from everywhere. It was all she could do to prevent herself from casting spooked glances all around.

Chill out, she ordered herself. Durand wasn't going to catch them with the money for the simple reason that they didn't have it.

Didn't matter, she realized grimly a couple of long strides

later. The money was gone, the team of thieves of which she was a part was on the premises and Durand could pin the crime on her father and the rest of them while whoever really had the cash made off with it scot-free.

It was the perfect crime. Only, it was someone else's perfect crime.

Go. Go. Go.

For all of their sakes, she couldn't allow herself to be caught.

Battling equal parts fear and fury, she called on every ounce of experience she'd acquired over a lifetime's worth of dealing with dicey situations to help her remain outwardly composed as she reached one set of the tall French doors that led from the ballroom to the terrace and pushed them open. Four dozen yards and a flight of twenty-three descending steps were now all that stood between her and escape.

After the air-conditioned chill of the ballroom, the wall of baking heat that she burst out into was welcome. Flames from the scented flambeaux set into sconces on the terrace's stone balustrade lit up the night. The bittersweet smell of frankincense-infused smoke blew toward her on the hot breeze, which was a mild precursor to the strong, sand-bearing *shamal* winds that were a feature of the months that would immediately follow this date in late May. Beyond the palace gates, traffic was still heavy on Bani Otbah Avenue. Lights, from cars, from offices, from the windows of the blocky apartment buildings that housed most of the city's residents, from the King Fahd Causeway bridge that linked Bahrain to its closest neighbor, Saudi Arabia, testified to the fact that the prosperous, well-populated city of Manama continued to bustle even as midnight approached. Ultramodern skyscrapers towered above the spires of ancient minarets against the star-studded night sky. The murmur of the sea could be heard beneath sounds of traffic.

Rushing across the terrace without, she hoped, giving the

slightest appearance of rushing, she barely noticed any of it. For once, the exotic beauty of her surroundings was lost on her. Her focus was all on the enormous stone lions that crouched with their backs to her, guarding the head of the stairs: her immediate goal.

We've got to get gone. Her pulse thundered with the urgency of it even as she silently counted down the remaining distance. *Thirty-two yards, thirty-one...*

Whoever was behind this could have found out about their plans, tipped off Durand to his old enemy's intentions and taken the money themselves.

Or maybe the whole thing had been a setup from the beginning. Maybe Durand had arranged it. Maybe the money had been bait, designed to lure her father and their team in and then moved for safekeeping before they could steal it. Maybe the only reason law enforcement hadn't been downstairs waiting in the vault when she'd reached it was because at the last minute Richard had shifted the entire operation forward by exactly one hour so that he could get back to England in time to see his other daughter—Bianca's seven-year-old half sister, Marin, who had no idea Bianca even existed and whom Bianca had never officially met—perform in some ridiculously cheesy little-girl dance recital and Durand had somehow missed the time-change memo.

Forget about the heat. Bianca felt cold all over again.

No way were they going down for something they hadn't even actually done.

Twenty yards. Nineteen...

Theft in Bahrain was punishable by a public lashing. Many of those upon whom the sentence was carried out didn't survive. Picturing it was enough to make her dizzy, which was stupid and counterproductive and something she absolutely did not have time for.

Reminding herself of why she really didn't need to worry about that particular fate provided a quick cure. Given the dirty nature of the missing money, it was unlikely that, if captured, any of them would live long enough to go to trial, much less come face-to-back with a lash. They'd be murdered within the hour to keep them quiet about what they knew.

She made an unamused sound under her breath. What was that saying about dark clouds and silver linings?

"Miss Ashley!"

Every tiny hair on the back of Bianca's neck shot upright. Jennifer Ashley was the name she was currently using. Without looking around or slowing her stride or giving any indication whatsoever that she'd heard, she pulled her small compact out of her evening bag, flipped it open as though to check her makeup and used the mirror to identify the man calling to her, *chasing* her, as one of the prince's personal bodyguards. Her stomach clenched. This could not be good.

He was close. Too close, head-and-torso-filling-up-the-mirror close, his heavily accented voice sharp and distinct as it cut through the waves of music and laughter and conversation that spilled from the French doors he'd left open behind him. Oh, God, she needed to *move*, without making it look like she was running away.

Snapping the compact closed, she thrust it back into her purse and lengthened her stride, silently cursing her four-inch heels for slowing her down.

"Miss Ashley, stop!"

Her skin crawled. He was catching up fast, she could tell from his voice.

Two yards. One...

The stairs were right *there*.

Reaching the backside of the lions, she picked up her full skirt

with both hands in preparation for a hasty descent to the limo—
her limo—that was at that very moment pulling up below.

"Miss Ashley!"

A hand clamped onto her arm.

3

Bianca's heart lurched. Her stomach plummeted.

Making like Cinderella and fleeing the ball before the clock struck midnight, when the security guards were scheduled to make the next of their every-thirty-minute checks of the now-empty vault, at which time they would inevitably discover that the money was missing and raise the alarm, had seemed like the best thing to do at the time, she reflected grimly as the body-guard's meaty hand tightened around her bare, slender upper arm, forcing her to a halt only a quick run down a flight of stairs short of freedom. But then again, Cinderella hadn't had to contend with the mother of all disasters combined with a Mossad-trained bodyguard coming after her as she tried to slip away from the ball.

And Cinderella's life hadn't been on the line if she didn't quite make it out of the palace, either.

In hindsight, Bianca thought in the eternity-long-seeming split second she had before she needed to react to being grabbed, maybe it would have worked out better if she'd simply gone ahead and returned to the prince's side and tried bluffing things out until she could excuse herself. After all, she didn't *know* the prince knew that she was there to rob him. In fact, she didn't know for sure that he'd been robbed. Maybe he'd simply had the money moved. Maybe this was all just a Mount Everest–size misunderstanding.

Yeah, and maybe she was Little Bo-Peep, too.

The thing was, Durand was there. And her instincts were screaming at her that this whatever-it-was was directed at her father, their team, herself—and it was bad. As in, potentially fatal.

The fingers clamped around her arm dug in painfully. Bianca gritted her teeth. There was nothing to do now but deal with whatever curveball came hurtling her way next.

Going for a gambit from the wide-eyed, innocent blonde playbook, and never mind that tonight her hair was a sexy, shoulder-length fall of flaming red waves, she whipped around as if startled at the contact, shot her captor an alarmed look and gasped, "Who are you? What do you want?" while making a deliberately feeble but hopefully desperate-appearing attempt to free her arm.

No surprise, he didn't release her. She could have made him let her go, but going all ninja on his ass was just about the best way she could think of to blow her cover.

And blowing her cover was the last thing she needed to do. At least, as long as there was still a chance she could escape without doing it.

Besides, there were four more bodyguards behind him.

"His Highness requests that you rejoin him immediately." The bodyguard's grip on her arm eased. It was still meant to be unbreakable, she could tell. His bald head gleamed in the golden light spilling from the arched windows behind him. His large, bulky frame towered over her slender five feet six inches, which when she added in her shoes was actually about five-ten tonight and made him a solid six foot six. His evil genie face could have served as an illustration for the word *intimidating.* The fact that he and the other equally large bodyguards fanned out behind him were clad in immaculate black tuxedos did nothing to disguise the danger they represented. These were single-mindedly loyal men armed with deadly weapons. They would do whatever their master ordered, including killing her, without a qualm.

"His Highness sent you?" She infused her voice with what she hoped was just the right, squeaky combination of girlish surprise and relief. Instead of continuing to resist, she let her arm relax in his hold as if the notion that his accosting of her had occurred at the prince's instigation had gone a long way toward allaying her alarm. She knew that he was seeing a milky-skinned, fine-boned young woman in an haute couture ball gown complete with long black evening gloves and a small fortune in diamonds around her neck and at her ears. Even her wristwatch, anachronistic in this digital age but necessary to her line of work, was the centerpiece of a diamond bracelet that she wore fastened over her glove. Wide green eyes, carefully sculpted features and bee-stung scarlet lips completed the picture. She looked exactly as she'd meant to look tonight: beautiful, expensive, a fragile flower of high-end femininity. All of which was working for her. She could see it in his eyes.

Woo-hoo. The pretty wrappings were doing their job.

For now, much as it galled her, her best bet was to play Fay Wray to his King Kong.

His grip loosened even more. It was clear that he did not consider her any kind of a threat. Nodding in a silent affirmative, he said, "Please come with me, Miss Ashley."

"I was leaving. I'm feeling ill." It was worth a try, she thought as she swept a furtive, longing glance down the graceful steps falling away inches beyond her toes. The wide marble staircase exiting the palace looked like something straight out of Disney. So did the beautiful light pink palace itself with its pearl-colored, onion-shaped, artfully lit dome glowing against the midnight-blue sky. In front of her, the limo waiting at the foot of the stairs, the shooting fountain in the middle of the motor court and lush gardens and wide avenue lined with palm trees, the gilded palace gates and pale stone wall washed by the light of the three-quarter moon, all added to the fairy-tale illusion. Unfortunately, she didn't think she was looking at a fairy-tale ending to her night.

The rusted garbage truck that was her father and his crew's ride, the one that should have been carrying the cash away from the vault but was instead presumably still filled with the bogus bills they'd meant to leave behind, lurched into view on the side road that fed into the Al Fatih Highway from the palace's back gates. Trash was collected late at night in the city, which made a garbage truck the perfect vehicle for spiriting the money in and out. The three men inside the truck were on their way to the harbor, to the faux garbage scow that would take them across the gulf to Qatar, where a private plane was standing by to whisk them all away.

A corner of Bianca's mouth quirked upward in wry acknowledgment of the fact that her father was making his escape while she was caught up in the rapidly disintegrating web he'd spun. He would never wait for her. *Don't be a hero* was practically his mantra. Richard *always* landed on his feet, world without end. He was famous for it. Lucky for her that in the course of their long collaboration she'd become adept at the same thing.

Her gaze dropped automatically to her watch. Oh, God, she had just under twenty-five minutes to make it to the boat, which would be pulling away from the dock at precisely 12:10.

Be on time: that was another of the rules, and it was strictly enforced. Whoever wasn't at the extraction point precisely when they were supposed to be was out of luck. If she didn't handle this, manage it, fix it, quickly, she would be left behind to make her own way to the plane, or worse—if she missed that ride, too—home.

Which was a problem to worry about *after* she avoided being arrested *now*, or, alternatively, fourteen minutes, thirty-one seconds from now when the guards discovered the empty vault at midnight and raised the alarm.

"I am sorry. But it is His Highness's pleasure that you rejoin him," King Kong said.

Do they know who I really am? Do they know about my father, and the missing money, and the rest? Bianca could read nothing in his dark gaze. Flutters of panic curled through her stomach, which she instantly squelched.

If they did know, her best bet was to make a run for it. Now.

She calculated what it would take to break free of King Kong, make it down the stairs and into the limo and through the gates and—

It could be done, but not quietly. And in the wake of what she would have to do to get free, the hounds would be coming after her in full cry.

"I'm afraid I'll be poor company for His Highness, feeling as I do," she said. If she could talk her way out of this, life suddenly became way simpler.

King Kong shrugged. "I am sorry," he said again. "His Highness has sent me for you, and bring you to him is what I must do."

All righty, then. So much for talking her way to freedom. She could see in his face and in his body language that he meant to convey her to the prince by force if necessary.

Make the wrong decision here and she could die. If His Highness Sheikh Mohammed bin Isa Al Khalifa thought that she so much as knew about his ill-gotten millions, much less had planned to steal them, she was pretty sure she could kiss her fanny goodbye. Because His Highness couldn't afford to let anyone know about the cash in his vault, and that would be because he had stolen the money just as surely as her father had intended to steal it from him.

The personal fortune that Muammar Gaddafi was rumored

to have spirited out of Libya during the so-called Arab Spring in hopes of living out his life in cushy exile was more than a rumor, as it turned out. The money was not supposed to have ended up in Bahrain, in the hidden vault of an ancient palace, right beneath the noses of the US Fifth Fleet, but that was where it was.

Or at least that was where it had been until sometime less than six hours ago.

In the motor court below, the limo driver got out to open the long black car's rear door. He was one of her team, the fifth man as it were, and the plan was for the two of them to leave together. With the door open and his hand still on the handle, he looked up at her.

"Mam'selle?" he called. Despite a crash course in the language, his French accent was by way of the Bronx. That was why he'd been ordered to speak as little as possible while acting as her driver, but she doubted the bodyguards would notice. Unlike the chauffeurs and waitstaff who had been hired especially for this occasion and were all French nationals, the bodyguards were locals and, if anything, their French was probably worse than his.

Poised at the top of the long flight of stairs, Bianca met her confederate's gaze through the flickering shadows cast by the flaming torches that lit the way down. She was fairly sure that if she gave him any kind of sign, he would come running up the steps to her assistance, but that would only get him hurt or worse. Five-ten, well north of three hundred pounds, with dark brown frizzy hair and a baby face, Miles Davis "Doc" Zeigler, known as Terry Brown to everyone except herself and her father for this job, was an affable marshmallow of a computer genius whose many talents did not include anything approximating hand-to-hand combat. As she could think of no kind of computer magic he could work to extract her from her current situation, there appeared to be nothing he could do to help her. They were almost the same age—he was twenty-five to her twenty-six—but he'd been committing crimes on this kind of grand scale for only the past six months and change, when he'd been recruited onto their team for this one specific heist, instead of for most of his life as Bianca had been. From his ad hoc workstation inside the limo, it was Doc who had remotely disabled the motion detectors and vibration receptors and infrared sensors that had been part of the security apparatus protecting the vault. That, plus conducting electronic surveillance as needed, providing fake web histories for them all, vetting the web histories of those they came into contact with and driving the getaway car that would take himself and Bianca to the boat, was a bare-bones summation of his part of the job. The other members of the team—forger Thomas Findley and muscle Nate Grangier—were with her father and, as she'd just witnessed, safely away. She and Doc were the last.

And now the most at risk.

Backlit by the limo's interior lighting, Doc was wide-eyed and pale in the black chauffeur's uniform as he stared up at her from his place beside the open door, his awareness of the unfolding disaster visible, at least to her, in every rigid line of his body.

"*Ça va,*" she called back to him airily. *It's okay.* "*J'en ai pour une minute.*" *I'll just be a minute.* Now, there was an optimistic statement if she'd ever made one. In case he was having trouble translating her French, she warned him with a gesture to stay where he was, stay in character, stay cool, as she shifted her attention back to the frowning bodyguard.

"Whatever His Highness wishes, of course," she conceded with a smile, and a pointed look down at the thick-fingered hand digging into her arm just above the edge of her satin glove. When with only the slightest hesitation his hand fell away, she knew that her cover was not blown, at least not completely.

If His Highness had had any idea that Jennifer Ashley, the art expert whom he'd brought in to authenticate his Matisse collection, was an impostor who had in fact made his acquaintance and was attending tonight's gala for the sole purpose of relieving him of his ill-gotten fortune, King Kong wouldn't be treating her so courteously. She didn't think. Unfortunately, one never knew anything for certain when it came to interactions with megalomaniacs such as the prince.

It was very possible that King Kong hadn't been clued in as to exactly why he'd been sent to fetch her. It was equally possible that this semblance of courtesy was a ploy to keep her from panicking and making a scene until His Highness and his minions could get her alone. There were a lot of rich and influential people in attendance tonight. The prince might not want them to be upset by the sight of a screaming, struggling woman being dragged off to his dungeons (and, oh yeah, he did have dungeons).

Even more important, he wouldn't want his guests to know about the money in case she should start to babble before he could shut her up.

"Please come with me." King Kong's hand was back on her arm, but this time it was in the guise of a pseudo-gentlemanly cupping of her elbow.

Like she was fooled by *that*.

Making the call, Bianca allowed him to escort her back inside the ballroom. When she shivered as she stepped through the French doors she'd so recently exited, she told herself it was because of the renewed onslaught of air-conditioning. She could find no such excuse for the fierce pounding of her heart.

Tony Bennett—yes, *the* Tony Bennett, alive and in person— had taken the stage, which had been newly constructed at the far end of the ballroom for this particular event, while she was out getting collared on the terrace. He was crooning "It Had to Be You," one of her favorites. In the context of Music to Be Possibly Led to Your Death By, however, she discovered she wasn't liking it quite so much.

Ordinarily she would have stopped whatever she was doing to soak up the performance with pleasure. Tonight what it meant to her was that a large portion of the crowd was focused on the stage, which could be useful if at some point she decided she needed to cut and run, or equally not useful if the prince decided to have her discreetly clobbered over the head and carted off.

A singer and song she loved became background noise as her quintet of keepers escorted her through the crowd. She was hyperaware of her surroundings now, observing and mentally cataloging everything that might be of use to her. The ballroom was enormous, what seemed like acres of white marble and soaring ceilings held up by dozens of Doric columns. The intense, saturated colors of the paintings on display stood out vividly against the all-white background. Small knots of admirers surrounded each work of art.

Despite its size, the venue was packed to overflowing with a cross section of the jet-set version of high society, the nouveau megarich, minor royalty and a motley collection of celebrities, who mostly had been paid to appear. A wide selection of nationalities was present. Hijabs and kaffiyehs were less numerous than designer gowns and tuxes, but only because there were *a lot* of designer gowns and tuxes. Nick-worthy jewels were being worn by the yard.

The only windows were tall arches interspersed with the French doors at the far end of the room. Other exits led to inner corridors like the one she'd used to access the cellars. Not ideal for escaping. She noted the location of the security guards, all of whom were armed. The gentleman whose pocket held her phone was not far inside the entrance. He was nodding vigorously in response to something one of his companions was saying as he chowed down on what looked like a crab cake, still clearly unaware that there was a foreign object in his pocket. If he found it, *when* he found it, there was nothing that could connect it to her.

She could not see Durand, or the prince.

Not seeing them was worse than seeing them. It made her feel edgy, like she could jump right out of her skin.

She grimaced to herself. So much for "Ice Ice Baby."

"Please come this way." As they skirted the group that was murmuring admiration of the sapphire blues and jade greens of *Woman with a Hat*, King Kong indicated a narrow sliver of open floor space snaking away along the nearest wall.

"Certainly."

At least she *sounded* cool and untroubled. Guided by the hand gripping her elbow and flanked by the gorilla-size bodyguards, Bianca figured that at this point going where they took her was the only thing to do. She'd made her choice out there on the terrace. Still, she continued to try to identify every possible threat and exit.

Just in case.

The young, attractive waitstaff wove in and out among the crowd, offering drinks and canapés. Couples danced in the center of the room. Even where she was, walking so close to the wall that her arm practically brushed the cool marble, the crowd kept getting in the way. King Kong finally had to release her elbow and move in front of her to clear a path. For an instant after he let go of her arm, Bianca again considered making a run for it, but another hand belonging to another bodyguard captured her elbow almost at once. That and awareness of the four bodyguards still behind her discouraged her, as did the thought that if she tried and failed to escape, her situation would be made infinitely worse. There would be no easy way of coming back from that.

Keep your game face on: it was another one of the rules. She could almost hear her father's voice whispering it. The first time he'd said that to her she'd been six years old and the two of them—a handsome, well-dressed forty-four-year-old man with his blond-haired, blue-eyed, Alice in Wonderland looka-like daughter—were walking hand in hand out of a New York jewelry store where they'd supposedly been picking out a present for Mommy, who in reality by that time had been dead for almost two years. The bright blue bag containing the inexpensive locket they'd purchased had been clutched in Bianca's small hand. The numerous pockets of her specially designed dress had been filled with jewels Richard had lifted from the display cases. The manager had stopped them just before they reached the door, said, "Wait right here," in a stern voice and stepped behind a counter. Scared to death, horribly conscious of her weighted-down dress, Bianca must have started to look as panicky as she felt, because her father had leaned down to murmur in her ear, "Keep your game face on."

She'd managed to do so, the store manager had returned with a lollipop for her and she'd given him a big beaming smile in her relief before her father had led her on out of the store.

So, game face on one more time, twenty years later.

As Tony's gorgeous voice slid over her without even regis-tering, her gaze skimmed the beautiful people in their beau-tiful clothes who were laughing and drinking and eating and dancing, all unaware of this life-and-death drama unfolding in their midst.

She was searching for Durand. She didn't find him.

Not knowing his whereabouts was driving her around the bend.

"Where is His Highness?" Raising her voice, Bianca directed the question to King Kong, who was obviously in charge of the group of bodyguards. She couldn't ask for Durand; she ostensibly didn't know of his existence. Locating the prince was the next most reassuring thing.

King Kong glanced back at her and jerked his head toward the far right end of the ballroom, not far from the stage.

"There."

Looking through the throng of milling guests in the direction he indicated, Bianca caught a glimpse of the prince, a tall, portly man in traditional Middle Eastern garb. He was standing in front of one of the Matisses she had authenticated for him after having originally won his trust by approaching him in a Paris auction house and telling him that the painting he was getting ready to buy for millions was a forgery. She had known it was because, as part of the setup for tonight's debacle, she'd stolen the real painting and personally replaced it with the forgery not long before approaching the prince. Having already had it authenticated by his own expert, the prince had not believed her until a subsequent reexamination of the painting confirmed that it was, indeed, a forgery. After that, her bona fides were firmly established with the prince, and the upshot of the whole thing was that she had been invited here tonight to celebrate the first public showing of his collection.

Which had been her goal all along.

The crowd shifted.

Durand was standing with the prince. Their heads were close together as they talked in front of *Woman in a Purple Coat*.

The shock of it ran through Bianca like an electric current. Goose bumps raced over her skin. The sudden surging of her pulse made it pound in her ears.

The two of them knew each other. Of course they knew each other. What, had she ever really thought that Durand's presence tonight was some kind of terrible accident of fate?

Keep walking. Keep breathing.

As an Interpol agent, Durand didn't actually have the power

to arrest anyone. Instead he got the job done through local authorities—like the prince and his men.

A person less used to finding herself in deadly peril might have out-and-out panicked at that moment. Bianca didn't, because she had learned long ago that panic could get you killed. She did experience a rush of adrenaline, but what that resulted in was a focusing of her mind, a sharpening of her senses, a kind of revving up of her body. After all these years she was a pro, and in the face of what felt like extreme danger, her training kicked in.

Head up, shoulders back. Walk like you own the place.

Meanwhile, her mind worked at breakneck speed.

It was possible that neither Durand nor the prince had a clue about who she really was, had no idea that a robbery was going down, had met by chance and were simply discussing the painting. The prince had sent King Kong after her because he wanted Jennifer Ashley to clarify some point about the canvas or Matisse's technique.

Right. Keep dreaming.

It was possible that they were aware that Traveler had targeted the money in the vault but neither of them had any idea who she really was or knew about her connection to the crime in progress. They were still in the ballroom idly discussing the painting in front of them because they thought that the robbery would happen on its original timetable. In that scenario, the trap would still be in the process of being set. It was now nine minutes, sixteen seconds until midnight. If Richard hadn't moved things up, she wouldn't be heading for the cellars, and the surprise that awaited her in the vault, for another forty minutes, forty-four seconds.

Maybe. If the planets are aligned and the stars are in your favor.

It was possible that they both knew exactly who she was and what was happening, and she was being brought to them as a precursor to being hauled away, tortured until she spilled everything she knew and then finally murdered after some present-day proclamation of "off with her head."

That was the one she really didn't like.

Durand's primary target would be her father, not herself.

To her knowledge, Durand had never actually seen her father, who was a master of disguise, in any identifiable form. No clear pictures of Traveler were known to exist. Durand had also, to her knowledge, never seen *her.* The only other time she had seen Durand in the flesh was when she was ten years old and he was waiting outside a hotel where her father was taking her for a weekend outing (actually, a heist for which he had required her help) after picking her up from her boarding school. Bianca remembered the occasion well, because her father, who rarely used profanity, had sworn furiously upon spotting Durand and, to her great relief, abandoned his plan, returning her to her school and disappearing until he'd needed her for another job.

Durand's face had been emblazoned in her memory ever since.

Durand might not know that Traveler had a daughter, or that she was frequently part of his team. But he would know that Traveler had confederates. Her father kept an extensive dossier on Durand, including all known associates. She didn't doubt that Durand had an even more extensive dossier on Traveler. Would it include information about her, *pictures* of her? As Traveler's confederate, if not his daughter? She would be a fool not to assume it did.

The question thus became, would he recognize Traveler's confederate, or, alternatively, Bianca St. Ives, in Jennifer Ashley? Since the beginning of this job, she'd been in disguise, her features altered into exotic beauty by makeup and prosthetics, the color of her eyes changed by contacts, her luxurious mane of red hair a wig, chosen because the prince had a notorious weakness for redheads. She had a foolproof false identity in the art expert she was pretending to be. But was she willing to trust her life, her freedom and a whole host of other things she held dear, to the hope that Durand wouldn't be able to identify her, anyway?

No.

Bottom line: whatever the prince's motivation in having her brought to him, she could not come face-to-face with Durand.

Her body vibrated with barely suppressed tension. Time to shift gears.

4

Doing her *Crouching Tiger, Hidden Dragon* thing would probably attract too much attention, Bianca concluded reluctantly as her gaze swept the ballroom. Besides, given the abundance of guards with guns, she could wind up getting shot.

Not the outcome she was looking for.

Subterfuge was the key. Quick, dazzlingly effective subterfuge.

Surrounded by her goon squad of escorts, she was approaching a side-by-side pair of alcoves. What they were, basically, were shallow, dead-end corridors with a single door at the end. Those doors led to restrooms. Discreetly hand-lettered signs propped on gilded easels outside each alcove directed gentlemen to the left, ladies to the right. She had known the restrooms were there, of course. She'd memorized floor plans and photos documenting every square foot of the palace down to the location of each light switch and thermostat, just as she always memorized every possible detail connected with a job.

It was not in her nature to leave anything to chance. Preparation, she'd learned, was the key to success—and survival.

A tuxedo-clad waiter—handsome, dark-haired, twenty-something—wove his way through the crowd just a few yards away. Balanced above his head on the flat of one hand was a silver tray loaded with drinks: red and white wine in goblets and champagne in flutes along with various cocktails and liquors in their appropriate glasses.

Bianca's eyes widened slightly. What she was looking at was opportunity. It shouldn't be difficult to—

Right in front of her, one of the male guests stepped back to make room for the waiter, inadvertently getting between her and King Kong, blocking her path and providing her with the opening she needed. With the lightning reflexes that had been honed by a lifetime of having to react fast, Bianca bumped into the guest hard, careened away (not incidentally jerking free of the bodyguard's hand on her elbow at the same time) and stumbled sideways into the waiter.

"Ah! *Merde!*" the waiter yelped as she sent him staggering. The tray upended and, drinks and all, came crashing down on top of Bianca.

"Oh, no!" Ducking, she thrust an arm above her head in self-defense as a deluge of chilled liquid, maybe half a dozen crystal glasses and the tray itself hit her, light blows that caused no real damage. Jumping back to the sounds of shattering glass and clanging metal as everything subsequently smashed to the floor, she looked down at herself in feigned dismay. What previously had been the contents of the glasses rolled down the cascade of sequined ruffles that formed the outer layer of her skirt, soaking the tissue-thin material, dripping around her feet. "Oh, dear!"

Having scattered, the people nearest her were now exclaiming in a variety of languages as they came together again to gawk.

"*Verdammt!*"

"Would ya look at that!"

"Clumsy idiot!"

"*Ahmaq akhraq!*"

"I say, are you all right?"

"*Mademoiselle!* A hundred million apologies!"

"Miss Ashley!" Obviously caught by surprise, King Kong had spun around to survey the scene with consternation. She was free now, with no one holding on to her and a circle of gaping, tsk-tsking onlookers to provide a—brief and temporary, she knew—buffer zone.

Fortunately, the noise seemed not to have carried too far. Tony continued to sing, the band played on and only those guests in the near vicinity had turned to look. She could not see Durand and the prince through the crush of people all around her, but unless she was officially the unluckiest person on the planet, which at this point was not outside the realm of possibility, they were too far away to have seen or heard anything and would remain unaware that this little contretemps was going down.

"Ce n'est pas grave." *It's all right*, she comforted the lamenting waiter, who wrung his hands as he spouted a babble of nearly incomprehensible French at her. *"Accidents arrivent."* *Accidents happen.*

Swiping ineffectually at rivulets of what looked like red wine rolling down the front of her dress, she took a few more steps to the side, ostensibly to get out of the mess of broken glass and spilled drinks but really to put more distance between herself and the bodyguards. The smell of wine was strong. Spreading puddles of multicolored liquid made the marble treacherous underfoot; fortunately, her custom-made shoes had nonslip rubber soles. Everyone was stepping back, taking care. Gazes darted from her to the abashed, still-apologizing waiter to the floor.

She was now the center of a small open circle. Along with the milling onlookers and the scattered debris, the space the accident had given her provided a measure of protection from the bodyguards.

A lightning glance down told her that it was eight minutes, twenty-five seconds until midnight. Her breathing quickened along with her pulse. She mentally clamped down hard on both.

"My *dress*." Bianca started shaking out her skirt at the same time as she began to edge unobtrusively toward the restrooms.

Near-instant response to the airborne droplets: more space around her as everyone drew farther away.

"I have a hankie." A white-haired gentleman with a plummy British accent leaned forward to proffer it.

"Thank you." Accepting the monogrammed linen square, Bianca used it to dab at the splotches on her dress as she took a few more steps closer to her goal.

"Mademoiselle, que puis-je faire...?" What can I do? The waiter, sounding agonized, followed her.

"Range ce désordre." Clean up the mess. She just managed not to say it through her teeth. The last thing she needed was him calling attention to her movements.

The alcove where the ladies' room was located was maybe ten feet away on her left. She had to get past the alcove where the men's room was located to reach it. Still applying the handkerchief to her dress, she took care to keep as many of her fellow guests as possible between herself and the bodyguards as she edged away.

A stirring in the crowd nearby caught her and everyone else's attention. Some of the staff hurried toward them. One pushed a mop in a bucket. In a bit of good news, the bodyguards were distracted, glancing away from her in response to the bucket's rattling wheels.

Bianca broke for the restroom.

"Je suis vraiment désolé," the waiter called after her. *I'm really sorry.*

Bianca's shoulders tensed. His raised voice, to her at least, made it obvious that she was now some distance from him.

King Kong apparently caught the verbal cue, too. His head snapped around. His face tightened as he saw where she was, and that she was walking away. "Miss Ashley—"

Damn it. Bianca picked up the pace. Now she was fast-walking away.

"I can't possibly appear before His Highness like this. I'm going to duck into the ladies' room for a tiny moment and see if I can't do something about my dress," she called to King Kong over her shoulder. The man's pit-bull eyes widened.

"I do not think—" His tone made it clear that he was getting ready to object.

Bianca didn't give him the chance. With a bright "I'll be right back," she ducked into the alcove.

She walked so fast as she made for the white-painted ladies' room door that her long skirt swished behind her like an angry cat's tail and her legs flashed in and out of the thigh-high slit. A hand on the knob, a turn, a push, and she was inside and pivoting to face the door.

"Miss Ashley, *wait*—" King Kong barreled into the alcove after her, looking big as a semi, his hands outstretched to grab her even as she put her weight into closing the door. Approximately three long strides away, he was coming after her like a heat-seeking missile and closing fast.

Not quite fast enough, turkey.

The door thunked shut practically in his face, blocking him from her view. Securing the laughably flimsy lock with a twist of her wrist, she ignored her racing heart as she called through the heavy panel, "I'll be quick."

She was pretty sure she couldn't really hear him leaping across the last few feet of floor space, or the sound of his breathing as he fetched up on the other side of the door. Imagining him doing so, or standing there with his hand on the outer knob, only served to ramp up the stress hormones that were already pouring into her bloodstream.

She was under no illusion that he would have any real difficulty breaking through the door—one good kick would do it—but not without making it obvious, to her and any observers, that she was being taken to the prince under duress as opposed to being escorted courteously to rejoin him. Which she didn't think King Kong was prepared to do, at least not without clearing it first with his superiors. In any case, whatever he was or wasn't going to do, she'd bought herself some precious time.

It was exactly seven minutes, forty-nine seconds until midnight.

Oh, God, this was going to be close. When the empty vault was discovered, all hell was going to break loose. She needed to be long gone by then.

A comprehensive glance around confirmed what she already knew: it was a single-user restroom. No windows, no obvious way out except for the door she'd just closed and locked. If King Kong knew that, the lack of alternate exits should make him feel better because in theory he had her trapped. There was no way she was getting past him.

The room was about twelve by fourteen feet, as large as a decent-size bedroom and as opulent as everything else in the palace. The white porcelain fixtures were modern. The amber-veined marble walls and floor, the pink velvet fainting couch and the intricately carved gilt-framed mirror that took up most of the wall above the sink were not. Neither was the crystal chandelier that hung by a gold chain from the twelve-foot ceiling.

The room was cold as a refrigerator. The sandalwood-laced smell of potpourri—there the aromatic stuff was, in a little open-weave gold ball on top of the toilet tank—was strong.

Crossing to the sink, Bianca dropped the wine-stained handkerchief in the nearby trash can, then quickly turned on the taps so that King Kong, if he had his ear to the door, would think she was busy tending to her dress. For a moment Jennifer Ashley's reflection looked back at her: deep red waves framing a high-cheekboned, square-jawed, porcelain-pale face in which

Bianca's own delicately chiseled features had been altered just enough so that if her picture should happen to be run through facial recognition software the only hit would be to the fake but extremely convincing identity of the Yale-educated art expert she was pretending to be. Wide bottle-green eyes. Slight, sexy overbite. Dainty ears and long neck dripping diamonds. Fragile-looking collarbones and narrow shoulders above the curved neckline of her frothy dress.

Nothing but sweetness and light here, folks.

The only identifying mark that she was not able to change from identity to identity was a two-inch-long, fishhook-shaped scar on the underside of her jaw near her ear. It was faintly puckered and pinkish still, even though she'd had it for as long as she could remember. Covering it with makeup helped but wasn't foolproof. What made it a nearly nonissue was its location. Surveillance cameras were routinely positioned looking down on a scene. The scar was so far under the edge of her jaw that she had to tilt her head back to see it in a mirror. No lens was going to be picking that angle up.

All along, the intention had been for tonight to be Jennifer Ashley's swan song. The fact that the job had gone so monumentally wrong didn't change that. She would not be sorry to see Jennifer Ashley go. Holding the prince at arm's length while giving off enough of a sexual vibe to keep His Highness interested had been exhausting.

This wasn't the time to think that it had all been for nothing, or to dwell on the fact that they were going home (always presuming they got home) empty-handed.

She set her teeth against the gut-wrenching knowledge that, for the first time ever, they had failed.

So cry me a river. Only, do it later.

The doorknob rattled ominously.

"Miss Ashley—"

Turning her back to her reflection, Bianca snatched up a handful of the linen guest towels that were stacked near the edge of the sink and headed toward the fainting couch, which was against the opposite wall from the sink.

"Blast this red wine!" she exclaimed, confident that King Kong could hear both her raised voice and the water that still rushed from the taps through the door. "My dress is *ruined.*"

The gilt-framed fainting couch was shaped like a wave, with a low curled arm leading to an arching back ending in a high curled arm that at its top was approximately three and a half feet off the ground. Reaching the couch, surprised at its weight, she put her back into it and tilted it so that she could insert a guest towel under each leg (to make moving the heavy piece of furniture easier and to cut down on the noise as the legs slid across the floor) before dragging it into the position she needed: a few feet to the right.

"I will take you to one of the maids. They can see to your dress," King Kong called through the door.

"I'm handling it, thank you."

With the couch in place, Bianca reached up through the slit in her skirt to free the small but serviceable screwdriver concealed inside one of the narrow ruched straps of the black satin-and-lace garter belt she wore. A garter belt, she'd found, made an excellent tool belt for a woman in her line of work. Properly constructed and equipped, it was an indispensable aid to defeating X-ray machines, metal detectors and pat downs. Male security personnel were instantly agog when they discovered a garter belt, and the ridiculous amount of sexual steam the silly scrap of lingerie engendered in them seemed to fog their brains. The result was classic misdirection: their attention was focused on one thing, while something entirely different was going on right under their noses.

She had her garter belts specially made by a woman in Macau

she'd found through a serpentine tangle of connections. Officially the owner of a busy tailor shop that sold cheap custom-made clothes to tourists, SiuSiu Tseng had a select list of highly confidential clients with more exacting requirements. SiuSiu called them spy clothes, although to Bianca's knowledge none of her customers were actual spies. They all just operated on the wrong side of the law. Bianca's garter belts were lined so that an X-ray machine couldn't pick up the tools inside. The tools themselves were made of plastic polymers as strong as steel that were undetectable by even the most hypersensitive metal detector. Besides the screwdriver and lock pick, other custom-designed items included a combination hacksaw/pry bar and a stun gun, all wand-thin and miniaturized to fit in the straps that clung to her thighs. The stun gun's metal-containing battery was hidden inside the open metal clasp that fastened her evening bag; no surprise when a metal detector detected *that*. She removed the battery from the clasp and inserted it into the weapon once she was through security as needed, which tonight had been when she was on her way down the cellar stairs, because one never knew where one might encounter a stray security guard who needed to be instantly silenced.

The clips at the end of the dangly straps on her garter belt, the ones that fastened to the tops of her black fishnet stockings, also concealed essential items: a button-size flashlight, a locator beacon to be used only in case of extreme emergency because when turned on it obviously could be tracked, and two hundred feet of dental-floss-thin, two-hundred-and-fifty-pound rated cord that would spool out from a hook (the clip itself, which among other things was designed to serve as an anchor) so that she could rappel down as much as nineteen stories if necessary, a length arrived at by space considerations coupled with the theory that if her exit needed to encompass more than nineteen stories she could break through a high-rise window or find some other alternate means of descent by the time she, um, reached the end of her rope.

The fourth clip contained a tiny switchblade with a wicked, lethal blade.

Whoever it was who'd said *Never bring a knife to a gunfight* was dead (probably literally) wrong. It was more like *Never bring a gun to a knife fight*. A gun was a distance weapon. By the time it was drawn, aimed and fired, she could gut its owner like a fish. Not that she went around gutting people. But she *could*.

She liked to think her garter belts gave the Girl Scout motto of Be Prepared a whole new meaning.

An air-conditioning vent was now located directly above the repositioned fainting couch. As it was the only alternate means of getting out of the room, she was going into that vent if there was any possible way of squeezing herself inside.

5

Bianca knew where the vent ended up: the men's restroom in the alcove next door, a distance of twenty-two feet.

Clambering up onto the top of the high arm, she evaluated what she had to work with even as she flipped her small screwdriver into Phillips mode and started in on the screws.

The vent was not large, maybe a foot high by eighteen inches wide, but she was slim and agile and *had no choice*, which was the most important part of the equation. A slight additional degree of difficulty was added by the fact that the lower edge of the vent was about two feet above her head when she balanced on the high arm of the fainting couch in her four-inch heels, which meant that getting herself inside it was going to require some major acrobatics.

Fortunately, she was good at acrobatics, major or otherwise.

The air-conditioning system had been installed nine years previously. She knew that, just like she knew where the ductwork ran, just like she knew the location of every vent, just like she knew where the restrooms were and the exits and all about the warren of secret passages beneath the palace and every other thing she could possibly learn about the building, because it was her job to know. Her life, and the lives of her team, could hang on the minutest detail—see her current situation as a case in point.

The screws came out of the metal grate without much difficulty. Dropping them in her purse and tucking the grate beneath her arm, she scrambled down, slid the screwdriver back into its slot and, careful to make no telltale noise, hid the grate inside the toilet tank. Ideally she would have replaced the grate once she entered the vent so that it would be harder for anyone coming into the restroom after her to figure out how she had escaped from the locked room with the big beefy guy plastered against the door outside, but once she was inside, there wasn't going to be room to turn around. Hopefully she would be out the other end and gone before King Kong decided to burst through the door, but there was no way to be sure. Hiding the grate might keep him from instantly realizing where she'd disappeared to. At some point he undoubtedly would notice the grate-less opening, but it might take a while. In her experience people rarely looked up. It might buy her a little more time, and at this point time was the name of the game.

She was backing away from the vent to give herself a running start at it when King Kong rattled the doorknob again. Her heart kicked up a notch. With the goal of harnessing her body's natural reaction to danger and making it work for her, not against her, she exhaled. Mindfully.

Feel the air leaving your lungs…

It was a classic calming exercise that she did more as a result of her training than because it actually worked, which, in general, for her, it didn't. Patience, as it turned out, wasn't her strong suit.

"Miss Ashley, His Highness is waiting! We cannot spare any more time!"

Whoosh. Okay, she was officially airless. A glance at her watch told her that it was six minutes, thirty-two seconds until midnight. *Go.*

"I'm almost finished!"

Muscles already bunched in preparation for takeoff, she caught a glimpse of her reflection in the mirror.

Wait, stop.

Poised to run, quivering with the force of hastily aborted momentum, she looked down at herself in dismay. No way was she getting through that narrow metal chute in the gown she was wearing. While the bodice was sleek and formfitting, the skirt was as wide around as a Hula-Hoop. Crawling through the duct in it would be impossible.

A lightning flash from her fog-shrouded past hit her. Herself at maybe three years old huddled with her mother under a blanket on the well-worn couch in the living room of their small apartment. It was cold and dark outside, the curtains were drawn and the two of them were watching a Winnie the Pooh cartoon. She was giggling hysterically because poor Pooh, crawling headfirst through a hole, had gotten stuck when his backside had proved too big to fit.

Remembering made her mouth go dry, made her dizzy, as remembering anything from the very earliest years of her life always did. Much of it was a blur. She had vague recollections of being called something else—Beth McCoy or Mulloy, something like that. Blinking, she shook her head in an effort to clear it.

Never look back: another of the rules. She mentally grabbed on to it with both hands.

Wallow later. Survive now.

Given the size of her skirt and the size of the vent, she'd been on the verge of doing a Winnie the Pooh.

Bottom line: death by poufy dress just wasn't going to happen.

Swearing silently, one eye on the doorknob, which was twisting as King Kong tested the lock, Bianca ignored her still-elevated heart rate as she shimmied out of her gown. Everything else she left on. Her shoes were specially designed to leave footprints that misled about her shoe size, height, weight and the provenance of her shoes, because footprints could be almost as telling as fingerprints, which her gloves were intended to prevent. Plus the spike heels were specially hardened so that they could be used to, say, kick out a high-rise window or deal a kneecap a crippling blow.

"Please unlock the door." Frustration was obvious in King Kong's tone.

The wooden panel rattled ominously as she snatched her dress up off the floor.

"I have my dress off." Which had the advantage of being true. If he was thinking about bursting in, the thought of catching her in her underwear should be enough to give pause to a man whose view of women was as deeply conservative as she was guessing King Kong's had to be. "I'm rinsing it out."

Dress in hand, she sprinted on the proverbial little cat feet to the couch. Leaping back up on the arm, she crammed the dress and her purse into the vent, shoving them as far inside as possible.

She couldn't simply leave the dress behind. If all went well, she would be exiting the ballroom shortly. Doing so in elbow-length black satin gloves, skimpy black bikini underwear, a matching strapless bra, a garter belt, fishnets and heels would definitely attract attention, which was the last thing she wanted to do. Anyway, when she came out on the other side, the gown would serve a purpose. Like all the clothes she wore on a job, it was made to be functional in case a situation went south and a quick getaway was required. To that end, the gown was lined in lavender silk. Once through the vent, she would turn it wrong side out and put it on again, and anyone scanning the crowd for the redhead in the billowy black ball gown wouldn't find her.

Because by that time she would be a blonde in lavender.

Five minutes until midnight. Talk about cutting it close.

She could feel the anxiety leaking into her system, revving her adrenals, making her tight.

Forget about the time. Focus.

Clearing her mind of everything except what she intended

to do, trusting that the drumming of running water from the taps would be enough to cover any sounds that might otherwise make it through the door, she took off. Racing toward the couch, counting off the steps in her head as she went, she vaulted onto the arm. Launching herself upward, she flew toward the ceiling, jackknifed in midair like a champion diver, thrust her hands inside the vent, pressed her palms hard against the smooth metal sides for leverage and heaved.

She executed perfectly, shooting headfirst into the narrow opening and scraping belly-down along the chute.

Ouch. Her wig caught on something, nearly yanking the extremely well-secured accessory off, jerking her to a stop. Eyes watering from the unexpected pain, she managed to release the remaining clips and pull the wig off, freeing it from whatever it was caught on. She stuffed it up in front of her with her dress and purse, all the while kicking and scrambling as she dragged herself the rest of the way inside.

Losing the wig wasn't really a problem, she thought as she ran a quick, soothing hand over her stinging scalp and through her short cap of naturally baby-blond hair. She'd meant to take it off before reentering the ballroom, anyway. Although with the wig off, she could kiss goodbye any hope of continuing in the Jennifer Ashley identity. Which meant that her situation was now exponentially more dangerous. If she got caught, good luck bluffing her way out of turning from a redhead into a blonde.

So don't get caught.

Losing the wig might not be a problem, but her watering eyes, combined with the dust disturbed by her explosive ingress, *were* a problem. Her eyes stung and her vision blurred.

Keep going.

Blinking her contacts out and thereby changing her eye color from bottle green to crystalline blue as she inched along, she thrust them into her purse. *Leave nothing behind* was another of the rules.

The space was so confined that her elbows and knees were practically useless at providing forward momentum. Instead she had to wriggle like a snake in the squashed-flat version of a soldier's crawl. The metal compressing the curve of her rear and the sides of her arms and thighs was almost painfully cold everywhere it touched her skin. She was pretty sure she was collecting enough scratches and bruises to leave her marked for weeks. The frigid air continually blowing at her had a metallic smell, bore dust on it and made her want to sneeze.

Do. Not. Sneeze.

Her eyes continued to water. Blinking, she tried to clear her vision. She could hear nothing from the restroom behind her. She didn't know if that was because of the drumming of her pulse in her ears or the slight scratching sound her dress made as she shoved it in front of her or because of the insulating properties of the metal and marble with which she was surrounded. She would like to think that the reason she heard nothing was because there was nothing to hear.

The problem with that was, she couldn't hear the water rushing from the taps she'd left running.

The knowledge set her teeth on edge.

What was King Kong doing? There was no way to know. Everything she could imagine was counterproductive, so she shut that down. All she could do was scoot and slither and belly-crawl away as fast as she could while praying that "as fast as she could" would be fast enough.

Squirming past the spot where the duct she was in connected at right angles to another duct that ran directly to the ballroom, Bianca thought about trying to use the new channel to turn around so that she would be approaching the vent she meant to exit from feetfirst, which in theory would make getting out without cracking her skull easier. It would also give her the added advantage of being able to kick the vent out, because the screws on that vent would be on the outside, which meant she wasn't going to be able to reach the screws to unscrew them. But she didn't want to waste the time required to complete the maneuver, plus the advantage of being able to see who or what was in the men's room she intended to drop down into before she did it trumped everything else.

The cross vent meant she had only another eight feet to go.

How long would it be before King Kong lost patience and forced the restroom door?

The question got her adrenaline spiking, accelerating her breathing and forming a knot in her chest. *Not helpful.*

Using her tongue to flip out the acrylic insert that gave her Jennifer Ashley's charming overbite while altering the shape of her mouth and jaw, she added that to her purse. Working her mouth and pursing her lips to relax her lips and cheeks into their natural, more finely drawn contours, she made use of the momentary bit of extra space afforded her by the opening where the secondary vent branched off to reach down and free her hacksaw/pry bar and her spool of cord from their storage units in her garter belt. She would use the pry bar to pop off the grate. The cord would allow her to lower it gently to the ground, thus preventing it from crashing down on the marble floor and alerting anyone (like, say, King Kong) who might be close enough to hear.

As she neared the end of the chute, Bianca discovered that her dress posed a massive problem: it completely blocked the last few feet, including the vent itself. She couldn't see around it or reach the vent.

Swearing silently, she got her arms over the damp, prickly, wine-smelling thing and tamped it down as much as she could, wedging parts of it beneath her chest as she struggled to gain a reasonable degree of access to the vent. Pressing her face close to the grate, blinking as she tried without a whole lot of success to clear her still-blurry vision, she squinted out at the men's room.

Like the women's restroom, it was large and white. It was also single user: toilet, urinal, sink—she couldn't see everything, but she could see those essential components clearly enough.

It was empty.

So go already.

Latching the hook that was attached to the cord to the vent, she edged her small pry bar between the wall and the grate and popped the grate off. She quickly lowered it with the cord and shoved her dress out at the same time. Her dress landed with a soft plop. She dropped her purse on top of the dress.

There was no fainting couch in the men's room, of course. Such a convenient aid to getting out of the vent would be too much to ask. From her prone position some two feet below the ceiling, it was an eleven-foot drop straight to the marble floor. She was going to have to go out headfirst, which fortunately shouldn't pose a problem. Piece of cake to do a backflip on the way down that would allow her to land on her feet.

Wriggling head and shoulders out of the vent, she pressed the flat of her hands against the slick marble wall to get some momentum behind that flip.

Then she pushed, squirmed, kicked—and fell. Straight down.

Backflips, half twists, somersaults—none of the moves she might have used to land on her feet were forthcoming.

Because her attention was fatally distracted by the man standing in the corner nearest the vent watching her fall.

6

Bianca couldn't have been more shocked if somebody had thrown a bucket of ice water over her. How the hell had she missed him? How—

Having dropped like a rock with her gaze riveted on the man, she barely managed to get it together enough to catch herself with both out-flung hands in time to save her head from smashing into the floor. Dangerously off balance in her impromptu handstand, she flopped over and smacked down flat on her back on the barely there cushion of her dress.

"Ooph!" The sound was surprised out of her as the impact sent the breath rushing from her lungs.

For a split second after she hit, she lay there, dazed and winded, the back of her head resting on the unforgiving marble floor, the rest of her sprawled inelegantly atop her dress. Her eyes were still blurry as she gazed blankly up at the ceiling. She arched slightly as her purse dug into her spine and found herself gritting her teeth against the pain shooting from her tailbone, which had hit first and hardest.

"Well, hello there, beautiful." He had a low, deep voice, rich with amusement and something else. He spoke English with the faintest of underlying accents, the origin of which she was in too much distress to even try to place. Shoving away from the wall he'd been leaning against, he moved to stand over her.

Her pulse skyrocketed. Her heart thumped. Her fight-or-flight response had jumped directly to fight even before she landed, but to her horror she discovered that both options were beyond her. She couldn't move. Forget harnessing her body's reactions. She was struggling to suck in air.

"You know, when I first heard scratching inside the wall here, I was thinking rats." He gave her a slow once-over, blatant male interest warring with the twinkle in his eyes. "This is much better."

By way of a smart comeback, she wheezed. God, she needed to breathe!

"Take your time," he advised, his eyes on her legs, which were bent at the knees and all akimbo, giving him an unfettered view all the way up to her crotch.

Eat dirt and die, she thought. Good thing she couldn't talk.

"Is this like spelunking? Only, in your underwear? Very nice underwear, too, I might add." His eyes were doing a slow crawl over the rest of her.

Wheeze.

He was tall, probably around six-three, although it was difficult to be certain, since she was looking up at him while lying flat on her back. He was about thirty, lean, with broad shoulders, narrow hips and long legs, and he looked good in a classic black tux, which was what he was wearing. His hair was coal black and wavy, brushed back from his face and long enough so that it curled up a little on the ends, which just reached the collar of his white shirt. He had a wide forehead, broad cheekbones, a square, clean-shaven jaw. His brows were straight black slashes above caramel-brown eyes that were, at the moment, checking her out with an unmistakably carnal gleam in them. His nose was aquiline and had been broken once. It had a bump on the left side of the bridge. His mouth was a little thin, a little cruel-looking despite the hint of humor in the curve of it as he looked her over. His skin was deeply tanned, leading her to conclude that he'd spent a great deal of time outdoors in either this or some other sunbaked locale.

He was handsome, sexy even, but that wasn't what sent a shiver snaking down her spine. Her instincts screamed that he was dangerous. Underneath the humor and the sexual interest, he was looking at her like a predator eyeing prey.

Armed? She couldn't tell, but it was better to err on the side of yes. A pistol in a shoulder holster, maybe, or tucked into his waistband at the small of his back.

No way was his presence in the men's room at this particular moment an accident.

Was he one of the prince's men? Or Durand's?

Her heart lurched.

Then adrenaline—and ice water—flooded her veins as survival mode kicked in.

She finally managed to suck in air.

If he'd moved quicker, he might have succeeded in capturing her while she was helpless, handcuffing her or tying her up or whatever it was he had in mind to do to subdue her.

Too late. She wasn't helpless any longer.

His weakness was right there in front of her, in the hot gleam in his eyes as they moved over her, in his obvious assumption that he could take his time with her, that he was bigger and badder and stronger, that he had her and she couldn't get away.

The scraps of black lingerie, the strapless bra offering up her breasts as way more of an eyeful than they actually were, the filmy panties, the sky-high heels and long gloves, but most of all the blatant suggestiveness of her garter belt and (now torn at the knees, but still working for her) fishnets were doing exactly what they were supposed to do: getting him to think with body parts other than his brain.

Well, everyone was entitled to a mistake now and then.

"Help me up?" Her voice was husky, suggestive, its sexy

breathiness aided by the fact that she still didn't have her breathing completely normalized. He abandoned his slow perusal of her body to meet her eyes. Projecting sultry invitation for all she was worth, she gave him a small, intimate smile and held up her hand.

Come into my parlor, said the spider to the fly.

He did.

"My pleasure," he said and took her hand. His was big, long-fingered, strong. He pulled her to her feet easily.

She let him, smiling at him even as her bruised tailbone sent a twinge up her spine, resisting the urge to flip him over her hip, throw him to the ground, use a blood choke on him and have done. First, because there was something in the way he held himself that made her suspect he might be able to launch a counter to such a move, and second, because fighting was noisy and King Kong, supposing he hadn't gone in search of orders or reinforcements, wasn't far away. The last thing she wanted to do was bring him into the picture again.

Best to string this guy along until she could take him out silently. The only problem with that was, she didn't have a lot of time. A discreet glance at her watch told her that it was two minutes, forty-one seconds until midnight.

She needed to move this along.

"Thank you." On her feet now, she was able to verify that he was, indeed, around six-three, and that despite the appearance he gave of leanness he was broader and more muscular than she had at first supposed. She estimated his weight at around one-ninety, which meant he outweighed her by a good seventy pounds. A glance at the pair of them in the mirror over the sink confirmed it: he seemed to dwarf her. He was inches taller, twice as broad, a good-looking guy in a tux looming over a slim, blonde girl who looked like he'd special ordered her from Hookers R Us.

Their comparative sizes actually worked to her advantage. The fact that he was so much physically larger meant that he wasn't on his guard with her, because he was confident he could overpower her at will.

That thing people said about assumptions? His were about to bite him in the ass.

"Usually you find condom dispensers in men's bathrooms," he said. He was having fun toying with her, she could tell. He was still holding her hand, his fingers wrapped firmly around her gloved palm, and she suspected he didn't mean to let go. Of course, it was always possible that he was being careful because he wasn't quite sure she was his target. After all, she was now a blue-eyed blonde in slutty undies instead of the green-eyed redhead in a ball gown he must have been expecting. On the other hand, how many women could possibly be sneaking around inside the palace's air-conditioning system? And said ball gown formed a very visible heap on the floor. Fortunately, the heap was mostly lavender instead of black. "I like this Bahraini custom of dispensing beautiful, half-naked women through the air vents much better."

"Oh, my." She gave a wide-eyed glance around, playing confused innocence to the hilt on the off chance that it might keep him, or throw him, off balance. "Is this the men's room? I'm embarrassed."

"Probably hard to tell where you're going to come out when you start crawling through the ductwork." His tone was all sympathy. His eyes as they met hers—well, she no longer had any doubt at all that this guy was major bad news.

"It is."

He smiled at her. "What's your name?"

She smiled right back.

"Sylvia," she said, because the Jennifer Ashley identity was now gone with the wig, which, a quick glance at the floor told her, was fortunately hidden by the crumpled folds of her dress. She made big bedroom eyes at him while trying, subtly, to free her hand. Her best bet was probably to chop him across the throat. That would shut him up and put him out of commission at the same time. The only problem: she did her best chopping with her right hand, which he was holding. And she needed to make this quick, silent and not messy. "What's yours?"

"Mickey."

"Hi there, Mickey."

"Right back at you, Sylvia."

Okay, so subtle wasn't going to do it. He was holding on to her hand like he never meant to let go—which, she suspected, he probably didn't, at least not until he had her secured in some other way.

He said, "Don't tell me, you're the air-conditioner duct version of a chimney sweep."

She gave a flirtatious little nose wrinkle as she debated the merits of sweeping his legs out from under him and then taking him out with an elbow to the temple. "Not quite."

"An exterminator, then. With a very enticing uniform."

"You are funny."

"So you want to tell me what you were doing in that vent?"

"Escaping," she admitted, because sometimes honesty really was the best policy. At least, as far as it went.

He hadn't expected her to actually tell him the truth. She could tell from the flicker of surprise in his eyes.

"Escaping?"

"From the man I was with. I would have used my words, but he was a little too...insistent."

"*He* being the big guy rattling the knob of the ladies' room next door," he said, as if he were guessing. Only, she was as sure as it was possible to be that he didn't need to guess. She didn't know who or what he was exactly, but he'd clearly seen

King Kong, and since he wasn't yelling some version of "She's here, I got her" to him, she felt it was unlikely that he was part of the prince's team.

So was he with Durand? That possibility was actually worse. It dried her mouth, made her stomach twist. The prince and his men were murderous thugs, but they were mostly dumb murderous thugs with a local reach. Durand, on the other hand, was smart, relentless and global.

She gave an elegant little shrug, made a small moue with her mouth.

A kick to the chin was what she was going with, followed by a knee drop to the solar plexus once she had him on the ground.

"He's not really my type," she said. Stepping closer, she vamped him with her eyes.

He smiled, a slight, sensual curve of his mouth, but before either of them could say or do anything else, the sound of heavy footsteps outside caused them both to glance in that direction. Bianca's breath hitched as she realized that someone was seconds away from reaching the door. Her gaze flew to the knob. It was unlocked.

Had King Kong breached the ladies' room? Had her absence been discovered and were the prince's men now looking for her? She didn't know, and she didn't want to find out.

Unfortunately, there was nowhere to go, nowhere to hide.

Except in plain sight.

Tightening her grip on the hand imprisoning hers, she stepped toward Mickey, looked up into his eyes that were just starting to frown down at her and whispered a panicked-sounding "Oh, no, he's coming! Please, you have to help me hide! Kiss me!"

Then she threw herself against him, wrapped her free arm around his neck and kissed him for all she was worth.

He didn't kiss her back, just stood there like a statue while she teetered on her tiptoes and urgently plied his mouth with hers and pressed her nearly naked body right up against the long, solid, fully clothed length of him and used him to keep whoever might be coming through that door from getting a good look at her. His hand gripping hers tightened and he folded her hand against his chest. That was all the reaction she got. Deepening the kiss, she licked into his mouth, slid her fingers up into his hair and closed her eyes.

The closing-her-eyes part was the hardest, because she really, really didn't like to render herself blind, but she figured she had to do what she had to do to sell it.

Two things happened almost simultaneously: he turned so that his back was fully to the door, pulling her around with him and shielding her from the view of whoever would enter, and the door opened behind them.

There was a pregnant silence. Bianca could feel the weight of the intruder's gaze on them. She imagined the scene from his perspective: a man's broad back; a blonde girl in her underwear, her lavender dress puddled on the floor; the two of them, a couple, alone in a restroom, locked in a kiss—

Nothing to do with the escapee you might be looking for, she told the onlooker silently. *Nothing at all.*

Mickey's hand slid across the bare skin of her rib cage, big and hot and strong. His mouth slanted over hers as he started kissing her back. He backed her into the wall—the marble felt smooth and cold everywhere it touched her skin—and pressed himself against her.

The firm warmth of his mouth, the glide of his tongue between her lips, the pressure of his body against hers, all caught her by surprise. Focused as she was on the urgent need to get out of there, she still felt an unexpected tingle of electricity, a shaft of heat, a pulse spring to life deep inside her body. He tasted faintly of whiskey, his body radiated heat even through his clothes and either his job kept him very fit or he was religious about working out. He was all long, powerful muscle.

He was also turned on. As he kissed her, she could feel his erection through his pants, growing larger by the second, bulging against her stomach.

Nice. But she could hardly complain. Not without reason, he was clearly under the impression that she was majorly on board with the program. And he was tall and broad enough so that now she was almost completely blocked from being seen by whoever was looking in on them from the door.

Fair enough.

She answered the probing of his tongue with some serious tongue probing of her own. She kissed him like he was sweeping her off her feet, like she was maybe five minutes away from slithering out of her remaining clothes and getting down and dirty with him on the restroom floor.

"Maazrat chahta hun." I'm sorry, a deep male voice said in Urdu from the direction of the open door. It took Bianca a second to process the translation, and that would be because her blood was pounding in her ears, and *that* would be because, whatever else this guy was, he was a really good kisser.

He still held her hand. It was pressed against his chest. She tugged, and—*hello, masculine brain fog*—he let go. Still kissing him, she wrapped both arms around his neck and arched up against him—

The intruder left. The restroom door closed. She heard the swish of its movement followed by the click of the latch. A quick peek through barely parted lids confirmed it: she and Mickey were once again alone.

Relief bubbled up inside her. Having heard the language in which the intruder had spoken, she'd braced for an imminent invasion by the palace security guards, and she hadn't been at all sure that her current (lack of) disguise would be enough to save her. But now the intruder was gone.

Cue Operation Get Out of Here.

As quickly and quietly as possible.

Mickey didn't seem inclined to stop what he was doing to attempt to apprehend or do whatever it was she was ninety-nine point nine percent sure he was there to do to her, proving yet again that men came equipped with two brains but could access only one at a time.

Which was fine by her. Keeping the make-out session going was as good a distraction as any.

She stroked the nape of his neck, ran her hand down the strong muscles of his back—if he was carrying a gun, it wasn't anywhere on his torso.

"You taste like sugar," he murmured, lifting his lips from hers to slide his mouth along her cheek toward her ear. He had one arm braced against the wall beside her head, presumably to keep his weight from crushing her. His other arm was wrapped around her waist.

"Margarita." Her reply referred to the cocktail she had drunk with the prince just prior to slipping away to open the vault. The glass had been rimmed with sugar.

The warm crawl of his mouth down the sensitive skin at the side of her throat had her tilting her head to grant him greater access and making sexy sounds.

Her stroking hand slid down over what was, actually, a really nice, tight ass.

"I bet you taste like sugar all over." His voice had a growly quality now.

"Um." It was a soft, sensuous sound that could mean whatever he took it to mean. Her hand stroked its way down his hard-muscled thigh. Sensuously she slid her leg up the outside of his to meet her hand.

"I want you," he said.

"Do you?"

Even as his lips found hers again, kissing her with the hungry intensity of a man who was getting down to better things, she slid her leg back down his until she was once again standing firmly on both feet. Then she slipped her questing hand around his neck, found the vulnerable skin of his nape—and let him have it with her stun gun.

A sizzling sound. An electric tingle in the air. The slightest of burning smells.

As the voltage hit him, Mickey's head jerked up. His eyes widened, collided with hers. In that split second in which their eyes locked, Bianca saw comprehension, fear and fury flash into his. Then he gasped, stiffened, shook. His eyes rolled back in his head. He went limp, collapsing on top of her and nearly taking her down with him.

Staggering under his weight, conscious of a momentary twinge of regret—how long had it been since a man had kissed her like that, anyway?—she grabbed him around the waist and lowered him carefully to the floor.

If there was anyone out there listening, the kind of thump he'd make crashing down on his own might be all that was needed to bring them in here.

Snapping her stun gun back into place, dragging her dress out from under his head, she sized him up as he sprawled facedown at her feet. She saw no reason to doubt her previous assessment of him: he was almost certainly some kind of law enforcement type, probably working for Durand.

Not that it mattered now. He was handled. And it was one minute, twenty-six seconds until midnight.

She had bigger fish to fry than Mickey.

She took ten seconds to frisk him—useless: no ID, no gun, nothing—then whipped her dress lavender-side out and pulled it on. There was a trickle of blood on one of her knees, she saw as she zipped the dress up and adjusted the skirt so that the few wet splotches that had soaked through weren't so visible. She must have scraped it coming through the vent. It didn't hurt, and she had no time to deal with it. Later, when she was safe, she could slap on a Band-Aid. The wine smell—it wasn't *that* noticeable, she decided as she snatched her clip from the fallen grate, pushed the button to rewind the cord and restored the clip to its place on her garter belt. Grabbing her purse, she stuffed the red wig inside.

Time to go. Fluffing her hair with one hand in hopes that it wouldn't look quite so much like it had spent most of the night smashed under a wig, she headed for the door.

The Urdu-speaking guy who'd popped in on them—was he gone, or waiting nearby? What about King Kong? Was he still outside the ladies' room door or—

Behind her, Mickey stirred and groaned, causing her head to whip around. The long fingers of his right hand, bronze against the white marble, flexed warningly.

Oh, God, was he regaining consciousness? It usually took much longer.

She couldn't have him waking up and raising the alarm, so she took a second to run back and zap him again. As he spasmed, she hurried back to the door, listened briefly—nothing—and eased the door open just enough to make sure the coast was clear.

It was. At least, the alcove outside the men's room was clear.

Nervous tension tightened her stomach as she made for the ballroom. In the alcove next door she could hear the lowered but urgent-sounding voices of King Kong and several other men. From certain unmistakable sounds that accompanied the voices, she gathered that they were at that moment forcing their way into the ladies' room. Had it been one of their number who'd surprised what he'd clearly thought was a couple getting it on in the men's room moments earlier? If so, it was evident that he hadn't recognized Jennifer Ashley in the half-naked blonde he'd seen. But as soon as he beheld the empty ladies' room, he might well make the connection.

Her number-one worry was that Mickey would recover his senses and stagger out of the men's room shouting for help before she was safely away.

There wasn't time to go back and take additional precautionary measures, like, say, tie him up and gag him. There wasn't time to create a diversion, or do anything except make for the exit as fast as she could go.

Stepping out into the ballroom, she instantly ducked her head. She knew where the surveillance cameras were, and she chose her route to avoid most of them. For those she couldn't avoid, keeping her face down was standard tradecraft. For foiling the unexpected, like, say, a new installation or a stray snap from a cell phone camera, she assumed a wide smile. What most people didn't know was that smiling was one of the simplest, most effective techniques for defeating facial recognition software that existed, because it significantly altered the contours of the face.

Of course, you might look like a grinning fool on the playback, but they wouldn't know who you were.

Thirty-one seconds until midnight, and she still had a quarter of the crowded ballroom to bob and weave her way through before she reached the doors.

Clenching her fingers tight around the strap of her purse, moving as fast as she could without calling attention to herself, Bianca felt pulses of anxiety fluttering through her bloodstream as it became clear that she wasn't going to make it out of the ballroom in time.

7

Bianca kept a wary eye on the top of the ballroom, where the prince still stood with Durand. The ebb and flow of the crowd around the pair interfered with her view, but she was able to see enough to discern that they were still talking, still seemingly unaware that anything was wrong, as her watch ticked down the seconds until midnight.

When it happened, when the little digital numbers on her wrist proclaimed the hour, she was still maybe thirty yards shy of the door.

Down in the vault, security guards would be making their regular check and discovering that it was empty.

All hell would be breaking loose, but it would be breaking loose discreetly. More guards were no doubt swarming the cellars at that very instant. The prince would be notified. Under some seemingly innocuous pretext—an outbreak of violence in the streets, say—the palace would be locked down tighter than a maximum security prison.

No one would be allowed to leave.

The hunt would be on.

She had to get out—of the palace, of the grounds—before then.

As Tony ended his set and the room erupted into applause, Bianca found that her nails were digging into her palms.

The crowd largely stopped in place as they clapped, their

attention focused on the stage. She had to edge sideways, bump shoulders, push to get through.

She was maybe ten yards away from the French doors when she caught a glimpse of a small wedge of men in traditional robes and white kaffiyehs emerging through an interior door on the same side of the ballroom as the kitchen and slicing across the assembly toward the prince. The speed and determination of their advance made her stomach drop toward her toes. She had no doubt, no doubt at all, that this was the contingent sent to inform the prince that his money was gone.

Cheshire cat smile firmly in place, blond head down and legs flashing in and out of her silky lavender gown, she made for the nearest set of French doors like a Walmart shopper zeroing in on a Black Friday bargain.

The men reached the prince, pulled him aside, spoke rapidly. At the same time, she saw to her horror, King Kong and his crew burst out of the restroom alcove, looked wildly around—

She reached the French doors.

Security guards posted inside near the exits, clearly not yet alerted to the disaster, glanced at her incuriously as she pushed through the doors and strode out onto the terrace.

A blonde in a lavender dress: no one was looking for that woman—yet.

All it was going to take for that to change was for Mickey to recover his senses and start talking. In retrospect, she should probably have done something to make sure he wouldn't wake up for hours. Like stomp his head.

The heat, the smells, the flickering flambeaux—nothing about the terrace had changed since she'd tried escaping across it the last time.

Fearing to find King Kong or one of his ilk on her heels with every step, she kept her head high and her pace fast but steady as she headed toward the stairs. Every atom of her being urged her to run, but she was afraid of the attention that might attract. It would take just one guard, one worker, one curious observer, to spot a woman sprinting across the terrace and report it.

She could only trust that Doc hadn't gotten cold feet at her detention and would still be waiting for her. If he wasn't, well, she would improvise. If nothing else, she would lose herself in the dark of the gardens until she could figure a way out.

Whatever happened, she could not allow herself to get caught. There would be no bluffing her way out this time. With the money gone, and her impersonation of Jennifer Ashley obvious, if she was hauled in front of the prince, she was as good as dead.

A prickle of fear slid over her skin.

There'd been no way to alert Doc that she was coming. Reaching the stairs, she ran down them, her shoes barely touching the steps, her gown billowing behind her. A line of limos snaked around the fountain at the center of the motor court. A thousand pinpricks of stars twinkled in the night sky. The moon hung directly above the immensely tall, sail-shaped towers of the Bahraini World Trade Center near the center of downtown. Traffic was lighter on Bani Otbah Avenue than it had been earlier, but it was still heavy enough so that the limo would blend in.

Assuming the limo was there.

To her huge relief, she spotted the vehicle with Doc behind the wheel before she reached the bottom step. It was first in line.

He must have seen her coming, too, because the headlights came on, the motor revved and the limo pulled forward to meet her. As she reached the motor court, Doc got out and hurried around to open the rear door for her.

His eyes moved over her anxiously.

"So, like, you changed your hair," he said under his breath when she reached him. "And didn't your dress used to be, like, black? I almost didn't recognize you. Except, you know, who else is gonna come running down the stairs at midnight?"

Doc had known her only in her red-haired Jennifer Ashley incarnation, Bianca remembered. To see her as herself was a surprise to him. Only she and her father knew the real identities, etc., of the rest of the team—no one knew theirs. It was Security 101: people couldn't reveal what they didn't know.

"Later," she responded, looking back at what she could see of the still-closed French doors before ducking into the car. A glance confirmed that Doc had done as instructed and moved her small duffel from the trunk to the back seat. "We need to go."

Doc looked in at her, his bushy black brows drawn together. "You're tripping me out here."

"Now."

"Going." Doc obediently shut the door and walked around the car. It couldn't have taken more than a few seconds, but by the time he clambered behind the wheel, Bianca was ready to jump out of her skin.

"Don't drive too fast, but we have to get through the gates as quickly as we can."

The stretch limo was sized to seat twenty. The interior was beige leather and carpet and still had that new-car smell. The rear windows were tinted. No one could see her in the back. Having moved into the long, rear-facing seat closest to the driver, she turned and leaned forward, one hand on the back of Doc's seat as she spoke to him through the open partition that separated the two sections of the vehicle.

"O-kay," he said, putting the car in gear. His black-gloved fingers flexed as he gripped the wheel. "Drive slow but fast."

The limo pulled away from the steps and started around the wide circle at a stately pace. They still had to make it down the long driveway and get through the closed, guarded gates.

Glancing back at the palace, Bianca felt her stomach twist. Its domed beauty was deceptively serene. Inside, a volcano of fury would be erupting. Looking forward again didn't help. At the end of the palm-lined drive, the gates waited under bright white security lights. It was—Bianca glanced at her watch—one minute, fifty-three seconds after midnight. How long would it take before word to stop all exiting vehicles reached the guards at the gate?

She couldn't count on it being much longer.

She wanted to scream at Doc to drive faster. She didn't dare.

"So what happened?" Doc asked.

"The vault was empty."

"Empty?" He looked at her through the rearview mirror.

"Empty. As in, the money was gone when I got it open."

"The money was gone? Gone where?"

"No idea."

"We don't have it?"

For a smart man, Doc was being remarkably slow to catch on.

"No, we don't have it," Bianca said. "That's what I meant when I said it was gone."

"So who has it?"

"I don't know."

"You kidding me?"

"Do I look like I'm kidding you?" Their eyes met in the rearview mirror.

What Doc saw there must have convinced him, because he said, "No! No, no, no! I was supposed to walk away from this and never have to work again!"

"Life's a bitch," Bianca said. Actually, she knew where he was coming from. She just hadn't had time to process it yet.

"We did all this for nothing?"

No point in sugarcoating it. "Yes."

"Shit!" Doc sounded as poleaxed as she felt. "Wait. If we

didn't steal the money, why are we running away? We didn't do anything."

"Because the money's *gone*. It's possible that someone else beat us to it, and we were set up to take the fall. At this point I don't know for sure. Anything's possible. But the prince knows our team is here, and he knows the money's missing. He's going to blame us. He's going to come after us. He's going to shut the palace down at any second, and if we're not out of here…"

"We're all gonna die." Doc's voice was hollow. Under better conditions Bianca might have smiled, but these weren't better conditions. She was just glad she didn't need to spell things out. Like the rest of the team, Doc had been well briefed on possible consequences if the job should go wrong.

"Pretty much," she agreed.

There was a moment of appalled silence. Then Doc said, "This totally sucks, you know what I mean?"

"Yeah, I do."

They were approaching the security checkpoint, a small stone guardhouse that stood just to the left and in front of the enormous gilded gates. The guardhouse was lit from within as well as from without. Through its mullioned window, Bianca could see one of the two heavily armed sentries looking out at them. Then the sentry turned his head sharply. A second later it became clear why. He walked away from the window to pick up the phone.

Bianca felt her insides constrict.

"If they don't let us through right away, tell them you have a medical emergency," she said. Her first instinct if they weren't allowed to leave—ram the gates—was problematic. The gates were heavy iron. The car might not make it through. There were airbags. The sentries had guns. "I'll sell it from back here. I hope." If she couldn't sell it from the back seat—the ability to vomit on cue was one of the many minor talents on which she prided herself—she was going to get out and collapse, moaning, in the grass. When the sentries came over to check on her, she would take them out and open the gates. Or something. "Whatever happens, you stay in the car and be ready to take off."

"Medical emergency," Doc repeated. His shoulders were tense. He looked doubtfully at her through the rearview mirror. Of course, having never seen her in action, he had no way of knowing what she could do. He gave a curt nod of agreement as the limo reached the guardhouse and braked to a stop. The guard who wasn't on the phone came to the open window and looked out at them.

Doc smiled and waved.

No problems here.

Bianca watched the other guard's face turn toward them. He was still on the phone. She held her breath—

The gates started to open. Slowly. So, so slowly...

Her stomach felt tight as a clenched fist.

"Get out of here," Bianca breathed. The limo inched forward in the wake of the parting gates.

"Trying," Doc replied through the wide smile still stretching his face.

The limo was through.

A moment later they were making a sharp turn onto Bani Otbah Avenue.

"Good job," Bianca said.

"I almost crapped my pants."

The limo changed lanes as Doc did his best to get themselves lost among the motley collection of vehicles traveling along the six-lane boulevard that ran through the mixed-up jumble of garishly lit modern skyscrapers and centuries-old buildings and mosques that made up the downtown. Bahrain was one of the few gulf countries that didn't have much in the way of oil. Given that lack, they'd been forced to build their economy on something else, and that something was banking. Manama was a banking and financial hub for the region, and on this main thoroughfare there were banks on just about every corner. Banks complete with ATMs, which came with security cameras. She had mapped the route they would take to the dock with those cameras in mind.

"Don't look back here." She was in the process of stripping off her dress and shoes, replacing them with jeans and sneakers and a black hoodie from the duffel: the world's universal uniform. The gloves, jewels and garter belt stayed on. The gloves to prevent fingerprints, the jewels because if she found herself in a tight spot they could be sold for cash or used for bribes and the garter belt because, well, you never knew.

"You know we got kind of a time crunch going here." Doc's voice was hushed, as though he feared being overheard.

"I know." They actually had five minutes, eleven seconds to make it to the boat. Bianca could feel the tension in her neck and shoulders as she tossed her purse in the duffel on top of her discarded clothes. They were moving with the flow of traffic, but still, to her, the limo felt as conspicuous as a party bus with strobe lights firing. A glance back at the palace made her feel slightly better. The gates were closed and the guard hadn't run out into the middle of the street to brandish his rifle threateningly or fire after them, which she took as a good sign.

The fastest thing to do would be to take the limo directly to the dock. It would also be the stupidest.

"Hang a left at the alley before the next light," she said.

She'd deliberately selected a limo that lacked a GPS, because if the shit hit the fan and they had to make a run for it, a GPS made tracking the vehicle too ridiculously easy. She didn't need a GPS to know where she was going, anyway. As part of her prep for tonight's job, she had memorized a map of the city and had walked the streets until she knew the parts of Manama that mattered like the back of her hand.

Doc turned where she'd told him.

The alley, an ancient one that was now primarily used for deliveries and trash pickup, had existed since long before cars were invented. Its single lane was stomach-churningly narrow. Bumping over the cobblestones, the limo barely avoided scraping the earth-toned, stucco-and-stone back walls of the small shops on either side. At this hour, fortunately, they were the only vehicle on the street.

"Turn in here," she said.

8

"Here" was a ramp that led down to the underground parking garage beneath the Gulf Hotel. The security gate opened automatically to let them through. The limo, one of a fleet that primarily serviced the city's big hotels, had a bar-coded sticker on its windshield that allowed access.

Leaving the limo at the dock would be like leaving a flaming sign announcing where they'd gone, in Bianca's estimation, so she'd arranged alternate transportation to the boat and this was where the vehicle exchange happened. They were in the lowest level of the garage, the one employees used. At this hour it was only partially full. The one security camera had most unfortunately broken earlier in the day.

Following Bianca's directions, Doc drove to the rear of the parking garage and stopped.

Jumping out, Bianca glanced around: poured concrete walls, round support columns, dim lighting and the faint smell of gasoline. Security camera gone dark and hanging from the ceiling by its wires. Parked vehicles. Not a soul in sight.

"Come on." Jerking her head to indicate the direction she meant, she slogged toward a spot two vehicles over. She opened the duffel bag and swung it in Doc's direction as he trotted behind her. "Drop your hat and tie in here."

Doc did. Bianca zipped the bag up. As she reached the Kawasaki 250 motorcycle that she'd parked in the garage shortly after she'd taken out the camera, she threw the bag on the back. The plan had been for her to arrive in this garage in the limo with Doc. They would then part, making their way separately to the boat, because if/when the hunt for them heated up, the searchers would be trolling surveillance video and questioning witnesses looking for a couple. Separating was intended to confound the search, or at least slow it down. She'd planned to get to the boat via motorcycle, while Doc caught a cab at the hotel entrance. That plan was now out the window. Doc was going to have to stay with her. They were almost out of time.

"Here." Having secured the bag with a bungee cord and freed the two helmets fastened to the bike, Bianca held a helmet out to Doc even as she pulled the other one on. No more worries about cameras. The helmets were full face. Wearing them provided total anonymity.

"Me?" Doc looked at the helmet like she was offering him a spitting cobra. Holding both hands up in rejection, he shook his head. "I don't ride motorcycles."

"Take it." She smacked the helmet into his chest. He took it, holding it like it was a live grenade. "All you have to do is sit down and hold on." Securing the helmet strap beneath her chin, Bianca swung a leg over the seat. Starting the engine, she looked at Doc, who was frowning down at his helmet in mistrust, and yelled over the sudden noise, "Get on. Do you want to miss the boat?"

"Oh, jeez." Cramming the helmet on his head, Doc hitched himself on and wrapped his arms around her waist. It was kind of like being caught in the death grip of a giant, sweaty teddy bear. As he plopped down and the back of the bike sank under his weight, Bianca had an instant, hideous vision of the two of them popping a never-ending wheelie through the streets of Manama.

Inconspicuous wasn't the first word that came to mind.

Sometimes you just had to work with what you were given.

Yelling, "Scoot up," she revved the gas and took off.

He scooted, and the balance improved. Slightly. Sitting practically on top of the gas tank in an effort to keep the front tire on the ground, Bianca gunned it out of there.

The roar of the 250's engine echoed off the walls. The headlight slashed through the darkness like Tinker Bell on steroids.

It wasn't far to the dock. Zipping through a maze of alleys, she felt exhilaration at their escape edging out the fear that had been gnawing at her ever since she'd discovered the empty vault. The cold hard knot of failure in her stomach she refused to acknowledge: something to face later. As they neared the gulf, she caught glimpses of its shimmering black waters through the gaps in adjacent walls. Almost all the old buildings they passed had been built with the tall, square, open-faced turrets known as wind towers protruding from the roofs to catch the sea breezes. The buildings themselves blocked any hope of those breezes reaching street level. That, combined with the day's accumulated heat rising up from the ground and the fact that her head was shrouded in a helmet, made it stiflingly hot. Like most of the small island nation, the city was flat, which was a saving grace as she cranked the speed until the bike was skittering like a wild animal over the cobblestones and vibrating so hard that her hands and thighs were going numb from hanging on. Careening around corners and opening up the throttle on the straightaways, she drove so fast that the collection of little shops and restaurants and offices that blocked them in on both sides became a blur.

"Will they really leave without us?" Doc's higher-pitched-than-usual voice reached her via the intercom built into the helmets. Pressed up against her like a gorilla-size backpack, his arms clamped around her waist, his body curved around hers, he was hanging on for dear life. Having never worked with them before this disaster, he didn't know that the Ten Commandments were more flexible than that particular one of Richard St. Ives's rules.

"Yes."

"What about that thing about never leaving a man behind?"

Bianca snorted. "You've got us confused with the US Marines."

"Oh, man."

A glance at her watch told her how much time they had before the boat left without them: one minute, sixteen seconds. It would be tight, but, she calculated, they were going to get it done. They were only about a block away from where the alley opened out into the road that ran along the plaza fronting the harbor. The garbage scow would be docked about three blocks to the left, at Pier 16. It was situated so they could drive right up and—

The quick flash of multiple headlights in the spaces between the buildings to her right caught her eye. What she was seeing was traffic on the next street over, she realized—and all of a sudden there seemed to be a lot of it.

"We got a plan B in case we miss the boat?" Doc's uneasy voice crackled in her ear.

"We're going to make it."

"Really? Boo-ya! I knew you could do it!"

It was touching, the amount of faith Doc seemed to have in her, Bianca reflected absently as she did her best to make sense of the sudden flood of vehicles that seemed to be racing down the main drag parallel to them. Almost from the beginning, when her father had recruited him right out of his two-year stay in a minimum security prison for hacking a defense department server with a job offer that, if successful (which obviously this fiasco hadn't been, but who could have foreseen that?), would have paid enough to make his felony conviction no longer a concern, Doc had latched onto her as the least likely one of the group to screw him over or murder him in his sleep.

Good call, because she was.

The last of the headlights that marked what seemed to be a speeding motorcade running parallel to them flashed past.

Bianca frowned. They were almost at the plaza—

Directly ahead, she watched a large truck zoom past the end of the alley, crossing the space where the alley emptied out into the road that ran along the plaza that fronted the dock. The road that the garbage truck would have taken, the road that the bike would be turning down in the next few seconds—

Bianca braked sharply as more vehicles rattled past the mouth of the alley. The bike's rear wheel skidded sideways before they shuddered to a halt mere yards short of the road. Putting her foot down automatically—Doc did the same thing, or the bike might have toppled over—Bianca stared. Her throat closed up as she realized that what she was looking at was a military convoy. Jeeps and covered personnel carriers and boxy trucks bristling with soldiers and fitted with big guns, all racing in the same direction she and Doc were heading. The same direction that her father and his crew had taken not so long before.

Coincidence? Oh, God, she hoped so.

"What's happening?" Doc was hopping a little as he fought to maintain his balance. He was in the awkward position of having one leg flung over the bike and one leg planted on the ground, which made it hard to stand still. Bianca's grip tightened on the handlebars as she struggled to keep the bike upright.

"Get off," she instructed, her eyes locked on the string of vehicles still speeding past the end of the alley. As Doc obediently hopped off, she pushed up the visor on her helmet to get a better look.

Her heart began to slam in her chest.

"You think they're after us?" Doc had clearly recognized the military nature of the convoy, too. He stood in the alley beside her with his helmet in his hands, his gaze glued to the clattering trucks.

"Not us. They haven't seen us."

"Whoa." The appalled way Doc drew out the syllable told Bianca that he'd reached the same conclusion that she had: the convoy's target was in all likelihood the garbage truck, or the boat. Or both.

"Yeah."

Doc said, "How about we just tell them we don't have their money?"

"They won't believe it. And even if they did, they'd kill us for knowing about it." She did a quick reconnoiter. The yellowish glow from the streetlights that illuminated the plaza and road in front of them didn't penetrate this far in. She and Doc were sheltered inside the alley, deep in the shadows cast by the buildings rising on either side of them, protected by darkness. A few dusty windows overlooked their position. None had lights on inside. Except for the bike's headlight—she instantly killed it—and the roar of the engine, there was no reason for anyone to so much as glance their way.

She killed the engine, too, and got off the bike. Pushing it close to the nearest wall, she leaned it on its kickstand. The smell of exhaust and the sea combined with the heat was doing her stomach no favors. She felt nauseous.

"Is this where we, like, have to go shoot somebody?" Doc asked.

"Since neither of us has a gun, probably not." Richard and the others had insisted that Doc have some firearms training. Occasionally looking in on their efforts, Bianca had formed the firm opinion that, armed, Doc would be far more of a danger to himself than he would be to anyone else. And she, personally, did not like guns. Guns tended to get people killed.

"Oh, yeah. Good point." Doc sounded relieved.

Removing her helmet, Bianca hung it from the end of the handlebar and flipped her hood over her head. Blonde in a world that was largely brunette, a woman out alone at night where that was unusual: those things would attract attention. She'd chosen the concealing hoodie with that in mind.

"I'm going to go check this out. You're going to wait here. I'll be back."

Careful to stay in the shadows, she jogged to the end of the alley, hugged a wall, looked cautiously around it.

The garbage truck was stopped in the middle of the road in front of Pier 16. Its headlights were still on and its motor was still running, but it wasn't moving. The boat was there, tied up at the dock, but what looked like a military vessel was idling behind it, preventing it from leaving. It was obvious at a glance that nobody was going anywhere.

What she'd suspected was true: the vehicles that had sped past the mouth of the alley were indeed a military convoy. She was just in time to watch as they surrounded the stopped garbage truck and the two jeeps filled with armed soldiers that were parked in front of it, holding it at gunpoint. Two more newly arriving jeeps boxed the truck in on the side facing the plaza. The rippling black waters of the gulf, the miscellany of freighters, scows and fishing boats that were tied up at this section of the wharf and the dock itself formed a barrier on the other side of the garbage truck. With two more jeeps and four covered trucks outfitted with what looked like heavy artillery bringing up the rear, Richard and the others were well and truly caught.

From the way the soldiers were behaving, Bianca thought the trio must still be in the truck, but she couldn't be sure.

Wetting her dry lips, she stepped out into the plaza. The open-air *souk*, or market, to her left was closed. The space out front where some of the merchants displayed their wares on wheeled carts was empty, the carts taken home for safekeeping until the market opened again in the morning. Iron gates fronted by canvas curtains protected the contents of the shops.

Careful to stay in the shadow of the wall, Bianca moved closer to where the garbage truck was being held. She wasn't alone. People craned their necks from the decks of some of the boats, and a small but growing crowd was gathering on the plaza to watch developments. Soldiers jumped out of the newly arrived trucks to form a barrier, ordering onlookers to move back.

"Atti alaolwyeh! Atti alaolwyeh!" The soldiers' shouts were in Arabic, confirming that this was almost certainly the Bahraini military.

Don't be a hero: the rule pounded in Bianca's head with the same staccato rhythm as her pulse.

Keeping her face down as she edged around the periphery of the crowd, she stopped in front of what she thought, from the smell, must be a fishmonger. She was now directly across from the garbage truck, doing her best to see inside the dark cab while her stomach twisted itself into a pretzel.

"What do we do?" Sidling up beside her, Doc almost made her jump. His voice was low, but he was speaking English. A wary glance around told her that nobody was likely to overhear. There was so much noise—the chattering crowd, the shouting soldiers, the throbbing engines of the stopped vehicles, the rush of the tide—that anything short of a screech was probably safe. And with his dark coloring and black suit, Doc blended in well enough visually.

"I told you to wait by the bike."

"I thought you might need help."

That was actually kind of sweet. Doc's particular skill set wasn't really suited to the occasion, but she appreciated his loyalty and willingness to put his own safety on the line for the team. As the newest member of the group and the only one she and the others had never worked with before, Doc was still a largely unknown quantity. At this point, with no payout forthcoming and a whole boatload full of trouble crashing down on their heads, he could have just cut and run.

Before she could reply, another truck roared up, passing the convoy at speed. Once on the other side of the garbage truck and the jeeps holding it at bay, it executed a neat one-eighty and positioned itself so that it was in front of and facing the garbage truck. Maybe a dozen armed soldiers jumped out of the back and advanced on the garbage truck, rifles pointed threateningly at the windshield.

"Holy shit." Doc's voice went high-pitched.

Two uniformed officers got out of the newly arrived truck's cab and walked toward the garbage truck in the wake of the advancing men. One of them yelled through a bullhorn, "You in the truck! Put up your hands and step out!"

She registered that he was speaking English. Her heartbeat quickened as she realized what that had to mean: the soldiers, and thus the prince, knew exactly who was in that truck.

Don't panic, Bianca told herself as she felt the prickle of cold sweat breaking out around her hairline. It was possible that her father was even at that point working some kind of angle that would lead to the trio's deliverance. A con man to his bone marrow, Richard wouldn't submit to capture without at least attempting to save himself.

Don't be a hero. Don't be a hero. Don't be a hero.

To hell with it. She couldn't just do nothing.

"I'm going to create a distraction," she said under her breath. "You go back and wait by the bike. I'll meet you there in a few."

Doc gave her a worried look. "What kind of distraction?"

"Go back to the bike." Bianca was already on the move. Her plan was to steal the truck that had just arrived. She'd watched the soldiers jump out of the back and the two officers exit the

cab, one through the passenger's door and the other through the driver's door. Chances were high that the truck, and more to the point the cab, was empty. The engine was still running. She would jump in, slam the transmission into Reverse, make a one-eighty of her own and floor it out of there. That should create enough of a diversion to give her father and the others a little bit of time when the focus was not on them. Time to do what? That was up to them. Bottom line was, escape.

"Hands up! Get out of the truck!" The officer in charge—Bianca assumed he was the officer in charge because he was the guy giving the orders—boomed through the bullhorn.

The garbage truck was angled in such a way that until that point she hadn't been able to see anything inside the cab. A spotlight switched on—it was mounted on the hood of one of the jeeps—and by its blinding glare Bianca was finally able to make out the three men inside: Findley, dark and compact, was behind the wheel; wide-shouldered, bald Grangier was in the middle; and her tall, silver-haired father was on the far side.

She couldn't see their expressions, but she knew they had to be grim. She was feeling pretty grim herself.

"Turn off the engine! Get out of the truck!" The commands thundered over the bullhorn. "You have until the count of five! One—"

She didn't dare run. She didn't dare make a beeline for her target. Keeping her head down and sticking to the fringe of the crowd, she moved toward the truck she meant to steal as fast as she could without giving herself away.

"Two!"

She could almost hear her father saying, as he did before every job, that if the situation went south, it was every man for himself and they'd meet back at base.

"Three!"

Wait, this was going down too fast. Maybe forty feet of open space separated her from the truck. Bianca looked around to make sure no soldiers stood between her and it, gave up on being careful and sprinted toward it. No time for anything else. No one seemed to be paying any attention to her, thank God. Everyone was focused on the drama playing out with the soldiers and the garbage truck. Out of the corner of her eye she saw the driver's-side door of the garbage truck open. *No, wait, stay where you are*, she wanted to scream at Findley as he started to emerge. Then she thought, *Maybe this is Dad making his play*. The inside of the cab was completely illuminated now as the interior light came on. She could see her father saying something to Grangier—

A weird whistling sound sliced through the air.

Boom!

The explosion almost knocked her off her feet. A blast of heat, a burst of blinding light, the concussive force of a wave of intense energy slammed into her. Thrown backward, she fetched up against the truck she'd planned to steal, caught herself with both hands against the grille—and then flung herself forward again, desperately.

Only to stop, swaying, because there was nothing she could do.

Except stare in horror at the raging fireball that the garbage truck had turned into.

Dad.

She screamed it internally, but not a sound emerged from between her shock-parted lips. The truck was totally consumed in flames. They shot skyward, reaching at least three stories high. Their brightness lit up the night, painted the street and the sky and the gulf and the surrounding buildings and the faces of the shouting, shoving, running onlookers orange. The soldiers who'd been surrounding the truck were on the ground now, blown back by the explosion. They were bathed in the hellish orange light, too.

"Aidhyn 'atlaquu alnnar alty?" the officer with the bullhorn bellowed. She automatically translated the Arabic: *Who fired that shot?*

If there was an answer, she missed it.

Some of the soldiers on the ground staggered to their feet. Two more raced from the convoy toward the burning truck with fire extinguishers. Futile, she could tell even before they tried shooting foam at the flames. Even from where she stood, she could feel the heat, intense as sunlamps turned on high. The roar of the fire was punctuated by a sharp crackling. The horrible smell of burning rubber—of burning *something*—was everywhere.

Screams. Through the roaring and shouting and all the other sounds—sirens wailing in the distance, coming closer fast; the incessant blare of a boat horn; pounding feet—Bianca thought she could hear screams.

From the men in the truck.

Her father.

Oh, God, please.

Her blood turned to ice in her veins. Her pounding heart seemed to freeze. It was as if she were watching everything happen in slow motion, as if she were trapped in a nightmare, as if—

A wave of dizziness hit her, stronger almost than the concussion from the blast. Inside her head, a burst of memory detonating through the fog that shrouded her early childhood nearly dropped her to her knees: another explosion, another fireball, other horrific sounds, smells, screams.

The long-ago screams she was hearing were *hers*.

Mommy.

For the first time in her conscious recollection, she remembered how her mother had died. It spun through her head in a lightning flash of terrible illumination.

No, no, no.

Her legs buckled. Pain twisted her insides, skewered her heart. She dropped to her knees on the uneven, baking-hot cobblestones and with a tremendous effort of will managed to thrust the hideous memories aside.

While she watched with tortured disbelief as her father died before her eyes.

It was, she realized as pain turned to soul-wrenching agony, the first time in a long time that she had been sure she loved him.

Mentor, teacher, taskmaster. Ruthless disciplinarian. Despot. Her constant in an uncertain world. Con man. Thief. Dad.

Oh, God. This was why she was always so cautious about letting herself love anyone, anything. It always went wrong, and when it did, it hurt too damned much.

Her breath rasped in her throat. She felt like her lungs were being crushed, like a heavy stone had been dropped on her chest.

"Jennifer. Jesus." Doc was there, hunkering down beside her, dropping an arm across her shoulders. He called her Jennifer because that was the only name for her he knew. His voice, his presence, the solid bulk of him, steadied her. It broke through the pall of horror that held her rooted to the spot. It reminded her of reality, of her own danger and his.

"We have to go," she said and stood up. It took every ounce of strength and determination she possessed. Fire trucks raced up the street, screaming to a stop beside the flaming truck. Firefighters jumped down, ran to connect their hoses to hydrants along the plaza.

Useless. Everyone in the truck was dead. There was no possibility of saving them.

The scene shimmied before her eyes.

Doc rose, too. "But we can't just—"

"Yes, we can. We have to go," she repeated more strongly

and grabbed his arm. Her tone turned fierce as Doc stared at her without moving. "We can't help them. We can stay here and die with them, or we can save ourselves."

People were coming from everywhere now, bursting from their buildings, running up the street, spilling from the alleys. More leaned out of windows and gawked from the decks of boats. They were yelling, calling out to each other. The officer with the bullhorn was still shouting, still giving commands, but she was no longer capable of translating anything.

Every moment that they stayed increased their risk of discovery.

"Move," Bianca ordered, giving Doc's arm a hard yank as she started to walk and he didn't. "Now. We've got to get out of here while we can."

As he moved off with her, finally, she was relieved to discover that her brain was regaining its ability to function. If she and Doc were to survive, she needed to make cold, clear, careful plans, and to hell with her bleeding, crying wimp of a heart.

9

The Four Seasons Seareinersma Bay Hotel was one of Manama's newest, and its finest. Built on a man-made private island in the most exclusive section of north Manama, it was a high-rise tower overlooking the lush gardens and swimming pools of the hotel grounds as well as the beautiful calm waters of the bay in which it stood. The city of Manama filled the skyline on all sides. At night, which it currently was, the garish neon lights of the newest skyscrapers lit up the sky and the smooth black surface of the bay with a kaleidoscope of colors: Vegas by way of the Middle East.

Driving from the city across the causeway to the hotel for this meeting a short time earlier, Colin Rogan had looked at the steel-and-glass column thrusting sixty-eight stories straight up from the tiny island toward the sky and been struck by the imagery. It was as if the hotel itself was giving the finger to the investigators who had worked long and hard to bring the man Interpol called Traveler to justice.

He personally was suffering from two burn marks on the back of his neck, the mother of all headaches and a bad case of the I-can't-believe-you-were-that-stupid's for letting himself get taken down by a babe in sexy underwear with a hot line in kisses. Especially since said babe was his ticket to Traveler and the multimillion-dollar reward being offered to anyone who brought him in.

The only saving grace was that no one besides himself and the girl knew. By the time he'd regained consciousness and staggered out of the restroom, Traveler had been cornered down by the docks and the rush had been on to take him into custody.

An endeavor that had failed spectacularly.

Rogan turned away from the window of the top floor conference room as the last member of the quartet who had been summoned to this meeting knocked briskly before being admitted by one of the support staff, which consisted of security officers and a pair of administrative assistants.

"Kemp." Interpol's Laurent Durand greeted the newcomer, John Kemp, deputy head of covert operations for the American CIA, with a handshake. In his early sixties, average height and weight, Kemp was solid and still muscular, a gray-haired, granite-jawed bureaucrat in a suit.

"Durand." Kemp looked past Durand at Rogan and then at the young, dark-bearded man in the Bahraini military uniform already seated at the far end of the conference table that was the centerpiece of the room. The table had a smooth wood top and chrome legs, and half a dozen black leather chairs were pulled up to it. Except for a credenza holding bottles of water, a coffeemaker and a selection of snacks, it was the only furnishing.

"This is Brigadier General Hamad bin Sequer Al Amiri of the Bahraini Royal Guard." Durand made the introductions. He then nodded at Rogan. "Colin Rogan. At present he is working for me."

As a private contractor recruited to help bring Traveler in, Rogan finished Durand's introduction silently. Kemp shook hands, then flung himself into a seat.

"Why am I here?" Kemp addressed the question to Durand. He looked tired and harassed, and his tone reflected that.

"If you will all excuse us," Durand said to the support staff. As they filed out, his gaze singled out a slender, black-haired young woman in a skirted suit. "Samira, all I do is push the button?"

"The touch pad," Samira corrected, giving him a small smile. "Tap the touch pad. The image will come up."

"The touch pad." Durand sighed. "Don't go far, would you, please?"

"I'll be right outside," Samira promised and followed the rest of the support staff from the room, closing the door as she exited. The four principals to the meeting were left alone.

"I repeat, why am I here?" Kemp drummed his fingers on the table.

"We have come across some information that we thought you might find of interest," Durand said. "Does the name Mason Thayer mean anything to you?"

Kemp's fingers stilled. He gave Durand an inscrutable look. "The question is, what does it mean to you?"

"We have reason to believe that Mason Thayer is Traveler."

Kemp stood up abruptly. The action thrust his chair back, causing its legs to scrape noisily over the floor.

"Impossible," he said. "You've had me fly halfway around the world to tell me *that*?"

"We found a fingerprint. A partial fingerprint. On the inside of a rubber glove that was discarded in a Dumpster outside the apartment building where Traveler spent time preparing for this job. Surveillance leads us to believe that Traveler dropped the glove in the Dumpster." Durand's eyes were watchful on Kemp's face. "We ran the partial, and the name that came up was Mason Thayer. One of *yours*."

By "one of yours," Durand meant CIA, Rogan knew.

"Impossible," Kemp said again. His voice was harsh. "Thayer is dead."

"Are you sure?"

"Yes. Dead twenty-two years. Sure beyond any possibility of mistake."

Durand walked over to a laptop that had been left on the table. Lifting the lid, he let his hand hover over the touch pad and tapped.

"Ah," he said with open satisfaction as an image appeared on the screen. He thrust the laptop across the table at Kemp. "If you will look at this."

This showed black-and-white footage of a man in a raincoat with a hat pulled down low over his forehead entering an alley on a rainy night. The footage, which Rogan knew was from a surveillance camera at an ATM across the street, was of poor quality and its efficacy was further marred by the falling rain. But the streetlamp on the corner provided light enough to see the man, and even read the address of the building he was passing in front of, which was affixed to the stone facade by a bronze plaque: 1801 Rue Saint-Honoré. Paris, he knew.

The man was carrying a white plastic trash bag, and as they watched he turned slightly sideways to sling it into…something. The footage didn't show the Dumpster, although that was where the bag, supposing it was the same bag, had been recovered. But despite the shading of the hat, that slight sideways turn revealed a partial profile: a long nose, firm, full lips, square chin.

"Could that be Mason Thayer?" Durand asked as the footage ended. "From the man's facial features, his size, the way he moves—are they consistent with what you know of him?"

Kemp's expression didn't change. "You're assuming I know what Mason Thayer looked like—twenty-two years ago."

"We know you worked with him on Cerberus." Durand made an apologetic face as Kemp's brows snapped together. The Cerberus Project was a top secret US government program.

Rogan knew that but didn't know the details. He wasn't sure if Durand did. "We have our sources."

Kemp looked back at the image of the man, frozen now at the end of the video. "It's difficult to say. Possibly. Except, and I repeat myself here, for the fact that Thayer is dead."

Durand shook his head. "He wasn't at the time that fingerprint was recovered. We were close, so close, to catching him. This is the man we were pursuing, and I see no other way Thayer's fingerprint could have found its way inside that glove if he didn't leave it there."

"As I understand it, the man you call Traveler is a high-end thief. The fact that he stole millions from Prince Al Khalifa? It has nothing to do with us." Kemp closed the computer with a quick snap and gave Durand a small, sardonic smile. "We have our sources, too."

"It wasn't only money." Durand looked at the brigadier general. "Tell him what else Traveler took."

The brigadier general looked uneasy. When Durand nodded at him encouragingly, the man grimaced and said, "Among other items that, uh, came to us along with the money, there was a small notebook. It contained the names and cover identities of all the American agents operating in the Middle East and those who were helping them clandestinely at the time of Gaddafi's overthrow. Gaddafi was going to use it to blackmail the Americans into getting him out of the country and securing for himself a safe place of asylum. As you know, many of the names are unchanged even today."

Kemp's eyes narrowed. His gaze shot to Durand. "It's my understanding that Traveler burned to death in a stolen truck last night along with his gang and Prince Al Khalifa's misappropriated fortune. If the notebook was taken at the same time as the money, it surely burned, as well. Thus Traveler's identity no longer matters, and your problem is solved."

Durand said, "One would think." His attention shifted to the other man. "Brigadier General Al Amiri, your role in this meeting is complete. I thank you for coming."

The brigadier general stood and came around the table toward Durand. Durand held out his hand to him in farewell. Taking it, Al Amiri said, "You understand that His Highness requires the utmost discretion in this matter. If word of what was lost should get out—"

"It will not. Please assure His Highness of that, and thank him for his cooperation."

The slightly bitter twist Al Amiri's mouth took on as Durand said that reminded Rogan that the prince's cooperation had been obtained under duress, and only because Durand had emphasized to him the consequences, not just worldwide but among his own family, if it should become known that Gaddafi's widely rumored missing fortune had wound up in the prince's possession.

"Yes, I will do that." The brigadier general allowed himself to be shown out. While he had the door open, Durand poked his head out into the hall.

"Samira—"

"Yes, sir." The woman entered and, with a quick smile for Durand, headed directly for the laptop.

"If you could pull up the other video." Durand sounded apologetic as he followed her to the table.

She opened the laptop, pecked at a few keys and said, "You need only tap the touch pad again."

"Thank you, Samira." Dismissing her with a nod, he waited until she had left the room and closed the door behind her. Then he looked at Kemp and said, "Over the years, but especially in the past five years or so, Traveler has stolen not only millions upon millions of dollars in cash and valuables but also secrets. Highly classified material like what is in this notebook that could cost the lives of many serving and former intelligence officers if the information in it should leak out. The items that he has taken—documents, photographs, recordings, computer files—are SCI and SAP level. You will understand that the hunt for him has grown increasingly intense."

SCI and SAP level were above Top Secret, reserved for the most sensitive government programs and information. Kemp's mouth thinned. "And what has Traveler done with this information?"

Durand shook his head. "We don't know. There has been no blowback that we know of, and so far we have not been successful in determining where the stolen material has ended up. But rest assured, Traveler took it for a reason. Identifying him, knowing now that he is most probably Mason Thayer, gives us even more cause for concern. As it should you."

"Thayer is dead," Kemp said.

"Yet somehow his fingerprint lives on. I am informally requesting your agency's cooperation in this matter. I can submit a formal request if you like, but, as you know, formal requests have a way of leaking. I think everyone concerned would prefer it if we worked together to resolve this quietly."

Kemp appeared to consider. Then he nodded curtly. "We'll do what we can."

"Time is of the essence," Durand said. "We are closer than we have ever been to bringing Traveler in."

"I thought Traveler was dead," Kemp replied. "Just as Mason Thayer is dead."

"I am not so certain about either." Durand beckoned both Kemp and Rogan closer. "Watch this. Tell me what you think."

He tapped the touch pad, and the laptop sprang to life.

Footage of a stopped garbage truck surrounded by soldiers closing in on it. A flash of light like a shooting star through the darkness, streaking toward the truck from out of frame. The truck erupting into a giant fireball that almost immediately consumed it—

Durand tapped the touch pad again, and the image froze. For an instant he looked pleased with himself before glancing up at the others.

"Traveler and at least two and possibly as many as four of his associates are thought to have perished in this blaze. Two hundred million dollars in untraceable US cash that was in the back of the truck burned to ash. My question to you is, in your opinion could this have been faked?"

"Are you sure Traveler and the money were inside the truck when it burned?" Placing one hand on the tabletop, Rogan leaned forward to study the still image of the blazing truck. It was impossible to see inside the cab, impossible to tell if anyone might have been in the back with the cash. Hardened as he was to the almost infinite forms violent death could take, he discovered that he didn't much like to think about the possibility that his scantily clad seductress might have burned alive in that truck.

"We have eyewitness testimony placing Traveler and at least two of his associates inside the cab at the moment of explosion," Durand said. "This is the only video that we have, and as you see it doesn't show much. The people on the garbage scow that was to take the truck to Qatar profess to know nothing. They are being questioned, but I do not expect a great deal of new information. We have people sifting through the wreckage as we speak who have confirmed that the ash inside the truck is consistent with US dollars. Unfortunately, the bodies inside were also reduced to ash. It will take time to recover the DNA and do an analysis so that the identities of the deceased can be confirmed."

"Why do you suspect it might have been faked?" Kemp asked.

Durand shrugged. "I do not so much suspect it as—how shall I put this?—wonder. It is very convenient that Traveler, his associates and the large fortune he was attempting to steal all go *poof* up in flames just as the authorities close in. If we believe Traveler is dead and the money burned, we stop looking for him—and it. Plus, if Traveler is in fact Mason Thayer, he has apparently successfully faked his death before. As you said, for twenty-two years."

"Impossible." Kemp's tone was harsh.

"Is it?"

"Who fired the shot that took out the truck?" Rogan had tapped the touch pad and gotten the video going again. There was footage—incomplete but interesting—of the military vehicles surrounding the truck. "The only thing I see that could cause anything approaching that level of explosion is the Mark 19 grenade launcher—" he pointed at the screen "—here, and it doesn't appear to have been fired."

Durand gave him an approving look. "That is a very good question. So far no one is taking responsibility, but then the word is out that the prince is upset at the turn events took and so it is possible that they may be keeping quiet. We are having the footage analyzed, of course."

Rogan said, "But you feel that it's possible that Traveler himself had the truck blown up to cover an escape."

Durand shrugged. "Anything is possible. It is an avenue I am prepared to explore."

"How could they possibly have pulled that off?"

"Perhaps by using doubles. Perhaps— I do not know. But we do know that Traveler is a master at the arts of misdirection and illusion. I am not willing to simply accept that he is dead without examining other possibilities."

Kemp took a hasty turn around the room. He stopped to look at Durand. "What's being done?"

Durand said, "There's a Red Notice out." A Red Notice being an international wanted-persons alert. "We found an old photo of Mason Thayer that we have had age-enhanced to present day. That is being run through facial recognition software to compare it with driver's license databases, pilot and all other license databases, government ID programs—anything anywhere in the world that requires a picture ID. Unless he has changed his appearance drastically, and it does not appear that he has, we will find him."

"Do we have IDs on his associates yet?" Rogan asked. "If we find out who they are, that might lead us to him."

"Not yet. We suspect that the woman who was advising the prince on his art collection was part of it. She slipped away from the prince's bodyguards while being brought in for questioning, and may or may not have been in the truck. The prince knew her as Jennifer Ashley, but we have ascertained that that was an alias. We have a description, a passport photo and pictures from security footage—here." Durand tapped the touch pad and looked delighted when images appeared of a red-haired woman walking through an art gallery and, at a different time, across a hotel lobby, followed by what appeared to be the same woman entering the Gudaibiya Palace ballroom the previous night. Unfortunately, in all instances her face was turned away from the camera. The slightly blurry passport photo that followed showed an attractive, thirty-ish woman with a wild mane of red hair obscuring the sides of her face and most of her wide jawline. She had narrowed eyes and a slight overbite as she faced the camera.

She bore little resemblance to the blonde beauty who had blindsided him in the restroom. But he knew they were one and the same.

This, Rogan reflected, was the moment to come clean, to

reveal what he knew about the woman's drastically altered appearance.

"We think there were two, possibly three others," Durand said as the screen filled with rows of what looked like passport photos. Unwilling to examine his motives too closely, Rogan let the moment pass. Durand continued, "We're cross-checking these known associates of Traveler's with security footage taken in Bahrain over the past few days. We'll let you know when we come up with some names."

Kemp said, "If Mason Thayer is dead—and he is—your whole strategy is a waste of time."

"This isn't our whole strategy." Durand met Kemp's gaze. Something in Durand's expression seemed to challenge the American, because his mouth tightened.

"Oh? What else do you have in mind?"

Durand said, "We're going to shake the tree."

Later that night, when Kemp was once again aloft in the private jet that had brought him to Bahrain, he made a call over a secure line. If what the Frenchman alleged was true, he would be blamed, he knew. Having failed to kill Thayer was the kind of blown mission that could cost him his career, maybe even his life. Annoying to discover that his palms were sweaty and his chest was tight as he faced the even more crucial question: Who else had he failed to kill?

It was 3:00 a.m. Bahraini time, 7:00 p.m. in Washington, DC, where the man he was calling lived. That man was Alexander Groton, Kemp's onetime boss and the recently retired head of the Defense Advanced Research Projects Agency (DARPA) under the Department of Defense umbrella, which among other things was charged with the research and development of emerging technologies for use by the military. The only person who had more to lose than Kemp did if Thayer was still alive.

"Looks like we may have a problem," he said to Groton when he answered.

10

Five months later

It was 5:30 p.m. on the Wednesday before Halloween. Bianca emerged from her office, a large corner space on the top floor of one of Savannah, Georgia's newest semi-high-rises (okay, so fifteen stories didn't seem to her like it should actually qualify for the term *high-rise*, so she'd added the *semi*), to find Doc waving at her frantically from behind his desk in his office just off the sleekly modern reception area. Bianca acknowledged him with an upraised hand and a quick, negative shake of her head. Silent message: whatever it is will have to wait. Gordon Kazmarek, owner and CEO of the worldwide megachain of mall-based Gordon's Jewelry Stores, and two of his associates had just walked through the front door into the reception area to hopefully seal the deal that would give Guardian Consulting—the security firm Bianca had established in this sleepy Southern town five years before, right after graduating from college, as part of the cover identity/bolt-hole that every prudent international criminal needs—an exclusive contract to provide all of Gordon's Jewelry's security.

It was a big deal, a big *legitimate* deal. And legitimate was important. The problem with acquiring money by questionable means such as theft was, what did you do with it once you got it? Stuff it in your mattress? Squirrel it away in tin cans buried in your backyard? Stash it in a secret bank account or safety-deposit box somewhere? That was fine—unless you wanted/needed to use the money, which was generally the point of acquiring it. Plus there was the little matter of taxes. Al Capone was taken down by the tax man, and Bianca had no desire to follow in his footsteps. The solution was obvious: come up with a means to make the money look like it came from somewhere that didn't involve anything illegal. Like an elderly aunt who died and left you an inheritance. Or a windfall profit on the sale of an object that turned out to be surprisingly valuable. Or the ongoing profits from your own thriving business, i.e., Guardian Consulting.

And when it turned out that your father had secretly, dangerously depleted all your bank accounts, hidden and otherwise, to fund the operation that had gone to hell on a slide, rendered up no profit whatsoever and ended with him getting killed and you barely escaping with your life, why, then your legitimate business, the one that you could actually work at and make a profit from, became doubly important.

Because a girl had to eat. And pay the rent. And make payroll. And—well, lots of things.

The opportunity with Gordon's Jewelry Stores had come about because Bianca had been able to illustrate gaping holes in the chain's security by robbing six of their stores. Kazmarek had challenged her to put her moves where her mouth was when she'd approached him at a conference with a pitch about the terrible state of his security. When he'd seen how easily she'd been able to make off with hundreds of thousands of dollars' worth of his merchandise, he'd been floored—and impressed. Tonight, Bianca was almost sure, would be the payoff.

"Mr. Kazmarek." Holding out her hand, Bianca walked forward to greet him with a smile.

"Kaz, please." Kazmarek took her hand, shook it, then held it a little too long and a little too tightly. Bianca was conservatively dressed in a black pantsuit and a white silk blouse, with her straight, not-quite-shoulder-skimming blond hair parted on the side and tucked behind one ear and her makeup minimal, but still he looked her over with open admiration. Five-nine and stocky, he was fifty-three, a twice-married, currently divorced self-made multimillionaire with an unabashed eye for the ladies. He was bullish in manner and appearance, with a bald, smooth-shaven head, coarse features, pale blue eyes and a brash confidence that had its own charm. That confidence was currently on full display as, once-over completed, his eyes rose to meet hers again and he smiled.

"Kaz, of course." Bianca hadn't forgotten that they'd progressed to a first-name basis during their last meeting, when she'd flown to his Memphis headquarters to present Guardian Consulting's proposal to him and his board. She just didn't want to encourage him to think that he was going to get anything out of this contract besides her firm's very best security consulting services.

She was shaking hands with Kazmarek's associates when, out of the corner of her eye, she saw that Doc was waving at her again and looking agitated. Lips compressing, she glanced around for Evie, who, she was happy to see, had risen from her desk beneath the big silver Guardian Consulting sign that took up most of the wall at the top of the room and was approaching.

"I don't think you've met my assistant, Evangeline Talmadge." Bianca introduced them. Evie turned on that megawatt Deb-of-the-Year smile of hers and shook hands. Five-three and curvy, Evie was dressed today in a sleeveless, colorful rose-print sheath that, like all of her clothes, had cost the earth, a coordinating cardigan, pearls and, atypically, flats. She had a round, pretty face with the magnolia-pale skin that had been prized in the Deep South since time immemorial, a riot of shoulder-length coffee-brown curls, a small, upturned nose, wide mouth and big brown puppy-dog eyes. The only daughter of a real estate magnate who owned a good portion of Savannah and a lot of the rest of the South and Savannah's leading blue-blooded social-ite, she'd grown up rich and privileged—and feeling unwanted.

Bianca had met her at Le Rosey, the boarding school in the Swiss Alps where really rich kids whose parents were too busy to be bothered with them were shipped off to be educated. Evie was at Le Rosey because her really rich parents were divorc-ing. Bianca was there because her father wanted an entrée to the really rich with the intention of robbing them, swindling them or, in some other iniquitous way, separating them from a portion of their wealth, although of course she hadn't realized that at the time.

Evie had been miserable at first, crying herself to sleep at night, letting her vulnerability show, making herself an easy target for the school bullies, who were numerous and vicious and who'd scented fear in the plump little newcomer. Bianca, who after years of Richard's take-no-prisoners upbringing had pretty much lost her fear of anything unlikely to result in her immediate death, had handily routed the bullies and taken Evie, one of the few other Americans at the school, under her wing. The cool, guarded blonde who opened up to no one and ex-celled at everything—sports, academics, languages, social graces, getting boys to fall at her feet—and the warm, impulsive, in-discriminately trusting brunette who was hopeless at sports and languages and no more than mediocre at academics but was actually pretty good at attracting boys, too, became un-likely fast friends.

Of course, Evie knew nothing about Bianca's double life. She had no idea that Richard St. Ives was not the independently wealthy businessman that was his cover identity, or that Bianca's life when she wasn't at school or helping her father steal some-thing consisted of everything from mixed martial arts training by a sensei master to physical conditioning by a pair of retired special ops to lessons in such varied specialties as the fine art of picking pockets and locks to the use of weaponry and explosives to gymnastics and boxing—and ballet. Because ballet, according to Richard, gave you grace and balance. Bianca mastered everything that was thrown at her, but she really loved ballet.

As time passed, at Evie's insistence, Bianca spent the majority of school holidays (if Richard didn't need her for a job, or training, she was left to make her own plans) with Evie and her mother, Rosalie, at their Savannah mansion. When Bianca was setting up her bolt-hole, she'd chosen Savannah because it was a continuation of the life she'd known, the one she considered her real life, the one she lived as Bianca St. Ives. She'd gone to boarding school as Bianca St. Ives, she'd earned her degree in English lit from Sarah Lawrence College as Bianca St. Ives and the minimal family life she'd experienced with her father had been as Bianca St. Ives.

She'd also chosen Savannah because no one in their right mind would look for a member of an internationally wanted gang of criminals in the Southern belle capital of the world, and because Evie had permanently settled down there. Evie had permanently settled down there because she had married William Wentworth Thornton IV, scion of a local textile dynasty, right after her and Bianca's sophomore year of college and Evie's star turn, at her mother's insistence, as Savannah's Debutante of the Year.

Two months ago, Evie had discovered that Fourth, as her husband was known, was cheating on her. Evie had filed for divorce. In doing so, she'd gone against the wishes of her father, her mother and Fourth himself and his family, all of whom insisted she was making a mountain out of a molehill and told her in their various ways that all men stray occasionally and that as the wife she should simply look the other way. For one of the few times in her life, Evie had refused to go along with the majority.

She took back her maiden name: Talmadge. She kicked Fourth out of their mansion in the historic district.

She was getting a divorce and taking her life back and nothing and nobody was going to talk her out of it.

What complicated the situation, what had her warring parents coming together in a rare moment of accord and made getting Fourth out of her life a whole lot harder than it otherwise would have been, was that she was pregnant. Five months and change now. Her baby bump was obvious and dictated both the loose sheath and the flat shoes she was wearing.

When Evie's crisis had dropped in her lap, Bianca was working to move past the shock of her father's death, which no one in her world except Doc knew about because at that point she wasn't up to concocting and living the lie that would be required to fake a funeral, explain how he had died, etc. Shaking off her own troubles, she'd offered Evie staunch support, a shoulder to cry on and a job at Guardian Consulting.

The job, as it turned out, was the important thing, because one of the first things Fourth did was cut off Evie's credit cards and drain her bank account. Evie's father, who had business dealings with Fourth's family and an old-fashioned view of single mothers, had refused to come to her financial assistance and had threatened to disinherit her unless she went back to her husband. Once started down the road of defiance, Evie grabbed on to it with both hands and told him what he could do with his money. Then she told her mother that she wouldn't be doing as Rosalie suggested and moving back into her old bedroom in the family mansion, either, and that furthermore she could take care of herself, thank you very much.

Having thus burned her familial bridges, Evie gritted her teeth, squared her shoulders and huddled with Bianca to take stock. She was a veteran of the volunteer/philanthropic/charitable circuit, but none of that was paid employment. Her new job with Guardian Consulting was the first paying gig she'd ever had in her life. Bianca would have kept her on regardless of how it worked out, but Evie was proving to be really good at it.

To what Evie confided in Bianca was her own surprise, the former Deb of the Year was efficient, hardworking and a hit with clients.

As Evie finished shaking hands with Kazmarek's associates, Doc beckoned insistently at Bianca behind the visitors' backs. Frowning at him, also behind the visitors' backs, Bianca said to Kazmarek, "If you'll go on into my office, I'll join you in just a moment. There's something I need to check on."

"Sure thing," Kazmarek said. "You take all the time you need."

"Can I get you gentlemen some coffee? Or tea? Or maybe something stronger?" Smiling graciously, Evie ushered the visitors toward Bianca's office like she'd been doing it for years, instead of the six weeks she'd actually been on the job. The men voiced their preference in drinks before disappearing into Bianca's office. After promising them that she'd see to it right away, Evie turned back to Bianca to say, low-voiced, "I made reservations at 700 Drayton for 7:00 p.m., by the way."

700 Drayton was one of the city's finest restaurants and also one of the hardest reservations to secure at short notice, which this had been. Here was the type of situation where having Evie on the payroll was turning out to be truly beneficial: she was Savannah aristocracy by birth and marriage, A-list all the way, with connections that paid off in large ways and small, including obtaining impossible reservations. The plan was that, after Bianca went over the contract and extolled the myriad benefits of signing on with Guardian Consulting here at the office, she would take Kazmarek and company to dinner to seal the deal.

"Thanks, that's perfect." Bianca's response was equally low-voiced. "Is Hay back yet?"

Hay was Haywood Long, her second in command, in charge of running the business when she was away and overseeing all but the highest level jobs when she was present. He'd been down at the docks that afternoon supervising the crew providing security for the unloading of a large quantity of electronic equipment for Dynex, Inc., another important client. Dynex had been losing an unacceptable percentage of their imports to theft, and it was Guardian Consulting's job to find out how it was happening, who was doing it, and stop it.

"Not yet," Evie said as she passed Bianca on her way to the small combination kitchen/break room where she would prepare the drinks.

"When he gets back, send him along to the restaurant, would you, please?"

Evie looked back over her shoulder to grin at Bianca in total comprehension. "You got it."

That was another thing about working with Evie: they knew each other so well that Bianca didn't have to spell things out. Hay would serve as Bianca's "date," which would hopefully keep Kazmarek from coming on to her to the point where Bianca had to outright refuse him, or worse. The firm badly needed his business, and thus keeping him happy was important. Bianca felt it would be much easier to do that if she didn't have to, say, break his nose at the end of the evening for putting his hands where they didn't belong.

"Boss," Doc hissed, giving her another come-here wave.

Bianca headed toward him. She shouldn't have brought Doc with her to Savannah, or into Bianca St. Ives's world at all, she knew.

Live your life in compartments: it was another one of the rules. The corollary being, of course, that the various life compartments should be kept totally separate, and the components should never be mixed. Doc had belonged to the Jennifer Ashley, Bahrain, two-hundred-million-dollar debacle compartment. He should have been left there, none the wiser about who or what Jennifer Ashley or Kenneth Rapp or any of the rest of them really were. But Bianca had discovered that it just wasn't in her to simply abandon Doc in Bahrain, and so she'd gotten him out of the country, then out of the Middle East. By that time she'd realized that he was clueless about how to evade the manhunt that was raging for them across Europe and helpless as a child at looking out for himself in any meaningful way that didn't involve computers.

She'd taken a chance and ignored one of the rules that her father had spent a lifetime pounding into her. Swearing Doc to secrecy, reminding him that he had as much to lose as she did if the truth were to ever come out, she introduced him to Bianca St. Ives, brought him back to Savannah with her and, under his real identity as Miles Davis Zeigler, reformed (sort of) computer hacker, made him Guardian Consulting's head of cyber security.

So far it was working out. His *dese* and *dose* accent and penchant for wearing all black clothing even when it was sweltering outside meant that he would never be mistaken for a local; any dish involving grits he regarded with deep suspicion, and he stayed pretty much permanently flushed and sweaty from the never-ending heat and humidity. But he liked his new apartment overlooking Monroe Square, he'd fallen madly in love with the pralines at River Street Sweets and he'd happily adopted Bianca as family. And he added a whole new element to the services Guardian Consulting could offer clients. Plus, she discovered, it was good to have someone around who knew the truth about what she was and what had happened and could help her keep tabs on any fallout that might be echoing around the globe from Richard's death.

"What's up?" Bianca asked quietly as she reached him. Doc's desk faced the door. She walked around it as he gestured toward the state-of-the-art computer in front of him.

"We got another Bat Signal. Look."

Leaning back precariously—Doc dwarfed his small ergonomic chair, which he stubbornly refused to let Bianca replace, and had a penchant for leaning back so far in it that she lived in constant fear that he was going to tip over and crash to the floor—he looked up at her with a worried frown.

Bianca's pulse picked up as she moved closer to check out the monitor. A Bat Signal, so called by Doc in honor of the sign that was flashed in the sky to summon Batman, was an email that came through an anonymous, highly encrypted account used to contact Richard by clients who'd been willing to pay large for his services. Since his death, he'd been approached by four such clients, all of whom had wanted him to steal something for them. He'd been offered a handsome payday in each instance, and Bianca had thought about taking the jobs on herself. But the *Live your life in compartments* rule had included keeping her life and her father's lives strictly separate. When he wasn't Richard St. Ives, he had multiple other identities, only a few of which she knew. In his other lives, he could be anyone and up to anything. She was wary about accidentally sticking her toe into what might turn out to be a pool of sharks.

Once she'd grown up enough to grasp the dangerous nature of what they did, she'd understood his insistence that they come together rarely, usually only when he needed her for a job. They communicated irregularly, mostly via email. Phone contact initiated from her end involved her dialing an always changing number, leaving a message and waiting for him to return her call. When he called her, which wasn't often, the calls always came through a blocked number that accepted no callbacks. His appearances at her major school events had been quick and tightly scheduled. They had no permanent home; when she visited him, which happened less and less often as she grew up, he was always staying in a different house or apartment or hotel suite in a different part of the world. That was necessary because security, he told her, was best preserved by his keeping on the move, and by maintaining strict separation of their lives except when they were actually working together.

She understood. But sometimes, especially when she was younger, like the first Christmas she'd spent with Evie when they were twelve years old and she'd seen the big sparkly tree and the decorations in every room and Evie's extended family had come for Christmas dinner, she'd felt a little wistful.

The only reason she was able to access this particular email account was because at the time of his death Richard had been having Doc work his magic to better hide the account's tracks from anyone who might be trying to follow them back to him. Bianca was fuzzy on the details, but she gathered that Doc had the account pinging through a maze of different countries, servers and IP addresses. Doc assured her that the account's point of origin would never be found, and they, who were monitoring it, would never be found, and she trusted him enough to believe him.

It still made her sick to read the incoming emails, because the very fact that she was doing so reminded her that her father was dead. She was having trouble coming to terms with it. Richard had always seemed indestructible to her.

It didn't help that questions from the night he died kept gnawing at her. What had gone wrong? How had Durand found out about the heist? And who had really taken the money?

She knew from the sources she very cautiously kept in touch with that authorities believed it had burned up in the garbage truck. She also knew that that was absolutely untrue.

The thought that someone else had secretly made off with

the stolen fortune that her father had died in pursuit of drove her around the bend.

Ignoring the hard knot in her chest, she read the email aloud, "'Your services are required.'"

That was it. No greeting, no signature, just those four words. She slanted a look at Doc. "Can you tell where this is from?"

"Close as I can tell it originated from somewhere in Hong Kong. 'Course, that's probably a bounce address, you know what I mean?"

She gathered he meant a fake address that resulted from the email being bounced around through various servers before it was delivered.

"When did we get it?"

"Like, five minutes ago. I have an alert set up so that I'm notified when anything comes into that account."

Bianca's lips tightened. The urge to reply, to reach out to whoever this was in an attempt to find out who they were, what they wanted and how they knew her father, was strong.

A soft *ping* announced the arrival of another email into the same account. Bianca's pulse quickened. She frowned at the words that had just popped up on the screen.

We need you to retrieve something that was stolen from us. We will pay one million dollars US.

Now, *that* was tempting. She needed the money. She could answer the email, take the job and—

Live your life in compartments.

The rule pushed its way into her mind. This email account belonged to her father. The smartest, safest thing she could do was leave it in his compartment and walk away.

"Don't answer it," she said, as she'd said about the previous emails. "We're not going to respond."

"Yeah."

As Doc nodded agreement, she turned and left his office.

Her throat was tight and her stomach churned. Ignoring those emails was one of the hardest things she'd ever done.

They felt like a last link to her father. Like she could somehow get to him through them. And she was walking away.

From the first moment she'd been able to pause to catch her breath after the harrowing journey she and Doc had undertaken to get out of the Middle East, she'd monitored every means of communication that had ever connected her to Richard—the email account that was only used for exchanges between the two of them, the last burner phone number she'd had for him that she did not dare call for fear someone besides Richard might be watching the other end, her business and personal phone lines that he had never used but that he knew, everything.

She'd done that because, Bianca realized, in her heart of hearts she still expected to hear from him again. And that would be because she was still having trouble processing the fact that he was dead even though she had watched him die.

She hadn't left the Middle East without making certain there were no survivors from that fire, despite another rule that Richard had drummed into her from childhood: *Never look back.*

She could still hear his voice lecturing in her head: *If an operation goes south, it's every man for himself. Your job is to get the hell out.*

That was what she'd done, but she was still paying the price in grief, regret—and the nightmares about being trapped in a fire that now haunted her sleep almost every night.

"Bee? You okay?" Walking by her with the tray of drinks, Evie looked at her with a frown.

Bianca realized that she had stopped walking just outside Doc's door and was standing stock-still with her arms crossed over her chest staring blankly into space.

Shake it off. "I'm fine. I was just thinking about something."

Plastering a hopefully not-too-fake-looking smile on her face, she followed Evie into her office.

11

The restaurant was as fabulous as always. Hay showed up just after they were seated and before Kazmarek could do much more than press his thigh suggestively against hers under the table, and over after-dinner drinks Bianca persuaded Kazmarek to sign on the dotted line, making Gordon's Jewelry Stores their newest client.

All in all, a good day. Except for the anonymous email, which was still taking up way more than its fair share of real estate in the back of her mind. The more she thought about it, the more obvious it became that whoever had sent it had an ongoing relationship with Richard that was different from her experience of his interactions with other paying clients. *Your services are required.* There was an arrogance to it. As if her father were obligated to—

"That ole boy was droolin' all over you the whole time we were eating," Hay said with disapproval. Six-one with short fair hair that had been blond when he was a kid, bright blue eyes that crinkled when he smiled and a muscular build, he had the all-American appeal of the high school football star he had once been. He was looking good in the navy blazer, tieless blue shirt and khaki pants that were a staple of the Savannah male business wardrobe. Twenty-nine, single and gainfully employed, he had a whole lot of women interested in him. Bianca might have been, too, but she considered him one of her closest friends.

Additionally, he worked for her and did a very good job at it. None of those things did she want to screw up by starting a romantic relationship with him that was doomed to fail, anyway.

She knew Hay well. He was a salt-of-the-earth kind of guy, with plenty of vices but no real vice in him. The thing was, he knew only a tiny part of her. And that was the way it had to be.

"We got the contract," she retorted.

"Yeah, we did. Congratulations, by the way."

She smiled at him. "You helped."

"I'm glad to play bodyguard." He looked her up and down and wiggled his eyebrows suggestively. "Especially to such a great body."

She made a face at him. "Ha ha."

"Wasn't joking."

After seeing Kazmarek and company off, they were walking down the sidewalk away from the restaurant, which was housed in the Mansion on Forsyth Park, a boutique hotel in the historic district, on the way to their respective vehicles. It was nearly 10:00 p.m., a clear night with a lot of people out and about, strolling along the sidewalks that fronted the rows of antebellum houses or through the parklike squares. Thanks to a salt-scented breeze blowing in from the ocean, the day's humidity was gone and the temperature was no more than a smidgen above pleasantly warm. Dripping tendrils of Spanish moss from the huge live oaks lining the street hung low overhead. Antique-looking streetlamps on the corners acted as beacons for a whole collection of flying bugs. The cicadas were doing their usual thing and providing a little night music.

Like Bianca, Hay had had to scramble to find parking because the redbrick, turreted former-mansion-turned-hotel was popular with locals and tourists alike and the lot was full when they got there. As they neared the intersection, Bianca spotted his dark green Chevy Tahoe beside the curb about half a block down Gwinnett. Her silver Acura with the magnetic Guardian Consulting signs on each of the front doors (itemized tax deductions were a wonderful thing) was parked a block farther along the street they were currently on, Drayton.

"Gordon's Jewelry has the potential to be an extremely lucrative contract." Her tone was serious as she looked up at him. "You'll get a bonus."

"That's why I didn't punch *Kaz* in the nose when he started trying to play footsie with you under the table." Hay's faintly sour tone told Bianca that Kazmarek's overattentiveness to her still rankled. It was an open secret that Hay, in the parlance of the Deep South, "fancied" her, but he wasn't pushy about it. They'd known each other since Bianca had started coming home to Savannah with Evie when she and Evie were twelve and he was fifteen. He was the proverbial boy next door (well, to Evie). That would be because his single mother, who worked for Macy's as a retail associate, i.e., salesclerk, had lived in the carriage house belonging to the place next door to Evie's parents' huge mansion on East Jones Street for free in exchange for keeping an eye on the Big House while the owners traveled the world. Hay had spent a good portion of those teenage visits hanging with Evie and Bianca and, as they grew older, trying to get Bianca to go out with him. She never had, holding out as he spent a year partying at the University of South Carolina and then joined the army, where he'd served a tour in Afghanistan. He'd been working as a cop in tiny Sandfly, one of the many small satellite communities around Savannah, and doing his best to cope with a bad case of the what-do-I-do-with-the-rest-of-my-life's by drinking heavily when Bianca had started setting up her bolt-hole in Savannah. When she'd run into Hay—she'd been speeding through Sandfly in her little red sports car and he'd pulled her over—she'd been struck by a flash of inspiration even as he was writing her out a ticket. Hay was just the man she needed to handle day-to-day operations at Guardian Consulting. A cop who was ex-military, someone she knew, liked and trusted—he was perfect for what she had in mind. So she'd offered him the job, he'd accepted and he'd been instrumental in helping to build up the business to where they were today.

Making a face at him, Bianca said, "I appreciate your forbearance."

"Much as it shames me to admit it, I can be bought."

"Can't we all." Bianca's tone was light. Truth was, he had no idea. She looked up at him as they reached the junction with Gwinnett and jerked a thumb in the direction he needed to go. "Your car's that way."

"I'm walking you to yours."

There was no arguing with him about it, she knew, and telling him that she could take care of herself was a waste of her breath. He knew she'd studied martial arts, and he knew that she knew her way around a punching bag, but he'd never seen her in action for real and she got the impression that he considered both endeavors as something along the line of cute little hobbies. Hay had no idea about her secret life as the elite sublegal operative she'd learned to be as her father's daughter, or anything about the way she actually made most of her money and found the funds to do things like, say, buy her condo or grow the business. Giving him a demonstration of exactly what she could do might have opened his eyes a little, but it would also raise questions she didn't want to answer.

Besides, she didn't mind the company.

"You get anywhere with Dynex this afternoon?" she asked as they proceeded through the intersection.

"Nope. Everything was present and accounted for. If I didn't know better, I might think somebody knew we were going to be there."

"An inside job?"

"That's what I'm thinking. I've got Latts and Harper—" two of the people who worked under him "—cross-checking time clocks to see who was present—or absent—when each of the thefts occurred. We're also looking at the logs of trucks that came into the dock area. Can't carry off that much equipment without a truck."

"Sounds like a plan. What about the Simpsonville deliveries? Did they go okay?" she asked. The Simpsonville deliveries involved supervising the dropping off of bags of cash to a chain of payday loan stores that had, unfortunately, attracted the attention of some small-time thieves who wanted the cash but no loan. After four locations in ten days had been robbed just as the stores were opening and the day's cash was being delivered, the owners had called in security professionals, i.e., Guardian Consulting. Guardian Consulting brought in retired cops to escort the money deliveries while police investigated the robberies. It wasn't a large gig, but the payday loan chain was expanding and it could grow.

Anyway, Bianca was a big believer in word of mouth. She did her best to make sure every job was done right and trusted that the word would spread. So far it had worked, both in the security business and in the extracurricular jobs utilizing her unique skill set that she took on individually. Advertising wasn't an option in the kind of circles where somebody wanted back the five million his business partner had embezzled and fled to Switzerland with, for example. She could get the money back, though not necessarily by legal means. Her fee for such services was usually twenty percent of the total, but it could be more or less, depending on the job.

"Like clockwork. Thieves like the ones that hit them spot a cop and take off after easier targets. As long as we're on the job,

I don't imagine they'll have any more trouble." Hay slanted a look down at her. "You going straight home after this?"

Sometimes they got a drink together at the conclusion of a long day. The Distillery was one of their favorite bars and it was nearby. Bianca knew what he was asking. But given the fact that she wasn't going to sleep with him because she valued their relationship the way it was, and it would get awkward if one booze-soaked night he was suddenly not okay with that, she tried to keep pub crawling with Hay to a minimum.

So she nodded. "Yes. Well, after I stop by the store. Evie texted me a list."

He accepted her decision without surprise. He knew the score. "Oh, that's right, she's at your place, isn't she?"

"For the time being. Fourth kept showing up at their house and making a scene. She's just staying with me until he gets it out of his system."

Hay snorted. "That'll be about the time the next bimbo walks by."

"Maybe. But see, there's the house. He really doesn't want to lose the house to Evie in a divorce. So I'm betting he keeps it zipped until he's convinced she's serious when she tells him they are never, ever, ever getting back together."

Hay grinned but said, "Shithead."

He was referring to Fourth, Bianca knew, and since their opinion of Evie's blue-blooded Southern aristocrat soon-to-be ex-husband was pretty much the same, she grimaced agreement.

"Think your boy Doc could hook us up with some ship itineraries and bills of lading?"

The way Hay referred to "your boy Doc" told Bianca that he had yet to fully accept Doc as a member of the Guardian Consulting team. He'd been dubious of the fast-talking Northerner from the time Bianca had brought Doc back with her from her last "vacation" abroad and opened up the new-to-them branch of cyber security with Doc as its head. For his part, Doc seemed to regard the drawling native Georgian as a refugee from *The Dukes of Hazzard.*

Bianca's diagnosis of the problem was, the two didn't speak each other's language. Doc was all about computers, and Hay was the quintessential man of action. Sooner or later, she was convinced they were bound to stumble upon common ground. If not, in her experience it wasn't so much absence but time that made the heart grow fonder.

"For the Dynex investigation? Why don't you ask him?"

"'Cause every time I say anything to him he looks at me like he thinks I ought to be strumming a banjo in the backwoods somewhere."

Bianca had to smile. "He does not."

"He does. And you know it."

"Ask him, anyway."

"You're a real hard-ass, you know that?"

"The knowledge keeps me awake at night." They had almost reached her car, and Bianca pulled her keys from her purse and hit the unlock button. The resultant *ding* and brief flash of her headlights had Hay glancing that way.

"You still planning on going to that Historic Savannah thing weekend after next?" Hay asked as they reached the car and she opened her door. As the car's interior light spilled out over the pavement, she looked at him over the top of the door.

By "that Historic Savannah thing," she knew he meant the annual autumn charity ball/auction/gala put on by the Preservation League. It was a costume event where all attendees were supposed to dress like residents of antebellum Savannah. All the Savannah Old Guard plus a select coterie of moneyed newcomers would be present, and as a local business owner Bianca was expected both to make a generous donation to the cause and to attend. On the bright side, it was an excellent networking opportunity.

"I think I might be Evie's date," she said. "She's the event cochair, so she has to go. She doesn't want to go alone, and, to quote her, she's sure as hell not going with Fourth. So at this point that leaves me."

"I'm sure you two will make a beautiful couple." Hay's eyes slid away from hers. For a moment he looked shifty. "The thing is, I have a family thing that weekend and—"

Bianca hooted. "Your mother's in Atlanta until January and your sister lives in California. Nice try."

"I'm allergic to costumes. The wig itches."

"Suck it up."

"I want overtime."

"Your paycheck clears, doesn't it?"

"*Hard*-ass."

"Damn straight. All hands on deck for this one, mister."

"Come on, Bianca."

"If I have to go, you have to go. It's community outreach. It's a way to drum up business. Anyway, I thought you were taking Susan Clemons."

He rubbed his nose. "When we went out last Saturday night, she said she was ready for us to be exclusive. Things kind of went to hell from there."

"So you're not taking Susan Clemons."

"Nope."

"Get another date. Or go stag. Or go with Evie and me. I know, I'll draft Doc and we can make it a foursome."

"Tickets are sold out. Too late to get one for Doc."

"He can go as your date. Instead of Susan Clemons."

"I'll get my own date, thanks."

"Works for me."

He narrowed his eyes at her. "You think you just won this argument, don't you?"

She grinned. "I do."

"This is not over," he warned as she slid into the driver's seat.

"You're just a sore loser." She closed the door, started the car, flipped on the lights, then waved to Hay, who stood on the sidewalk with his hands in his pockets watching as she pulled away from the curb.

She stopped by the store on her way home, so it was close to 11:00 p.m. by the time she pulled into the gated underground parking lot where she had two reserved spaces. Usually her second one stayed empty; tonight Evie's blue Volvo waited in the second spot.

She'd owned the condo, which was right outside the historic district, for four years now. The building was still under construction when she'd bought the three-bedroom, top (eighth) floor unit, and she'd been able to finish it to her specifications. Those included a steel-reinforced front door, a spiral staircase that provided access to a private rooftop garden (she could rappel off the roof, which meant it could serve as an emergency exit, if necessary), a specialized tool vault hidden behind a wall in the pantry, another vault for cash and valuables beneath the master bathroom floor and a state-of-the-art security system.

The parking area was concrete, dimly lit and deserted. Most everybody who lived in the building was home, she could tell from a quick glance around at the number of parked cars as she got out, but they were apparently all up in their apartments doing whatever it was they did at this time of night in the middle of a workweek. As far as she could tell, she was all alone in the garage. She started to unload the groceries from her trunk and almost jumped out of her skin when a voice piped up behind her.

"Miz Guardian, did you get it?"

She recognized the mode of address even before a sharp glance over her shoulder definitively identified the speaker as the eleven-year-old son of the live-in super, Angela Pack, a divorced mother of three who had a small apartment on the ground floor. He called her that, she could only assume, because of the Guardian Consulting signs on her car. She doubted if he knew her actual name. Bianca grabbed the last of the bags and turned to frown at the kid.

Quincy Pack was undersized for eleven, barely five feet tall with a thin build, buzzed black hair and a face that was all sharp bones and big dark eyes. The boy was the youngest of three sons. His older brothers, Trevor and Sage, were fifteen and seventeen, respectively. While they were also on the small and wiry side, they were a whole heck of a lot bigger than Quincy and inclined to bully their little brother when their mom wasn't around. Consequently, the kid spent a lot of time outside his apartment, lurking in the common areas, the small, manicured yard and the basement parking lot.

Juggling the bags, Bianca managed to close the trunk and turned to give him a severe look. "Shouldn't you be in bed? Don't you have school tomorrow?"

"We're out. The teachers have an in-service day. They go, we don't."

"Oh." The local school schedule wasn't something she was familiar with, although she supposed with Evie getting ready to have a kid it would be something she would be getting a lot better acquainted with in the future. Still, she had a while. "Shouldn't you be in bed, anyway? Or at least inside? It's late."

"You couldn't get it." Quincy's hopeful expression faded into resigned acceptance. It was clear his expectations hadn't been high.

At the look on his face, she relented. She'd known why he was there the moment he turned up.

"I got it."

His face brightened instantly. "Really?"

"Yes, really." Bianca juggled the grocery bags so that she could reach into her purse and pull out the handheld Nintendo 2DS that she'd retrieved for him. It belonged to fifteen-year-old Trevor, who'd just been given it for his birthday. Quincy had unwisely taken it without permission the previous day and made the further mistake of carrying it outside, where Shawn Torres, also known as Snake, the NFL-linebacker-size, eighteen-year-old scourge of the local streets, had taken it from him. Money was tight in the Pack household and the game system represented weeks of saving up by Angela, so it was a significant loss. Anticipating Trevor's reaction when he found out and knowing that even if he came clean neither of his brothers had a hope of getting the prized game system back from Snake, Quincy had watched Snake tuck the toy away in his backpack, then tried a snatch-and-run. Snake had caught him, beat him up and told him that he would do it again every time he saw Quincy for the rest of the eleven-year-old's life.

That was where the situation stood when Bianca got home from work last night. Walking to the elevator, she'd come across Quincy crying in a corner of the parking lot. Reluctant to get involved but equally reluctant to walk on past a weeping kid with a bloody lip and a swollen eye who was huddled in a corner near her car, Bianca had stopped, extracted the story from him and promised to help. He didn't know her as anything other than a building resident who waved when she saw him and occasionally exchanged chitchat with his mother, and he'd been visibly skeptical of her ability to retrieve the game system when she'd promised to do so. To learn that she had succeeded clearly dazzled him.

"No shit?" He looked at her with wide-eyed respect as she

handed the small plastic console to him. "How'd you get it away from Snake?"

"Don't swear," she said automatically, because he was a kid and she was pretty sure kids shouldn't. "I asked nicely. Never underestimate the power of *please*."

And that was the truth—or at least a small sliver of the truth. Actually, it hadn't taken much more than finding Snake—not that difficult, since he was big and loud and spent a lot of time swaggering around the square out front—and asking him to please (see there?) hand over the game system he'd stolen from the little boy in the building on the corner. When Snake had responded to that with a derisive look, a laugh and a contemptuous "Get out of my face, you crazy bitch," she might have had to go a step further, by, say, downing him with a leg sweep and pinning him to the ground with what she liked to think of as her Vulcan death grip while telling him what would happen to him if he ever came anywhere near Quincy and his brothers in the future, but it had all turned out well in the end. Snake had handed the purloined game system over, made so many blubbering promises that Bianca couldn't remember them all and then, when she'd let him up, stumbled away as fast as he could go.

What had made it especially fun was that her conversation with Snake had taken place with the two of them all alone in a dimly lit alley around 1:00 a.m. just after he'd left his entourage behind in the square to head home. Because she really didn't want anyone in Savannah associating local businesswoman Bianca St. Ives with the kind of takedown she'd suspected she was going to need to unleash on Snake, and because it was almost Halloween, which made getting one easy, she'd been wearing a cartoon character costume complete with mask at the time.

Have fun telling your homies all about getting jumped in an alley by Hello Kitty, tough guy.

Quincy looked at the game system like it was the Hope

Diamond. "You saved my life! Trevor's been hunting for it all day!"

"Yeah, well, go give it to him."

He looked up at her again. "You kidding? If Trev ever found out I took it, he'd kill me! I'm going to go stick it down between the couch cushions. When he finds it, he'll think it dropped out of his pocket or something."

Cradling the game system in both hands, he started toward the stairs that led to the ground floor. Bianca was shaking her head as she watched him go when he stopped, turned around and said, "Thank you!" so fervently that she smiled.

"You're welcome."

Then he hurried away to the stairs and disappeared up them.

Score one for the good guys, Bianca thought as she took the elevator to her apartment.

The lights were on, the drapes were drawn and she could hear Evie talking, she assumed on the phone, from somewhere in the depths of the apartment, but the foyer and living area were empty as she walked through them. As always, the soft eggshells and creams and taupes in which the apartment was done soothed her. The floors were highly polished longleaf pine, the lighting was recessed and soft, and the accessories were minimal. This was a quiet place, a place for her to recharge, a refuge to which she retreated. It was the safest place she knew, the place she felt most at home. Still, the few personal items on display had been carefully chosen to showcase Bianca St. Ives's public persona only, and in the walk-in-closet-size vault behind the wall in the pantry was a grab-and-go bag packed with essentials, including cash and a number of false identities, in case she should ever need to flee on a moment's notice.

Because, in her experience, shit happened.

She was putting away the groceries—along with the eggs and spinach and canned salmon that were staples in her kitchen, there were squirt cheese and Oreo cookies, whole milk and ice cream and peanut butter from Evie's list—when Evie appeared. She was, indeed, talking on her cell phone, so Bianca heard her coming, then looked up to see her in her pink zip-up bathrobe with a white towel wrapped around her head as she padded toward the kitchen in terry slippers. But what she hadn't expected was to see tears sliding down Evie's cheeks.

12

"…can have it, all right?" Evie choked out, speaking into the phone as her tear-filled eyes met Bianca's. "I don't *want* the house. I don't want *anything*. I just want—"

She broke off, lips clamping together as she listened. Bianca watched Evie's chest heave, her tears turn into a waterfall and her face go crimson at whatever was coming at her from the other end of the line. Her mouth opened and closed a couple of times as she tried and failed to produce a reply. It was clear she was so upset that she was no longer able to speak.

"Fourth, right?" Bianca asked. Evie nodded miserably. Putting down the strawberry ice cream she'd been getting ready to stow away in the freezer, Bianca came around the table, said, "May I?" and took the phone Evie handed to her.

She put it to her ear just in time to hear Fourth say, "…bring the papers about the house over to you tomorrow. All you have to do is sign. Then I'll know you're serious about—"

The thing about Fourth was, besides being a low-life cheating scumbag, he was a sneaky weasel and as tightfisted as they came. Bianca got instantly that he was trying to browbeat Evie into signing over their house and God knew what else to him.

"Evie does want the house," Bianca told him crisply. "And if you don't leave her alone, besides demanding child support and spousal support, she's going to go after half of everything you own. Not just your stock portfolio, not just your bank accounts and your trust fund, but your Porsche, Fourth. And the Zephyr. If she doesn't get it outright, you'll have to sell it."

She said that last with relish, because as much as he loved his Porsche Carrera sports car, he loved the Zephyr, his forty-eight-foot speedboat, more.

She actually heard him gasp. Then he said, "You stay out of this. This is between Evie and me! She—"

"Wants all communication from you to go through her law-yer in future," Bianca interrupted, her eyes on Evie as her friend sank down in one of the spindle-back chairs that surrounded the round kitchen table and rested her head in her hands.

"This is none of your damned business," Fourth growled. "I can talk to my own wife."

Evie looked up at that and mopped her still-streaming eyes with a corner of the towel that turbaned her head. It was obvious to Bianca that her friend had just gotten out of the shower. Probably to answer this call.

"Soon-to-be ex-wife," Bianca pointed out when Evie showed no sign of wanting the phone back.

Fourth said, "Maybe not. I'm hoping we can work things out." Clearly able to hear both ends of the conversation, Evie shook her head in violent repudiation. Fourth continued, "This conversation about the house is just to make her think, just to make her realize how much she needs me. How much we need each other. We're going to have a *baby* together. She's being ri-diculous about this whole..."

Evie's hands, which were now resting on the table, fisted as Fourth expanded on her folly in refusing to overlook what he termed *the one little mistake* he'd made. Her eyes narrowed dangerously. She held out her hand for the phone, opened her mouth—and sobbed. Clapping a hand over her mouth, she waved the phone that Bianca held out toward her away.

Fourth was still talking: "...not in her right mind right now. It's all those hormones and things. I—"

Looking outraged, Evie swelled up like a toad. A weeping toad.

"By the way," Bianca interrupted Fourth's flow, "what do you think is going to happen if Drew Healey—" one of the richest men in town "—finds out that the woman you've been cheating on your wife with is his daughter?"

There was a moment of stunned silence. Evie, who'd been mopping her eyes with a corner of the towel again, gave Bianca a thumbs-up.

"What?" Fourth yelped. "She told you?"

"Maybe. Maybe not. You know small towns," Bianca said. "No secrets. Look, Evie wants to keep this civil. Believe me when I tell you that it's in your best interest to let her."

Disconnecting while Fourth was still sputtering, Bianca put the phone down on the table and slid it toward Evie, who gave it a baleful look.

"He's right about the hormones, damn him." Sniffling loudly, Evie picked up the phone, ostentatiously turned it off and put it in her pocket. "Look at me. I'm a mess. All I do is cry."

"You're pregnant." Tearing a wad of paper towels off the roll on the counter next to her, Bianca handed it to Evie, who wiped her eyes and blew her nose. "I think crying's part of it. Why did you answer the phone, anyway?"

"I don't know. I was just getting out of the shower and the phone rang. I saw his name pop up and I didn't even think. It was automatic, like...like...for a moment I forgot."

At least the tears had stopped. Looking at her friend thoughtfully, Bianca picked up the carton of ice cream she'd abandoned, meaning to stow it in the freezer.

"You know, if you want to give him another chance, I'd still support you. So would—"

"Give me that." Lunging forward, Evie grabbed the carton from Bianca. Settling back down into her chair, she ripped off the lid. "No! He's a cheater. This isn't the first time, and you know it as well as I do. Annabeth Healey just happened to be the one I found out about. I don't care what he says now, he'll do it again. And even if he doesn't, I'll never be able to trust him again. So—just no."

Extracting a spoon from the silverware drawer, Bianca handed it to Evie, who dug into the ice cream with grim determination.

"Okay," Bianca said and finished putting the groceries away as Evie spooned her way steadily through the ice cream.

"It's just hard, you know?" Evie said after a moment. She was no longer even sniffling, but her eyes were swollen and the tip of her nose was red. Looking up, she met Bianca's eyes and hers narrowed. "Of course you don't. You've never been in love."

"Yes, I have," Bianca countered. Snagging her own spoon from the drawer, she sat down opposite Evie and dug out a bite of ice cream. "What, have you forgotten about Gabriel Thomas? Or Ben Moss? Or—"

"That was while we were in school," Evie replied scornfully while Bianca savored the sweet, creamy strawberry goodness of the treat she rarely allowed herself to eat. "They don't count. Anyway, they were way more into you than you were into them."

"What about—" Bianca was prepared to start enumerating other, later boyfriends when Evie cut her off.

"You didn't love them, any of them, and you know it." Evie's voice was tart. This was a running discussion between the two of them. Evie thought that the distance Bianca always kept between herself and the guys she dated was unnatural. Bianca thought it was smart.

"Thank God," Bianca responded and stood up to finish putting the groceries away.

"It'll happen one day." Evie was more than halfway through the carton of ice cream. Knowing her friend for a stress eater, Bianca reached over and took the carton from her.

"Hey," Evie protested.

"You're going to hate yourself in the morning."

It was true. Evie was already bemoaning the amount of weight she had put on with her pregnancy. The situation with Fourth was not helping. She had developed what she called a fatal attraction to sweets. Ice cream and Oreos were two particular weaknesses.

"You're right." Evie watched gloomily as Bianca put the lid on the ice cream carton and put it in the freezer. Getting up, Evie carried the spoons toward the dishwasher. "How'd it go at dinner?"

"Great. We got the contract."

Evie opened the dishwasher and stuck the spoons inside. "That guy—Mr. Kaz-what's-his-name—has a thing for you."

Bianca said, "Okay, I'm going to bed now."

Evie followed as Bianca left the kitchen, turning off lights as she continued to talk to Bianca's retreating back.

"He's a little old, but he's cute. He's really rich. And he seems nice. You ought to at least give him a chance, see if it goes anywhere."

"Bad idea to date the clients," Bianca said over her shoulder. Her bedroom, the master, was the farthest from the kitchen. It stretched across the entire far end of the condo.

"That's what you said when I told you that Hay's got a thing for you." Evie was following her down the hall.

"No, I didn't. I said it was a bad idea to date an employee."

"Oh, I see. No clients, no employees. That basically leaves out anybody work related. What was wrong with Tod Schuster?"

Tod Schuster was a handsome, charming and successful stockbroker they both knew. Who'd recently asked Bianca to dinner.

"I didn't feel like going out with him?"

"You never feel like going out with anybody."

Bianca had reached her bedroom by this time. Pivoting to close the door, she locked eyes with Evie, who had stopped outside the door to the bedroom she was using and was regarding her with a frown.

"What is this, misery loves company or something? You of all people should be seriously off men about now."

Evie pulled the towel from her head and fluffed her damp curls. "Believe it or not, I still believe in love. Just because Fourth turned out to be a turd doesn't mean that all men are. And I want you to be happy. All I'm saying is, you should say 'yes' to at least some of the guys who ask you out."

"I will, just as soon as the right guy asks. Quit using my love life as a distraction and go to bed."

"You mean your lack of a love life?"

"Whatever you want to call it." Bianca started to close the door, remembered something and paused to give Evie a hard look. "And no more lame attempts at matchmaking."

Right before Evie's marriage had broken up, she'd invited Bianca over for what Bianca had thought was a dinner party. As it turned out, the only other guest had been one of Fourth's newly divorced friends. Awkward didn't begin to cover it, especially since the guy had been calling at roughly one-week intervals ever since.

"Les Harding was a mistake," Evie conceded.

"Yes, he was. If you need a distraction, concentrate on Hay. He could use fixing up."

"He's dating that Susan Clemons."

"Not anymore. They broke up. Last Saturday night."

Evie perked up. "Oh, yeah? What happened?"

"Apparently she started to get too serious for him. Now he

doesn't have a date for your costume ball. That's all I know. If you need more, ask Hay."

"He needs a date?" Evie was definitely perking up.

Ruthlessly throwing Hay under the bus, Bianca said, "He doesn't have one."

"Hmm." Evie's expression turned speculative. "You know, you and Hay—"

Bianca's frown was dire. "No. No, Evie. There is no me and Hay. Don't even *start* to go there. Understand?"

"Fine."

"Good." Bianca stepped back and closed her door, then remembered something and called through it. "What time is that appointment with Claybourne Realty tomorrow?"

In the wake of an assault on a local Realtor, Claybourne Realty was coming in to talk about possibly arranging security for their sales agents who were hosting open houses.

"Leona Tilley?" Evie had a facility with things like names, times and dates that she was putting to good use on the job; Bianca was once again impressed with how well her friend had taken hold. "Nine a.m."

"Thanks. Good night."

"Night."

Bianca heard the click of Evie's door closing and turned to cross the bedroom to her closet, which was a large walk-in that she loved. Like the rest of the apartment, her bedroom was decorated in neutrals. Taupe walls, white drapes and bedspread. The queen-size bed, twin nightstands and mirrored dresser were smooth walnut in a stark, clean design. The lamps and big armchair also had a stark, clean design and were graphite gray. The rug beside the bed, like the rug on the gray-tiled bathroom floor, wasn't stark anything. It was cream-colored and fluffy.

Because it was pretty and felt good to her bare toes.

Bianca undressed and hung up her clothes. She never left

things lying around; Evie, who once upon a time had been her roommate and was messy as all get-out, accused her of being compulsively neat. Which was an exaggeration, Bianca thought, but honesty compelled her to admit, not by much. Her closet was arranged by type of clothing, color, appropriate occasion. Accessories had their own area. Her shoes were positioned on racks, side by side, sorted by style and color and heel height.

Wearing her bathrobe as she padded back into her bedroom to stand barefoot on the fluffy rug, she began the mindful meditation exercise that was supposed to prepare her for sleep. Staying very still, she pressed her feet into the floor until she was conscious of her own weight and placed her hands flat against the center of her chest. Clearing her mind of thought, she focused inward, on her breathing, the beat of her heart, the rhythms of her body. Taking a deep breath, she lifted her arms over her head and rose up on her toes, stretching upward—

An image of the folder she'd tucked away in the file cabinet at the office just before Kazmarek's arrival popped into her consciousness. *Had* she tucked it away, or had she left it out? Leaving it out wasn't like her, but she'd been looking through the information it contained for what must have been the hundredth time and getting frustrated because there was so much of it and absolutely nothing in it leaped out at her. The folder contained the research she'd been doing and having Doc do into house fires and/or explosions that had resulted in the death of a woman approximately twenty-two years previously. Since she didn't know the actual date, the place where the fire or explosion had taken place, what exactly had burned or exploded, or anything about the woman besides a few illusive recollections that might or might not be accurate, she was drowning in the sheer number of cases. A similar search into obituaries of women who had died in a fire or explosion twenty-two years ago had yielded relatively few results. Most obituaries didn't list cause of death. And she wasn't having any luck gleaning anything more concrete out of the memory that had surfaced on the night of her father's death.

For some reason, it felt vitally important that she remember.

According to Richard, her mother had been named Ann Johnson St. Ives. She'd died after being hit by a car when Bianca was four. The framed picture he'd given her when she was little had been of a blonde, blue-eyed, smiling young woman. Bianca had never felt the slightest degree of connection to it, and as she grew older she'd put it away, never to be looked at again. She suspected the reason was because the woman had been another of Richard's cover stories. The vague memories she had of her mother included a ruffle of black hair brushing her own little-girl cheek, a pair of laughing dark eyes and an elusive vanilla-ish scent. And a Winnie the Pooh movie. And an explosion.

And a possible last name of McCoy or Mulloy.

Richard and Ann Johnson St. Ives were the names listed for her parents on her birth certificate. If the name her father had given on the document was false, and Bianca was ninety-nine point nine percent sure it was, then it stood to reason that the name her mother had given was false, too. She'd seen her purported birth certificate maybe only twice in her life, and she had never before been curious enough, or brave enough, to ask questions about it. Now she was both curious and brave. She only wished her father was still around so that she could demand the truth from him.

Then she smiled a little wryly at herself. If he'd been standing in front of her, she *would* have demanded answers, and he *would* have provided them.

The only thing was, the answers he gave her would almost certainly not be the truth.

Her father lied as easily and convincingly as he breathed.

"Damn it." Dropping her arms and coming down off her toes, Bianca said it aloud. Meditation was not, and never had been, her best thing. When her father or one of his hired minions had been around to supervise, she'd faked it, but the truth was she could never turn off her mind for long enough to get the job done. Trying to close it down just seemed to *invite* disturbing thoughts into her head.

Face facts: as far as meditation was concerned, she was a total dud.

And yes, she *had* put the damned folder away. Now that her mind was back to doing the whole thinking-as-usual thing, she perfectly remembered putting it back in the file cabinet before going out to greet Kazmarek.

Ordinarily she would have tried again, but she was too tired to put the effort into it. Giving up, she went into the bathroom and turned on the taps in her big soaking tub before putting her hair up in a ponytail and brushing her teeth. Since her father's death, she'd found sleeping difficult. Mindful meditation was supposed to help with that. For her, it didn't. What did help, she'd discovered, was a hot bath and a big dose of NyQuil.

Especially the big dose of NyQuil.

At least, after that, if the nightmares came, they didn't wake her, and she didn't remember them.

Bianca was up at 5:00 a.m. As was her routine, she went for a run. On the way back she stopped for a workout in the small gym she'd set up for herself in the basement of the Dance Dreams Ballet School, which she owned and leased to the operators, sisters Lori Huddleston and Kathleen Groves, who taught ballet and other dance classes for a living. The rent she received was a pittance, but owning the school had other benefits. First, it added to her cover identity—badasses did not own ballet schools—and second, it gave her an excuse to set up a state-of-the-art private gym in a place where no one would think twice about it if she was seen going in and out on a daily basis.

It was autumn. Didn't matter. The day was going to be a hot one. By the time Bianca showered, dressed in navy slacks and a white linen blazer over a thin white cotton tank, and walked into Guardian Consulting with a copy of the *Savannah Morning News* tucked under her arm and a cup of coffee in her hand at a few minutes before eight, the sun was already a hazy yellow ball climbing the sky, and the leaves on the sweet gum trees in front of the office building were starting to wilt.

Inside, the office was blessedly cool. Bianca gave the gray-walled reception area with its black leather, stainless-steel-and-glass furnishings an assessing glance and concluded that everything was immaculate. A good way to start the day.

Hay was already there, in Doc's office, his back turned to Bianca as he took the thick sheaf of papers that Doc was handing him. Looking professional in a white dress shirt tucked into belted gray slacks, Hay stood in front of Doc's desk. Standing behind his desk, Doc looked even more rumpled than usual in a short-sleeved black shirt with a clip-on black tie and saggy black jeans. His curly hair was tied back in a ponytail at his nape. His forehead was furrowed as he frowned at Hay.

Hay said to Doc, "This is a hell of a lot of paper."

"You asked for all the closed trucks that entered the port of Savannah on the dates in question. That's what's in there. You tell me a little more precisely what you're looking for, I could maybe narrow the information down for you, you know what I mean? It's all about the paradigm. You want different results, you change the paradigm."

"At this point I'm not sure how to narrow it down, but if I come up with something, I'll get back to you." Hay turned away with the papers in his hand. "Thanks."

"No problemo."

Hay walked out of Doc's office. Doc settled back down behind his desk. They both spotted Bianca at about the same time.

"Coffeemaker's on the fritz," Hay said to Bianca, eyeing her cup as he passed her. "Care to share?"

"Oh, dear," Bianca replied to the first piece of information. To the second, she pulled the cup in closer to her body. "Go get your own. You know where the Starbucks is. Straight down the elevator, two buildings to the right."

"Selfish. That's two strikes. One more and you're out." Hay disappeared into his office. Bianca guessed he was counting last night's "hard-ass" as the first strike and made a face at his open door.

"Morning, boss." From his chair, Doc beckoned to her urgently.

Oh, joy.

Bianca's stomach tightened. She knew that urgent beckoning. It never meant anything good. At the very least, she was pretty sure she could say goodbye to the quiet fifteen minutes she had been looking forward to with the paper and her coffee.

She was heading for Doc's office when Evie pushed through the front door carrying a box in both hands. They both did their own morning thing, then made their way to work separately, so Bianca hadn't seen her since she'd closed the door on her the previous night. Evie was looking perky and surprisingly cheerful in a seafoam-green trapeze dress with beige flats. Her shrunken, half-sleeved seafoam cardigan had chiffon roses in the same shade of green blooming all around the neckline. Not a look Bianca could ever envision wearing herself, but it suited Evie perfectly.

"I brought coffee," Evie trilled to announce herself. "And doughnuts." To Bianca, she added, "I forgot to tell you, the coffeemaker broke last night after you left for dinner. I tried fixing it, but no luck. If you want, I can pick up a new one over lunch."

"You know where the petty cash is," Bianca responded, holding up her own cup in explanation as Evie proffered the box, which she saw now contained coffee cups. And doughnuts, stacked in the center. She'd already had a protein bar for breakfast, so she shook her head.

But she eyed the doughnuts covetously. They looked good.

"Coffee?" Hay emerged from his office, spotted Evie and made a beeline for her. Grabbing a cup and hooking a doughnut with a finger, he flicked a censorious look at Bianca and said to Evie, "Why am I not working for *you*?"

"Doughnuts?" Doc came out of his office with the cautious air of one not quite sure of his welcome. Evie held the box out toward him, and he took one, along with a cup of coffee. "Thanks, Evie."

The smile he gave her was tentative. Evie beamed at him, and his smile widened.

"I'll put the rest of these in the kitchen," she called as a kind of general announcement and walked away with what was left of her booty. Hay had already retreated to his office.

Bianca followed Doc into his. It was simply furnished: a teak-and-metal desk, a wall of bookcases crammed with books, framed black-and-white prints of some famous people who had died on the walls. Right now they included JFK in the motorcade moments before he was shot, astronaut Neil Armstrong taking the first steps on the moon, Princess Diana and Dodi Fayed emerging from the Paris Ritz on the night they died, union leader Jimmy Hoffa walking into the restaurant he supposedly disappeared from, whistle-blower Karen Silkwood inside the power plant where she worked not long before she was killed in a car crash. Not exactly the artwork Bianca would have chosen, but this was Doc's office to decorate as he would (within limits) and he was a major conspiracy theory buff. The pictures on the walls represented the cases he was currently researching in his free time. *Free* being the word to remember, as Bianca occasionally had to remind him. While he was in the office, he was on the clock, and his time wasn't free, it was expensive. As she knew, because she signed his paycheck.

"I'm glad you were able to help Hay out," she said. "Before you came along, he would have ended up paying off somebody at the docks to get that information. Then somebody might have talked, and somebody might have heard, and—well, it's just better if we can keep as much as possible about what we're working on in-house."

Doc shrugged. "He asked for it when he got in this morning. It took maybe fifteen minutes. I got algorithms that'll find anything if you ask the right questions. It's all about what you put in. It's all about the paradigms."

Bianca frowned as the concept struck a chord. Maybe if she changed what she was looking for in her search for her mother and what had happened to her, she would have better luck getting the information she sought.

"Could you do a search through newspaper archives for four-year-old girls mentioned in news stories twenty-two years ago?" she asked.

She hadn't told Doc why she wanted the information she'd had him help her with, and he hadn't asked. She'd searched for Ann Johnson St. Ives herself, with no results.

"Sure. How soon do you want it?"

"Sometime today?"

"Piece of cake."

"Thanks."

As Doc settled down into his seat, they both heard a soft tap on the doorframe of the office beside his—Hay's—followed by Evie calling out in a dulcet tone, "Oh, Ha-ay…"

Bianca's lips curved into a wry smile despite the serious nature of what she feared Doc had to tell her. The coffee, the doughnuts, the sugary approach: Evie was clearly turning her matchmaking efforts to Hay.

Sorry, friend, she apologized to Hay silently.

"So what's so important?" She closed the door and walked behind Doc's desk.

He looked up at her. "The Bat Signal—we got more from those same people."

"We're ignoring them, remember?"

Doc was already punching keys. "I think you ought to see this." He gestured at the monitor as the screen went black for a moment before going live again. "Check it out."

An image of her father striding across a London street hit Bianca like a fist to the stomach. It was all she could do not to wince with pain. There were too many visible landmarks for her not to instantly recognize the city: a Debenhams department store on the corner, a distinctive London taxi amid the traffic, a sign with the open red circle and blue Underground banner of the tube. In fact, she realized, she was looking at Oxford Street. She knew it well. The day was damp and overcast and it looked cold—well, it *was* London—and the Christmas lights were out on the shops, which narrowed the time frame down to mid-November through early January. Her father was wearing a trench coat with a hat pulled down low over his forehead as he splashed through puddles.

Despite the fact that his face was hidden, Bianca recognized him instantly. Everything from his tall, slim build and erect carriage to his way-too-youthful-for-his-years stride to his bespoke leather shoes made him impossible to mistake. She knew those shoes well. A derringer was concealed in the left heel and a compartment in the right heel was loaded with tear gas so if his shoes were searched whoever succeeded in opening the heel to expose the hidden compartment would be sprayed, thus giving Richard the opportunity either to run or to do whatever the situation called for.

As she watched, a gust of wind caught his hat and blew it off. For a moment as he looked after the hat in surprise, a three-quarter image of his face was captured, the features clear and recognizable.

Bianca's heart contracted painfully.

Richard chased the hat down, caught it, clamped it back onto his head and strode on toward his original destination, a café on the other side of the street just out of the frame. Bianca knew that, too, because it was a favorite of his and she'd often met him there. They would eat and talk, although rarely about anything personal. When they met, it was all about upcoming or past jobs. Still, it was time spent together, and now, looking back, she realized how much that time had meant to her. She was so caught up in watching him that for a moment after the video ended she completely missed the email message that appeared on the monitor in its wake.

Then she regained enough focus to read the words on the screen.

You screw with us we screw with you. Do the job or we send this to authorities who'll get their first good look at Traveler. If we don't hear affirmative from you within twelve hours, video will be on its way to them.

13

"Your father's dead," Doc said. That broke through the last of Bianca's laser focus on the screen and earned him a sharp glance. "Sorry, I guess that wasn't so sensitive."

A flutter of Bianca's hand said *don't worry about it.*

Doc continued. "What I mean is, since that's the case, this can't hurt us, right? Even if these guys do what they're threatening, we're in the clear."

With all her heart Bianca wanted to believe that was true. But a cold little shiver slid down her spine.

"I don't know." She considered possible ways the video could burn them. "Once his picture is in the system, it might be possible for authorities to uncover one or more of the identities he's used." Still thinking it through, she spoke slowly, reluctant to give voice and thus substance to her thoughts. But facts had to be faced, and the facts weren't pretty. "They might be able to use facial recognition software to tie him to a driver's license photo, for example." Or a passport photo, or a company ID, or a fishing license, or even something as obscure as an ID for a club like the Loyal Order of the Moose, which she knew he'd pretended to be a member of once as part of a cover.

Anything like that would give investigators a lead to follow. Sometimes that one lead was all it took.

The email said they—Richard, because that was who it was

meant for—had twelve hours to respond. That meant she had twelve hours to decide what to do.

Bianca looked at the screen again, trying without success to find a time stamp. "What time did this come in?"

"At 5:03 this morning. I saw it as soon as I got to the office."

She frowned. That seemed to indicate that whoever had sent it was not in the eastern US time zone, because 5:03 a.m. was not the most likely time for sending and checking email. Unless her father had an arrangement with whoever this was for their emails to be sent at that specific time. Unless—

Unless who knew what. There were so many different variables that it was impossible to be sure of anything. Doing some quick calculations, she came up with 2:03 a.m. Sacramento time, 10:03 a.m. London time, 11:03 a.m. Rome time, 1:03 p.m. Moscow, Istanbul and Riyadh time, 6:03 p.m. Hong Kong and Beijing time, 7:03 p.m. Tokyo time, 9:03 p.m. Sydney time. The most likely scenario, therefore, was that the email originated from outside the United States.

Unless the original time was wrong, because the email was scheduled to be sent at a specific time. Or—

"Is there any way to find out where this came from or who sent it?" she asked. The email's wording struck her as not being American in origin, but, like everything else in the freaking Hall of Mirrors world she lived in, that could be misleading. The surest way to handle a threat like this was to identify the source and neutralize it. She was, Bianca realized grimly, prepared to do whatever it took to maintain the layers of protection that kept everyone associated with Richard safe. But she couldn't neutralize what she couldn't find.

Doc shook his head. "I got a trace going. It's going to come up Hong Kong again, ten to one, because these are the same people. But like I said, bouncer address. So no way to be sure."

Bianca's lips tightened.

"Let me see the video again," she said. Something about it nagged at her.

"Sure."

Doc did something with the keyboard. A few seconds later Bianca was once again watching her father stride across the screen. This time the image was not such a shock and she was able to concentrate on details. The pedestrians on the sidewalk, the vehicles on the street—

That was it: the black Peugeot parked curbside at the far edge of the frame. Even as Richard recovered his hat and clapped it back onto his head, a woman and a young girl emerged from the car. They were small figures, background to the primary scene of a man losing his hat as he crossed the street. Amid all the extraneous vehicular and pedestrian traffic, they were insignificant. Bianca would have never given them a second glance, except—

She recognized them.

The little girl with the long nut-brown hair pulled smoothly back from her face was her half sister, Marin. The slim, attractive brunette with her was her father's wife, Marin's mother, her own (as difficult as she found it to wrap her head around the concept) stepmother, Margery Humphries. The film footage had probably been recorded sometime during the previous holiday season. She knew because Marin's looks had scarcely changed. She was round-faced, rosy-cheeked, happy-looking. A sturdy child in the plaid skirt and navy jumper (Brit-speak for sweater) that was her school uniform. She skipped a little as she closed the car door, then headed toward her mother, who was rounding the trunk. A normal child, with a normal life. For whatever reason, Richard had chosen to raise his two daughters very differently. Bianca was glad of that, for Marin's sake.

As her mother joined her, they both looked toward Richard,

who didn't glance their way. The impression Bianca got was that he wasn't yet aware of their presence.

Bianca's stomach tightened. What she was looking at was a rendezvous in progress. Richard used that café as a hub.

Marin and Margery were most probably on their way to meet Richard there. From the shadows cast by the buildings, from the busy stores and the number of people and vehicles out and about, it was around lunchtime. Possibly Marin and Margery were early, because Richard clearly was not expecting them yet. It couldn't be the other way around, because Richard was never late. From the eagerness in the little girl's face as she looked toward him, she was excited about seeing him. From Bianca's own knowledge of him, she guessed that he had most likely been away doing what it was he did. He would have changed identities en route and was now on his way to meet up with his family.

Live your life in compartments.

Those two belonged to a part of Richard's life that was completely separate from the compartment in which he was Richard St. Ives, her father.

To them, he was Edward Humphries, Margery's husband and Marin's father. They had no idea that he had any other life, any other identity. They had no idea about *her.*

Knowing that they would join him in the café, that the three of them would sit together as a family at a back corner table (Richard always sat in back corner tables in restaurants and took care to take the seat that kept his back to the wall) and that Richard would order the banoffee pie, which was what he always ordered at that café, was beyond unsettling.

Bianca suddenly felt the same way she had the first time she had walked into Evie's house to behold that big Christmas tree with all the ornaments and tinsel and piles of presents beneath. Like she was on the outside looking in. Like she was standing in the cold with her nose pressed up against a big plate-glass window, yearning to be part of what she saw in front of her and knowing that she never could be.

Much as she hated to acknowledge it even to herself, it hurt.

Pushing past the useless, idiotic emotions stirred up by realizing that her father was going to eat with his other daughter, his *family*, who had no idea that she even existed, in the café where the two of them customarily met, she forced herself to concentrate on details.

First, like her father's, Marin's and Margery's faces were perfectly visible to the camera, which she thought must be one of the many now posted around London as a reaction to the past few years of heightened terrorist threat.

Second, so was the Peugeot's license plate.

She knew that it was registered to Edward Humphries, Framlingham, Suffolk.

She knew because once upon a time, after one of their café meetings, she had followed Richard to the home in Framlingham that he shared with Marin and Margery. She'd spent an embarrassing-to-remember hour trailing him and Margery as they took toddler Marin to a neighborhood park, then lurking anonymously in a nearby shop watching through a window as her father pushed her little sister on the swings.

But the point, *the point*, was that the car, the child, the woman, outed Richard's bolt-hole, the cover identity that was the main compartment in which he lived his everyday life. It was a dangling thread that astute investigators could pull and follow until, possibly, they unraveled the whole.

Richard was in all likelihood dead. The video couldn't hurt him.

There was no way to know if Richard in his Edward Humphries identity possessed anything that might lead investigators to Bianca St. Ives.

But it was possible.

There was no way to know, if whoever had sent this email carried through on their threat and sent the video to investigators, whether investigators would even notice the child and the woman getting out of the car among all that busy background, much less isolate them and do the work required to establish their identities and/or trace the Peugeot plates.

But it was possible.

There was no way to know if whoever had sent this email was already aware of the identities of the child and woman in the background, or if they had picked up on the Peugeot's license plate and traced any or all of those through to Edward Humphries.

But it was possible.

What was indisputable was that the video represented a terrifying breach of security.

It was a loose end that might prove dangerous to her.

It might prove dangerous to Marin and Margery, if whoever had sent the video went looking for Richard and found them instead.

It might prove dangerous to Doc, and to any and all members of the underground network of Richard's associates around the globe.

The question was, then, what to do?

Did she dare ignore the threat and hope it was a bluff?

Did she dare to take the chance that, if it wasn't a bluff and the video was sent to the authorities, it would bring no harm to Marin or Margery? That it wouldn't be used to hunt her, Bianca, down?

That it wouldn't be used to hunt down the whole loosely connected web of Richard's contacts?

What would happen if, say, she were to reply and simply

inform whoever had sent the email that Richard couldn't do what they wanted because he was dead?

That answer was easy. First, she would expose the fact that *someone* was on the receiving end of Richard's most private emails. The senders might believe Richard was dead, but they'd worry because their communication with whoever had received their supposedly secure emails had revealed their existence, their reliance on Richard and the types of activities that he undertook, and created a giant loose end that left *them* at risk. And, like her, they might feel the need to eliminate loose ends.

Second, they might believe that Richard was simply trying to get out of whatever it was they wanted him to do. That they clearly felt he had an obligation to them to do.

Neither scenario was good.

So what if she swooped in and scooped Marin and Margery out of harm's way? *Tried* to scoop Marin and Margery out of harm's way, because of course they had no idea who she was and no reason to listen to her. If anybody was watching, attempting something like that might even endanger them more, bringing attention to the fact that they were important to Richard—and it wouldn't do anything to protect anyone else.

Bianca asked, "What happens if we reply? Is there any possible way, any tiny sliver of a chance, that the email could be traced back here?"

"You kidding? With me on the job? No way."

"You're absolutely sure?" She trusted Doc, but caution had been bred in her DNA, she supposed, and reinforced a million times over by the life she'd led. Right now, she and Doc were safe. After what had happened, sending even the smallest feeler out into the world felt like a risky thing to do. But on the other hand, if whoever was behind this did as they threatened, would the video be the means of bringing the dogs sniffing around the life she had built for herself here in Savannah, around Guardian Consulting, around Bianca St. Ives? And around Marin and Margery and Doc and the rest?

Doc said, "You ever hear of Tor encryption?"

"No."

"It lets you hide out on the web. We're using it. Trust me, nobody's going to find us." He frowned at her. "You thinking about replying?"

"I'm thinking about a lot of things." She gave herself a mental shake and headed toward the door. "Twelve hours, which means 5:00 p.m. We've got some time. Let me know if anything else comes in. And keep trying to trace those emails back to whoever sent them."

Doc's expression was troubled as he watched her go. "Will do."

It was, Bianca saw as she walked into her office, exactly five minutes until nine. Setting her nearly untouched coffee cup down on her imposing glass-and-steel desk, she walked past it and her big black leather chair to the wall-to-wall expanse of windows that looked out over the muddy green waters of the Savannah River. Staring blindly down at the familiar scene as her mind raced, she barely noticed the brown pelicans flying in formation and dropping like kamikaze planes into the water as they fished, or the tanker-size barge gliding past under the guidance of the much smaller tugboat escorting it to the mouth of the river, or the flotilla of other boats zipping busily to and fro.

Her insides were still in a knot. Seeing that on-screen image of her father so unexpectedly had knocked her for a loop, as much as she hated to admit it even to herself. Her feelings where he was concerned were a mess. A tangle of grief and anger, love and hate, hurt at his clearly stronger emotional attachment to his other daughter, his new family—and a terrible emptiness at the idea that she would never see him again.

Buck up, she ordered herself fiercely. How she felt didn't matter. What mattered was what she was going to *do*.

"Bianca?" Evie's quick knock on her open door interrupted her thoughts. "Leona Tilley with Claybourne Realty is here."

"Thanks." Pasting a smile on her face, Bianca turned away from the window and went out to greet Guardian Consulting's newest prospective client.

By 3:00 p.m., after getting a near commitment to provide a security guard at all Claybourne Realty open houses from Leona Tilley, who had to clear the expenditure with her partner before finalizing the deal, then schmoozing management at the Savannah Civic Center over lunch and concluding with a tour of the facility in hopes of persuading them that a locally owned company—Guardian Consulting—would be a better, more responsive alternative for their security needs than the Atlanta-based firm they currently used, Bianca was tired, sweaty (okay, glow-y in Savannah parlance) and still mulling over what to do about the threat posed by those anonymous emails as she walked back into the thankfully air-conditioned environs of her office.

The situation with all its implications had been churning away in the back of her mind, and the direction her thoughts had taken hadn't made her feel any cheerier.

She'd been struck by the unsettling notion that the emails might constitute a trap. Although if they did, they were meant as a trap for Richard, not her. She was certain of that because the job, and the threat, had been sent to Richard's private email account that she would have had no access to if Doc hadn't been upgrading it at the time Richard had been killed.

If it *was* a trap, then whoever was behind it clearly either didn't know or didn't believe Richard was dead. When she asked herself who would go to such lengths, Laurent Durand immediately sprang to mind as the most viable candidate, but he had been there in Bahrain and must be aware of the explosion and fire.

So either Durand didn't believe Richard was really dead or there was someone else who wanted Richard really, really badly.

Who? She didn't know.

Which led her to another question: Why? Why would Durand or anyone else go to such lengths to attempt to capture Richard?

And that brought her to the most disturbing realization of all: as the video with Marin and Margery had underlined, she was actually acquainted with only a small part of her father's life.

Who was he when he wasn't with her?

She knew some—many, she liked to think—of his identities and activities. But she didn't even try to fool herself that she knew them all.

So what didn't she know?

That was the question that was niggling away at her when she walked back into Doc's office shortly after three. Hay was out, probably checking on what was going on with Dynex down at the docks. Evie was in the kitchen setting up the new coffeemaker, and from the look of things when Bianca glanced in at her, she was going to be busy for a while. Still, Bianca closed Doc's door.

"All quiet on the Hong Kong–ese front," Doc said, looking up as the door clicked shut.

Knowing he was referring to the emails, she nodded. "I figured." Because she knew he would have let her know immediately if anything else had come in.

Doc raised his eyebrows at her in silent question as she stopped in front of his desk.

"I want you to do something for me," she said. Her mouth was dry, but she consciously chose not to swallow or wet her lips because she didn't want Doc picking up on how uncomfortable what she was getting ready to ask him to do made her. "I want you to get a still picture of my father off that video and use facial recognition software to run it through every database you can think of. I want to see what turns up."

Doc nodded. "Smart. Then we'll know what the cops might find if they were to get hold of it and run it."

"Right." Bianca agreed as if that was her primary motivation, which it wasn't. *She* wanted to learn as much as she could about her father. Checking him out felt like a betrayal in a way, but it was something that she needed to do. His death and everything associated with it had raised urgent questions in her mind. The wonder was that she'd never attempted to look into his background before. Loyalty, love, familiarity with him and the way he worked, acceptance of her life and his because it was all she had ever known—those were some of the reasons she'd come up with over the course of the day to explain to herself why she had simply accepted everything he'd told her without really questioning it. But those reasons were no longer operational.

She needed to know—who was Richard St. Ives?

"Oh, by the way, I got that information you asked me for this morning." Doc nodded in the direction of the printer, which rested on a table between the two tall windows. Rolling away from his desk, he scooted in his chair over to the table, grabbed a manila folder that was beside the printer, twirled around once with the glee of a six-year-old and scooted back to hand it to her.

"You're going to kill yourself in that chair." She said it in the absent tone of someone who'd said the same thing many times before. Opening the folder, she saw a printout of a newspaper article headlined Tiffany Brady, 4, Named Little Miss Hamilton County Fair. The story was accompanied by a picture of a beaming blonde child having a crown placed on her head.

Fantastic.

The file was an inch thick. Anticipating many more such

stories, Bianca closed the folder again in resignation. It was going to take a while to go through it, and right now she had bigger fish to fry.

"So?" Once more behind his desk, Doc leaned back to look up at her expectantly.

Bianca knew what he was asking.

"I'm going to take the job." She wasn't even sure when she'd made up her mind. As she'd finished weighing the pros and cons, she'd found an answer for the most compelling reason *not* to answer the email: it might be a setup orchestrated by someone hoping to capture a thief.

The thing was, if that was the case, then the thief they would be trying to capture was Richard. No one would be looking for her. She could nip in and get the job done without anyone even realizing she was there.

Because she was really very good at what she did.

And when she had her hands on whatever it was they wanted her to steal, she would put a tracer on it before handing it over. Then she would follow the tracer back to whoever had sent the threatening video and do whatever she had to do to eliminate the threat.

That, plus keeping the video from falling into the hands of the authorities until she could take care of the problem, was the "pro" that had convinced her that she needed to take the job.

Not that, in this particular case, the money had had any real bearing on her decision, but the prospect of earning some major bucks hadn't hurt, either.

"You sure?" Doc was looking worried again.

"I'm sure." He didn't need to know any more than that. She was still playing by her father's rules, and this one was *Keep your cards close to your vest.*

"Can you pull that email up again, please? Skip the video." She walked around behind him as she spoke.

"Yeah." The email popped up on the screen.

"If I have a seven-figure payment sent to a numbered bank account in Switzerland, you can get it out of there fast and stowed away in another bank account I give you in a way that can't be traced, right?"

He nodded. "Five minutes in and out. Just give me the account numbers and log-in information."

"All righty, then." Bianca felt the familiar quickening that she always experienced going into a job. She thought it must be equivalent to that of a soldier getting ready to go into battle. Her muscles tensed, her pulse sped up, her mind homed in on the objective to the exclusion of everything else. "You mind if I sit there for a minute? It'll be easier than me telling you what to write."

Doc pushed his chair back and stood up. Edging around him, Bianca sat down, hit Reply and typed, The fee is quadruple your offer. Four million US, half up front to the bank account following and half when the job is complete.

"Whoa," Doc said, reading over her shoulder. Bianca hit Send.

"Go big or go home," she said and waited. As she had expected, the *ping* announcing the arrival of an incoming email didn't take long.

It was one word: Agreed.

Send two million US to this account. She typed in the sixteen-digit number to the Swiss account, along with the other necessary information. When receipt is verified, I'll be in touch.

"Hard-core." Doc's tone was admiring.

"Never let them think you're running scared," she said.

That sounded so much like something her father would have said that she would have felt all sentimental if she'd had the time. She didn't. This was going down *now*. She scribbled the log-in information, routing and account number on a Post-it pad next to the computer and added identifying information for the Caymans account that the funds would be transferred into. At that point she hesitated, as it occurred to her that giving all that information to Doc meant that she was opening herself up to being majorly ripped off. Just because of the way she'd lived her life, she felt a wary disinclination to reveal so much. Then she remembered Bahrain, and how much Doc already knew, and how loyal he'd been—and how much he had to lose. And she thought, *I'm going to trust him. Unless and until he gives me a reason not to.*

"This is where it's coming in, this is where it needs to end up." She tapped each set of numbers in turn, then stood up and said, "Let me know when the money hits that account. And when you're finished, destroy that piece of paper."

"You got it."

Doc sat back down behind the computer and started pecking away at the keys.

Nerves on edge, Bianca returned to her office and resumed going through the file Doc had given her. Four-year-old girls apparently had amazingly eventful lives—who knew?

This one had saved her diabetic granny by calling 911, that one had gotten trapped in a revolving door and had required the entire population of tiny Glendale, Oregon, to free her, and a third, along with her eight-year-old sister, had opened a lemonade stand to help Save the Whales.

Bianca flipped that page over and found herself looking down at a picture of a slender, petite young woman with long black hair who was sitting alone at a picnic table biting into an enormous sandwich beneath a banner that proclaimed World's Biggest Fish Fry. The picture's background appeared to be some kind of local carnival.

The headline read Death of Local Family Ruled Murder-Suicide.

Bianca's breathing suspended as she read the accompanying story.

Ozaukee County coroner Tamara Biggar has ruled murder-suicide in the deaths of a local family whose bodies were found in the burned-out ruins of 2420 Lake Road last Tuesday. Sean McAlister, 40, shot and killed his wife, Sarah, 26, and their daughter, Elizabeth, 4, before setting his house on fire and turning the gun on himself. Motive is unknown at this time. The McAlisters had lived in the area for approximately six months. Funeral arrangements are pending.

The caption beneath the picture identified the subject as Sarah McAlister.

Bianca looked closer. The woman was wearing jeans and a green tee with writing on it that, due to the position of her arms, was impossible to read. She was in the act of chomping into the sandwich—not an elegant pose—but it was easy to see that she was pretty, with big dark eyes and a faintly Asian cast to her features.

A woman with long black hair. Elizabeth—*Beth*—McAlister. A fire.

Could it be? At the very least, it was quite a coincidence.

There's no such thing as coincidence. Her father had said that so many times she'd gotten tired of hearing it.

Without consciously deciding to do it, Bianca touched the picture, her index finger making barely there contact with the woman's face.

Sarah—the name didn't ring a bell. Just like Ann, the name her father had said was her mother's, never rang a bell.

Issa. The name whispered through her mind like a breeze from a just-opened door. Then, *Mommy.*

Bianca went all light-headed. Her hand fell away from the picture. She had to push back from her desk, drop her head into her lap and close her eyes.

Breathe, she ordered herself.

As she sucked in a series of deep, regular inhalations, it almost seemed as if she could smell the faint scent of vanilla.

What the hell?

Battling the dizziness that gripped her, she grabbed for logic with both figurative hands.

The story in the newspaper didn't match the facts as she knew them. If she was Beth McAlister, then obviously she hadn't died. And her father hadn't died then, either. He hadn't committed suicide, and he hadn't shot her mother and—

A dark, enclosed space. The smell of bleach. A man's voice calling "Beth" in a way that made her sick with fear. The boom of a shotgun being fired—

Oh, God, she remembered.

14

Beth. She was Beth, small and terrified, hidden by her mother in a cabinet that smelled of bleach. A shotgun went off, and a man—a bad man—came searching for her, Beth, calling her name in a way that made her skin crawl even now. A huge explosion a hundred times louder than the boom of the shotgun sent the cabinet with her in it catapulting skyward. She must have blacked out, or been knocked unconscious, because her next memory was of lying facedown on a slippery, cold carpet of evergreen needles. She remembered being in pain, her arm and side aching, how much it hurt to breathe. She remembered the strong smell of pine—and the horrible burning smell that was even stronger. Her father—Richard, although that wasn't his name—crouched beside her, his hand on the side of her neck as, she realized now, he felt for a pulse. It was dark, night, but there was this weird orange light and scary shadows leaping everywhere. Looking past her father, she saw the burning wreck of what had been their house and started to cry. He picked her up and carried her to a car. A strange car, not theirs. They drove away, the two of them.

Without her mother. She didn't remember saying a word, asking about her mother, anything, and she didn't remember her father talking, either.

What she did remember was lying in the back seat of that car crying from pain and fear and the horror of knowing that her mother was dead. She'd *known* that, without question, but she didn't remember how.

She did remember the car stopping after what seemed like hours and her father carrying her inside a long, low metal building that was so cold her teeth chattered. She remembered lying on a table and a man—a doctor, she thought—giving her a shot.

Then nothing. Nothing for a long time. Her next memories belonged to Bianca St. Ives.

All that came back to her in a flash, as though a lightning bolt had suddenly illuminated a dark and hidden part of her brain. The memories unspooled with a vividness that left her shaken. Still bent over with her head resting on her lap, Bianca tried to make sense of them, to reconcile them with what she knew about herself and her father and their life.

She battled the dizziness, the pain and shock of uncovering this terrible part of her life that she'd somehow totally *forgotten*, by forcing herself to focus and homing in on what she knew to be true.

Because most of what had been reported in the story in the paper wasn't.

The names—Sean, Sarah and Beth McAlister—were almost certainly fiction. Probably another of her father's cover identities extended to cloak the three of them. Her father hadn't shot her mother. He hadn't set the house on fire. He hadn't even been there when any of that had happened.

Another man, a stranger, had murdered her mother, had tried to murder her. That man had caused the house to explode.

Her father must have used the explosion and fire to fake his own death and hers, to make it appear that they had perished along with her mother. He had taken her away with him and forged new identities for them both.

That was how Bianca St. Ives had come to exist.

Why? That was the question that screamed through Bianca's

mind. Why would anyone commit such a horrible crime? *Who* would commit such a horrible crime?

And if her father had faked his death and hers twenty-two years ago, was he somehow faking his death now?

Her breathing steadied and her pounding heart—she only just then realized that her breathing was ragged and her heart *was* pounding—slowed as she realized that it all came back to a question she'd already started asking: Who, exactly, was Richard St. Ives?

A rap on her doorframe had her shooting upright in her chair.

She'd left the door open. Doc stood in the aperture frowning at her. Their eyes met. Doc looked surprised and concerned, and she—well, she didn't want to think what she looked like.

"You okay?" he asked.

"Fine," she replied, maybe a little brusquely, then pulled herself together and said, "Something I should know?"

"Yeah." He jerked his head back toward his office. Obvious message: *come with me.*

She instantly got it and got, too, that he was being careful not to say too much where he could be overheard. Evie was at her desk complaining over the phone about the nondelivery of some supplies she'd ordered, from the snatches of one-sided conversation Bianca could hear. Of course, if they could hear Evie, Evie could hear them, too.

Standing up—God, that was a mistake, her knees felt wobbly; she had to brace herself for a moment with a hand on her desk—she said, "I'll be right there."

He was watching her closely. Probably seeing her with her head on her lap had freaked him out.

Never show weakness: it was another of the rules. One she had just blown to hell.

"I'll be right there," she repeated.

He still looked uneasy, but to her relief he nodded and left.

Bianca took a few seconds to compose herself. The newly recovered memories were both painful and precious, but right now they had no place in her thoughts. Prioritizing had always been one of her strengths, and she prioritized now. Number-one problem: bad guys threatening to expose Richard. Everything else could be dealt with later.

Still, she couldn't quite let finding her mother go. Finding her, remembering her and the truth of what had happened to her, was such a big deal, so momentous, that she knew she needed to take some time to absorb it and process the emotions and everything else that went along with it.

But not now.

Grabbing her cell phone, Bianca took a photo of the news article with its accompanying picture for no more reason than she just wanted to have it, then slid her phone in her pocket, picked up the article and headed out the door.

"Excuse me one minute," Evie said into the office phone as Bianca appeared. Pushing the hold button, she grinned at Bianca from her seat behind her desk. "Leona Tilley called. They're ready to sign a contract. And she's recommending to the Board of Realtors that we provide security for all Savannah area open houses. Somebody's supposed to call tomorrow to set up an appointment to talk to us about it."

"That's great." Bianca summoned a smile and a thumbs-up as she followed Doc into his office. Evie apparently noticed nothing amiss, because Bianca heard her resume her castigation of whoever was on the other end of her phone call as she closed Doc's door.

He was already standing behind his desk. She looked a question at him.

He said, "Money's where you wanted it. I ricocheted it around the world like I was knocking down points in a pinball game. The route's untraceable."

"Good job. You da man."

"Walk in the park."

"You destroy that piece of paper?"

"Ate it."

"You didn't."

"Tore it up and put the pieces in the shredder, which is practically the same thing." He seemed to hesitate before saying, "You sure you're okay? You don't look so hot."

"Thanks." Her response was dry.

"You know what I mean."

"Yeah." She almost said, *I must have had some bad fish for lunch.* But she didn't. Instead of lying, instead of dissembling, she decided to go with the truth, or at least a portion of it. Some of the story was just too personal to reveal. "I came across this in the file you gave me." Walking toward him, she held out the article. "I think I recognize her. Only, not as Sarah McAlister. I'm almost certain that's not her real name. I knew her as Issa." Merely saying the name out loud made her chest tighten, Bianca discovered as Doc took the paper and glanced down at it. "I want you to run a trace on her, find out everything you can about her. She was…connected to my father, if that helps."

"It might. I'll run her through some databases and see what turns up."

"I knew there was a reason I didn't leave you behind in Bahrain."

"You just wanted somebody whose pretzels you could eat while they were sleeping on the flight home."

Bianca smiled. "That, too." For the moment she'd done all she could to uncover the circumstances behind her mother's death. It was time to concentrate on the job at hand. She came around Doc's desk. "Now that the initial payment's been made,

I need to get back in touch. See what kind of bang our friends are wanting for their megabucks."

"Here you go." Doc gestured at the computer as she joined him. The emails were on the screen.

Bianca sank into his chair, frowned at the screen, hit Reply and typed, Initial payment received. Send job details.

It took a few minutes, but then an email arrived with a file attached.

The message accompanying it read, You have seventy-two hours. Contact us when it's done.

Across the pond, it was a few minutes after 9:00 p.m.

"We have something." Durand's voice was full of satisfaction as he strode into the conference room where Rogan waited. A young man carrying a laptop scurried after him. They were in London, because the latest intelligence they had on Traveler had led them to believe he might be in London. They were still following that lead, but they'd been scouring the city for six days without any luck. To be more precise, they were in the Vauxhall section of London, in the MI6 Building, a postmodern fortress on the bank of the River Thames that was popularly known as Legoland by those who served in Her Majesty's clandestine services. Having formerly been one of that number, Rogan preferred to call it the clown factory. Although not in the hearing of Timothy Cowles-Parker, the senior MI6 officer who'd been sent by "C," as the head of MI6 was known, to sit in on the after-hours, hastily called meeting. The office they were using was also provided courtesy of "C." The courtesy being extended to Durand rather than Rogan, who, having left his post as an intelligence officer several years previously to go the freelance route, was still in the agency's black books.

Durand continued. "He's made a mistake at last. *Connard.* I knew he would."

"Are you saying that Traveler accepted the job?" Cowles-Parker's tone expressed disapproval of the other man's bad language. He was around sixty, with a florid, jowly face and a body to match. His black business suit almost exactly matched the color of the sky outside the window. The view was only slightly enlivened by the fog-obscured lights of the adjacent Vauxhall Bridge.

"That is exactly what I am saying." Durand motioned to the young man, who immediately set the laptop on the conference table in the middle of the room. The table was wood veneer with metal legs and six cheap folding chairs. Cowles-Parker occupied one and Rogan sat in another. It was uncomfortable, but then Rogan wouldn't be in it long. "He wants four million US. Half up front, half on completion. The initial payment has already been made, and shifted out of the account it was sent to."

"He's alive, then." The flat voice belonged to Kemp, the CIA agent, who was in the room via a tablet computer and some secure version of FaceTime, the connection having been set up by an assistant in anticipation of Durand's arrival. In Washington, DC, where Kemp was, the time was a little after 5:00 p.m. The man was in a suit and tie, probably still at the office.

"Look at this." Durand gestured at the laptop, which was now on and positioned in front of Cowles-Parker. Rogan stood up and moved around behind Cowles-Parker to get a look. From the tablet, Kemp complained, "I can't see squat," so Durand obligingly read the message aloud.

"'The fee is quadruple your offer. Four million US, half up front to the bank account following and half when the job is complete.' As I said, we paid the stipulated half."

"How do we know that's Thayer?" Kemp asked.

"Who else could it be? It is his private account. Highly encrypted. So far, our people have found it impossible to hack or trace. Used exclusively by select clients to solicit his services.

We were able to lean on one of those clients who is currently in custody to provide that contact information."

"So you set up a phony theft to lure him out?" Kemp said. The bare bones of the operation had already been described to him. "I'm surprised he bit."

Durand said, "Let us say, we added a sweetener. Also, it is not a fake theft. Traveler has too much experience and too much of an ear to the ground for us to think it wise to attempt that. No, the theft is real enough. Fortunately, the nature of what was stolen is such that the intelligence community was immediately made aware of what had happened. It provided us with the perfect opportunity."

"So you've hired Thayer to steal whatever it is back for you. When and where is he supposed to do the deed?" Kemp frowned impatiently out at the room.

Durand said, "He was given a seventy-two-hour deadline. At this point we've intercepted enough chatter to make us think the thief is heading for the States. We're working with real-time information as it comes in, and as of right now that's all we know."

"So you're telling me the plan is for someone to take down Thayer as he attempts to steal whatever it is back from wherever it winds up. Only, you don't know who stole it or where it's going to go." Kemp's words held a derisive edge.

"If by 'take down' you mean 'kill,' the answer is no. We want Traveler alive," Durand said. "We need to know what he's done with the information he's stolen. We need to know what he knows."

"If Traveler is Thayer, good luck with taking him alive. The man's a killer, among many other things. One of the most proficient we ever had," Kemp said.

"That's Rogan's job," Durand said, nodding at Rogan. Kemp gave Rogan a long look.

"It is, and if there's nothing else, I'll be on my way. I expect I'll be getting updates as they come in?" Rogan had been read into the situation by Durand via the phone call in which Durand had summoned him to the meeting, which was being held at the clown factory because the information being discussed was deemed sensitive enough that a secure facility was needed. Having gotten all he had expected to get from the meeting, which was nothing, Rogan headed for the door. His question was addressed to Durand, who nodded.

"I'd say that concludes our conference," Cowles-Parker said as Rogan left.

Groton's house in Great Falls, a swanky neighborhood just outside of DC, was impressive: a two-story, ten-thousand-square-foot brick mansion with white columns and five acres of well-groomed lawn. To Kemp, it looked like every light in the place was on, including the three massive chandelier-like ones dangling two stories on the wide front porch. Pulling up the oak-lined driveway about two hours after the conference call, he experienced a pang of envy. Groton's wife came from old money, and that allowed him to live far more lavishly than Kemp, who was forced to get by on his not overly generous government salary.

They don't pay me enough for this, Kemp thought, not for the first time. Three more years until retirement, and he was looking forward to it. Parking behind the line of cars that filled the top third of the driveway, he got out and walked around the back of the house to Groton's study, which had a separate entrance. Groton didn't want Kemp to be seen by his wife, who was entertaining her book club. Likewise, Groton no longer wanted any information on the topic that was prompting their get-together to be discussed via email or over the phone.

In person only.

Groton had been on the alert for him, heard him coming, met him at the door, ushered him inside. Groton was a tall, spare man of seventy-five, his face was deeply lined, but his blue eyes were sharp and he had a full head of white hair. He was dressed in a blue-checked shirt tucked into a pair of dark slacks.

"Drink?" Groton asked, gesturing at a silver tray holding a bottle of Maker's Mark whiskey, an ice bucket and some glasses.

"Yes, thanks." Kemp glanced around the study while Groton poured. Dark green walls, plaid curtains drawn over the windows, a leather couch and chair, a massive desk. Hunting prints on the walls, plus a few family pictures. Groton handed the drink over, Kemp sipped the fine bourbon appreciatively and they sat and got down to business.

When Kemp finished relaying the gist of the conference call to him, Groton said, "The solution is simple. Find out where this comedy is taking place, get there and take out Thayer."

"There's a concern about the top secret material he may have in his possession."

Groton shook his head. "Not our problem." He gave Kemp a level look, one that Kemp remembered from many years of working under him. It still had the power to make Kemp nervous. "I don't have to tell you that our asses are on the line here. And not just ours. Some very important people's."

"I know." Kemp tossed back the last of his whiskey and set the glass on the table beside him, careful to use the coaster Groton had provided because, he'd said, his wife went nuts about things like that. He had one more piece of bad news to share, and he hated like hell to have to do it. There was no help for it, however. Groton had to know. "The lab got back to me today with the DNA analysis we had run on those spots of blood that were found in the air vent in Bahrain. We assume it came from that woman who was working the robbery with Thayer." Kemp hesitated, wishing he hadn't been so quick to finish his drink.

He could use another shot of whiskey about now. He bit the bullet, came out with it. "It's definite. The DNA matched our sample. It's her."

Groton's face whitened. His fingers tightened around his glass until Kemp thought it might shatter in the old man's hand. He carefully put the glass down and stood up.

"I've been understanding. My God, I've been understanding. But this is on you." Groton towered over him, his eyes burning, his fists clenching. Reminded of what the old man had once been—an operative with more successful missions and kills under his belt than Kemp had himself—Kemp had to consciously stop himself from cringing. "How the hell—how the *hell*—did you screw this up so badly? How the *hell* did you let her live?"

Kemp licked his lips. "I, uh—"

Groton shut him up with a slashing gesture.

"Fix it," he said.

15

In Savannah, approximately three hours later, Bianca was in her office frowning down at the information contained in the open folder in her hand.

The emailed file, printed out now for convenience, included exactly three pages and a photo. To say that it was not as complete as Bianca would have liked was an understatement, but after requesting additional information, including as many details of the actual theft as were known, she was able to put together the broad strokes of a plan.

Of course, it was a well-known principle of war that no plan survived the firing of the first shots in a battle, but it was a start.

The first vital piece of information in its formulation was that the theft involved a physical object of a size and weight that could be carried in a briefcase, which meant that she would easily be able to transport it herself once she acquired it. A prototype weapons defense system was how the target was described, which didn't tell her a whole lot. The accompanying photo was more helpful. The object was about the size of a hardback book, with a remote-control-shaped electronic center complete with buttons, lights and a small digital display encased in a clear plastic box. It was shown cushioned by dark foam inserts inside a silver titanium briefcase with a six-digit combination lock. The specifications provided were complex, but what the object boiled down to was, in Doc's words, a drone detector.

"It works like one of those things drivers use to bust cops lying in wait on the freeway, you know what I mean? A radar detector." Doc's enthusiasm for the technology involved bubbled over as he studied the specs that were included in the file he'd printed out. Because this job belonged to the part of her life that couldn't be shared with Evie or Hay, Bianca had returned to the office after hours to do the prep work that needed to be done before going after the target. Doc had been waiting for her there, and he was with her in her office at that moment as they went over the information. His technical expertise was proving to be a surprisingly good fit with her more practical abilities. "Some Afghan warlord can just stick it in his jeep and it'll start beeping and give him, like, a two-minute warning if there's a Predator with a Hellfire missile overhead locking in on him."

"Yay?" Bianca replied. She was sitting in her office chair; he was in the visitor's chair across the desk from her. Once she'd ascertained the size, weight and not-dangerous-to-her status of the target, she was more interested in grappling with the identity of the thief.

Because that was the second vital piece of information she needed. Couldn't steal the thing back if she couldn't find it, and, presumably, the thief had it. The good news was, all thieves had a signature, a way of going about certain jobs that made it possible for someone who knew the players in that world to narrow down the pool of suspects if given enough of a description of the job. Plus most thieves specialized in objects of a certain type, which thinned the pool out even more.

This individual—Bianca never assumed the gender of a thief, for obvious reasons—had done it *Mission: Impossible*-style, dropping down through a hole cut in the ceiling to snatch the briefcase off a desk in a locked, secured office on a locked, secured floor in a locked, secured building where it had been left for no more than an hour while the businessman who'd had possession of it had run out to grab dinner. The alarm had been circumvented by the ceiling access because whoever had wired the building had not considered the possibility that someone might enter through it. Cameras had been thwarted by the same means. They filmed in arcs designed to detect intruders at normal human heights.

Bianca allowed herself a moment of professional admiration for the mind behind the planning and execution of the theft before once again getting down to business.

The style was flashy, the thief was an athletic pro and Bianca was as sure as it was possible to be that he/she already had a buyer lined up before he/she pulled the job.

The buyer was the third vital piece of information.

There was a limited market for a prototype weapons defense system with a low- to mid-eight-figure price tag, which was, she thought, a reasonable estimate for the price it would fetch given the amount she was being paid to retrieve it.

The fourth piece of information was that the theft took place in Southeast Asia. The client—thinking of them as "the client" was better than thinking of them as "the blackmailers," because the latter just made her angry and this kind of operation called for a cool head—refused to be more specific about where the theft had taken place than that, presumably so as not to give away their own location, but it was enough to point Bianca in the direction she needed to look.

Since Richard's death, she'd been reluctant to tap into the sprawling network of contacts her father had developed over the years that were now, she supposed, hers by inheritance in case it should somehow draw the wrong kind of notice. But for this she did, reaching out cautiously over the Dark Websites they used with what she knew and asking for help filling in the blanks. The information she got back yielded no more than a handful of possible identities for both the thief and buyer. By having Doc run a computer search on the names and known aliases of their thief candidates and then having him cross-check for last-minute flights booked by passengers with those names and known aliases to the areas where the possible buyers were located, she was able, with what she considered a high degree of certainty, to identify both thief and buyer.

Justin Lee, traveling under the alias Austin Hunt, was at that moment a passenger on a flight from Bangkok to Singapore, where he was scheduled to board United Flight 2, a nonstop flight to San Francisco. He was the thief.

Allied Industries in San Jose was the most likely buyer. It was the only major player in weapons systems development in the area. Its founder and CEO, Walt Sturgeon, was almost certainly the one who would be making the buy. According to her sources, he ran the company with an iron fist, and neither buying stolen property nor forking out millions of dollars for it was going to happen without his say-so. Who would actually take physical possession of the prototype, though, was open to question.

The simplest thing to do would be to intercept Lee at San Francisco International Airport and relieve him of the prototype before he got anywhere near his buyer.

United Flight 2 was scheduled to take off in three hours, and the flight was slated to land in San Francisco at 4:50 p.m. Pacific time the following day, Friday, which was 7:50 p.m. Savannah time. It was currently just after 6:30 p.m. Thursday Savannah time. She had approximately nineteen hours to get to San Francisco.

Piece of cake.

"Could you see if you can find me a direct flight from Atlanta to San Francisco International that gets in before 2:00 p.m. tomorrow?" she asked. Because flying was flying, after all, and she wanted a time cushion to leave room for any possible mishaps, like, say, tarmac delays. On the other hand, too long an interval wasn't good, either. She wanted to remain inside the gate area behind security after her plane arrived so that she could pick Lee up when he exited the international arrival area. It would be a lot easier than trying to pick him up as he left the busy airport. And there was only so much in-airport shopping and eating she could do without risking attracting unwanted attention.

With a grunt of assent, Doc stood up and headed for his office. A few minutes later he was back, rattling off flight times.

"The 11:15 one," she said. The flight time between Atlanta and San Francisco International was five hours, ten minutes, which meant she would arrive at 1:25 p.m. Pacific time, giving her a three-hour-plus window to allow for things going wrong. It was a three-and-a-half-hour drive to Atlanta from Savannah and she needed to be at the airport at least an hour and a half before the flight, which meant she needed to leave home around six tomorrow morning. Yes, she could make that work.

"You want me to book two tickets?"

She frowned at Doc as he stopped in front of her desk. "You can't come with me."

He looked affronted. "What? I can help."

If it had been a full-fledged heist, that would have been true. Doc's expertise with surveillance and alarm systems and anything computer-related or virtual that could be hacked was an ace in the hole that could make a difficult job a whole lot less complex. Plus it was always good to have backup, just in case. But what she was planning was a simple snatch-and-replace as the target exited the airport. The broad strokes of the plan were to distract Lee with something like, say, a hard stumble against him that made him fall down and drop the briefcase that he would be carrying with him because it was too valuable for him to do anything else with it, apologize profusely, help him up and in the process exchange the briefcase he was carrying for the nearly identical one she would have with her. Then she would disappear before he discovered the switch.

She said, "We can't travel under our own names. I don't want to leave a trail that could be traced back here once the job goes down. Any legend—" thief-speak for a false identity, including passport, other ID such as a driver's license, credit cards and accompanying backstory "—you used before can never be used again. And there's not enough time to get you a new one."

In fact, all the identification documentation connected with the disaster in Bahrain was sleeping with the fishes; once they'd made it safely back to Savannah, she'd collected everything, burned it and thrown the ashes in the river.

The key was to make it as close to impossible as she could for anyone to retrace her path from Savannah to San Francisco after she completed the job. Protecting her identity and her bolt-hole from discovery and her friends from being involved was of paramount importance. She had a selection of legends to choose from; he was back to being Miles Davis Zeigler.

Doc made a scoffing sound. "You think I don't have a fake ID? I've got a drawer full."

The look she gave him was incredulous. "How?"

"I made them. I've been making fake IDs since high school. I made decent money selling them back then, too."

"You're getting on an airplane, not trying to sneak into a bar."

"They're as good as anything you've got. Want to see?"

"They're here?"

"Like I told you, I got a drawer full. A *desk* drawer."

"Show me." Bianca stood up and followed Doc into his office. When he opened one of his desk drawers to show her his collection of driver's licenses—he had more than a dozen, featuring his picture matched with different names, addresses, birth dates and states—she picked them up one at a time, examined them closely and was impressed. "These are good."

"Told ya."

"*Why* do you have these?" She was examining the bar code on a Texas license with Doc's picture and the name Blake Warren—if she hadn't known the thing was fake, she never would have been able to tell.

He shrugged and looked shifty. Bianca's attention was caught and her gaze sharpened on him.

"Well?" she said.

He sighed. "When I first got here, I wasn't sure how long I was going to stay. I mean, I was tripping out over what happened, and I thought—well, I thought I might need to take off and fend for myself, you know what I mean? Go north again, or something. I might be fresh out of family, but New York—that's still home."

Okay, she got that. "And now?"

"I like it here. As long as the AC doesn't go out."

Bianca had to smile.

Seeing that, he added, "So I can come?"

She hesitated. Her gut instinct was to keep the operation as small as possible, but on the other hand, going in naked—more thief-speak for alone—had its hazards, too.

"You know you're safe here in Savannah, and you can stay here and stay safe," she said. "I don't expect anything bad to come out of this job, but—"

"Shit happens," he finished for her and grimaced. "If I'd wanted to stay safe, I never would have hacked into government computers to begin with. Anyway, now—we're kind of a team. I think."

He said it almost shyly.

"I'll book the tickets," she said. She'd brought the credit card she intended to use with her tonight for just that purpose. It was in her purse, which was in her office. For the flight, she was Laura Green. When it landed, she would turn into somebody else. "Pick an ID. Two, because you'll need a change once we land. Oh, and lose the black. You need to look like a tourist. You have anything like a gaudy Hawaiian shirt in your closet?"

"You kidding?"

"Nope," Bianca said and headed back to her office to book the tickets.

"You brought coffee," Doc said with sleepy-eyed appreciation when Bianca, all touristy in a pink button-up shirt over a pair of jeans, picked him up in front of his apartment at 5:50 the following morning.

He was wearing baggy black cargo shorts, black high-tops and a brown T-shirt that read Got Milk Duds? above a picture of the candy.

Okay, he'd made an effort.

"Loving the duds," she said.

He gave a grunt that said *aren't you witty* as he slid into the passenger's seat beside her and picked up one of the two coffee cups in the holder between them, having already deposited his bag in the trunk. She already had two bags of her own in the trunk, a carry-on and a larger one to be checked that contained, along with various items of clothing and miscellaneous, commercial-airliner-friendly selections from her weapons vault that she'd thought might come in handy and a silver metal briefcase. She'd found it after a quick search of the local open-all-night Walmarts. It was aluminum rather than titanium, but the dimensions were roughly the same as the target and she'd weighted it so that it matched the target's weight specifications. She didn't expect the switch to go unnoticed for long, but then she didn't need it to. Lee only had to remain unaware of what she'd done for long enough for her to get away, which would take a matter of maybe two minutes.

"We're on our way to Memphis to see Regions Bank about improving their cyber security, by the way." Headlights slicing through the predawn gloom, she headed up the ramp to I-16 West as she spoke. The sun wasn't yet up, but the sky to the east was glorious Technicolor. "I told Hay that you knew a guy in their tech department, and when they had a problem yesterday, he contacted you directly."

Coming up with a cover story that would account for both the sudden nature of her departure and the fact that she was taking Doc with her had required a little work. Fortunately, Hay had been too indignant with her—"You told Evie that Susan and I broke up, didn't you? She's trying to fix me up with Grace Cappy for that historic thing!"—to ask many questions. To Evie, she'd said the same thing, asked her to postpone the meeting with the Realtors until Tuesday and added that she would be back no later than Monday night. Since this was Friday, that gave her time to recover the target, follow it back to its source and do what had to be done to make sure the video, and the threat, was dealt with.

"Guy I know at Regions Bank had a hacker emergency. Got it." Doc winced as an 18-wheeler rumbled past them, practically blowing them into the other lane, which, fortunately, was empty. So early in the morning, traffic on the expressway was light. Doc took another swallow of coffee and slid a sideways glance at her. "Uh, I got some information for you."

Bianca picked up her own coffee and sipped at it. From the nervous look Doc gave her, she gathered that he preferred she keep both hands on the wheel. Well, too bad. She really needed coffee. "What kind of information?"

"That computer search you had me do? It came up with two identities for your father."

"Hmm." Since she, personally, knew of at least two dozen identities Richard had used over the years, she could only suppose he'd been very careful about not having a recognizable picture taken. "What were they?"

"One was Andrew somebody, a Texas oilman. That one came up because he got his picture in the paper at the scene of a car crash. Easy to give a fake name, which I'm assuming that was. The other—" he drank some more coffee "—was a CIA badge. Issued, like, thirty years ago to an active field agent named Mason Thayer. Boss, I think that one was real."

Another 18-wheeler rattled up beside them. Bianca carefully set her coffee back in the cup holder and wrapped both hands around the wheel to hold the Acura steady. When the behemoth passed, she asked, "What makes you think so?"

"I found it in the agency archives, in what's kind of the dead agent file. It's a hard place to get to. You have to worm past all kinds of firewalls and encryption and shit. But a fake badge— it wouldn't be there. It just wouldn't."

"How on earth did you manage to get in there?" Easier to think of the difficulty involved in breaching the CIA's—the *CIA's*—computer network than to come to grips with the possibility that her father had once been a badge-carrying CIA agent.

Doc smiled. "That thing I got arrested for? With the DoD computers? I left myself a couple of back doors in case I ever wanted to get back in. They've increased their protection, like, a thousandfold, but the back doors are still there."

"I'm impressed." She was thinking of Richard, of his wideranging skills that included everything from breaking and entering to running cons to martial arts to crack marksmanship. She thought of the training he'd given her, of the experiences and instructors he'd provided, of the skills he'd made sure she'd acquired. "When you say the badge was in the dead agent file, did you mean that literally? That badges were put in that file because the agent died?"

Doc nodded. "Yep."

Bianca gripped the wheel so hard she could feel the vibrations of the road through it. She stared unseeingly at the cars in front of her as she considered that information in the context of the story about Sean McAlister killing himself and his family and what she knew of her own life. And she thought, *That fits.*

For whatever reason, CIA agent Mason Thayer apparently had been declared dead when he wasn't. He had also pretended to be Sean McAlister and then faked his own and his daughter's—*her*—death. After that, he had become master criminal Richard St. Ives.

Why? That was the question that was starting to eat at her.

"Here's the other thing," Doc said. He'd waited, Bianca noted, until she'd successfully negotiated the merge onto I-75 North, which as the sun rose was bristling with traffic zooming toward Atlanta. "I got an identity for that Sarah McAlister, too. Just one, but I'm sure this one's legit. Her real name's Anissa Renee Jones. I found her in two places. First, the University of Maryland yearbook archives. She was only there one year. The year after that, when she was nineteen years old, she was working full-time for DARPA. I found her ID badge."

Anissa. *Issa.* Bianca clenched her teeth and took a deep breath and *focused*, because while she was driving a car that was barreling down the expressway at seventy miles an hour was absolutely not the time to wig out.

"DARPA?" she asked. When she could trust herself to speak—and think, and function—normally.

"The Defense Advanced Research Projects Agency. It operates under the DoD. Just like the CIA. That's the connection with your father. Anissa Jones and Mason Thayer both worked for agencies under the umbrella of the DoD. At the same time."

16

Anything that can go wrong, will go wrong. It wasn't one of the rules, but it should have been. By the time the Boeing 777 touched down at San Francisco International Airport, Bianca was willing to accord it honorary status at the very least.

Because of a medical emergency on board that had caused them to be diverted to Phoenix, they were more than four hours late getting into San Francisco. As they disembarked at 5:38 p.m., the airline had employees standing by at the gate offering help to any passenger who had missed a connection. Suppressing the urge to ask them if that included putting out an APB on an absconding thief, Bianca checked to make sure that United Flight 2 had arrived on time—of course it had, more than an hour earlier at 4:25—then rushed to pick up her bag and the rental car.

Although, she realized as she pointed the nondescript white Hyundai Accent toward 101 South and the hotel where they had reservations, rushing was no longer necessary.

They'd missed Justin Lee and his titanium briefcase by a mile. Or, more accurately, an hour, thirteen minutes. Given the size of San Francisco and the amount of traffic zooming everywhere, it might as well have been days.

Shit, shit, shit.

"Any luck on the rental car?" she asked Doc, who was wedged in beside her with his knees almost under his chin and his laptop open on his knees. He did not fit in the tiny front seat, but unfortunately by the time they got to the rental car counter, the car they'd reserved was gone, given to another customer whose flight had arrived on time, and they'd had to make do with what was left.

Which was fine with Bianca, but Doc looked like a Saint Bernard crammed into a hamster wheel.

"Not under the names Justin Lee or Austin Hunt or any of the other aliases I have for him."

"Hotel room?" Bianca asked without much hope. Doc had hacked into the reservation systems of the major hotels in the area, but the problem—well, one of the problems—was that there were a lot of hotels in the area, and not all of them used a hackable reservation system.

"Nada."

Big surprise. Considering how her day was going, the surprise would have been if Doc *had* been able to find him.

Okay, she was tired and hungry and crabby and *had lost the object of her cross-country flight.* In the back of her mind she was busy processing the minimal information in the file Doc had given her on Mason Thayer—basically the CIA equivalent of name, rank and serial number; Doc said that everything else had been scrubbed—and the slightly more extensive information in the file on Anissa Jones. Mechanic father, schoolteacher mother—thinking about them as her grandparents just messed with her objectivity, so Bianca did her best not to. Perfectly normal life growing up in Bethesda, Maryland. Until Anissa's parents were killed in a car crash during her freshman year of college. By the following year, Anissa—*Issa*—was working for DARPA, and presumably on the path that had taken her into the orbit of CIA agent Mason Thayer.

When he was thirty-eight and she was nineteen. With an almost twenty-year age difference between them, working for agencies under the DoD that should presumably have had little if any contact, they'd somehow managed to hook up and have her.

Something to wrap her mind around later, when there weren't at least half a dozen more urgent things to think about. She'd asked Doc to keep looking into the two of them, their connection, anything he could possibly find, and he'd set up programs that were running searches on thousands of databases even as they attended to the more immediate matter of the recovery of the prototype.

"Think you can locate Walt Sturgeon?" Finding the likely prospective buyer wasn't as sure a thing as finding the thief when it came to recovering the prototype, but under the circumstances Bianca was ready, willing and able to settle for whatever she could get.

"I'll try."

While Doc did things with his laptop, Bianca was briefly distracted by the view as the road curved and she suddenly found herself looking out over the sparkling blue expanse of San Francisco Bay. The boats skimming across the water trailing white ribbons of wake, the cloudless sky, the buildings studding the green hills that rolled away into the distance—the sight was breathtaking. San Francisco, with its iconic scarlet bridge and cable cars and trolleys and Victorian houses and steep, crooked streets, was one of her favorite cities in the world. She'd been there a number of times with her father, and not always to pull a robbery or scam. She'd actually had a couple of days to enjoy the area and explore.

"Got him." Doc shot her a triumphant look. "He's having a party tonight on his boat to celebrate his daughter's engagement. Apparently it's a really big deal, because it rates half a page in the *San Francisco Chronicle*. The engagement, I mean. On the Society pages."

"His boat?"

"He's got a Gulf Craft Majesty 135. It's like this huge yacht." Doc's tone made it clear that he was impressed. Bianca guessed he was looking at pictures. "It's docked at the St. Francis Yacht Club, and the party's from 6:30 to whenever. You think Lee will go there?"

Bianca did a quick calculation. Lee had deplaned at 4:25. Give him twenty minutes to get out of the airport, and there was a gap of one hour, forty-five minutes before Sturgeon's boat party. Sturgeon—or somebody working for him—could have met Lee at the airport, or at any point thereafter, and relieved him of the prototype. On the other hand, since the kind of person who would pay millions of dollars for a stolen item tended to be unscrupulous and often downright dangerous, a prudent thief usually preferred that the handoff be conducted in a public place, or at least a place with plenty of witnesses. Otherwise, there was nothing to prevent the would-be buyer from shooting said thief, taking the object and saving his money. Win-win for the buyer, not so much for the thief.

She said, "I don't know. But right now it's the only lead we have."

"If you're going to try to make it, you need to turn around. The St. Francis Yacht Club is the other way, straight up 101 North."

"Tell me what else it says about the party." Bianca would have made a U-turn, but a barrier prevented that. Anyway, she needed a place to change clothes. A Chevron sign caught her eye. Perfect.

"Two hundred guests, dinner cruise around the bay— Ah!" Doc broke off with an alarmed exclamation as Bianca whipped the Hyundai off the expressway and around the bend that led to the Chevron service station.

"You have to go potty that bad?" He looked at her in disbelief as she zipped past the crowded gasoline bays and braked beside the building.

"I'm going to change clothes," she told him. "I'll be out in five minutes. While I'm in there, you find directions to that boat."

Twilight was falling as Bianca pulled the Hyundai over within sight of Sturgeon's megayacht, the *Conquistador.* It was docked alongside other equally impressive yachts in individual slips at the St. Francis Yacht Club. Beyond the curving row of multimillion-dollar boats tied up at the dock, Bianca could see the Mediterranean-style clubhouse and, beyond that, the Golden Gate Bridge. To the west, Alcatraz rose from the smooth waters of the bay like the bony head of a grim, gray sea monster.

The yacht itself was a huge, streamlined, gleaming white triple-decker with a flybridge and satellite equipment that stood tall against the pink-and-purple sky. With the blazing orange ball that was the setting sun dropping behind it, the jetty on which the yacht club was located was swathed in lavender shadows while the bay itself was glossy purple blue. How much of that was natural and how much of that was a result of the flashes of purple neon that pulsed from the yacht in time to the blaring music Bianca didn't know, but the result was spectacular. Bianca could have stayed where she was—parked beside the promenade overlooking the dock—for a long time and admired the view, but it was already 6:30 and the golf cart brigade that had been dropping off guests was empty now and speeding away out of sight.

"You think Lee's in there?" Doc asked.

"No idea. I hope the briefcase is." Bianca watched the embarkation process through a pair of pocket-size binoculars.

The white-uniformed security guards around the *Conquistador*'s gangplank were busy screening several milling groups of festively dressed partygoers that totaled twenty-two individuals— she counted; knowledge was power—before allowing them on board. From what she could see, the vetting process involved a cursory check of a printed invitation presented by the guest before said guest was waved up the gangplank and onto the boat, which already appeared to be teeming with people.

"Uh, problem. You don't have an invitation." Squinting through the gloom, Doc was watching the same thing.

"I will have." She'd already instructed Doc to drive to the hotel and check in once she was on board. He'd protested—"I'm not just gonna leave you!"—but as she'd pointed out, there was nothing he could do to help her once she was on the boat. And getting him on board, too? Not going to happen. To begin with, sneaking two on was a lot harder than doing the same thing with one. And Doc would stick out in that California-hot company like a frog in a birdcage. "I'll call you if I need you to pick me up. Otherwise, I'll see you at the hotel later. Definitely by breakfast. Nine in the café."

"What do I do if you don't show?"

"I will."

Before he could argue further, she slid out of the car. The brief flash of interior light might have presented a problem if there hadn't been so much activity on the dock below. For the next few minutes, she needed the cover of relative darkness.

Stopping by the Chevron had given her a chance to do more than change clothes. As she'd passed the car service bay on the way to the outdoor-access restrooms, she'd spotted an old-fashioned Bic cigarette lighter, difficult to find in the United States now because they were fueled with compressed rather than liquid gas, which made them a fire hazard—and also very useful. Coupled with duct tape, a roll of which she'd purchased in the adjacent convenience store after snagging the lighter, she had the makings of a small incendiary device.

Because you just never knew when you were going to want to blow something up. Like now.

The duct tape was in her evening bag, which hung by a slender diamante strap from her shoulder. Fishing it out, tearing off a long strip, she attached the strip to her purse, leaving the silver tail of tape dangling but handy. Then, sliding the ratchet on the top of the lighter to the max on position, she lifted the ratchet to separate it from the flame adjustment gear and held the lighter with the top tilted downward at an angle so that the vaporized gas would start to leak out.

Shivering a little as the brisk sea breeze hit her despite the long sleeves of the high-necked, baby-pink, all-over-sequined mini that she wore with kicky little pink lace gloves (the better to keep from leaving fingerprints behind, my dear), sexy pink lace stockings (to give her loaded and lethal baby-pink satin garter belt something to attach to) and silver spike-heeled (literally) pumps, she ran down the narrow stone steps that led to the dock. The silky strands of her stick-straight, shoulder-length black wig blew back from her face; the long bangs felt cool and smooth as the wind ruffled them against her forehead.

For this operation she was black-haired, blue-eyed (no contacts needed), twenty-eight-year-old Cara Levine, fledgling restaurateur, LA resident and friend of Gemma Sturgeon, the bride-to-be.

The plan—get on board the *Conquistador*, determine if the prototype was on there, too, and, if it was, steal it.

Anything beyond that, she was going to have to wing it.

Her previous plan to switch briefcases, for example, was toast. To begin with, she wasn't even sure she was going to find the briefcase with the prototype in it on board. She *was* sure that as a girlie, pretty-in-pink partygoer she'd look way out of place trying to carry a big metal briefcase onto the boat.

An open-topped metal trash can was conveniently located near the bottom of the steps and was just as conveniently blocked from the view of the yachts by a trio of well-trimmed bushes.

Bianca stopped and flicked the Bic until the flame caught. Careful to keep the Bic tilted at the precise downward angle that would allow the small flame to ignite the cloud of leaking gas as it grew, which would then, just a moment or two later, melt the lighter's own plastic casing, causing the remainder of the trapped gas to explode with a bang as loud as a mortar and a subsequent fire as the piled-high trash in the can caught, she duct-taped the lighter to the inside of the trash can.

Leaving the flickering flame to do its thing, she skipped down the remaining few steps and hurried the ten or so yards up the darkening road to attach herself to the end of the line of the fourteen people who still needed to get past security and onto the boat.

Sidling up next to a tall, slim brunette in a red satin romper who along with her friends was grooving to the dance music blasting from the boat, Bianca smiled at her, said, "Totally awesome," in response to the Dancing Queen's exuberant "Isn't this the best?" and waited for it—

Bang!

The flash of the explosion was followed by flames roaring out of the top of the trash can. The Dancing Queen screamed and stopped dancing. A flock of seagulls that had been cruising past squawked and scattered in a dozen different directions. A maintenance worker who'd been pushing a wheeled cart down the road threw himself on the pavement and covered his head with his arms.

"Oh, my God!"

"Fire!"

"What the hell...?"

"Something exploded!"

"Look at that!"

"Quick! Throw me a fire extinguisher!"

Under the cover of the confusion and noise, Bianca lifted the

Dancing Queen's party invitation from her purse. She knew where it was because, while she'd been reconnoitering with the binoculars, she'd seen the girl look at it and then stow it away. A hand beneath the bucket-style bag to stabilize the weight, a quick lifting of a flap, and then her fingers were in the bag and closing on the gilt-edged invitation and the thing was done. The diversion had accomplished its mission: focus attention away from her small theft.

Tucking the invitation away in her own purse, Bianca moved quickly away from the mark, skirting the line until she was the next one set to be let through, all while everyone else was still ogling at and exclaiming over the blaze. By this time the flames were being extinguished by the timely application of two fire extinguishers, the maintenance worker was getting to his feet and brushing himself off, and the seagulls were wheeling out over the bay. A little harmless excitement to add variety to the evening.

Airily waving her invitation at security, Bianca was motioned through. She was up the gangplank and being offered a mimosa as she stepped onto the boat even as the flames subsided into a smelly column of smoke.

Accepting the drink with a smile, she made her way across the sheltered exterior deck that was crowded with knots of the young and the beautiful standing around drinking and shouting to be heard over the chest-thumping music. Sliding glass doors festooned with a banner that read Congratulations, Gemma and Greg opened into a saloon. She walked through them, ducking her head a little to avoid the confetti dripping from the dangling letters of the pair's names.

Glancing around, she saw rich-looking paneling, a built-in white leather sectional, a quartet of club chairs surrounding a glass coffee table, a pub-worthy bar with dark green leather bar stools and enough liquor on the mirror-backed shelves behind it to intoxicate an entire NFL team—and people everywhere. Glamorous people in gorgeous clothes talking, dancing, knocking back drinks, inhaling unknown substances from smooth surfaces with rolled dollar bills, making out in corners.

Unfortunately, none of those people was Walt Sturgeon.

She looked for surveillance cameras. There didn't seem to be any, probably because a boat like the *Conquistador* was the kind of private environment where owner and guests could indulge themselves and nobody who was participating in anything questionable, whether legal or illegal, wanted to record it.

She also checked for security and found it: two men in black suits with impassive faces and name badges clipped to their breast pockets unobtrusively walking around. Probably there were more. At a guess, for a two-hundred-strong crowd on a yacht the size of the *Conquistador*, a pair on every deck. So, three decks, probably six private security types.

Okay, then. Stay away from the men in black.

"Hors d'oeuvre, miss?" a steward asked. He had to raise his voice to be heard over the noise.

"Thank you." Snagging a crab ball and a napkin from the tray he held out to her, Bianca bit into the delectably crunchy mouthful and sipped her drink as she followed her ears to what, from the sound of it, was the heart of the party.

That involved making her way up a spiral staircase that had been turned into an obstacle course by the dozens of white and silver balloons tied to the rails and the sheer number of guests trying to go up and down it at the same time.

Reaching the next level, she glanced around and chose what seemed like the most promising option, heading out through open glass doors to the exterior deck. Having finished the truly yummy crab ball, she dropped her napkin on a tray a steward wordlessly held out to her for that purpose but kept her half-empty glass as silent proof of her party spirit to anyone who might glance her way.

Once outside, she took an appreciative breath of the cool, salt-tinged air and strolled casually across the deck, where dozens of guests eating dinner crowded around small tables. A buffet had been set up at the stern, and a line of people clutching plates patiently waited their turn to fill them. The food smelled wonderful—the crab ball had been appetizer-size, after all—but she kept her focus on the people, her growling stomach be damned.

She searched the entire deck: another large, dark-paneled saloon filled with dancers and make-outers, briefly illuminated by a strobe light that was enough to give people prone to seizures a seizure. Another, smaller room where a pretty blonde—Gemma, Bianca recognized her from the picture in the *Chronicle* Doc had shown her—was having photos taken. Four staterooms, all locked. Unless he was in one of the secured staterooms—possible; something to be checked out later if necessary—no Walt Sturgeon and no sign of the briefcase. Two security types in black suits, as she had supposed: laid-back, careful to be unobtrusive, clearly not expecting trouble, a rich crook's insurance policy. No threat to her, but best avoided. Still hanging on to the unfinished mimosa—from what seemed like time immemorial it had been drummed into her head that alcohol on a job was a bad thing, so she deliberately didn't finish it—she made her way up an outside staircase to the top deck.

There was a lot of exterior space where she came out, a huge open-air deck with lounge chairs and a pool and people everywhere, including up on the built-in banquettes that lined the low walls, dancing like wind socks in a hurricane. By that time it was almost full dark, and she had to make a pretty up close and personal tour of the revelers to be sure that her target was not among them. The revving of the boat's engines followed

by a surge of forward motion had her bracing herself to keep
her balance and then glancing out over the smooth teak rail
she'd grabbed.

The *Conquistador* was pulling away from the dock in a froth
of white wake. The sun was gone, the sky was navy blue with
a scattering of stars beginning to appear and only a crimson
rim on the western horizon to mark the day's passing, and the
Dancing Queen was down on the dock with a man beside her,
staring disconsolately after the departing boat.

Bianca had only a moment to feel bad about ruining the other
woman's night when her attention was drawn to a second man
walking past the couple. The dock's security lights had come
on, and he was caught in the unforgiving white glare.

Her pulse kicked it up a notch as she recognized him: Justin
Lee, aka Austin Hunt, aka just the thief she was looking for.

He'd looked younger and cuter in the photo Doc had found
of him.

He could only have come from the *Conquistador*. He must
have disembarked right before the boat pulled away from the
dock.

The prototype had to be on the boat. Delivering it was the
only reason Lee would have been on board.

Spiraling excitement twisted through Bianca's bloodstream.
A smile just touched her lips. The hunch she'd followed had
paid off.

Now to find the prototype.

A good-looking blond surfer type blocked the doorway as she
tried to leave the deck to head into the adjoining saloon, which
a bright blue neon sign flashing on the room's right-hand wall
announced was called the Sky Lounge. The guy was wearing
a polo and khakis and holding a beer. He looked her up and
down before smiling at her.

"So what's your Patronus, baby?" he asked her.

Seriously? Harry Potter's your pickup line?

"Scooby-Doo," Bianca said without blinking an eye and pushed past him.

There was more dancing in the Sky Lounge, girls boogy-ing singly and in groups to the pulsing beat, couples wrapped around each other swaying and groping in a blue-light-bathed version of *Dirty Dancing*. Bianca checked each face as she walked through, but given the wonky lighting, she would have had to go nose to nose with everybody present to make one hundred percent certain she wasn't overlooking Sturgeon. Although he was in his midfifties, a stocky guy with a bad toupee, she was pretty sure she would be able to pick him out of this group by silhouette alone.

She could feel the movement of the boat, the slight bounce of it cutting through the water, as she walked through the gal-ley, which was occupied by half a dozen caterers—no mistake there, the lighting was fine—and into the next saloon. It was outfitted as a library with three walls of built-in shelves in rich mahogany. The shelves were filled with books and ornaments behind glass doors. The music was slightly muted here, the room smelled faintly of cigars and soft lighting from sconces set into the walls made it bright enough so that when Bianca spotted Walt Sturgeon standing with a group at the far end of the room there was no mistake.

The titanium briefcase rested on the floor right beside his left leg.

For the briefest of moments, as her gaze riveted on that brief-case, her stomach tightened and her breathing quickened. She was sure her eyes widened and her face changed, as well.

Bingo.

Then she got a grip, remembered her surroundings and forced herself to glance away even as her mind raced.

Stealing the briefcase right now is out. The location is too exposed. Too many potential witnesses.

Cordovan leather club chairs were scattered in pairs around the perimeter of the room. They were full of people, just like the room was full of people. The hum of their chatter rose and fell like the floor beneath her feet. Three older women, meticulously groomed and obviously affluent, stood talking in the nearest corner. A gaggle of pretty young women—six, by count—huddled in a group next to them, sipping wine, giggling and nudging each other, their focus on the rear of the room where Sturgeon stood talking to a number of younger men. On the other side of the young women, a gray-haired man helped himself to a drink from a tray being passed by a waiter. He was only a few feet away from Sturgeon.

Never go in without an exit strategy. It was one of the rules. Before she did anything, she needed to plan how she was going to get away. This was complicated by the fact that she was on a fricking boat in the middle of San Francisco Bay, which made any kind of quick exit problematic. A snatch-and-run, for example, was definitely not going to work. A snatch-and-swim, maybe. Except the boat was a long way from shore, the water in the bay was cold and she had no idea what being immersed in salt water would do to the prototype.

Hmm.

One thing for sure, standing frozen just inside the doorway while she figured things out was not a good move. Getting it together, she strolled around the edge of the room, careful to attract no special attention. She headed toward the gray-haired man. He was alone, would probably be receptive to female attention and was close to the briefcase.

"This kid and me, we're going to be family," Sturgeon boomed, drawing all eyes. He held up a glass of what appeared to be Scotch on the rocks while wrapping an arm around the shoulders of a dark-haired, thin-faced twentysomething man who nodded and looked faintly sheepish as Sturgeon pulled him close. The men surrounded them, twentysomethings, too, nodding along with the first guy.

Sturgeon swept his gaze over them and said, "Since Gemma's busy getting her picture taken right now and isn't with us to hear this, I can speak straight from my heart. Greg here screws this up, I'm not just coming after him, I'm coming after all of *you*."

He used his glass to encompass the eight-strong group. Bianca deduced that she was looking at the male portion of the wedding party.

They all laughed, but nervously, like they weren't sure he was kidding. Bianca didn't believe he was. She felt sorry for the prospective son-in-law as Sturgeon released him, clapped him on the shoulder and said, "My girl says she loves you, God knows why."

Still moving in the direction of the gray-haired man, Bianca was scoping out the terrain—the room had two exits, the door she'd just entered through and one at the opposite end of the saloon that opened into a short hallway, which, from what she'd been able to ascertain from the layout of the boat, probably led to the master stateroom, and three side-by-side windows that were curtained, closed and useless to her—and coming to the conclusion that getting out of there with the briefcase was going to be next to impossible, when prospective son-in-law Greg found his courage and replied, "I love her, too."

What she needed to do, Bianca decided as the young women responded with a collective "Aww," was go ahead and plant the tracking device on the briefcase. She'd meant to save it for when she was ready to hand the recovered prototype over to the client, but now worked, too. At some point Sturgeon would take the briefcase away, hopefully to somewhere more private, and she could move in and retrieve it from wherever he put it. Locating it was the hard part, and she'd done that. What she didn't want to do was lose it again.

She'd brought the shirt-collar-button-size tracking device with her. It was part of one of what would appear to any outside observer to be several purely decorative charms dangling from the zipper of her purse.

The adhesive required to secure it had the consistency of gummy-bear candy, came in a tiny tin that looked like it held breath mints and was kept in her purse. Slipping off her right glove, she tucked it inside her purse, located the tin with a groping hand, pinched off a Tic Tac–size amount of the adhesive and withdrew her hand from the purse, manipulating the tiny ball between her thumb and forefinger until it was soft and pliable. When it was ready, she popped the tracking device out of the back of the concealing charm and pressed the small metal circle into the adhesive.

All actions low-key and under the radar, nothing anyone would notice or remark on.

Planting the device would require a distraction. She was, regrettably, fresh out of incendiary devices. She was, however, in a prime location just a few feet away from Sturgeon and the briefcase.

So, okay, use your words.

"Tell us how you proposed, Greg," she called to the prospective groom, then looked at the other women in the room for support. "We want every little detail, don't we, ladies?"

Her impromptu street team immediately responded in exactly the way she'd hoped. A couple of them clapped their hands; they all looked eager, and one cried, "Yes, how did you do it? What did you say?"

The others chimed in.

"Did you go down on one knee?"

"What did Gemma say?"

"Where did you do it?"

"Is that when you gave her the ring?"

"Tell us everything!"

Stammering and blushing, Greg was pushed to the center of the room. "Well, I, uh…"

Bianca tuned him out. What she needed to do had to be done fast, and there was no margin for error. When the adhesive set, which it would do within seconds of leaving the warmth of her fingers, it would be like concrete. Letting her purse slide off her shoulder—it was satin, so it hit the floor with a barely audible slither rather than a plop—she crouched down ostensibly to retrieve it, positioning her body between the briefcase and the rest of the room so no one could see what she was doing.

All eyes were on Greg, who was saying something schmaltzy about a grape arbor and violins. A lightning glance around confirmed it: no one was paying the least attention to her.

Hold the briefcase steady. Only touch it with your left hand so as not to leave fingerprints.

Quick as the thought, she steadied the briefcase and slid the tracking device into the small crevice created by one of the two hinges that attached the handle to the briefcase. The smooth metal surface would have made any other placement too obvious.

Then she tucked her purse beneath her arm and stood up again, pulling her glove back on as she rose.

To find that she was being watched from across the room.

By a frowning pair of caramel eyes set beneath straight black slashes of brows. In a deeply tanned and handsome face. Atop a leanly muscled, broad-shouldered, six-foot-three-inch frame.

His hair was coal black, wavy, but shorter than she remembered. He was looking at her like he thought he recognized her from somewhere.

The terrifying part was, Bianca definitely recognized him. She was locking eyes with the guy she had kissed, then zapped in the men's room in Bahrain.

Mickey.

17

For a moment Bianca felt as if she'd just been kicked in the stomach. She felt blindsided, off balance, thrown off her game.

She'd never been made before.

The circumstances were less than ideal. She was on a boat. The only way she was escaping was to immediately dart through three crowded rooms and take a flying leap into the bay—

But wait. She recognized him because except for the shorter haircut he looked exactly the same.

He might be staring at her with interest and looking like he was trying to place her in his memory, but that didn't mean he recognized her.

She'd been a short-haired blonde with Jennifer Ashley's vividly exotic makeup the last time they'd encountered each other. In slutty undies, yet. To which he'd paid an inordinate amount of attention.

What were the chances that he actually remembered her *face*?

Her black wig concealed her forehead and ears and hopefully visually lengthened her face and neck. Combined with her softer, pinker, more naturalistic makeup, it gave her an entirely different look.

Her eyes were the same, although last time he'd looked into them they'd been framed by the lashings of mascara and eyeliner that had belonged to Jennifer Ashley.

How likely was it that he would remember the exact shade of her irises?

Or that he could even discern their color while staring at her from across a crowded room?

The good news was, she'd tagged the briefcase. She didn't have to stand around and babysit it. Time to take herself out of Mickey's orbit. Get out of the room and lose herself among the crowd.

Now.

Because their eyes were locked, she gave him a slight, polite smile of disinterested acknowledgment and let her gaze seemingly wander away.

Her feet followed her gaze. Slowly, casually. Not as if she were escaping or anything. Skirting the perimeter of her side of the room, heading for the door she'd entered by, because the other door might lead to a stateroom and a dead end.

The goal was to put as much distance as possible between herself and Mickey, who was on the opposite side of the room. The side she'd never gotten around to vetting because she'd spotted the briefcase and thereafter focused all her attention on getting to it.

Mistake.

Greg was still holding the floor and creating a nice little barrier that prevented Mickey from crossing the room directly to get to her as he rhapsodized about how unbelievably wonderful it was that Gemma had said "yes." Most everybody in the room was listening raptly to him.

Most everybody did not include her. A stealthy sideways glance informed her that it also did not include Mickey. He was moving, too, around his side of the room, with a little more obvious purpose than she was. In fact, his purpose seemed to be intercepting her at the door.

Maybe he thought she was hot. Maybe he wanted to make

her acquaintance, try a pickup line, see if he could score. A typical guy wanting to hit on a random girl.

Or maybe not.

She could feel adrenaline flooding her system as it occurred to her how unlikely it was that Mickey was even here. From Gudaibiya Palace in Bahrain to this particular yacht in the middle of San Francisco Bay?

What were the chances?

Yeah. The proverbial snowball in hell came to mind.

On the other hand, Mickey couldn't be here because of her, because there was no way he could have known that she would show up. So why *was* he here? For her father? Was this whole thing a trap? She'd suspected from the beginning that Mickey was some kind of a cop.

Durand—was he with Durand? As soon as she had the panic-making thought, Bianca cast a harried glance around. But Durand wasn't in the room. Was he somewhere on the yacht? She hadn't spotted him, but then she hadn't spotted Mickey until just now.

Her alarm subsided only marginally as she reminded herself that Durand was hunting her father, not her. The trap, if a trap it was, was designed to catch Richard St. Ives.

The kicker was, it was one hundred percent guaranteed to fail, because her father wasn't present. Or, um, alive.

And, Mickey or no Mickey, she could slip discreetly away.

Without the prototype? That was the question that she needed to answer.

If this was a trap, was the prototype even real? Was the threat to expose her father real?

The yacht, the party, Greg and Gemma and the engagement announcement in the *San Francisco Chronicle*—the setup was too elaborate. *That* had to be real.

Walt Sturgeon and his company were real.

Justin Lee was a known entity in the circles that were aware of such individuals. *He* was real.

The theft of the prototype was known in those circles, too. *That* was real.

Okay. So whatever this was, it was definitely not entirely a setup.

Had Durand/Mickey/whoever somehow learned that Richard was going after the prototype, tracked it themselves and decided to show up here, too, to catch him?

That seemed possible. Even plausible. If so, though, the plotters were screwed, because she, not Richard, was the mouse taking the cheese. If Mickey et al. were after the fame and glory, or the large monetary reward, that went along with capturing Traveler, they were destined for disappointment. There would be no fame and glory from capturing her. Likewise, she didn't have a price on her head. Oh, and one more thing—she had no intention of being captured.

Bad luck, buttercup, she said silently to Mickey.

The way Bianca saw it, she had two choices. She could abandon the job, leave without the prototype, retreat to Savannah by the most circuitous route possible, hunker down and hope for the best.

Or she could steal the prototype, follow the tracker back to wherever it led, get some answers and, depending on what they were, go ahead with what she'd planned and eliminate the threat.

She wasn't a big believer in hoping for the best.

If Mickey and whoever he was with were here to prevent the prototype from being stolen and/or to catch the thief, it would actually be kind of fun to steal it out from under his/their noses.

Which she could do. She really was *very* good at her job.

Bottom line: running scared wasn't her style. And in this case there was a lot at stake. She was going to go for it.

Eluding Mickey was the first step.

Shooting another sideways look at him—he was maybe three steps behind on the other side—it hit her that he was wearing the same kind of black suit, open-collared white dress shirt and name tag on his breast pocket as the security team.

Mickey was *security*?

Her mind boggled at the possibility. She thought, *No.*

Even if by some wild stretch of the imagination she was willing to accept that he was acting as security here, it didn't explain his presence in Bahrain. No way had he been security there, too. What, Walt Sturgeon and Prince Al Khalifa shopped in the same security provider store?

Anyway, he didn't look like security. He looked like a thug in a business suit.

Pure bad news. On the hoof.

Mickey had longer legs and he wasn't trying to pretend he wasn't moving with purpose toward the door. Bianca realized with some dismay that that gave him an advantage. Unless she broke into a run, he was probably going to beat her to it.

She needed a plan B *now.*

Greg concluded his story by saying, "I'm so happy we're getting married," with a disarmingly sweet smile. Applause filled the room.

Everyone was still oohing and aahing over Greg as the pulsing music rolling into the room changed styles, growing appreciably louder while transitioning to a staccato beat she vaguely recognized. Bianca glanced through the open doorway in the direction of the music's source, which was the Sky Lounge, and instantly was struck by a way to escape Mickey without making it look like that was what she was trying to do.

"Conga line," she cried with a gleeful clap of her hands, in anticipation of the one that was already snaking toward her through the galley. Making a come-on-in-here gesture at the guy shuffle-kicking at the head of the twisting line, she grabbed the hands of the nearest male—one of the wedding party boys— and whipped around so that her back was to him, placing his hands on her hips and holding them there as she shook her booty and danced away from the door.

"Oh, yeah, conga line," her victim echoed happily, getting into the spirit of it. His hands molded the sides of her hips with loving attention and he danced along behind her, a little closer than she might have liked but doing what she needed him to do.

One, two, three, hip bump. One, two, three, hip bump.

"Conga line!" Sounding thrilled, two of the young women grabbed partners and fell in just as the dancers from the galley conga'd into the room.

One, two, three, hip bump. One, two, three, hip bump.

In minutes most of the room had linked up with the weaving, hip-swiveling line. Mickey wasn't one of them, although another of the young women had tried to pull him in. Big surprise, he was a good-looking guy. As the dancers circled the room, he'd been forced to move back against the wall. Bianca was conscious of his eyes on her as she led the line in an *S*-shape away from him, then circled back until she was exactly where she wanted to be: conga-ing on out the door.

Of course, she had about five dozen boozy, laughing, swaying revelers attached to her like a tail to a kite, but that was a mere detail.

The good news was, as they passed through the doorway their hip-swinging moves blocked it so no one else was getting out.

The better news was, once they'd danced their way into the galley, she was able to detach wedding-party-boy's way-too-feely hands from her hips. With an encouraging "Keep it going!" she fled toward the Sky Lounge, where she was immediately swallowed up by the identity-obscuring blue light.

A moment later the conga music ended with a flourish and a shout.

The conga dancers started spilling into the Sky Lounge.

Thus adding the whole safety-in-numbers thing to the protection of the wonky blue light.

The music started up again. This time it was another throwback to the fifties: "Love Is Strange."

In a hurry to get gone, Bianca cut across the middle of the floor, dodging around the dancers, taking the most direct route possible toward the door that led to the outside stairs, meaning to go down to the main deck and lose herself among the partygoers there until she could figure out her next move.

A hand caught her arm. She was maybe six feet from the door. All around her couples swayed and dipped to the music, but she was pretty darn sure she hadn't just been grabbed by a Mr. Lonelyhearts meaning to ask her to dance.

Her stomach sank.

She knew in her gut who it was. Everything from the size of the long fingers to the strength of the grip on her arm to the prickly warning of danger that ran down her spine gave her the bad news.

Short of throwing him over her hip—tempting!—there was no avoiding the encounter.

Maybe, she thought without much conviction, she could bluff her way through it.

Pasting a surprised smile on her lips, she turned. It was Mickey, all right, way too close, looming over her like she was Red Riding Hood and he was the Big Bad Wolf. She lifted her eyebrows at him. Questioningly. A little haughtily. As in, *Hey, stranger, why would you think it was a good idea to grab my arm?*

He was considerably taller, even with her in her spike heels. She had to tilt her head back to look up at him. That was a good thing actually. She wanted him feeling all strong and powerful.

That predatory thing he had going on? It worked for her. He just had the wrong idea about who, ultimately, was the predator and who was the prey.

The bigger they are, the harder they fall.

A maddeningly cocky smile appeared as his eyes slid over her face. He said, "Well, hello there, beautiful."

It was the exact same thing he'd said to her before. Was he repeating himself on purpose, to remind her? She thought so, but she couldn't—totally—be sure. It was always possible that that was his standard pickup line. The words, the husky voice, the barely there accent that she couldn't quite place, gave her a bad case of the déjà vu's.

Her fingers itched for her stun gun.

His gaze slid from her eyes to her lips. Despite the pulsing blue light, she could see the hot gleam in them.

Was he remembering how he'd kissed her? How she had kissed him?

Damn it. Her heart picked up the pace, and she realized that *she* was remembering. *Not* what she wanted to be doing.

"I bet you say that to all the girls." If they hadn't been standing so close, he wouldn't have been able to hear her over the throbbing music. She suspected that one of the reasons they were standing so close, besides the fact that the dance floor was crowded, was that he was bent on intimidating her with his size. Fat chance, but he didn't know that.

"Only the beautiful ones. Although I confess I liked you better as a blonde. Without your clothes on." He looked her over assessingly before his gaze returned to her face. The tingle of attraction she felt as their eyes met? She hated that. "Sylvia, isn't it?"

So much for him not recognizing her. She considered pretending she had no idea what he was talking about, then thought, *To hell with that.*

"My goodness, is it—Mickey?" Her eyes widened in fake astonishment even as her smile mocked.

"Good memory. And here I was thinking you might have forgotten."

"Yes, well, some things are unforgettable." She reached up to give his cheek a playful pat. It was shadowed with maybe half a day's growth of stubble and felt warm and faintly rough even through the lace of her glove. The blatant masculinity of it made her fingers curl in an unexpectedly sensual reaction as she withdrew her hand. The displeasing discovery of how that small contact affected her put a little extra snark in her tone as she added, "Such as the sight of you twitching on the bathroom floor."

His eyes narrowed. "Probably not smart to remind me of that."

"I doubt you needed reminding. Like I said, some things are unforgettable." She gave her arm a tug. "Let me go, please. I have somewhere I need to be."

"An urgent appointment with your confederates?"

She lifted her chin. "Confederates?"

"The gang you came here with to steal our Mr. Sturgeon's newest acquisition."

Bianca felt a chill slide down her spine. So he knew. Well, she'd suspected as much. She thought about saying, *I have no idea what you're talking about.* But that was clearly a waste of breath. Anyway, something about this guy made her want to get all up in his face.

She batted her lashes at him in exaggerated flirtation. "If I tell you where my confederates are, will you summon your confederates and hurry off and arrest them? Or do security guards actually have the authority to arrest people?"

"Security guards have the authority to do whatever they need to do."

"But you're not a security guard, are you? You're just posing as one. What are you really, some kind of undercover cop?"

"Is that what you think?"

She nodded as her tangled thoughts on the ramifications of his presence here started to unknot themselves. "I don't think Sturgeon has any idea who you really are. He wouldn't have you around if he did. What, are you here to bust him *and* catch a thief? A two-for-one deal?"

"Depends. Would that thief be you?"

She laughed, a throaty, deliberately sexy sound. "Let's not forget my confederates."

"Not even going to try to lie your way out of this?"

"Why should I?"

"To save your beautiful ass?"

"Believe me, it's not *my* beautiful ass that needs saving."

His eyes widened in surprise, and then to her annoyance he looked amused. "A woman who appreciates a nice set of buns. I like that! Just between you and me, kumquat, it's all in the squats."

"Kumquat?" she repeated, revolted.

"Beautiful fruit, slightly sour."

"I know what it is." Recovering from the unexpectedness of his little foray into stupid humor, she got back to the business at hand: figuring out how best to get away from him and make off with the prototype. "What do you suppose would happen if somebody told Sturgeon that one of his security guards is actually a cop looking to bust him?"

"About the same thing that would happen if somebody told him that one of his party guests is actually a thief looking to rip off his newly acquired merchandise."

They exchanged measuring looks. Silent, mutually acknowledged message: *touché.* His gaze dropped. She stiffened with indignation as she realized that he was giving her a slow and comprehensive once-over.

"What I want to know is, what's under that pretty pink dress."

"What?"

"You had that stun gun on you somewhere. From what I recall of those sexy little scraps of lace you were wearing the last time we met, there weren't too many places you could have concealed it."

"Wouldn't you like to—"

Before she could finish, she was knocked into from behind by a couple bumping and grinding past to the beat of the pounding music. The girl of the pair called out, "Sorry!"

Thrown off balance, staggering slightly, Bianca cast a startled glance over her shoulder to discover that the couple who'd hit her was just one of dozens in the room who were gyrating to the throbbing beat of "Love Is Strange." She'd been so intent on Mickey she'd almost forgotten they weren't alone. Trying to regain her footing, she pitched into something solid—Mickey, she discovered as her attention refocused in a hurry—and grabbed hold. His arm clamped around her waist, pulling her all the way up against him. She thought it was to steady her, but then he didn't let go.

"Hey," she protested. He held her so tightly that they were practically fused together. For all his leanness, he felt as solid as a stone wall. Her breasts tingled from being flattened against the firmness of his chest. She could feel every tiny detail: the hard nubs of his shirt buttons, the protrusion of his belt buckle, the long, powerful muscles, the heat of the hard body beneath. And yes, the man was aroused.

As she made that discovery, her body gave a deep throb of instinctive—unwelcome!—response.

It occurred to her that if she could feel the fine points of his body, he could feel the fine points of hers. Then she felt his hand moving over her, down her back, across her ass, sliding around to her thighs—

He was searching her.

"Stop that!" She grabbed his wrist. And fought the urge to break it.

"Loving the garter belt. Sexy."

"Let me go." She dropped his wrist to shove at his chest. He didn't let go. He did stop feeling her up, which was the point.

"Pure self-protection, kumquat."

Her lips thinned.

"If I had a stun gun on me, you'd know it by now, guaranteed," she said, lying through her teeth.

"That's actually oddly comforting."

His hand that had been gripping her arm slid along it to grip her hand instead. He brought her hand up so that it pressed against the smooth white shirt just above his heart and held it there, his fingers wrapped around hers. He'd held it that same way before, and once again the memory of how they'd kissed crowded into her head, unwanted but impossible to shake.

She looked up, met his eyes. What passed between them caused her lips to part and her breathing to quicken. It was, she realized with an inner shiver, an arcing of electricity, a flare of heat.

What was even scarier was, it was mutual.

"What do you think you're doing?" Her tone was sharp.

She asked because he'd started to move, walking her backward whether she wanted to go or not. His knee pushed into the space between her legs, his thigh parted her thighs, his pelvis tilted against hers as he pulled her even tighter against him—

Her senses went a little haywire then as she confirmed that he was now *majorly* aroused.

She felt all hot and flushed suddenly and didn't know whether she wanted to kick herself or him more for what she considered her over-the-top response to what he was doing. Luckily the darkness and the weirdness of the blue light almost certainly concealed what had to be her shell-shocked expression. She was wary of him, she didn't like him and yet she somehow found herself wildly attracted to him.

Her skirt was hiked up too high for decency, she feared. She could feel the rasp of his trousers against the sensitive skin of her inner thighs and the hardness of his leg beneath the trousers. Then he leaned her backward and rocked into her. As her body clutched and pulsed in unexpected, charged reaction, she made up her mind: the kick was definitely destined for him.

"It's called dancing. I'm surprised you don't recognize it." He straightened with her but kept her locked against him as he took a few more gliding steps that, courtesy of his leg that was still positioned between hers—letting that happen was an error, the rocking pressure of it against her was making her feel things she absolutely did not want to feel—had her moving backward against her volition *again*.

She would have put him on the floor, but she wasn't quite ready to let him know she could. Besides, this wasn't the right place. What she had in mind for him required privacy. Somewhere in the middle of all those sexy feelings he was engendering in her, it had occurred to her that Mickey was the only person who knew who she was and why she was on that boat. And as long as she kept him occupied, he wasn't telling anybody. If she could put him out of commission, she could steal the prototype and be gone with no one to interfere.

Cue Operation Spider to Fly, Part Two.

"I don't want to dance with you." But she hooked an arm around his neck and hung on as he swung her around and dipped her again. All around them other couples were dipping and swaying, too. She realized that they were dirty dancing just like everybody else, which made them practically indistinguishable from all the other couples on the floor.

Good to know. Just in case anybody came looking.

"Better than other things we could be doing. Well, most other things." He bent over her, his mouth warm as it just brushed her cheek.

Her breath caught. Her heart sped up. Her body melted. It had been a long time since she'd found herself getting turned on like this. Since she'd *let* herself get turned on like this. Under the circumstances, with him—bad, *bad* idea.

But it couldn't be helped.

"I'm hot. Let's go outside," she said.

18

"In a minute. They're playing our song." Mickey's mouth skimmed the side of her neck.

Bianca shivered. This time, though, she didn't bother to try to hide it.

"Our song?"

He lifted his head. The pulsating blue light made his chiseled features look like they were all hard angles and shadows. His pupils had dilated until his eyes appeared black. The look in them was intent—and sexually charged. The unexpectedness of what he'd said threw her a little as she tried to make sense of it.

He said, "Keep listening."

She moved with him automatically now, her steps the reverse of his, then found herself practically riding his hard-muscled thigh as he bent her backward over his arm once more. Arching up against him, she clenched her teeth in an effort to keep her focus on the big picture in the face of all that quaking, burning heat.

When he pulled her upright again, she was weak at the knees. Also, she probably wasn't thinking clearly, but as far as she could tell, the song was nothing special. It had a wailing bluesy edge and the singer was moaning something about her baby and sweet lovin' and all Bianca could think was that it was about as fifties generic as it could get and definitely in no way qualified as "their song." Not that they had a song or ever would have a song, because they were barely even acquaintances and in any case their acquaintance wasn't friendly and wasn't destined to go beyond the brief period of time it was going to take her to rid herself of him *again*.

Then she heard it: the semispoken lyrics made her eyes widen.

First came her name. Well, her fake name: Sylvia.

Then it went on to say something about calling your lover boy, but by then she was beyond listening. Because she remembered the names of the singers—the fifties R & B duo whose hit this was, whose names were even spoken in the song, who called to each other in the song.

Sylvia. And *Mickey*.

She froze—well, *she* froze, while he kept moving, pulling her upright, swaying with her as she hung like a coat hanger from his broad shoulders, which meant she actually kept moving, too, but without any cooperation on her part at all as she processed what she'd heard with growing indignation.

Her eyes shot to the ID badge clipped to the breast pocket of his jacket.

She had to squint to make sure, but…beneath his picture was the name Zane Williams.

Not Mickey.

Her gaze collided with his.

"Made the connection, I see," he said and smiled that cocky smile of his at her.

"Funny." Amazing how much bite could get crammed into a single word.

"Hey, if role-playing's your thing, I'm into it. You be Sylvia, I'll be Mickey, and—"

"*Really* funny." If her tone was short, it was because he was annoying the life out of her—and also because she was annoyed with herself for not making the name connection sooner. Her only excuse was that she wasn't all that familiar with obscure fifties songs—and she hadn't expected the dark and dangerous man she'd bested in Bahrain to be prone to making idiotic jokes at her expense.

He said, "You look mad."

"Is your name really Zane?"

"You tell me yours, I'll tell you mine."

"Cara."

"Thomas."

Sway, turn, dip. He rocked his thigh right up against her crotch. The resulting wave of desire made her catch her breath.

"Let's get out of here," she said when he pulled her upright. And did her best to keep her rising temper out of her voice.

This time he went for it.

Steadying her with his hands on her waist as she found her balance—being plastered against him like jelly on bread took a moment to recover from—he grabbed her hand and pulled her behind him toward the door she'd been making for before he'd stopped her, the one that led to the outside stairs.

The rush of fresh, salt-tinged air as they stepped out onto the narrow walkway that led to the stairs went a long way toward clearing her head. This outside area was strictly utilitarian and completely private, which was why she'd chosen to head for it in the first place. As the door closed behind them, cutting off the tail end of "their" song, Bianca curled a hand around the white iron rail. The motion of the yacht was as smooth as a rocking chair, but it was still motion, and without not-Mickey's support, she needed a moment to rediscover her sea legs. They were on the uppermost deck, three stories above the surface of the bay. Looking down, she saw that the walkway was directly over the water and she could see a line of white froth as the hull cut through it at speed. The sky was midnight blue with a frosty sliver of moon and what looked like thousands of twinkling stars. The bay was an even darker blue, its surface reflecting the stars and the lights from the bridge and the other boats that were out there flitting around like fireflies. The buildings on the shore glowed through the night like dozens of Japanese lanterns. White ruffles of surf framed what she thought had to be Treasure Island maybe a couple of hundred yards off the port side, which was the side they were on.

Music and laughter from the parties on the decks, the churn of the engine, the slap of waves against the hull, made it necessary for her to raise her voice as she turned to him, smiled a lovely, charming, completely false, prey-lulling smile and said, "It's a beautiful night."

He didn't say a word. Instead his hands came up to cup her face and he backed her up against the smooth fiberglass wall of the cabin behind her and kissed her.

His lips were warm and firm and way too expert, clearly the man was no novice when it came to women, and as they slanted over her mouth her heart lurched. She'd had firm intentions about what she meant to do when she got him outside—knock him out with a chop to the side of the neck was at the top of the list—but the kiss caught her by surprise and took her out of her game. Electricity shot through her, making her pulse race and her body tighten and her toes curl.

Chemistry, that's what this is was her last rational thought as she closed her eyes and clutched at his trim and toned waist and kissed him back with an intensity that she never would have expected to feel.

Not for somebody like him. Not for anybody, really. Until now, the only kind of chemistry she'd believed in had been of the science lab variety. When she got involved with a guy, it was because she liked him, because he was cute, because he satisfied a need, not only sexually but for normalcy. Normal girls had boyfriends. Thus, so did she.

She didn't feel sparks. Didn't get swept off her feet. Never had.

Until this moment she would have said she was constitutionally incapable of it.

But…his kiss was making her dizzy. It was making her stupid.

He leaned into her, pressing her against the wall with his not-inconsiderable weight, covering her body so that she could feel the entire muscular length of him, and kissed her some more, like it was something he'd been waiting to do all his life. His kisses were deep, sexy, arousing. They ignited a hot flare of passion that had her kissing him back every bit as hungrily as he was kissing her. She molded her lips to his, licked into his mouth, slid her hands up over the wide, firm contours of his chest to lock around his neck, arched up against him as his grip shifted and he slid a hand down to caress her breast.

Oh, God. She thought her bones might melt from the heat.

By the time he broke it off, she was aching with need. She wasn't sure she could stand without support. Her pulse pounded in her ears. Her breathing was uneven. She felt all soft and shivery inside.

He took her right hand and tugged it down from around his neck and she opened her eyes just to check out what was up with that. Silvery moonlight streamed over the pair of them. The star-studded sky, the bay and the boat and the darkness, the handsome, impossibly sexy man who was looking at her with—was it tenderness? Yes, she thought it was. The newness of this, of *him*, of *them*, was almost…dazzling. It was the stuff of every romantic dream she'd never had.

Because she didn't believe in romance. Romance wasn't something she did. But her heart was beating way too fast, and as she watched him carry her hand to his mouth and press his lips to the back of it she found that she was holding her breath.

When he lowered her hand, she could still feel the imprint of his lips on her skin. She smiled at him. A little tentative, a little—really? So unlike her—shy.

Then he snapped something cold and hard around her wrist.

Bianca's eyes widened. Her gaze dropped to discover that the cold, hard thing was one bracelet of a set of handcuffs. The other bracelet was fastened to the rail.

The SOB had just handcuffed her to the rail!

Like romance, fury wasn't something she did. But she was doing it now. She could feel it shooting like fast-moving lava all the way from her toes to her brain.

"Sorry, kumquat, but I need you safely out of the way while I go search the premises for your boss." *He chucked her under her chin.*

Fury didn't even begin to cover it.

"You *bastard*." Her right hand was her preferred chopping hand. He'd chained it to the rail. So she didn't chop.

Instead she stomped her spike heel into his instep—he yelped and jumped like she'd fired a bullet into his foot—elbowed him under the chin as he hopped in pain, snatched his name tag from his pocket, then executed a spinning back-kick that sent him over the rail with a cry.

Bianca still had fire in her eyes as she watched the splashdown. A small geyser went up as he disappeared beneath the shiny dark water.

"Man overboard," she said with savage satisfaction even though there was no one to hear. Glancing down at the name tag in her hand, she saw his face and the name Zane Williams and practically snarled. A present for Doc, she thought and stuffed it into her purse.

Recollecting where she was, she cast a quick look around. She was out there all alone and it was dark. There were no cries echoing her "Man overboard" from anywhere on the boat. No untoward commotion of any sort to indicate that anyone had seen anything. The darkness, the sounds of the party and the sea, their isolation on this little-used walkway, had kept anybody from noticing anything. The music and laughter and voices continued unabated. The *Conquistador* continued to plow through the bay.

No one had seen Lover Boy fall.

A bright spot in what, so far, had been a really sucky day.

Looking out toward where he'd gone in, Bianca saw his dark head bobbing in a patch of moonlight. From what she could tell, he was treading water. She didn't know whether to be glad or sorry that apparently he could swim. Then the pale oval that was his face turned her way, and she realized that he was looking after the boat, which was leaving him behind at a pretty good clip.

There was a life preserver hanging from a hook not far from where he'd had her pressed up against the wall.

Retrieving her lock pick from her garter belt, she freed herself from the handcuffs in just a few seconds.

Snagging the life preserver, she held it up and waved it so presumably he could see it. Then she threw it in his direction. It didn't land anywhere near him, but—how to put this?—too damn bad.

Casting one last baleful glance toward where he was presumably swimming toward either the nearest island or the life preserver, she pulled her phone out of her purse, hit the locator app and went back inside.

Time to find the briefcase and get the hell on with her life.

Unfortunately, her no good, very bad day just kept on keeping on. Following the locator beacon to amidships on the lowest deck, Bianca got there just in time to watch a tender pull away from the yacht.

According to the beacon, the briefcase was on board.

Along with Sturgeon. Clapping her binoculars to her eyes as she hung over the nearest rail, she was just able to make out what she was almost positive was his stocky form behind the wheel of the small open boat.

Thrusting the binoculars back into her purse, she stared after the retreating vessel and tried to keep her cool. She needed her thinking to be clear and collected. No telling what Sturgeon had in mind for the prototype. For all she knew, it would be whisked far away within hours. Likewise, there was no telling when Lover Boy, for want of a more accurate name, would be fished from the bay. Would he tell his rescuers all about her? Who knew?

Meanwhile, here she was, stuck on the damned boat.

She could almost hear her father recommending a calming spot of mindful meditation before she did anything else.

This was how people developed high blood pressure.

Okay, one thing at a time: come up with a plan C.

Anytime now.

She stole a Jet Ski. Right out of the *Conquistador*'s toy garage, pressing the button to lower the thing into the water and then steering it quietly away from the boat before juicing the throttle and heading out in hot pursuit of the tender.

She might have caught it, too, or, more feasibly, reached the place where Sturgeon was docking in time to snatch the briefcase away before he could do whatever he meant to do with it, except for one thing.

The Jet Ski died. Just sputtered and quit. While she was still a good distance from shore.

After trying everything in her considerable arsenal of tricks to get it going again, she was happy to accept the offer of a tow from a passing fishing boat.

By the time she clambered up on dry land, Sturgeon and the briefcase were long gone. She checked the locator beacon—it was still tracking. At that point the briefcase was maybe fifty miles away, heading south.

Plan C had just officially crapped out.

At least she would be able to find the thing again. If she wanted to. Knowing for sure that the briefcase was being watched and was the bait in a trap for her father put a whole new spin on the situation. While the threat posed by the video was real, the threat posed by Lover Boy and whoever he was associated with was more immediate.

She'd feared that the video might lead investigators to her, to Doc, to Savannah and Guardian Consulting and everything that constituted her ordinary life.

If she was caught here as she attempted to steal the briefcase, they wouldn't need the video to lead them to her. They would have her.

She faced the fact that it was time to call it a day—and might be time to call it an operation.

It was after 4:00 a.m. She was exhausted and absolutely not thinking clearly enough to make a final decision.

Better to get some sleep, think the situation through in the morning and then decide.

Two of the very nice fishermen gave her a ride to her hotel in their pickup truck.

Getting a key from the front desk, she went upstairs, showered and fell into bed.

And refused to even allow herself to wonder whether that jackass was still out there swimming around in the bay.

19

Bianca sank down in the black vinyl booth across from Doc. It was 9:00 a.m. and they were meeting for breakfast in the hotel café as arranged. The small restaurant was crowded and noisy and smelled of bacon and syrup.

"We're going home," she said. "We're leaving right after we eat."

He'd been looking at his phone. At her words he glanced up, blinking at her as if he was only at that moment becoming aware that she'd joined him. His Brillo-pad hair hung loose in a kind of modified pyramid shape that almost reached his shoulders; he needed a shave, and his eyes were puffy. He looked like he'd been up most of the night, which should make him feel right at home in her company. His T-shirt was a bright orange abomination that read Fat Guys Try Harder.

Next time she'd know better than to tell him to try to look like a tourist.

He said, "Uh—what?"

"Would you get off the internet for a minute and pay attention?" She gave him an impatient look. "We're going to drive to Vegas and take a plane from there. I want to make it as difficult as possible for anyone to track us."

Doc's face brightened. He sat up straighter in the booth. "You got it? You got it! Way to go, boss!"

He was referring to the prototype, she knew. Bianca hated

to admit the truth. Failing was hard for her. Quitting was even harder.

"I didn't get it. I failed to get it." That last carefully enunciated clarification was just to rub her own nose in it, she supposed. "It was there, but…I ran into a problem. A cop—at least I think he's a cop—was on the boat. I've run into him before—" she hadn't told Doc or anyone about that episode in the restroom in Bahrain, and she wasn't about to start now "—and he recognized me. Oh, not as me—Bianca—but as—" casting a quick glance around, she lowered her voice "—a thief. I managed to get away, but now he knows we're here. Going after that prototype is just asking to get caught. I'm making the call—it's not worth the risk. After we eat, I'm going to have you send an email to the client telling them the job's off."

"Coffee?" A waitress appeared beside them, a steaming pot of coffee in her hand. At Bianca's nod and Doc's "Yeah, thanks," she turned over the two cups that were already waiting upside down on saucers in front of them, poured and at the same time asked, "You know what you want?"

Bianca ordered a fruit plate. Doc looked conflicted but hurriedly ordered eggs, bacon and pancakes. The waitress went away.

The instant she was gone, Doc said, "Oh, jeez. This is bad. Like, way bad."

Bianca frowned at him. "What's bad?"

"You didn't get the briefcase. Somehow they must know you tried and something went wrong. They upped the ante. I don't think we can go home."

He sounded agitated. He looked agitated.

"What are you talking about?"

"This." He thrust his phone at her. "It came early this morning. I didn't see it until I sat down here to wait for you and started checking email."

Taking his phone, Bianca glanced down and then nearly went into shock at the face that stared up at her from the paused video on the small screen.

It was Marin.

Numbly Bianca hit the play button.

"Daddy, please do what they want." Tears welled in the little girl's wide blue eyes. Her face was pale. Her mouth shook. Her long brown hair was loose, and from what Bianca could see of her, she appeared to be wearing a pink flannel pajama top or nightgown with a ruffle around the neck and bunnies on it. It was a head-and-shoulders shot, dimly lit, with her up against an unpainted, poured concrete wall. Looking at her, listening, Bianca felt the blood slowly freeze in her veins. "I don't like it here. I'm scared. Hurry."

Marin disappeared, to be replaced by another image: Margery. Head and shoulders, up against the same background. She wasn't crying, but it was obvious that she was afraid. The look in her eyes—they were blue, like Marin's, Bianca noticed for the first time—was stark; she bit her lower lip as her face came on the screen, and her hands were steepled in front of her chin as if in supplication. Her face was scrubbed clean of makeup. Her coffee-brown hair was pulled back from her face. She appeared to be dressed, although haphazardly, as if she'd gotten ready in a hurry, grabbing the first clothes that came to hand.

"Edward." Margery's voice cracked as she stared into the lens. "They say your name isn't even Edward. I don't know. I don't care. These people—they have Marin and me. Please, do whatever they say."

The video shut off abruptly.

"There's a message with it. Hit the arrow to go back," Doc said.

Bianca did. An email took the place of the video.

Your wife and child are being held as collateral. If you want to see them alive again, you will satisfy the terms of our agreement. Contact us when you have the object and we will provide instructions for its delivery. The original timetable still stands.

Reading it, Bianca's heart started to slam in her chest. Her stomach knotted.

The scared little girl in the pink bunny nightdress was her *sister*. Bianca didn't know her at all, had never had the chance to develop the smallest relationship with her. She'd even occasionally felt jealous—God, that was hard to admit!—of the child's seemingly warm and affectionate relationship with their father.

But now she felt outrage, anger—and stark, cold fear. The outcome she'd most dreaded had happened: whoever this was, whoever was hunting Richard, had found a trail that led them to his family.

Doc was right: going home was no longer an option.

Think the problem through before you make a move: it was another one of the rules. Bianca had always considered it Richard's version of the builders' mantra of *Measure twice, cut once.*

It was possible that there were two different entities at work here: the client who wanted his prototype back, and the law enforcement contingent who were using this as a trap for, as they thought, her father.

She didn't think any kind of legitimate law enforcement agency would kidnap a woman and child, but that left all kinds of illegitimate ones. Richard had many powerful enemies.

A terrible possibility struck her: Was Mickey/Lover Boy/ whoever part of the group that had taken Marin and Margery? If so, what kind of man condoned the kidnapping of a little girl?

Bottom line, though, at the moment it didn't matter who had done this. What mattered was that it was done.

The question now was, what to do about it?

Contact the police, the FBI, Scotland Yard, Interpol, whoever, for help?

If she did, she would ruin her life, go to jail, the whole nine yards. Ruin Doc. Bring exposure to the whole criminal web in which Richard had operated. Make many, many more dangerous enemies than even Richard had. Enemies with long arms and longer memories.

None of that mattered when weighed against Marin's and Margery's lives.

But going to law enforcement would eat up time. It would be cumbersome. Whatever agency she went to would have logistical issues, because she was American, Marin and Margery were British citizens, and while she had no idea where the kidnappers actually were or where Marin and Margery were being held, she doubted that it was the United States. Jurisdiction would have to be established. Multiple investigations would be launched. And all the while the authorities would be agog over who she was, what she had done and her father.

While all this was happening, she would be in custody and helpless. And every contact she had inherited from her father who might be able to help would be running for the hills.

On the other hand, if she went through with the job, if she delivered the prototype as agreed, the kidnappers might actually let Marin and Margery go.

But whether they did or not, she would be able to track them down. She could follow the briefcase wherever it went. Hopefully that would be directly to where Marin and Margery were being held. If not, at least she would find out who was behind this.

That would be the time to call in the favors her father was owed by some very bad characters. Which would give her plenty of backup if needed when she went in to get her little sister and her sister's mother out.

Richard was gone. They were her responsibility.

I'm coming for you, she promised Marin and Margery silently.

"Here you go." It was the waitress, setting the fruit plate in front of Bianca with a clatter. Then, to Doc as she put his food down in front of him, "Hon, you want to be careful—these plates are hot."

By 4:00 p.m., the plan was almost at the execution stage, awaiting the completion of a few minor details. Bianca sat in the passenger's seat of a white panel van with Doc behind the wheel in a parking garage in beautiful downtown San Jose, carefully surveying the top (sixteenth) story of the building across the street through her binoculars. The adhesive-backed listening device she'd planted on the reinforced concrete "skin" of the building via a crossbow shot from the roof of the parking garage seemed to be holding well. From the walkie-talkie-size receiver she'd placed in between the seats, she and Doc had already been treated to a conversation of the "How about them Raiders?" variety. For the listening device itself she'd had to improvise, but the solution—a modified baby monitor the size of a pack of cards—seemed to be working beautifully.

"You think one of those guys in there is Williams?" Doc asked. He was looking down at the thermal imaging camera app on his phone, which was linked to the thermal imaging camera that was among the supplies that Bianca had purchased earlier in the day. A quick trip to a Walmart, another to a medical supply store, a third to a uniform shop and a fourth to a controlled demolition company (that last was more in the nature of a burglary than a shopping trip) and she had everything she expected to need.

Right now, Doc was watching the movements of a pair of what Bianca thought must be security guards patrolling the sixteenth floor.

Hacking the security cameras would have been easier than resorting to the far-less-clear images provided by thermal technology, but although the rest of the building had video coverage, there were no security cameras on the Allied Industries floors.

The only reason for that would be that Sturgeon didn't want any record of who, or what, went in and out of there.

Which worked for her. As far as she was concerned, the fewer cameras she had to fool, the better.

Doc's question was pertinent because Williams was the only one who might recognize her despite her disguise.

"His name isn't Williams," Bianca said. Neither of the voices coming over the transmitter sounded like his, but given the distorting effect of the device, it was impossible to be sure. Her earlier anger and fear had hardened into cold resolve: she was prepared to do what she needed to do to rescue Marin and Margery. She'd given Doc a highly edited version of last night's encounter with "the cop" and had passed the badge she'd taken off him to Doc as well so that Doc could check out his identity in hopes that it might lead to some scrap of information that could help her figure out who was behind this. What Doc's internet search had come up with was a complete backstory for Zane Williams. Bianca had barely begun to glance through it before she recognized it as a total fabrication. She'd used enough legends herself that she knew them when she saw them, and this one in particular had Zane Williams working personal protection in New York when she had firsthand knowledge that he'd been in Bahrain. The information Doc had uncovered was the false flag that had allowed Zane Williams to infiltrate the ranks of Sturgeon's security, and that was it. It told her nothing about who *not*-Williams really was.

Subsequent facial recognition searches yielded zero hits. *That* told her that whoever-he-was had worked really hard and had enough specialized knowledge or help with specialized knowledge to cover his tracks.

What she did know, what the fact that Mickey (calling him that was just simpler) had been there on the boat told her, was that whoever was behind this had the ability to anticipate her moves.

They'd been expecting an attempt to steal the prototype. Where they'd gotten it wrong was that they were looking for her father, not her. If the briefcase babysitter had been anyone except Mickey, she never would have been made, and she would have the prototype now.

After getting out of the bay—supposing he had gotten out of the bay—had Mickey told them about her? She had no way of knowing. The kidnapping of Marin and Margery had certainly been aimed at Richard, not her. It told her that they were still expecting Richard to show up.

As she had several times already that day, Bianca experienced a nearly overwhelming urge to reach out through every channel she had in an attempt to contact her father. And once again, she talked herself down off that particular ledge. At this point she had to assume that some or all of his communication links had been compromised. To attempt to reach out to him would only bring the hounds to her own door.

Besides, if by some miracle he wasn't dead and was free to do so, her father would be monitoring his communications himself.

These people clearly thought he was alive. The knowledge brought a flutter of hope with it. Was it possible?

Dismissing all such speculation as nonproductive, she focused instead on the problem in front of her.

The thing to keep in mind was that whoever was behind this was absolutely expecting another attempt on the prototype. After kidnapping Marin and Margery, they were all but assured it was going to happen, and happen today. She would be stealing the thing in their teeth.

Inside that building, they would be locked and loaded, waiting for their sitting-duck target to appear.

Well, she was locked and loaded, too.

And she was nobody's sitting duck.

Doc said, "Remember, once I cut the power to the building, you have two minutes before the generator kicks in." His tone was uneasy.

Bianca nodded. "I know."

What that meant was, there were two minutes when all of the very elaborate security systems Allied Industries employed on the sixteenth floor would be down. That was her window to get the prototype and get out.

"You know what to do if something goes wrong," she said.

He nodded reluctantly. They'd gone over it (argued about it) several times before he had agreed. Doc was to return the van to the rental lot, walk from there to the nearest hotel, take a taxi to the airport, rent a car at the airport and drive to Vegas. Once he was in Vegas, he was to call the FBI and report Marin's and Margery's kidnapping, giving their address in England so the fact that they were missing could be verified, without giving them his name or any identifying information. Then he was to fly to Chicago, take a train to New York, fly from New York to Atlanta and from there drive back to Savannah, switching out IDs along the way. Doc had protested, but she was adamant. If she was arrested, caught or killed, there was nothing he could do to help her. And the people behind this were bad. They would be searching hard for any trail she might have left behind, for any associates, for a path to Richard.

"Don't worry," she added. "So far, my record of coming back alive is one hundred percent."

"Ha." The look Doc shot her said he wasn't amused.

The parking garage was aboveground, with open sides, and she and Doc were on the sixth floor, a viewpoint that allowed them to see much of the downtown area. Surrounded on three sides by hazy blue mountains, San Jose was a charming juxtaposition of Spanish colonial-style buildings, mid-nineteenth-century Italianate architecture and the contemporary skyscrapers that announced to visitors that they had indeed arrived in the heart of Silicon Valley, tech capital of the world.

Today being a Saturday, and a beautiful sunshiny day in the upper sixties at that, there were lots of people out and about on the palm-tree-lined streets below. They were shopping in the funky little shops, eating at the sidewalk cafés with their colorful umbrellas that were plentiful in the area or browsing the art show that had been set up in the nearby Plaza de César Chávez Park.

What was pertinent about the parking garage was that it was directly opposite the Thurber/Wilkes Building, a sleek high-rise tower that was part boutique hotel (on the lower eight levels) and part office complex (on the upper eight.) The locator beacon had brought them here and pinpointed the briefcase's location as the sixteenth floor.

A little research had done the rest.

A building directory had identified the sixteenth floor as being part of the four floors occupied by the executive offices of Allied Industries, Sturgeon's company. The top four floors were stacked like a wedding cake, with the sixteenth being the smallest. Floor plans coupled with the locator beacon had yielded the information that the briefcase was inside a wall in a room in the southwest corner of that floor. Building permits issued when Allied Industries had modified the sixteenth floor indicated significant reinforcing of that interior wall, the removal of exterior windows from the entire floor and the installation of a state-of-the-art motion detection system along with a barrier containment unit that descended to seal that particular southwest corner room if security was breached.

Oh, yeah, and once the containment unit was in place, all the oxygen was sucked out of it by a vacuum system, leaving the intruder to suffocate if not rescued with sufficient speed.

In other words, nothing but fun on the agenda today.

Credit card records for Allied Industries indicated that a Fallon 230Z-series fire-rated safe with a six-digit combination lock had been purchased at the time of the renovations.

Bianca considered it very likely that the safe had been installed in the reinforced wall, and that the prototype was now resting inside it.

She could get into a Fallon 230Z in under a minute. That left her thirty seconds to get to the safe, and thirty seconds to get out.

She was ready. Doc was ready. Everything was ready. All they were waiting for now was the "go" signal.

Which would be a phone call from Allied Industries to their preferred plumber, identified by phone records as Hagan Brothers on Senter Road.

The thing is, some things in life are universal. We all need to eat, we all need to sleep and we all need to go to the bathroom. For that last necessity, every floor of Allied Industries had two gender-neutral, single-user units.

When Sturgeon renovated his office space, he equipped it with all the latest features, including smart toilets. Smart toilets, as it turned out, were hackable. All it required was a Bluetooth connection and the code 0000, and a competent hacker (lookin' at you, Doc) could turn a bathroom into a house of horrors (or a fun house, depending on which side of the hacking you were on). Toilets could be made to scream, to snap their lids open and closed like the shark in *Jaws* or to spray you with water when you sat down on them, among many other disconcerting things.

While he was setting the hack up, Doc had chuckled and

said, "Man, I bet we could win a bundle on *America's Funniest Home Videos* with this."

Bianca gave him a pointed look—*don't try this at home, kiddo*—and replied, "Yes, and while we're picking up the winner's check, we could also get arrested and go to jail."

Forty-three minutes after everything was in place, one of the presumed security guards on the sixteenth floor went into a room identified on the floor plan as a bathroom. They waited a moment as from the look of the image he relieved himself. When he turned away from the toilet, after having presumably flushed, Doc did his thing.

They couldn't see the water in the toilet shoot up like it was coming out of a fire hose, but they could hear the guard's startled yell and the blurry green image of his frenzied reaction.

"He shoots, he scores," Doc chortled in self-congratulation as they watched the guard try to contain the water, watched as he bent over, presumably looking behind the toilet for a way to shut the water off, watched as he burst out of the bathroom. Over the transmitter they heard a muffled shout of "Marco! Help! The damned toilet broke!"

"What are you—" the second guard said as he moved toward the first, then broke off as apparently the problem became clear. "What the hell did you *do*?"

"Nothing! I took a leak and it exploded!"

A string of curses followed as the second guard joined the first in frantic darts in and out of the bathroom. Listening, watching, even Bianca succumbed to a smile.

The easy fix—turn off the water to the malfunctioning fixture, the bathroom, the floor—wasn't possible. All that was computerized, too. And Doc had blocked the signal that allowed it to work.

Two more images joined the original two. More security,

from the panic-stricken exchange that ensued. From the sound of things, that toilet was gushing like Old Faithful.

Then they called building maintenance.

Bottom line: building maintenance couldn't fix it, either.

Bummer.

Out went the call to Hagan Brothers. Bianca listened to the one-sided, desperate plea for immediate help but didn't even try to intercept the call. No way were the plumbers getting there in under fifteen minutes, which was the outside amount of time she would need to get in, do what she'd come to do and get out.

"Let's go," she said. Doc gave her a look.

Then he put the van in gear and drove her down to the front of the building.

"Be careful," he said as she got out, her orange metal tool-box in one hand and a large canvas tote with tools in multiple outside pockets hanging cross-body from her shoulder. He added, "Two minutes," as an obvious reminder of the dangers of the most crucial part of the operation, and she gave him a thumbs-up.

He drove away, to wait in the underground parking garage for her to rejoin him.

Bianca looked at her watch, taking note of the time.

Then Brenda Smolski, master plumber, strode through the door of the Thurber/Wilkes Building into the busy lobby. Brenda was the same height as Bianca, but poor posture and flat black work boots made her appear inches shorter. Thanks to the figure-enhancing qualities of a layer of foam padding duct-taped around her torso, she looked pleasantly plump. From beneath a blue baseball cap, dull brown hair straggled to her shoulders. She wore a loose blue coverall-style uniform that zipped up in front and had a name tag fastened to it just above her heart, and brown leather work gloves. Brown-framed glasses that were too large for her face gave her a slightly bug-eyed look. Her makeup was colorless and bland.

Bianca's goal was to make it impossible for Mickey to recognize her at a casual glance, or from any distance farther away than, say, ten feet. If he got a close-up look at her face, all bets were off, she knew. But she hoped to keep that from happening.

Actually, she hoped he wasn't in the building. But she had to assume that he was.

There was a dedicated elevator that bypassed the hotel portion of the building. It stopped on the ninth floor, where she had to be cleared by security before she could proceed to the sixteenth.

The reception desk faced the elevator so that when the door opened anyone inside it was immediately in full view of whoever was on duty at the desk. Right at the moment, that was two men and a woman dressed in black suits with name badges attached to the breast pockets of their jackets.

Shades of Mickey. Getting a load of their outfits, it was all Bianca could do not to grimace. Except for security, which these three clearly were and which appeared to be present at full capacity, the rest of the floor seemed to be empty, and Bianca was reminded that it *was* Saturday.

"Hear they've got a toilet emergency up on sixteen," she said with hearty good cheer to the woman behind the reception desk, who was the first to greet her as she approached.

"Allied Industries. They've already called down," the woman replied. "Last elevator on the left. Just hit sixteen. I'll call and tell them you're coming."

"Thanks." Bianca proceeded to the elevator, hit sixteen and went up.

20

When the elevator stopped on the sixteenth floor, Bianca was careful to keep her head down in case Mickey should be standing there on the other side of the door when it opened. Her heart rate was up; her muscles were tensed for action.

Go time.

"Thank all that's holy you're here." The guy who greeted her as she stepped off the elevator was maybe fifty, balding, average height, stocky. Black suit, white shirt, name tag: security. He was all but hopping up and down with distress as he made a come-on gesture to her and turned to lead the way to the problem. "*Hurry.* We got to get this fixed."

He was walking so fast the sides of his jacket flapped. Bianca fell in behind him.

"What happened?" In case Mickey was somewhere where he could hear her, she changed her voice, making it deeper and rougher.

"The toilet—damnedest thing I ever saw. It just..."

While he described the erupting toilet to her, Bianca shot quick glances around, getting her bearings, scoping out the terrain. The entire sixteenth floor was about four thousand square feet, all of it open except for the back area, which was where the bathrooms were located and where she was being taken. That back part was walled off from the rest and took the form of a long corridor housing various utility-type rooms, including the bathrooms.

There were walls dividing the remainder of the floor into sections, but no section had more than three walls, which made it possible to see the entire floor just by looking around. That was what she did as she walked from the elevator bank, which was located in the center, toward the back hall. Then she realized that the sections did have four walls, the fourth wall in each case being Plexiglas. She could see right through it. The Plexiglas walls were part of the security system. She'd seen them on the plans without realizing they were Plexiglas. They could be raised during business hours and lowered when the office was closed, to keep intruders out. They were down now. Inside the closed-off sections, motion detector sensors would be monitoring the space.

The solid walls were different lengths and widths. Their colors—purple, red, fuchsia, orange—were vibrant and eye-catching. The ceiling was navy blue. The floor was polished concrete. There were no windows, but the recessed lighting in the ceiling made the space plenty bright. Large, abstract canvas-on-frame oil paintings adorned the walls, adding more color. Bright poured concrete pedestals held objets d'art. Plexiglas desks, some with work on them, some without, were in a number of the room spaces. Several seating groups—couches with chairs opposite them—were scattered around.

Bianca found the southwest corner. About twenty feet in, running perpendicular to the front wall of the building, an orange wall protruded from the adjacent outside wall, twenty feet long, six feet thick. A large pink-and-gold painting took pride of place in the center of the wall.

Beneath that painting, if her calculations were correct, was the safe.

A Plexiglas wall sealed it off.

The southwest corner space was approximately twenty by twenty, four hundred square feet.

Bianca stepped in water and her attention refocused in a hurry. They were just reaching the back hall, she discovered. Water rolled out of the doorway that led into it, spreading out as it moved into the main part of the sixteenth floor. She could smell the dampness, hear the slosh of it.

"…floods the entire floor." Splashing into the hall through the inches-deep water that was flowing down it at a terrifying clip even as he spoke, her guide, who'd been talking the entire time she'd been looking around, gestured toward the open bathroom door in front of them. Alarming gurgling sounds and the continual rush of water could be heard through it. Two more black-suited security guards, one with a mop and one with a large plastic trash can, were in the hall trying to contain the deluge that was rolling out of the bathroom. The guy with the mop was sweeping waves of water into the trash can, which the guy with the trash can ran to empty in, presumably because Bianca couldn't actually see it, the bathroom sink.

They were big, solid ex-military types. They were not Mickey.

"Plumber's here," her guide called.

"Thank God." Trash Can Man was back in action. He was, she saw, soaking wet.

Looking up at Bianca beseechingly, Mop Guy said, "All I did was flush the damned toilet. I didn't put nothing down it. *Nothing*, I swear." All the while he was frantically pushing more water into the can. He was soaking wet, too.

"You had to have done something," her guide said. *He* wasn't soaking wet. He must have had the good sense to stay back. "You can't tell me you—"

"I can fix it," Bianca interrupted. The water rolling out of the bathroom was six inches deep; she was thankful for her boots. Splashing up behind the men, she saw that the fourth guard was inside the bathroom trying to put a lid—literally—on the fountain of water shooting up from the open toilet. He was bent over the toilet trying to force the lid shut in the teeth of the blasting geyser, with the result that water was spraying all over the room.

The good news was, he wasn't Mickey, either.

"Sir, *stop*," Bianca said sharply, because she really didn't want to end up as wet as three of the four. They all looked at her. She gestured at Mr. Toilet Lid. "*You*. Let go. That's not helping."

He let go. The lid flew up and hit him in the chin. He squealed and fell back. Literally. Landing on his ass in the lake on the floor. Looking dazed and confused.

The toilet fountain shot toward the ceiling again.

Her guide clapped both hands to his cheeks *Home Alone* kid-style.

Mr. Toilet Lid swore and clapped a hand to his chin.

Trash Can Man bounded into the bathroom with his water-filled trash can, dumping its contents in the sink, which was too small to hold all that water, which meant that about half of it ended up back on the floor.

Bianca sighed and took charge.

"I'm going to need you two in there," she said to her guide and Mop Guy, who were still outside the bathroom, and pointed inside.

Putting her toolbox down on the elegant console table that stood, legs awash, in the hall right outside the bathroom, she followed them in.

"We're going to try something," she said when they were all inside the bathroom. In there, the water was deep. It was creeping up toward the top of her boots. "If it's going to do the trick, we need to work together."

"For God's sake, make it stop." Her guide was wringing his hands as he stared at the gusher shooting out of the toilet. "It's going to flood the entire floor."

"I'm going to make it stop," she promised, which had the advantage of being the truth. "You're going to help." Which wasn't the truth, but oh well.

Meanwhile, Mr. Toilet Lid moaned, "My chin's bleeding," from his spot on the floor.

"You—" Bianca pointed at Trash Can Man "—put the trash can down." He did. "Come over here." She pointed to the toilet, where the white column of water was spouting six feet high and throwing off droplets like a wet dog. "When I tell you to, I want you to push the flush button on the toilet. Keep pushing it until I tell you to stop. But don't start until I say so."

As he got into position, she pointed at Mop Guy. "See that vent on the side of the toilet?" She pointed to the small grate in the white porcelain base. "I want you to press the head of the mop against it as hard as you can. When I tell you to."

Mop Guy nodded and splashed toward the toilet.

"You—" Bianca pointed at her guide "—are going to turn on the taps and keep the water pouring out of them at full blast. Don't let the sink overflow, though."

She looked down at Mr. Toilet Lid, whose chin now dripped blood, pulled a paper towel from the dispenser and handed it to him.

"You're going to sit there and hold this to your chin," she told him. Accepting the paper towel gratefully, he complied.

"Get ready," she told her troops and splashed toward the door.

"What's the purpose of this?" her guide asked. He was standing ready by the sink.

"We're going to try to equalize the pressure in the toilet," Bianca said. She had no idea if there was such a thing as pressure in a toilet, but it sounded good. By then she had reached the door. "Everybody ready? We need to work together on this. One, two, three—go."

They jumped to do her bidding. Water poured from the taps.

The toilet flushed. The mop hit the vent. Oh, and Mr. Toilet Lid applied direct pressure to his chin.

She walked out the door and shoved it shut, which was harder to do than one might expect against the force of the water pouring over the threshold.

"I'm closing the door so the whole floor doesn't flood while we get this fixed," she called to her helpers through it, just in case it should occur to them that maybe a plumber wouldn't be closing the door on them. "Keep doing what you're doing. We'll have it under control in no time."

Then she pulled a door jammer portable lock from her toolbox and, ignoring the water, thrust the bottom plate under the door, positioned the foot and screwed it in place.

Voilà. The sixteenth-floor security team was now locked in the bathroom.

The great thing about the device she'd used was, the torque on it was such that the more force that was applied to the door from the inside, the tighter and more secure the lock became.

In other words, her helpers weren't going anywhere anytime soon.

"I'm going to go flip some switches," she yelled through the door. Stripping off her wet gloves—she had surgical gloves on beneath—she dropped them in her toolbox, removed her glasses and tossed them in there, too, picked up the toolbox and walked away.

Battle won, no casualties, not a shot fired.

Her kind of operation.

She glanced at her watch. From street to now, that part of the job had taken less than five minutes.

Doc was in the van presumably listening in, so he'd know to start gradually dialing back the toilet fountain until it was eventually turned off. (Keeping it going for a few minutes more would serve to keep her helpers diverted until she was out of there, she hoped.) Talking to Doc directly was out. The rule about saying anything that might reveal that a job was going down was in force. For all she knew, she might not be the only one with ears on the sixteenth floor.

Although Doc's location in the underground parking garage made reception in the van a little iffy. But then it didn't really matter if he couldn't hear what was going on with her. They'd gone over everything he needed to do and established precise timetables. Right now, they were both on the clock.

In three minutes, seven seconds, the power to the building would go out. That would open the Plexiglas security wall on the southwest corner room and turn the motion detectors off.

When that happened, she would have two minutes to get in and out of there before the emergency generator kicked in.

Meanwhile, the next order of business was to lock down the fire exit door to prevent any surprise visits via the stairwell. After that, she would do the same thing to the elevator until she was ready to use it to go down.

Then it would be time to go get the prototype.

The fire exit was at the far end of the hallway with the bathrooms. She used a door jammer on it, too.

Heading toward the elevator, she paused to yell toward the bathroom, "I think I've found the right switch. Keep on doing what you're doing. We should see some improvement soon."

The walls were thick. And concrete. She barely heard the shouted reply that sounded like "We're on it."

Sometimes things were just that easy.

Water had begun to spread significantly throughout the main floor, she saw. But the seepage was shallow, and given that the floor was polished concrete, all it did was make the surface underfoot slick. Fortunately, her work boots had nonskid rubber soles.

Pulling from her toolbox the metal bar that she was going

to use to lock the elevator door open and thus imprison it on the sixteenth floor, she checked her watch again. One minute, fifty-three seconds to go.

She was right on schedule.

The elevator *pinged* when she was still some eight feet away from it. The *ping* meant somebody was coming up.

Alarm stopped her in her tracks. Her eyes locked on the rectangular, deep purple floor-to-ceiling column that held the single elevator servicing the floor.

Too late to stop it. Nowhere to hide.

Okay, then. She dropped the metal bar she needed to lock the elevator open in her toolbox. With one minute, twenty-nine seconds to go until the power was interrupted, taking out whoever emerged from the elevator was priority number one. She didn't need a metal bar for that.

Positioning herself opposite the elevator as if she was waiting for it to arrive so as not to spook her victim, she set her toolbox on the ground and pulled off her shoulder tote to rest on top of it.

The elevator door slid open.

Mickey stepped out. Big and tough-looking in his black suit. Handsome. Grim-faced. With a slight limp that favored his left foot. The one she had stomped.

Ha.

Forget the unholy tangle of emotions that erupted inside her at the sight of him.

She was on him like a tiger on a gazelle.

Chop to the neck, with the intent of disabling with a single blow.

Thunk. Her hand slammed into a rock-hard forearm as he deflected her blow with stunning quickness and a surprised "What the—"

The impact sent a tingle up her arm. So he *was* trained, she thought with savage satisfaction when he whirled away with an answering leg sweep that would have brought her down if she hadn't leaped over it like it was a jump rope and launched an ax kick to his chest. Special forces? Some kind of advanced military martial arts, for sure. She'd expected it. She *relished* it. She would dance on his head when her ax kick took him down.

But to her surprise, he caught her foot before it could connect, wrenching it up so that she found herself flipping head over heels in a backward somersault. It was, she thought, the fault of the foam body wrapping. It was throwing off her timing just that vital little bit.

As she three-sixty'd through the air, her hat fell off.

In a fight she was like a cat, always landing on her feet. That was what she did now before bouncing off her toes and delivering a double palm heel blow to both his ears.

Whomp.

"*Shit.*" He fell back, but instead of covering his ears with his hands as most recipients of that blow instinctively did and thus leaving himself open for a devastating follow-through, he yelled, "Damn it, kumquat," while assuming a defensive stance.

He recognized her. Of course he did.

Their eyes locked. Sparks crackled in the air between them. Anger, and something more.

"How was your swim?" Her tone made it a taunt.

"Cold. Wet. You left me to drown."

"I threw you a life preserver."

Her already bubbling anger was amplified a thousandfold by the thought that he might have had something to do with the kidnapping of Marin and Margery. That was the spur that separated itself from the emotional pack and threatened to derail the ice-cold concentration that dropped over her like a mantle whenever she fought. Powering through it, she fell on him like a chopping, kicking dervish even as he parried with body blows that might have actually done some damage if she hadn't been wrapped in layers of padding.

But she was.

He yelled, "Stop it! We need to talk," and grabbed her arm before it could connect as she let loose with a should-have-been-fight-finishing roundhouse to the temple. Yanking her off balance, he twirled her into him, trying to put her on the floor.

Inwardly she sneered. He didn't have the goods.

Driving her elbow into his stomach, she wrenched free with a backward kick to the kneecap that missed breaking his leg only because she was distracted at the last nanosecond by the lights going out and the Plexiglas doors rising and the knowledge that she was now on the two-minute clock.

"Save your breath for your inflatable doll," she hissed at him, leaping out of reach as he grabbed for her.

They circled each other like wary wrestlers. Bianca's eyes narrowed as she realized that, like herself, he wasn't even breathing hard. Whoever he was, whatever he did, he kept himself in fighting shape.

A distant, barely audible thumping reached her ears. Her helpers, pounding on the bathroom door, at a guess. Mickey paid no attention to the sounds. He probably thought they were coming from outside somewhere.

"I get that you're mad because I kissed you, then handcuffed you to the rail," he said. "What you want to keep in mind is, you kissed me, then Tasered me unconscious first."

"You think *that's* what this is about? Tell me something, what kind of man colludes in the kidnapping of a seven-year-old?"

"Wha—"

He didn't even get the word all the way out before she was on him. Aiming a round kick at his chest that deliberately missed, she used the momentum of the feint and his reaction to latch onto his arm and throw him over her hip.

The sight of his powerful body cartwheeling through the air brought her more satisfaction than anything had all day.

He landed with a thud and a curse and skidded on his back across the slippery-when-wet floor.

His foot caught the back of her knees as he slid past.

Damn it. To her shock, she went down, landing hard on her ass. Pain shot up her spine.

He dived at her. She rolled. He got a hand in her jumpsuit. She chopped his wrist. He yelled and let go. She followed up with a knife hand strike to the throat that he managed to partially deflect but that was still powerful enough to put him, coughing, on his back. She leaped to her feet, glanced at her watch, snatched up her toolbox, tote bag and hat, took another second to drop the elevator-locking rod in the door channel and sprinted away toward the southwest corner room.

She had—another glance at her watch—sixteen seconds left before the Plexiglas wall descended again and the motion detectors powered up and the whole security apparatus kicked back in.

And getting the prototype out of the safe got a whole lot harder.

She should have been in and almost out by now.

What to say? She'd gotten distracted.

The lights sputtered and came back on.

The Plexiglas wall was on its way down even as she reached it.

"Stop!" On his feet now, Mickey pounded after her. The fast slam of his footsteps matched the thumping of her heart. "Stay out of there!"

Sliding her toolbox and tote bag across the slick concrete ahead of her, she rolled under the edge of the wall seconds before it made jarring contact with the floor.

The wall was the barrier that turned the twenty-by-twenty-foot space into a containment unit. It was designed to keep whoever was trapped inside it in.

But it also served to keep whoever was outside it out.

In other words, her fight with Mickey was officially over. There was no way he was getting to her now.

The next sound she heard was the motion detectors beeping as they sensed her presence in the secure area. Then came the sound she'd been steeled for—the horrible sucking sound of the air being pulled from the room.

21

"No!" Mickey threw himself against the clear wall like a bug hitting a windshield. As Bianca got to her feet, he slammed a fist into the Plexiglas. He was a big, strong guy; he hit that wall like he meant to knock it down, and not only did it not crack, it didn't so much as shake. Bianca was impressed—with the wall. "There's a security device—it's sucking all the air out of the room right now. In a minute or two you'll suffocate!"

He sounded—and looked—panicked.

Bianca let her mouth go all open and round with horror and made big, terrified eyes at him. Just for the hell of it.

"Jesus. Stand back." Looking wildly around, he picked up one of the pedestal-style columns that served as display stands for the objets d'art. The columns were solid concrete, she was pretty sure; this particular one was hot pink and held—had held, it went crashing to the floor—a bust of Pallas. Or somebody.

The bust went rolling away as he slammed that concrete column into the wall.

Not a crack. Not a dent. Not a shiver.

In the meantime, the air continued to get pulled out of the room with a hiss that sounded like a giant deflating balloon. Somewhere deep in the bowels of the building, alarms from the breach of the area protected by the motion sensors would be going off. The entire security team would be assembling for a charge to the sixteenth floor.

Unfortunately for them, the doors were locked and the elevator wasn't going anywhere.

Could anybody say *access denied*?

"God*damn* it." Mickey slammed the column into the Plexiglas over and over again, huge crashing slams that would have made her jump if she hadn't been expecting them and would have knocked a hole the size of Texas in most walls, then flung it aside in disgust as he saw that he was making no headway at all. The wall hadn't suffered so much as a scratch.

Crouching, he pulled up his trouser leg to reveal an ankle holster—aha, so he *was* armed!—then stood to aim the Glock 27 he drew from it at a corner of the Plexiglas, taking care to aim away from her.

"No!" she shouted just before he fired, because firing a bullet into an enclosed space with nothing but concrete walls was dangerous. She winced as the bullet slammed into the Plexiglas— then went ricocheting around the room, whining, kicking up a chunk of concrete from the floor, whistling past Mickey and causing him to duck and cover.

The wall remained as pristine as ever.

Bianca's opinion of the wall, already high, soared higher.

"That was just stupid," she told him, picking up her toolbox and tote bag and carrying them over to the orange wall. Mickey jammed the pistol into his waistband.

"There's got to be a release switch." Sounding desperate, he pulled his cell phone out of his pocket and started to punch in numbers. Bianca would have been seriously alarmed—the last thing she needed was more witnesses for what she was about to do—except for the fact that, after the call to the plumber, Doc had started jamming all phone signals from the building. Really, nobody wanted to get the cops or the fire department or a SWAT team or anything of that nature involved. Or at least she didn't.

"*No signal.*" His fingers tightened around his phone. He stared down at it as if he wanted to crush it in his hand. His eyes shot to her. His face was hard with fear for her. She might have found his performance downright touching except for the whole he'd-possibly-had-something-to-do-with-the-kidnapping-of-her-sister and he'd-definitely-kissed-her-for-the-purpose-of-chaining-her-to-a-rail thing. So, not so much. "You need to try to find an air pocket. Maybe under the—"

He broke off as she lifted the big pink-and-gold painting from pride of place in the center of the orange wall and set it aside. Beneath it, as she had expected, was the safe.

"What the hell are you *doing*?" He had both hands pressed flat against the Plexiglas now. His feet were planted wide apart as he seemed to be trying to rock the wall out of its moorings by the application of sheer brute strength. His eyes were alive with alarm. "What part of 'you're going to suffocate' do you not understand? You've got to be just about out of air in there. Jesus *Christ*…"

The dislodged bust wasn't far from his feet. It was bronze, she saw as he snatched it up and hurled it at the wall.

When it bounced off without leaving a mark, he cursed and looked poised to hurl himself at the wall in its place.

Until he saw that she was crouched beside her toolbox lifting a small metal canister from it. A canister connected by a hose to a clear plastic face mask.

Bianca pulled off her wig, shoved it into the tote, ran her fingers through her own blond hair, tucked the silky fall of it behind her ears. He already knew what she looked like in several iterations, so she didn't see much point in complicating her life by trying to look like somebody else, and at this point her wig could only get in her way.

She put the face mask over her nose and mouth, securing it in place with the attached elastic band that went around her head.

Then she turned the knob on top of the canister, assuring herself a nice, steady flow of air.

See, she was a big believer in the Girl Scouts' motto of Be Prepared. Any halfway reasonable person would realize that even the most remote possibility of getting caught in an airless room equals the need to bring your own air.

And it really was starting to get a little stuffy in there.

"You—" Mickey broke off before he could add whatever pejorative had been on the tip of his tongue, but she could read the bad words he didn't call her in his eyes. His expression as he stared in at her was a combination of thunderstruck and murderous. She'd scared him badly, and it showed in his reaction.

Bianca smiled, pulled the tote bag over her shoulder, dropped the canister in the tote bag so that it stayed with her and she had her hands free, fished a stethoscope from the toolbox, stood, settled the earpieces in her ears and got to work on the lock.

"You're not getting out of here," Mickey said. He once again stood with his hands pressed flat against the Plexiglas watching her, but the fear was gone from his face. Instead he just looked pissed. "I'm right here, and this place is locked up tight."

Bianca ignored him in favor of listening for the distinctive clicks that would tell her which numbers would open the lock.

"You have any idea what kind of jail time you're looking at here?"

Click.

"Probably twenty years," he continued when she didn't answer. "You're what—thirty?"

That stung. She narrowed her eyes but refused to let him disrupt her concentration, which she guessed was his intent.

Click.

"I can make you a deal," he said. "You tell me where to find your boss. If the information you give me pans out, I might even find a way to let you go free."

Click.

"I'm betting you don't have any idea about the kind of man you're working for."

Click.

"His real name is Mason Thayer. He used to work for the CIA. As part of their Cerberus Project. You know what that was? A team of government-sanctioned assassins. He's killed more people than you are old."

Bianca's attention wavered. Her father, an assassin? Her mind ping-ponged through some shadowy places folded in with years of memories. Did it fit with what she knew of him? Maybe, although there was no way to know for sure if what Mickey was telling her was the truth. The name and the CIA connection jibed with what Doc had turned up. But she still didn't see how he could have gotten to know her nineteen-year-old mother well enough to make a baby with her. Bianca desperately wanted to hear more, to learn more. But she couldn't hang around and shoot the breeze with Mickey. There was far more at stake here than just uncovering her father's secrets. There were lives—Marin's and Margery's—on the line.

Click.

"He's using you," Mickey said. "He's using you to do his dirty work while he stays safely out of the reach of everybody who's looking for him. What kind of man does that?"

Click.

There it was, the last number. Taking off the stethoscope, Bianca dropped it in the toolbox and pulled the safe open. The briefcase was inside. With a tingle of satisfaction, she lifted it out.

Ordinarily she next would have closed the safe and replaced the painting, but, seriously, what was the point?

She was pretty sure that by the time she was through they were going to know she'd been there.

Anyway, she'd always thought stealth was overrated.

"The deal I'm offering you is a good one. Take it." Mickey's voice sounded strained.

Picking up her toolbox, Bianca headed toward the adjacent wall. As she went, she pushed the oxygen mask down and looked at Mickey.

"I'll make *you* a deal," she said. "You tell me where the little girl and the woman your people kidnapped are, and I'll tell you where my boss is."

"I don't know what you're talking about," he said as she slid the oxygen mask back into place. "If a little girl and a woman have been kidnapped, it's nothing to do with me or the people I work for."

Right. Like she was supposed to believe him? Her lips tightened. He looked, and sounded, like he was telling the truth.

She pushed the oxygen mask out of the way again. "So who is it you work for? Laurent Durand?"

His eyes flickered. She thought—maybe—he hadn't expected her to know that name. Of course, the only reason she did know it was because she was her father's daughter, a fact that Mickey and, by extrapolation, the people he worked for didn't seem to be aware of. She had no plans to tell them. Just like she had no plans to reveal that the kidnapped little girl was her sister. Her gut feeling was that both she and Marin were better off if no one knew.

He said, "You don't need to know who I work for. Except for the fact they're way more interested in bringing in your boss than you. And they don't kidnap little girls."

While he was talking, Bianca had pushed the oxygen mask back into place and started pulling the major component of her plan B from the toolbox. The thin coils looked like yards of ordinary clothesline, but they weren't. They were detonating cord.

Nicked from the demolition supply company because she'd foreseen that there was a sliver of a possibility that she might get trapped in a locked, windowless, doorless, airless room. And she really hadn't liked that idea.

Always have a plan B: it was another one of the rules.

Pushing her mask aside again, Bianca said, "Maybe you don't know the people you're working for as well as you think you do."

Then she restored her mask and started duct-taping the detonating cord to the wall, marking out the shape she needed.

"Tell me about the kidnapping. Maybe I can help with that."

Bianca considered. She didn't see that it could hurt to tell him, just in case he *didn't* know and his people *were* involved and he was a decent enough human being to try to do something about it. She pushed the mask down. "My boss's daughter—her name is Marin, and did I mention she's *seven*?—and her mother were kidnapped. Probably while you and I were playing our little games on the boat. Whoever did it is threatening to kill them unless they get what's in this briefcase. Or, more accurately, I think, until they get my boss." Finishing with the detonating cord, she fixed him with an accusing look. "Who does that sound like?"

"If Thayer's daughter and her mother have been kidnapped, it wasn't done by us."

Bianca's skeptical expression was her reply. Adjusting her mask and turning her back to him, she affixed the longish fuse to the blasting cap she'd crimped onto the cord, lit the end of it and scampered back to take cover behind the desk.

Oxygen was highly flammable. Since she was wearing it, she really didn't want to be too close when the blast went off.

"Damn it—" That was as far as he got when the detonating cord...well, detonated.

Boom.

It was a small explosion as explosions went, designed to open up a door-size hole in the wall.

It succeeded. Chunks of concrete blew outward, the pieces

crumbling away and falling to the roof of what she knew was the ten-story building next door. That building and the opportunity to keep the blast fallout away from the sidewalk and the pedestrians out front were why she'd chosen that particular wall. Well, that plus the fact that she was far less likely to be spotted going out the side of the building than the front. Looking through the hole, she saw nothing but blue sky and a variety of downtown buildings. Perfect.

She took off her oxygen mask, dropped it into the tote and inhaled. She hadn't realized how wonderful fresh air smelled until it billowed into the room.

Time to go.

"You don't want to do this," he said.

"You know, I think I do." Her tone mocked. She shucked her plumber's uniform as she spoke.

"You leave this room, you're asking to get shot on sight."

Looking at him, she discovered that she was gritting her teeth and getting a knot in her stomach and realized that it was from anger. He was part of this, part of the web of intrigue that had resulted in the kidnapping of her seven-year-old sister, that had almost certainly caused her father's death, and he had the gall to threaten her and try to make a deal?

The fact that he had kissed her and made her like him was just something else to hold against him.

"That *is* scary. But I think I'll chance it." Stepping out of the jumpsuit, she pulled the foam padding from around her middle. That left her wearing a cute pair of gray-plaid shorts with a black scarf belt, a black tee, black stockings and her work boots. *Très chic*, if she did say so herself.

Also, *très* handy.

For one thing, the shorts provided easy access to her way out.

She bundled up the uniform and foam and stuffed them into the toolbox.

"Is keeping Thayer safe worth risking your life?" His voice was tight as he watched her pull up the leg of her shorts to reveal the top of her stocking, a sexy black band below inches of slim, tanned bare thigh, and the clip that fastened it to her scarlet satin garter belt.

She said, "I'm pretty sure Thayer, as you call him, is dead. You were there in Bahrain. Did you somehow miss the whole blow-up-the-gang-of-thieves-in-the-garbage-truck thing? What I'm doing is trying to save a little girl and her mother, and yes, that's worth risking my life."

She undid the escape-cord holding clip attached to her stocking, then unclipped the top of the strap from the garter belt itself. Walking back to the safe, she fastened the clip around the door and made sure it was secure. She knew the specifications of the Fallon 230Z. That door would support a literal ton of weight before the hinges gave. Sliding her wrist into the shiny red strap, she moved back over to her toolbox and the briefcase. The cord unspooled behind her as she went.

Mickey watched her with a frown. He said, "You have proof he died? Because we haven't been able to confirm that."

Once again, hope flickered in Bianca's heart.

"Do you have proof he didn't?" She plucked her hat from the toolbox and put it on, pulling the bulk of her hair through the opening in the back and settling it firmly to make sure it stayed in place.

"No."

"But you're trying to find him, anyway." She wrapped a bungee cord around the handles of the briefcase and the toolbox so that they were fastened together. He watched her, tight-lipped.

"Yes."

"Good luck with that."

"Listen to me." His voice was harsh. It was clear from his expression that he knew what she was about to do. "You need to turn yourself in to me, right now. If you tell me everything you know, I'll make sure you're not charged with any crime. That you'll go free. And I'll get a crack investigative team on finding the little girl and her mother. I give you my word."

Bianca thought about it for maybe two seconds. Turning herself in to him meant giving him total control over what happened next.

"For me to even think about doing that, I'd have to trust you, and I don't," she said and smiled at him. "By the way, that pounding noise you've been hearing? That's some of your security staff trying to get out of the bathroom in the back hall. I locked them in. You might want to go let them out."

Then she picked up the briefcase and toolbox by the bungee cord handle she'd created, slid her hand into the satin strap and ran toward the hole in the wall.

And jumped.

By the time she reached Doc and the white van, fire trucks and police cars were racing up the surrounding streets. Sirens echoed through the parking garage.

"Go, go, go, go, go." Bianca scrambled up into the van, stowed the briefcase at her feet and shoved the toolbox and tote bag into the back.

"You got the prototype." Doc spared a glance for the briefcase as he put the van in Reverse and pulled out of the parking spot.

"Yep."

"You took longer than we planned. I was worried." Shifting into Drive, he hit the gas, and they were on their way toward the exit. Bianca's biggest fear was that someone would think to block off the area before they could get away. "What happened?"

"I ran into a problem." They were only one floor below street level. She fastened her seat belt as Doc swerved up the ramp at speed, but not so fast that it would attract unwanted attention. It felt good to sit down. She hadn't realized how amped up she was. Dropping six stories, then breaking in through the rooftop door, taking the elevator down like she was just one of many patrons of what had turned out to be a medical office building and then going outside and making her way along the sidewalk to the garage of the building she'd just blown a hole in had set her teeth on edge with the need to appear calm and unconcerned and not in a hurry. But she'd made it, and here they were. Almost home free.

"What kind of problem?" They were approaching the exit, which was blocked by one of those drop-down arms that required some kind of action before it would lift. This particular lot was pay in advance, so all Doc had to do was key in the number printed on the top of his ticket. The street was right in front of them, maybe six feet beyond the arm. Bianca saw the tail end of a fire truck shoot past. The reflections of the stroboscopic lights revolved in the windows across the street, where the beginnings of a crowd gathered. She and Doc were getting away with seconds to spare.

She said, "That cop I told you about? The one you were checking out earlier? He was there."

"Uh—" Doc had been punching in the numbers. *Beep beep beep.* He stopped; his voice pitching higher until it was almost a squeak. "That cop?"

Bianca glanced sharply in the direction in which Doc was nodding like an out-of-control bobblehead to discover that Mickey was crossing directly in front of them. He was clearly intent on reaching the sidewalk on the other side of the parking garage. Her eyes riveted on him. He looked tall, lean, formidable and way too handsome to suit her. His jaw was set and hard, his mouth was thin and he was squinting slightly as he scanned the sidewalk and street in front of him. She had no doubt that he was hunting something and that something was her.

It occurred to her that at the end of a fight with most of her opponents, they weren't up to walking anywhere. It then occurred to her that maybe, just maybe, the fact that her blows hadn't landed with their usual incapacitating force might not have been entirely due to the fact that she'd been encumbered by padding. In fact, she might have been pulling her punches.

Then she remembered how little his counterblows had hurt her and wondered if, maybe, he'd been pulling his punches, too.

She held very still, watching him.

"Keep punching in the code," she said to Doc, who audibly gulped but complied. *Beep. Beep.*

As a matter of good tradecraft, she'd taken off her hat and wrapped her head in the black scarf she'd worn as a belt as soon as she'd broken through the rooftop door of the building she'd landed on. The scarf covered her hair and forehead completely and gave her a vaguely ethnic look. It was also tied loosely enough that, as long as she kept her head down, the soft folds would conceal her face from any security cameras.

Now she pulled the scarf forward still more, casting her face in deep shadow, and lowered her head.

Just in time. Doc hit the last number, the restraining arm lifted—and Mickey looked their way.

"Holy moly, he's looking right at us," Doc said. Under his breath, as if Mickey could possibly hear them. He couldn't; he was too far away. Bianca dared to glance up, peering through her lashes without lifting her head. Mickey *was* looking at them, frowning at the windshield of the van. But there was no intent in his face, no recognition—she didn't think.

"Drive," Bianca said.

Doc did. As he pulled forward, Mickey glanced away, stepped

up on the sidewalk and kept walking. Her eyes followed his broad back until the van turned left out of the parking garage and she could no longer see him.

22

Bianca didn't like to steal cars. It inconvenienced the owners and it got the police involved (assuming that the owner wasn't into avoiding the police). But in this case, stealing a car was the best fix she could come up with for her problem.

Her problem was finding a secure, short-term spot to keep the briefcase. One that she could keep under surveillance until whoever came to get it showed up. In the movies, the solution would be stashing the briefcase in a temporary storage locker in a bus or train terminal while she lurked in a nearby dark corner and watched. The reality was that, since 9/11, all remaining lockers and similar units of that type were monitored. Any contents left longer than a few hours were checked on and/or removed.

And given that she suspected a Mickey-esque law enforcement type was going to show up to retrieve the briefcase, a rental car left too many potential leads behind: fake driver's license and credit card used to rent the car, possible security footage from the rental place, clerks that could be questioned, etc.

"You gotta be kidding me" was Doc's reaction when she'd dragged him out of bed before dawn while the fog was still rolling in from the bay to blanket the steep, crooked streets. He'd stood watch while she'd stolen a battered blue Ford Fiesta from a block in the Tenderloin area, which was one of those places that only a resident could love and tourists were advised to avoid if they wanted to go home with their valuables and lives intact. That particular vehicle had gotten the nod because the owner had been careless enough to leave a spare key in one of those little magnetic boxes under the car. A key was important because whoever came to get the briefcase would need it to unlock the trunk.

Unless they wanted to break in, but that seemed unnecessarily messy.

If she got the chance, she would return the car before leaving town.

If not, she was confident that it would be found. It was, at the moment, parked in a very public spot at the Vagabond Inn near San Francisco International Airport, because, when dealing with situations with a high potential for violence, public was good. If the car remained there longer than twenty-four hours, a security guard or patrol officer could be counted on to check it out.

She was in a rental car parked in the lot of the In-N-Out Burger two businesses down, conveniently situated so that she could keep an eye on the Fiesta. Alone.

She'd repositioned the car a couple of times so it wouldn't always be in the same place, but so far she'd been sitting in it watching the Fiesta for six hours. Six *long* hours, in which she had nothing to do but think.

Marin's face as it had looked in the video haunted her. The memory of the fear in the child's eyes was as corrosive as acid eating away at her concentration. Bianca's every impulse urged her to rush to the rescue. But there was nothing she could do until she knew where to go.

Speculating on the conditions in which the little girl and her mother were being held was useless. It made her angry. It made her sick to her stomach. It kept her from focusing on everything she would need to do to find them. On what she might need to do to get them out.

It was counterproductive.

Wondering if her father could possibly be alive, processing the apparent truth that his real identity was Mason Thayer, ex–CIA agent, and coming up with various scenarios in which he could possibly have hooked up with her mother was counterproductive, too.

Any thoughts of Mickey—not that she had any—were just a waste of brainpower.

She needed to stay alert, to keep her focus on her surroundings. It was possible that the client might be wary about approaching the Fiesta, might be hanging around keeping it under surveillance in an effort to spot her father.

She might not be able to physically recognize whoever it was, but she could recognize patterns of behavior. That was what she was looking for.

She couldn't read. She couldn't watch YouTube videos or play games on her phone. She couldn't turn on the car or even roll down her specially requested tinted windows because she didn't want to attract attention or be seen. She could watch the planes take off and land out of the corner of her eye. And count them. Unfortunately, the effect was like counting sheep, and she didn't need that. She could listen to her playlist of songs. She could sing (badly) along. She could eat, and she did. She ate a protein bar. She ate an apple. She succumbed to the temptation of the In-N-Out Burger and made use of the drive-through window and ate a burger, with cheese. She drank water. She drank soda. She drank more water.

And now, at 2:00 p.m. on a busy, sunny Sunday afternoon, she really, really, *really* had to pee.

There were restrooms all around her: in the burger place, the motel, the service station on the other side of the burger place.

She figured she'd be gone five minutes, tops.

What were the chances that whoever was coming to retrieve the briefcase would show up within those five minutes?

Probably, she decided glumly, about one hundred percent.

Two quotes—well, a quote and the hideous maiming of a quote—that summarized her situation kept chasing themselves through her mind.

A watched pot never boils and *bathrooms, bathrooms everywhere, nor any spot to pee.*

She was really starting to regret making Doc get on the motel's airport shuttle right after he (in the rental car) had followed her (in the stolen car) to the motel. If he was with her, he could watch the Fiesta while she ran inside.

"You might need me," he'd protested when she'd told him it was time for him to go.

She'd assured him she wouldn't, that she could take it from here. At the time, she'd thought it best to get him safely out of harm's way.

So now he was flying back to Savannah and she was stuck doing what seemed like never-ending surveillance in the hot, uncomfortable, bathroom-less front seat of a tiny little rental car.

James Bond, take me away.

Last night, she and Doc had holed up in a Quality Inn in Oakland. Even under a fake identity she'd been uncomfortable, because she was confident that Mickey and the Mouseketeers (her new name for the group he worked for) had launched an all-out search for her/her father/their supposed gang. There'd been nothing on the news about the theft or the hole she'd blown in the Thurber/Wilkes Building, but that didn't mean the police weren't after her. That just meant that San Franciscans were incredibly jaded, or Sturgeon/Mickey/somebody had come up with an explanation for the explosion that didn't involve theft. Which made sense, since what she'd stolen from

Sturgeon had been stolen property and he wouldn't want that getting out.

People went to jail for things like that.

She'd chosen to grab a few hours' sleep before notifying the client (aka threatening criminal kidnapper) that she'd recovered the prototype, on the assumption that there was no telling when she might get the chance to sleep again. Once the client picked up the prototype, all bets were off. The thing was, the previous email from them had explicitly stated that delivery instructions would be forthcoming.

She preferred an arrangement where they picked up.

Choose your ground: it was another one of the rules.

If she allowed them to dictate the terms of a delivery, she had no doubt that she would be walking straight into a trap. True, the trap would be aimed at her father, but she was pretty sure that once she showed up with the prototype, they weren't going to just say *thanks* and *oops, our bad* and let her go. She would be detained, possibly killed, depending on who or what was behind this. And then she would be no help to Marin and Margery at all.

By placing the briefcase in the trunk of the Fiesta and telling them to come and get it, she stayed free. And while whoever showed up might be ticked that they hadn't succeeded in capturing her father, they would have to take the briefcase *somewhere*. Hopefully it would be back to wherever Marin and Margery were being held. If not, at least it would give her a place to start looking.

She no longer had any doubt at all that her father's so-secure-the-NSA-couldn't-hack-it email account had been penetrated by someone bent on tracking him down. Who, she wasn't quite sure. She would have immediately suspected Durand, except Mickey, whom she was ninety percent sure worked for him, had seemed to genuinely not know anything about the kidnapping of Marin and Margery. So, was there another player in the game?

Considering the number and resources of her father's enemies, the list of possibilities was long and frightening.

One thing she was convinced of: the company from which the prototype had been stolen had not hired her father to recover it. They had nothing to do with this, had probably never been a client of his and had no idea that anything out of the ordinary was going down. Sturgeon had hired Justin Lee to steal the prototype in good faith, and Lee had done what he'd been paid to do.

Thieves' honor being what it was, she would have sent the prototype back to Sturgeon, but she needed it to find Marin and Margery.

The crux of the matter was, the emails, the threats, the money, the kidnapping, had all originated from an entity bent on hunting her father down.

A rich, powerful, dangerous enemy.

That morning, before they'd left the hotel room to go steal a car, she'd had Doc email the client and tell them that the prototype had been acquired. The message had included the place and conditions of the pickup.

Their reply: Unacceptable.

Her response: Take it or leave it.

So here she sat, waiting for them to take it.

For all she knew, they were coming from halfway around the world, which could account for the delay.

But she didn't think so. If she'd managed to track the prototype to San Francisco, and Mickey had managed to track the prototype to San Francisco, she was willing to bet that whoever this was had done the same thing. Probably they'd been hanging around since before she got here just like Mickey, waiting for her father to show up.

A woman came out of the In–N–Out Burger slurping a soda through a straw. She stopped to say something to the man with her, then took little sips all the way across the parking lot until she walked right past Bianca in the rental car to dump what was left of her soda out in the grass.

Bianca watched the long spill of liquid from cup to grass and grimaced.

To hell with it. She couldn't wait any longer. She was going to roll the dice, take a chance, tempt fate.

She had to pee.

"We've got eyes on somebody we think might be the woman." The voice in Kemp's ear was terse. It belonged to one of his team, who'd been monitoring the parking lot of the hotel where they'd been told the object was available for pickup and the area immediately around it. The blue Ford Fiesta that held the recovered prototype had been identified four hours previously. They hadn't approached it, hadn't gone anywhere near it, for fear of spooking Thayer or his team. Their surveillance was carried out by drone.

"Where?" The hours-long wait without anything happening was making Kemp edgy. He was as certain as it was possible to be that Thayer was doing the exact same thing he was doing—keeping the object under surveillance to see who turned up—and would spot one of the team, or especially Kemp himself, no matter how careful they were. If that happened, Thayer might disappear for another twenty-two years. Or he might renew old acquaintances by reverting to the crack sniper he'd once been and pumping a bullet into Kemp's brain. Or both.

What Thayer didn't have that Kemp did was access to the full surveillance arsenal of the US government.

Thayer could stake out the Fiesta all day and never spot the eyes in the sky that were watching for him.

The voice in Kemp's ear said, "Going into the burger place two doors down from the hotel."

"What makes you think it's her?"

"She's wearing a hat and sunglasses, but we got a close-up on the jaw, mouth and nose and they seem to match. She's about the same age, height and build. She got out of a car in a nearby lot that's parked so that anyone inside it can see the Fiesta. The car's a rental, with tinted windows. We're checking with the rental company for information on the renter now."

"Get me a feed of her. What about Thayer?" His team of six crack operatives had been given access to Thayer's picture, age progressed, along with a rendering of what the little girl he'd failed to kill all those years ago might look like today. Of course, there was no guarantee that either image was accurate enough to be helpful. Long ago, when Kemp had known Thayer, he'd been a master of disguise.

Kemp was five miles away from the Vagabond Inn parking lot, alone in a fourth-floor hotel room behind a locked door.

The thought of Thayer in disguise still made him nervous. He caught himself glancing warily around.

Thayer would perceive the taking of his wife and daughter as an act of war and respond accordingly. Unless the man had changed personalities in the intervening years, Kemp expected nothing less than scorched earth.

The voice in his ear said, "No sign of him."

So where the hell was he?

It was a zero-sum game. Kemp knew Groton well enough to know that if he came up empty on Thayer, or the woman, he could kiss his future goodbye. Not just his job, and the richly deserved retirement he was looking forward to. His life.

Groton wouldn't hesitate to kill anybody he had to kill to save his own skin.

The monitor on the desk in front of him sprang to life. He watched a slim young woman in a black baseball cap, sunglasses, a cobalt-blue silk tee and loose black slacks cross the last few feet of a parking lot, step up on a sidewalk, then push through the door of a restaurant. A curly thatch of dark brown hair tumbled to her shoulders from beneath the baseball cap.

The hair didn't match, but he disregarded that. Hair was an easy change.

The angle of the shot was such that he got a profile only: nose, lips, chin.

His breathing quickened. It could be her.

"You send a still shot of her in for verification?" Kemp asked.

"We did."

"Good."

In the mountain aerie where these things were handled, a biometric program would at that moment be running a point by point comparison of nodal points between the woman's face and the age-progressed face they were working with. Anything to do with the eyes or ears, which were covered by her hair, wasn't going to work. But the width and length of the nose, the shape of the cheekbones, the length of the jawline, the distance between the nose and upper lip and the lower lip and tip of the chin, could be measured by computer.

The voice in his ear said, "Results are back. They're on the way to you right now."

"Thanks."

Kemp's jaw tightened as he read the message that appeared on the monitor. It said, Absent all required markers, identity match probability estimate is eighty percent.

That meant it was his call to make.

If he got it wrong, he was very much afraid he would pay with his life.

★ ★ ★

Bianca was halfway back to her car when she saw the Fiesta backing out of its parking space.

Her eyes widened.

"Oh, no," she said aloud. "Oh, no, no, no."

First, that old saw about the watched pot was evidently true. Six hours of inactivity, three minutes and—she glanced at her watch—twenty-two seconds in the bathroom, and stuff was going down.

Second, this particular stuff should not be happening.

Her instructions to the client had been to retrieve the key from beneath the car and get the briefcase from the trunk.

Not drive the car with the briefcase in it away.

Alarm quickened her pulse.

Either the client was doing something unexpected or whoever was driving the car was not the client.

What were the chances that the damned car was being stolen?

Poor, Bianca judged as she beeped the door on the rental car to unlock it, opened it and slid behind the wheel. Although she *had* left the key in the little magnetic box attached to the car frame. *She'd* known to check there when she'd been looking to steal a car with a key. The types of people who might actually steal a car? They knew that, too.

The Fiesta shifted into Drive and headed out of the lot.

Holy hell, what to do?

Her first instinct—race over there as fast as she could, block the Fiesta from leaving, bang on the driver's window and demand to know who they were and what they were doing—was obviously not the best course of action.

Her choices boiled down to sit tight or follow.

She went with follow. Just for a little way. Just until she could get a glimpse of the driver. She might be wrong, but she felt that any agent of the client's who'd come for the briefcase would look very different from a car thief.

Whipping out of the In–N–Out Burger parking lot, playing dodge-the-T-bone with oncoming vehicles, she saw that the Fiesta was already comfortably ahead on the Old Bayshore Highway heading away from the airport. Between shoppers patronizing the strip malls and fast-food restaurants and people traveling to and from the airport, there was a lot of traffic. Keeping an eye on the Fiesta while weaving in and out of cars whose drivers all seemed intent on changing lanes or turning left or slowing down for no discernible reason was nerve-racking.

All her training in escape and evasion driving had not prepared her for this.

"Who *are* you?" she asked the unknown driver aloud.

Didn't help. She still had no clue.

Being careful not to get too close, Bianca shortened the distance between them, finally settling in when she was tailing the Fiesta from eight cars back. The good news was, she didn't have to worry about losing it, at least not as long as the briefcase with the locator was in the trunk. But if the person behind the wheel was a car thief, probably just about the first thing he was going to do when he stopped was check the car for valuables. The briefcase in the trunk qualified as a valuable.

It could end up anywhere.

Instead of this ridiculous chase up the highway, it would probably be better to simply pull up beside the Fiesta and look in at the driver, Bianca decided. After all, unless the driver was Mickey—what were the chances?—he or she was not going to recognize her.

The problem with staying eight cars back was red lights. Running them to keep up wasn't good. It was the kind of thing that might attract cops, to say nothing of attention. Driving up through the turning lane in the middle and then cutting sharply in front of a line of cars waiting at the light so as not to lose her quarry, which she'd just done, was a good way to end up—

The sudden wail of a siren as she shot through the intersection against the light was the only warning she got. Turning her head sharply in the direction of the sound, Bianca saw an ambulance barreling into the intersection from a cross street too late to do anything about it.

She didn't even have time to stomp the gas in an effort to get out of the way.

The ambulance slammed into the side of the car with a screaming of metal and the crash of shattering glass.

Bianca was flung violently against the driver's-side window, hit her head in an explosion of light and pain, and knew no more.

23

The next thing Bianca was aware of was the prick of a needle sliding into her left arm. And a god-awful headache. And a smell—rubbing alcohol?—that was sharp and strong enough to make her wrinkle her nose.

She opened her eyes. The world around her tilted and shimmied. Blinking, she tried to bring it into focus.

She was lying on her back on a bed. Metal bed rails boxed her in on either side. A woman leaned over her. Late thirties, pixie-cut dark brown hair, sturdily built but not overweight. A stranger. She was wearing a light gray jumpsuit with some sort of pattern to it and blue rubber gloves. The gloves accounted for the weird plastic feeling of the hand that lightly clasped Bianca's arm. The woman's other gloved hand manipulated a syringe that was—Bianca grimaced—drawing several tubes of blood.

Glancing down at her arm where the blood was being taken, she saw the cobalt-blue sleeve of the silk T-shirt she had put on—when? She had no idea how much time had passed since she'd gotten dressed. Bianca frowned. As far as she could tell, she was wearing her own clothing, minus the shoes. No wig. She could see strands of her own blond hair. Was she in an emergency room, then? And nobody had yet gotten around to getting her into a hospital gown?

The woman must have felt her movement, because she glanced up then and their eyes met.

"You're awake."

Bianca said, "What happened?"

"You were in an accident."

Bianca remembered driving through the intersection against the light, the ambulance shrieking as it bore down on her, the impact. All of that came back to her in a flash as the woman finished drawing blood. Withdrawing the needle from her arm, the woman capped off the last of what Bianca saw were three vials full. Swabbing the tiny wound with alcohol, she applied a square of gauze and a Band-Aid to the inside of Bianca's elbow where the blood had been drawn. Then she reached across Bianca to hit a button on what seemed to be an intercom unit built into the wall.

"She's awake," she said into it.

"I'll be right there." It was a man's voice, rendered slightly staticky by the machine.

"This is a hospital?" Bianca asked. The woman shrugged.

If Bianca sounded uncertain, it was because the room didn't actually look like a hospital. It looked like...a bunker. The walls were gray poured concrete. The floor was gray poured concrete. The ceiling was gray poured concrete. Fluorescent lights recessed into the ceiling beneath black metal grids provided indifferent lighting. Two small rectangular windows were set high in the wall to her right. The light that filtered in through them was thin, gray and cold-looking. A work light on a six-foot-tall tripod was positioned near the bed for the obvious purpose of providing additional lighting as needed. It was currently turned off. The wall to her left seemed to be covered in photos of some sort. She couldn't get a good enough look at them to determine their subject. Besides a freestanding IV unit—was she hooked up to it? A glance confirmed that she was—and the mobile cart holding supplies, there was no medical equipment.

Plus she seemed to be in four-point restraints. The arm that blood had just been drawn from was secured by a three-inch-wide white webbing strap that circled her wrist like a cuff and was fastened to the bed by another strap that seemed to pass all the way around the mattress and beneath it to encompass the frame. The thin blue blanket that covered her to her armpits had been folded back on that side to allow blood to be drawn, so she could actually see the cuff. Two silver buckles on the outside of her wrist where it would be impossible for even the most flexible fingers to reach it cinched the cuff closed. She tried moving her other arm and then her legs for confirmation that they were similarly restrained.

They were. She was strapped to the bed.

Bianca was starting to get a bad feeling.

"Why am I in restraints?" Her voice was sharper. She still was not quite hitting on all mental cylinders, and the thought of being tethered to a bed gave her the willies.

"I'm really not authorized to answer questions."

The sharp snick of metal on metal had Bianca shooting a glance in the direction from which it came. Moving her head so quickly it hurt, she winced at the pain but resisted the urge to close her eyes. All at once it felt very important that she gather as much information as possible.

The sound came from a heavy-looking metal door set into a corner of the wall opposite the windows. She watched as it opened. Beyond it she caught a glimpse of a hallway, more poured concrete but a narrower space than the large room she was in and with more light. A man stepped through the doorway and into the room, commanding her full attention. He closed the door behind him, locking it with a key and the same sharp metallic sound that had preceded his entrance. He then dropped the key into the breast pocket of his shirt. As he turned into the room, she saw that he was sixty-ish, of average height and weight, maybe a little on the beefy side. He was wearing a white dress shirt and tan trousers along with a shoulder holster complete with a—she squinted—Beretta 96 tucked inside.

Okay, Toto, we're definitely not in Kansas anymore.

"How's she doing?" The man addressed the question to the woman.

"Once the sedation wears off, she'll be fine."

Sedation? Bianca's spidey-sense, already quivering, went into overdrive. The IV dripping into her arm suddenly seemed beyond sinister.

"Good. Let me know those results when you have them."

The woman nodded and moved toward the door, bearing the vials of blood and the used syringe away with her in a handheld plastic caddy. Bianca watched her open the door. She first had to unlock it with a key that hung with a bunch of others from a ring at her waist.

The woman left. The clink of the key in the lock—Bianca knew what the sound was now—told her that she had locked the door behind her.

This just kept getting better and better.

The man loomed above her, looking down into her face. "Hello, young lady."

"Who are you?" Bianca asked. Most of the mental fog that had afflicted her when she'd first woken up had been swept away by her growing alarm. She was aware enough now to be careful. She made her voice breathy, weak. The details of the situation might be murky, but the big picture was becoming increasingly clear. Short version was, she was in trouble. Faking helplessness was a classic defensive move. Practically the only one available to her at the moment.

"My name's John Kemp."

"Are you a doctor?"

He shook his head: *no.*

Kemp had a pair of iron-gray eyes that were bright with intelligence beneath drooping lids. His hair was gray, too, cut short and thinning on top. His features were irregular but not unattractive. His jaw was square and a little jowly. Deep lines bracketed his mouth, formed a web around his eyes. The interest with which he looked her over—Bianca found it unnerving.

She found *him* unnerving.

Let's see how hard it's going to be to get out of here.

"I can't move my arms and legs." She shifted restlessly, as if she were in discomfort. "Why are they tied down?"

"It's standard procedure while you're under sedation, I believe."

"Can you unfasten my arms?" Bianca asked. "Please?"

"Not now. That—" he nodded at the IV "—is a saline solution, to flush the sedative you were given from your body. Once that's done, we can talk about it."

"Why was I given a sedative?"

He said, "We thought it was best, to give you time to recover from the car crash. And to make the flight easier on you."

Oh, wow. She really didn't like the sound of that.

"Flight?" The quaver in her voice was easier to fake than it should have been. Something about the man made her skin crawl.

"The one from San Francisco to Heiligenblut." At what must have been the look on her face, Kemp added kindly, "Austria."

Austria. Holy freaking disaster. Bianca had a hideous feeling that she knew exactly who this guy was—the client. Aka the threatening criminal kidnapper, the unknown player in the game, the not-Durand entity bent on hunting her father down, the rich, powerful and dangerous enemy she'd suspected was lurking in the wings.

A jolt of adrenaline chased away the last vestiges of her disorientation. Her pulse quickened and her muscles tightened in readiness for...something. All of which she took care to conceal.

"Austria." She looked at him blankly, as if she'd never heard of the place.

"Yes. We staged the accident with your car, then brought you all the way to *Austria* because we want to ask you some questions about Mason Thayer. He goes by any number of other names, but I'm confident you know who I'm talking about."

He'd staged the accident? Of course. If his people had been in the ambulance, they could have scooped her right up without raising any eyebrows at all. If she'd had any time to consider what had happened, she would have seen it.

Little bubbles of panic started to percolate through her system at the thought of how well connected and powerful Kemp must be to have been able to pull something like that off. But she refused to panic; she never panicked, and she wasn't about to start now. She reached for the icy calm that always came over her in dire situations and, thankfully, felt it settling around her like a blanket. It was imperative that she keep her head in the game. She wasn't sure how much he knew, but he obviously was aware that she'd been babysitting the prototype if nothing else. He knew she had a connection to Mason Thayer. Denying it would be foolish, but there were other ways to get around answering.

"I don't understand—*Austria?* I was in *California.* You *staged* the wreck...?" She let her eyes go slightly unfocused and then allowed her eyelids to droop. Snapping them open again as if she were trying her best to stay awake, she added in a faint, fretful voice, "This isn't making any sense. I...I can't think. My head hurts so badly. *Oh.*" That last was a moan, uttered as she closed her eyes.

He leaned over her. Inwardly she recoiled. But all he did was punch a button on the intercom.

"Yes, sir?" The female voice that answered almost certainly belonged to the woman who'd drawn her blood.

"How much longer until this damned stuff is totally out of her system?"

"With the saline running? Probably not more than another fifteen minutes."

"Do you have any results for me yet?"

"Not yet, sir."

"Let me know the moment you do."

His hand dropped away from the intercom as he straightened to look down at her. Bianca's lids were cracked open the teeniest bit, not enough so that he could tell, just enough to keep tabs on him, to see the way he was looking at her. No way could she make herself close her eyes all the way and go totally blind in his presence. Having him so close made every nerve she possessed jangle. It was as if her body could sense danger like an electrical charge. Under the current circumstances, though, there was absolutely nothing she could do about it.

A tremor of dread ran through her. She didn't fear often, and she didn't fear much. But somehow, in the scant few minutes he'd been in the room, this man had managed to touch a well of horror buried deep inside her that she'd never even suspected was there.

She drew in a soft, untroubled breath, as if she were falling asleep.

"I'll be back in fifteen minutes," he said.

To her enormous relief, he turned and left the room, locking the door behind him.

All righty, then. Get on with it.

She didn't even have to think about what course of action to take. Lying there strapped to a bed and waiting to see what fate or Kemp had in store for her was a nonstarter.

Whatever it took, she was getting out of there. Figuring out what to do when she was away from this place could wait until she was away from this place. The thought that Marin and Margery might be being held somewhere inside this same building gave her pause, but not for long. She had no idea of the size of the structure, the number of people inside, how many were armed, how fortified it was. She had no idea if Marin and Margery were even there. It was like the airplane guidelines for using oxygen: she had to save herself first, then work on saving them.

Her body was tense, bristling with alarm, with the need to act. She forced herself to remain motionless except for her eyes, which she slowly opened. First things first: scan the room for signs of remote surveillance.

There didn't seem to be any cameras. Given the stark nature of her surroundings, the only place to hide one would be in the overhead lights or the intercom, and she could find no sign of a camera in either place. Craning her neck, she assessed the photos on the wall. They seemed to be head-and-shoulder shots of people, with photos of infants paired with those of adults. The photos were numbered, but what interested her was that they were flat and seemed to be affixed to the wall with tape. There was no place among them to hide a camera.

The next thing she needed to do was get out of the restraints.

Not as easy as one might suppose. She wasn't wearing her watch; she'd had it on at the time of the accident, so she could only speculate that either she'd lost it or it had been taken from her. The relevant thing about no watch was, she had no way to judge the time.

Her best estimate was, one minute had already elapsed of her fifteen. And it was always possible that Kemp would return early.

She hadn't worn one of her garter belts when she'd left the hotel to go on surveillance detail, so she had no tools with her. Not that she would have been able to access them, anyway, tethered as she was, so she supposed it really didn't matter for this particular task.

Being careful not to make any kind of move that might cause the restraints around her wrists and ankles to tighten, she looked down at her left wrist. It was circled by a shackle of white canvas webbing of the type used in straitjackets. To test it, she wiggled her fingers, jiggled her wrist around.

It was loose enough so that she could move her wrist up and down inside it.

She *really* hated doing what she was about to do.

Gritting her teeth, she slammed her left hand hard against the metal bed rail and dislocated her thumb. The popping sound alone had once been enough to make her feel faint. Her father had made her practice doing it enough when she was young so that it no longer did.

But God, it still hurt.

"One day being able to do this may save your life," her father had told her when she'd cried and vomited the first time he had deliberately dislocated her thumb and shown her what it allowed her to do. She'd been ten years old.

He'd forced her to practice until she could dislocate her thumb herself without feeling sick and without tears.

Always on her left hand, which preserved the structural integrity and strength of her right hand and made the gruesome task that much easier to do, because the joint became more elastic with each repetition.

Today just might be that day her father had been talking about, Bianca reflected. Sweat beaded her forehead and her pulse rate shot through the roof, but she was able to worm her left hand out of the restraint.

Popping her thumb back into place hurt almost more than forcing it out.

But once it was done, the pain subsided to a dull ache and she was able to unstrap her right hand and then her ankles.

Ha! She was free. She slid off the bed.

For a moment after her bare feet touched down on the cold concrete, her legs wobbled. Her head swam. And ached. Her left hand hurt. She leaned against the bed for support, lifted a hand to check out her head.

As she had suspected, she had a bump just above her left temple. It was tender to the touch.

Get over yourself. Get it together.

Taking a deep breath, she did.

First, she turned off the drip on the IV. Then she lifted the tape on her arm and pulled the small needle from her vein. After she got back in bed, she would tape the dislodged needle to her arm. When the time came to move, she couldn't afford to be tethered to an IV unit.

Next she took care to refasten the restraints so that they were loose enough to allow her to get her hands and feet in and out of them with ease. Then she sabotaged the buckles so that they couldn't be undone and refastened. The last thing she wanted to have happen was for her to be lying there pretending to be strapped to the bed and have Kemp or someone decide to tighten the restraints and make her pretense a reality.

A glance up at the windows had already told her that she probably wasn't getting out of them, not in the amount of time she had to work with. They were too small, the glass was thick and they were barred from the outside.

Just to make sure, she climbed up to stand on the bed and looked at the closest one more carefully. Her breath caught when she realized that what she was looking at was bullet-proof glass. She wasn't breaking out through that, and no one was breaking in.

The view outside the window made her stomach twist. A gray day, cold-looking, light, blowing snow. A mountain vista. Jagged blue peaks wreathed in clouds falling away into the distance. *Austria*—the thought blew her mind. She seemed to be on the second floor of a building that was perched on the side of a mountain. It was situated just below the tallest of the peaks but above the drifting blanket of clouds. The ground sloped away from the side of the building she was looking out from. Snow covered everything—the ground, the few evergreens she could see, the bump of what she thought might be a low wall or fence. It piled in tall drifts around an outbuilding. As she watched, a snowmobile came into view, swooping around a corner of the building, then rocketing away down the slope. The man driving it wore a black ski suit with a gray stocking cap pulled down low over his ears. An assault rifle—she was too far away to tell which one—hung across his back.

The door was a better bet.

It was locked. She was almost one hundred percent sure.

Moving like the fog on little cat feet, she jumped down from the bed, rushed to the door and carefully tried the knob, just in case.

Yeah, no such luck. It was locked, with a formidable, military-grade double dead bolt. With a little time and a tool or two, she could defeat it.

She had neither time nor tool.

Ticktock, she reminded herself and looked swiftly around the room for anything that she could turn to her advantage.

Her best bet was to get back in bed, pretending to be groggy and weak and helplessly strapped down, then at the first opportunity jump up and overpower whoever was in the room with her.

The plan had a few weak points. First, Kemp was armed. If

she struck fast enough, and with enough ferocity, though, she was confident she could neutralize and take possession of the weapon before he could use it on her. Second, she was assuming only one person would be in the room with her, probably Kemp, possibly the woman. Even Kemp and the woman together should be doable. But what if there were more, a couple of guards, maybe, or—well, who knew?

Another weak point was, where did she go after she got out of the room? She had no idea of the layout of the building, how far outside civilization the building was located, etc.

For both of those, the only solution she could come up with was *Wing it.*

A third weak point was that she would be launching her attack from the bed, where she would be lying flat on her back. And no matter how quickly she moved, it would take her a few seconds to get out of the restraints.

When attacking a physically larger, armed opponent, the element of surprise was crucial.

First things first: what she needed was a distraction that would give her time to launch an attack.

In what was basically a concrete box with a bed, a medical supply cart that—she went through it quickly—contained nothing more than gauze pads, Band-Aids, surgical tape, a slender Bic pen and a plastic bottle of isopropyl alcohol, an IV unit, a work light and dozens of paper photos taped to a wall, there weren't a lot of options. The pen was a possible weapon. So was the alcohol, providing she wanted to throw it in someone's eyes. The IV tubing or the cords on the IV unit or the light could possibly be used as a garrote—

The light. She could use the light.

Snatching up the pen and the alcohol, she turned to the work light on the tripod that stood near the bed. Ever conscious of the minutes ticking away, she used the pen to chip off a small hole in the top corner of the rectangular pane of frosted glass covering the light bulb. Then she stripped out the inner workings of the pen until all she had left was the casing, which at that point became a hollow tube with a hole in each end. Using the casing as a funnel, she poured several ounces of alcohol into the light, then sealed the hole with a piece of surgical tape.

When the light was turned on, it should take only a couple of minutes for the bulb to heat up enough to ignite the alcohol.

Then—*boom*.

She had her distraction.

If Kemp didn't seem inclined to turn on the light, she would complain that she couldn't see.

She was returning the alcohol to the supply cart when the pen, which she had pocketed for possible use as a weapon as needed, fell out of the pocket of her loose black pants and rolled across the floor.

She ran after it. It came to rest against the wall with the photos. Bending down to scoop it up, she happened to glance at the pictures.

Four photos in a line: full face and profile infant, full face and profile adult.

Row after row of them.

Male and female, infants no more than a few weeks old, adults in possibly their midtwenties.

In the profile pictures, both infants and adults alike each had a number seemingly tattooed on his or her neck. The infant and adult photos displayed side by side had the same number, although the tattoo appeared much smaller in the adult. It seemed clear that the photos were of the same individual, first as a baby and then all grown up, and that the individuals had been marked shortly after birth with a number.

Who would do that? And why?

The numbers ran in order, from one to forty-eight.

Bianca was turning away even as her gaze skimmed the wall.

Until she saw something among the photos that stopped her cold.

Her own face.

24

She was in one of the photos.

Bianca stared, riveted.

It was her, all right. At least, the adult picture was. Her, with no makeup and her hair pulled back from her face and—here her hand rose to touch the scar beneath her jaw—the number 44 tattooed high up on the side of her neck.

Just below her jaw.

Where her scar was.

Bianca's stomach went into free fall. She looked disbelievingly from the picture of the infant, round-faced and blue-eyed, with a cap of downy blond hair, the number 44 tattooed maybe an inch below her small ear, to the picture of herself with the same tattoo, shrunken and blurred by the passage of the intervening years.

Beneath her fingers, her scar felt puckered and hard.

What the *hell*?

Her mind bounced from some kind of psychological ploy getting ready to be tried on her, to a possible doppelgänger, to...to...God knew what.

She didn't have time to think about it. Whatever this was, whatever it meant, she had a more urgent problem to deal with.

She had to get back in bed and get situated before anyone came.

She did, taping the IV needle down, pulling the blue blanket back over herself, inserting her hands and feet into the restraints. She practiced, just to be sure. Yes, she could get out of the shackles in a matter of seconds.

Then she lay there, waiting.

Her attention returned to the wall of pictures.

She looked at her own picture first. There were, she was relieved to see, some slight differences between her actual self and the photo. Her lips were fuller in real life than in the picture. Her eyes were a lighter, brighter shade of blue. Her cheeks were thinner, her cheekbones higher. And she definitely didn't have the number 44 tattooed beneath her jaw.

Although she had the scar.

In that exact spot.

Her heart thumped.

Then she realized that what she was looking at wasn't a real-life photo at all.

It was an age-progressed, computer-generated image. Extrapolated from the photo of the infant.

Was that baby *her*?

She'd never seen baby pictures of herself. If any had ever existed, they hadn't survived her transition to Bianca St. Ives.

Her pulse pounded. Her mouth went dry. Her hands curled into fists.

She didn't know what this was.

But she had a terrible feeling that it was something bad.

The snick of metal on metal warned her that her time was up.

She tensed, then forced herself to go all limp and boneless.

Kemp walked into the room. He immediately glanced her way and seemed to relax the tiniest little bit when he saw that she was still in the position in which he'd left her.

Watching him, she felt cold to her bone marrow.

He was closing the door when she heard it: the voice of a little girl crying out, "Mummy! Mummy, no! I don't want to—"

The door settled into the jamb, cutting off the rest.

Marin. Bianca tensed all over again. Marin and Margery were here. And close. Given the building's concrete construction, that was the only way she would have been able to hear Marin so clearly. The child had to have been out in the hallway, or else she and Margery were being kept in a room along this same corridor and the door to the room they were in had been open at the same time Kemp had entered.

Either way, their presence changed the situation, both simplifying and complicating it. She knew where they were, knew that they were alive and well, which was a tremendous relief. But escaping all by herself was going to be hard. Taking them with her would be infinitely harder.

She wanted to ask about them, but revealing her interest in their whereabouts would be a mistake, she knew. It would be too easy for Kemp to have them moved.

"I want to know where Thayer is," Kemp said. Bianca had been so distracted by the discovery that her sister and stepmother were close by that she hadn't noticed him moving until he was practically standing over her. One thick hand curled around the guardrail as he stopped beside the bed to look down at her.

There would be time to worry about getting to Marin and Margery later. For now, she had to focus on taking care of Kemp.

For starters, she wanted to make him think that she was prepared to cooperate with him.

Tell the truth—until you can't. That was straight from How to Lie Convincingly 101, courtesy of her father.

"He's dead." She kept her voice small, submissive.

Kemp's hand tightened on the rail. "You can drop the pretense. I'm not buying it."

"It's the truth." If possible, her voice was even smaller than before. Her eyes slid, for no more than a fraction of a second,

to the weapon in his shoulder holster. Could she free herself
from the restraints, spring from the bed and grab it, perhaps
administering a disabling chop or two along the way?

No. Not with an acceptable degree of certainty. He was looking right at her. He would see her coming in time to react. At
some point he would move away, turn his back—or she would
ask him to turn on the light. Either it was getting close to twilight or a storm was approaching. The light coming through the
windows was taking on a purplish cast. Turning on the light
would be a natural-sounding request.

Patience, grasshopper.

Kemp said, "You've lived with him all your life."

Bianca had to work to keep her face impassive. Not exactly
true, but close enough. What made him think that? Did that
mean he knew that she was her father's daughter?

He continued. "You know where he is." He leaned over
the bed, his face coming so close to hers that she would have
shrunk back—or punched him in the nose—if she'd been capable of either. *"Tell me."*

She made her eyes huge, her lips quiver. "Really. He's dead."

Kemp straightened as if she'd spat at him. His eyes went hard
and cold. His mouth contorted. "Don't lie to me. I can make
you tell me the truth, but you won't like how I do it."

Bianca believed him. Her insides twisted. Her mouth went
dry.

As much as she hated to face it, the fact was that in some
deep, atavistic, primordial part of herself, she was deathly afraid
of this man. She, who was never afraid of anything.

The intensity of her fear puzzled her. It made her angry.
Quickly she lowered her lids so he wouldn't see the emotions
blazing from her eyes.

The intercom buzzed, drawing Kemp's attention. He leaned
across her to punch the button.

She had to suppress a shudder of revulsion at his nearness.

"Yes?" His tone as he spoke into the intercom was impatient.

"We have the test results, sir. They're perfect. A score of one hundred percent."

"Ah." It was a sound of satisfaction. "Thank you."

He straightened and looked down at Bianca. He seemed to be closely examining her features. Then he nudged her chin to one side with his knuckles.

He was looking at her scar.

The tiny hairs on the back of her neck shot upright.

She jerked her chin away from his hand.

The picture, the tattoo, the scar, his reaction—something was up. Something big. Something she didn't want to know. She could feel it in her bones.

She hated being afraid. She *refused* to be afraid.

"What test results? And why is my picture on your wall?" Okay, that didn't exactly sound like the frail feminine flower she'd been portraying. But she couldn't help it. She had to take back that part of herself that never cowered away from anything—or anyone.

He gave a grunt that wasn't quite amusement and glanced at the pictures.

"How much did Thayer tell you about the Nomad Project?"

She was feeling her way here, but she didn't like the idea of admitting the truth: her father had never said one word about it. "Not a lot."

"You're part of it. You're Nomad 44."

Bianca thought of the number 44 tattoo on the picture that looked like her and on the corresponding infant and felt goose bumps ripple over her skin.

"What does that mean?"

"The Nomad Project was brilliant. Brilliant in concept, brilliant in execution. And it was—and is—badly needed. Human frailty is the biggest weakness on the battlefield, you know. If we could make soldiers stronger, more athletic, smarter, give them more stamina—well, that would give our armed forces a tremendous edge. Our scientists came up with a way to do it, got the funding, got the go-ahead and started the Nomad Project. Then somebody in DARPA blabbed to somebody on the National Research Council about it, and they got a burr up their ass about biomedical ethics and what would Congress think and killed it."

Bianca didn't like where this was going. She wet her lips. "Killed it?"

"The program. And the fruits of the program. Forty-seven out of forty-eight genetically enhanced test subjects ended up being destroyed. That's one reason I'm finding you so interesting. You're proof positive that what our scientists were doing was right on the money. The process worked." He crossed to the wall and tapped her picture. "We checked your blood—not an anomaly anywhere. You're flawless. Look at these pictures. You look exactly like you were supposed to. That's how all these subjects would have turned out. What a waste."

Bianca thought of the forty-eight pictures on the wall and felt cold sweat pop out around her hairline.

"Are you saying that all those people—" She broke off. What she suspected was so horrible she couldn't put it into words. It was nothing less than mass murder.

"That's exactly what I'm saying. *You* are the sole survivor of a program that was so far beyond top secret that the government doesn't even have an acronym for how classified it was. Only a very small number of people still alive know anything about it. The staff here? They have no idea that it ever existed, much less that you are what's left of it." He shook his head. "All these years, and Thayer never told you. I guess I shouldn't be surprised. Since he kept you with him when he ran, probably would have been a little bit awkward to tell you he'd originally been sent out to track you down and kill you."

"My father was sent out to kill me?" She'd just spilled the beans about who she was, but she was so stunned she didn't even care.

"Your father?" Kemp gave her a sharp look. "Is that what he told you? Mason Thayer isn't your father. He is—well, was, back in the day—a deep-cover assassin who was deployed to track you and the woman who ran away with you down and kill you both. Only, he failed to do it. Oh, he said he completed the assignment, but he lied. He was actually hiding and protecting you and the woman. Sleeping with her, too, of course. So the agency had to send someone else to do the job."

Bianca had a brief, terrible flashback to the night her mother died. The remembered pain and horror clutched at her heart.

"She wasn't a job." Her voice was fierce. "She was my mother."

"No," Kemp said. "She wasn't. Not your biological mother, at any rate. She was no more than your gestational mother, a rented womb who answered an ad in her college paper and came to work for the Nomad Project in return for a nice salary and the promise of a full ride back at college when the job was done. If she hadn't run away with you, you never would have known a thing about her. You and the other Nomads, had everything gone as planned, would have been sent to a special training facility and raised from infancy on as the supersoldiers you were meant to be."

"Supersoldiers—" Bianca couldn't finish. Mentally she was reeling. Her chest felt tight. Her heart pounded. Her pulse raced. The worst thing about it was, she didn't disbelieve him. If she looked at her life through the prism of what he was telling her, it all made a hideous kind of sense.

Didn't matter. She felt as if she were bleeding to death inside.

"The purpose of the Nomad Project was to make supersoldiers with the goal of giving us an invincible military. Like those of the other Nomads, your parents were selected from a bank of sperm and egg deposits donated by some of our finest military heroes. You were created in a test tube. Then Nomad Project scientists used what they called molecular scissors and cut and pasted in specific genetic modifications on our army's wish list—enhanced strength, enhanced intelligence, enhanced stamina. Athleticism. Fighting ability. A gift for languages. The list was long, and I don't remember most of it. But you're the result."

"No." The idea was too horrifying. Bianca couldn't wrap her mind around it.

"Yes. You should be proud. You're a living example of exactly what our scientists set out to do. They *succeeded*."

Whoopee. They succeeded—and she was what, Frankenstein? Or rather, the monster. She shuddered. Openly. Ordinarily she never showed weakness, but she was so overwhelmed she seemed to have lost all her self-protective instincts.

"Am I human?" She looked at him numbly.

"You're entirely human."

"What happened to the women? The other…gestational mothers?"

"When the project was terminated, they had to be terminated, too. It was unfortunate, but there was such an outcry at the time about human embryo experimentation that taking the chance that one of them would break their nondisclosure agreement and leak what they'd been involved with seemed entirely too risky."

"Is that why you're hunting my—" Oh, God, he wasn't her father. She felt like she was teetering on the brink of this huge chasm that had just opened up beneath her feet. "Thayer? Because he knows too much about your Nomad Project?"

"That's why I'm hunting him, yes. Others want him for other

reasons. I thought he'd show up here to retrieve his daughter. He hasn't yet."

It took Bianca a moment to realize he was talking about Marin, not her.

"Maybe that's because he's dead."

"I don't think so. Maybe he's smart enough to know his family's dead no matter what he does." His expression changed. Bianca could almost see the calculations going on behind his eyes. She was engaging in calculations of her own. He'd said Marin and Margery were dead no matter what Thayer did. There was no longer any question: she was going to have to get them out. "I brought you here with the intention of forcing you to tell me where Thayer is and then killing you. Cleaning up an old mess, in a way. You're living proof of an experiment that the powers that be want to forget ever happened. But now—I think we might be able to use you. Study you. Let you serve as a template for another, future Nomad Project. Maybe even put you in the field, once we've learned all we can from you." He looked at her thoughtfully, as if she were a bug he'd been about to crush underfoot but was starting to find interesting. "It seems a shame to destroy what we spent so much time and effort to create. The truth about what you are could never be allowed to be known beyond our small circle, of course, at least not for many years, but if you work with us—"

He was interrupted by a crackle of static from the intercom.

"Sir? Mr. Groton has arrived."

"Kemp? Where are you?" A man's voice replaced the woman's. Even over the intercom it sounded autocratic, like he was accustomed to being in charge.

Kemp stared at the intercom as if undecided for a moment, and Bianca got the impression that he was thinking hard. Then he leaned forward and pushed the button.

"I'm on the second floor. Room 203. Come on up. I have somebody with me you might find interesting."

"Not Thayer."

"No." He glanced at Bianca. "Do you still go by Beth?"

Beth? She'd only gone by Beth when she was a little girl living in Wisconsin with her mother. The memory was still hazy. How had he—

She nodded. Her gaze fixed on his face.

He said into the intercom, "Her name's Beth."

"How have you not taken care of that yet?" The voice was impatient, irritable. "Letting her live once was a mistake. Doing it twice is a decision."

Kemp's face tightened. She almost got the impression that he was afraid.

"Come up and see for yourself," he said and stepped away from the intercom.

Bianca shivered a little as cold chills raced over her skin. He'd called her Beth. His friend, boss, whatever, had said, *Letting her live once was a mistake.* From the moment he'd come near her, she'd reacted to his presence like a sparrow to a hawk.

She stared at him, and the world seemed to tilt on its axis.

"I remember you now," Bianca said, wanting proof for her theory. "You walked through my house calling my name, all those years ago in Wisconsin."

"You were a smart one. You hid. Where were you, by the way?"

"Does it matter?" The sturdy metal cabinet she'd been hiding in had protected her from the blast, which had sent it hurtling through the air and away from the subsequent raging fire. She remembered the shock and terror she'd felt as the world had exploded around her, remembered instinctively curling into as tight a ball as possible as she was launched skyward. She remembered crying out for her mother—

Keep emotion out of it: that was another of the rules.

To hell with that. She made no attempt to stem the hatred that swamped her as she looked at him.

"No, I don't suppose it does." He was beside the lamp, bending over as he reached for the toggle on the cord. "It's too dark in here. Why don't we turn on this light so that Groton can get a real look at you?"

The lamp came on. With one hand on the tripod, he turned toward her, adjusting its position so that the light fell directly on the bed.

Bianca waited and breathed.

Boom.

She was on him in an instant, plunging the hard plastic pen deep into his carotid artery.

25

Kemp didn't scream. He squeaked, started to clap a hand to his neck, started to totter sideways, then grabbed on to the bed and leaned against it and went completely still.

Smart man.

"You move, you're dead," Bianca warned him, holding the pen steady in his neck. She stood behind him, her body close against his as she steadied him until he got used to the idea that one wrong move meant he would die. She wanted to make sure he understood his situation. He was breathing so heavily that his whole body heaved with the force of it. With her other hand she yanked his pistol from its holster, thrust it into the front waistband of her pants. "I've punctured the outside wall of your carotid artery with an ink pen. I can feel the back of it against the tip of the pen. If I puncture that back wall, you're dead. If I pull the pen out of the hole in your neck, you're dead. You'll bleed out in about two minutes either way, nothing any-one can do. Oh, and I took the insides out, so the pen's hollow. I have my thumb over the end of it, or your blood would already be shooting out like a fountain. Thing is, my thumb's prone to getting cramps."

"You'll be sorry." His voice was punctuated with those heavy breaths.

Being a supersoldier means never having to say you're sorry. Okay, she was officially shell-shocked. Her mind was going places it had never gone before.

"I don't think so."

"I was going to let you live."

"You killed my mother. Be glad I'm letting you live. For now." Bianca plucked his key from his pocket, then twined the hand that wasn't holding the pen through the back of his belt. "We're going to walk out of here together, you and I. You're going to take me to Marin and Margery Humphries, and then you're going to get us some transportation out of here. And you're going to tell anybody we come across to stay the hell back, because if I get shot, if I get grabbed, if I stumble, if I so much as twitch wrong, you're dead." She paused to let that sink in. "Understand?"

"There's no transportation. Helicopter...dropped us off. Won't be back until I call."

"Move. Toward the door. Very carefully." She steered him around with her hand in his belt. They started walking. "So call."

"Phone's...on the first floor. No cell signal this high up."

Bianca thought about going to wherever the phone was, thought about waiting for him to call and a helicopter to show. No telling how many armed individuals between here and there. Plenty of opportunity for somebody to get stupid, or for something to go wrong. Plenty of opportunity for wherever they were holed up waiting for the chopper to get surrounded and cut off. Plenty of opportunity for the word to get out, and the chopper to end up as a no-show. Or if the thing did show, for it to get shot down.

By herself, she might have made another choice. But she couldn't chance taking a kid out in the snow and cold and trying to get off the mountain. If a chopper was the only transportation there was, she was going to have to wait for the chopper.

Probably she would need more hostages to hold off any sabotage attempts, and to travel in the helicopter with them, in case something should go wrong with Kemp.

Like a stumble. Or a sneeze.

Because of her bare feet, she had to be careful not to step on any of the glass pebbles scattered across the floor as a result of the exploding light. She needed shoes; a glance at Kemp's confirmed that they were way too big. In them she would be clumsy, prone to tripping over her own feet. At some point that might be the best she could do, but not yet.

They reached the door without incident. She unlocked it, opened it, and together they stepped out into the hall. No one in sight.

Her heart should have been beating a mile a minute. Her pulse should have been racing.

They weren't.

She'd gone into warrior mode, stone-cold.

"We're walking sideways," she told him. That was so she could keep both ends of the hall in sight while keeping her grip on the pen. The hall was maybe sixty feet long, poured concrete like the room they'd just left, three metal doors to the left, two to the right on the side they'd just emerged from, the same number—six—on the side opposite. Down staircases at both ends of the hall. No windows. Light from overhead fluorescents.

Kemp was sweating now. She could see the droplets beading on the sides of his face, feel the heat coming through his clothes. She could feel the stickiness of his blood seeping out around the pen against the heel of her hand. She could smell it—raw meat.

The sound the blown light had made—had it been heard beyond the room? If so, they wouldn't be alone for long. Plus there was Kemp's intercom exchange with Groton, who should be on his way to join them.

"Careful," she cautioned Kemp, who seemed to be sagging

at the knees. Blood loss was not a problem; she had the hole in his neck plugged up. Shock was. "You know where Marin and Margery Humphries are. Take me to them. And you don't want to mess with me, because it would be easy for me to decide I could make it out better on my own."

"They're in there." He stopped outside a door, leaned a hand against the wall. He was trembling now. Bianca wasn't sure how much longer he was going to be able to keep moving. But she'd told the truth. If she took the pen out of his neck, or let go of it, he was dead.

"Are they alone?" she asked.

"Don't know."

"Same key unlock all the doors?"

"Yes."

She handed him the key. "Unlock the door. Open it. Say, 'It's Kemp,' as we step inside."

That way, if anyone besides Marin and Margery was in the room, at least she'd have a moment to do something about it—like shoot them. The reason she was having Kemp do the unlocking and the pushing-the-door-open thing was because she now had his Beretta in her free hand.

"Be careful," she warned him. "You don't want me to lose my grip."

He unlocked the door, pushed it open, said, "It's Kemp."

The overhead lights were off. With only the gray light of the two small windows for illumination, the room appeared cold and gray. Marin and Margery, looking terrified, sat on the edge of a cot against the left wall. They huddled together with their arms around each other. The mother bent protectively over the daughter as, moving in tandem, Kemp and Bianca stepped inside. The door started to swing shut behind them. Marin whimpered; the fierce *"Shh"* that followed presumably came from Margery.

There was a flurry of movement in the corner behind the door.

"*Freeze.*" Bianca snapped the pistol toward the corner, cross-body, ready to fire at the shadowy figure that, fortunately for whoever it was, froze. Her movements were restricted because of her need to keep a grip on the pen, but not so restricted she couldn't have gotten off a shot. Or three.

"Ah," Kemp moaned, clutching at his neck, at the same time as Marin whimpered, "Mummy, I'm scared," and her mother said, "Hush."

"*Bianca.*"

The most welcome voice in the world, chock-full of pleased surprise. Bianca looked at the man who stepped out of the dark corner into the meager natural light and felt as if a great weight had been lifted off her chest.

Her father was alive.

She discovered that she wasn't even all that surprised. He always had been one to land on his feet.

Richard St. Ives—no, Mason Thayer—had movie-star good looks, if the movie star was in his midsixties with a few wrinkles and thick silver hair. He had blue eyes, high cheekbones, a long, straight nose, well-cut lips, a square chin. He was six foot one, with a slim, elegant build. Bianca had always thought she looked like him.

Nope.

She almost said, *Dad,* before she remembered that he wasn't.

The sudden hollowness in the pit of her stomach was a stark reminder of how much everything had changed.

"Mason Thayer, right?" was how she greeted him instead, because showing emotion had never been what they did. She thrust the Beretta back into the waistband of her slacks. "And here was I thinking you were dead."

He was wearing a ski parka, boots, gloves, and he smelled of fresh air and the outdoors. The weapon he'd slung over his shoulder upon recognizing her was a submachine gun. A machine pistol hung over his other shoulder. From the looks of him—his shoulders were wet with what was presumably melted snow—he had arrived scant moments before she and Kemp had stepped through the door.

She couldn't help it. Despite everything, she was really glad to see him.

"Long story," he responded, as if the ordeal he'd put her through was no big deal. "Short version is, the only way you ever get away from them is to die."

"You could have filled me in on the whole test-tube thing," she said.

He looked at her, and she could see the truth of what she'd been told in his face. She hadn't even realized that she'd been cherishing a tiny little sliver of hope that the story was a lie until it died.

"Strictly need-to-know. And you didn't." At his brusque reply Bianca felt a stab of hurt, a flicker of anger, and pushed both aside in favor of focusing on the urgency of the here and now. His gaze shifted to Kemp, who was partially turned away from him. "What's this, the catch of the day?"

"Daddy." Marin drew his attention by breaking away from her mother to run to him, throwing her arms around him, hugging his legs. Bianca looked down at her little sister—no, not little sister—this child she'd *thought* was a sister, and felt another twinge, this time of emptiness. "I want to go home."

Watching her not-father hug her not-sister and say something comforting to her, it hit Bianca, forcefully, that she was once again on the outside looking in. She had no one and nothing of her own.

Pity party at seven. Emergency confab for now.

"You have transportation?" she asked Mason (calling her erstwhile father by that name was going to take some getting used to, but apparently that was his name and she couldn't call him Dad anymore).

"Chopper. ETA fifteen minutes. East slope."

That was the best news Bianca had heard in a while.

"I need shoes," Bianca told him. "And a coat."

He glanced at her bare feet. "There were piles of boots by the door I came in through. You can grab some on the way out. A bunch of coats hanging there, too."

Marin looked around at her. The little girl's round-cheeked face was pale and streaked with dried tears. Her hair had been finger-combed and plaited into a single braid that hung down her back, presumably by Margery.

"What happened to your shoes?" Marin asked.

Bianca met wide blue eyes. "I lost them."

"I'd get in trouble if I lost my shoes."

"Stay with Mummy." Mason gave the kid a gentle shove in her mother's direction. To Margery, he said, "Bundle her up. We've got to go."

"Edward, who is this?" Even as Marin ran into her arms, Margery was looking at Bianca. Her expression was wary. Well, fair enough, Bianca thought. It probably wasn't every day that her husband teamed up with a young blonde who was armed with a pistol and was leading a bleeding man around by a skewer in his neck.

Plus Margery was probably traumatized from the kidnapping.

Mason said, "Margery, Marin, this is Bianca. She's...a friend."

Okay, that hurt, too.

"I need to sit down." Kemp tottered a little. His voice was weak, strained. Bianca could feel the rapid pulsing of his neck beneath her hand. More blood leaked out around the pen.

Bianca said, "You can't. We're heading out."

"I have to." His knees sagged. He sank to the floor, first kneeling, then sinking back on his haunches with his hands

braced on his thighs. Hanging on to the pen, cursing silently—
she didn't want to curse in front of Marin—Bianca shifted po-
sitions along with him. She'd meant the thumb-cramp thing as
a taunt, but turned out it was a real problem and her position
was starting to get untenable.

"John Kemp." Mason drew the name out. He walked around
in front of the man as he seemed to recognize Bianca's prisoner
for the first time. Across the room, Margery zipped Marin into
a coat. The sound caused Bianca to glance their way. Marin's
back was to their gruesome little tableau with Kemp. Bianca
thought Margery had turned her daughter away from it deliberately. "Long time no see."

"Thayer." Kemp's voice was labored.

"Flying pretty high these days, I hear," Mason said. His voice
was soft. Bianca suspected he didn't want Marin to overhear.
"Apparently killing women and children does wonders for the
career."

"How are you alive? Twenty-two years ago, I damned well
blew off your head."

"You screwed up. See, I got word that somebody was coming for me. I thought they might try to take me out on that
long, lonely drive from the airport, so I picked up a hitchhiker,
let him drive, rode ducked low in the passenger's seat. We get
close to the house, I see flames shooting up everywhere. I tell
him to punch it, he does. We get to the house. He jumps out
the driver's-side door, I roll out the passenger's side. He gets
his head blown off. I don't." As he looked down at Kemp, his
eyes were blocks of blue ice. "Your bad."

"You should have done your job."

"You kidnapped my family. My little girl. You knew I'd
come."

"I did. I wanted you to come. I put the word out through all our old sources. I made it so easy for you to find us, I practically painted a Day-Glo path to this place."

It was obvious to Bianca that Kemp thought he was done for. His defiance in the face of his growing distress told the tale. He was pale and sweating, and shaking in long tremors. Enough blood had leaked out from under her hand to turn the shoulder of his shirt shiny red.

"We need to go," Bianca said. A glance at Marin and Margery told her that they were ready. They'd clearly been allowed to grab some outdoor gear before they were taken from their home. Both wore coats and in Marin's case a fuzzy blue scarf that her mother had wrapped around her head.

"Yeah, we do," Mason agreed.

Bianca looked down at Kemp. He was too big. She wasn't going to be able to physically haul him to his feet. "You, stand up."

Kemp said, "I'm not going anywhere."

"He'll slow us down too much. We're better off without him." Mason glanced at Bianca. "He can hold the damned pen himself." Grabbing Kemp's hand, he brought it up to the pen and pressed it around Bianca's fingers. "Now let go," he told Bianca.

She did, slowly and carefully. Kemp slumped forward, but his hand stayed tight around the pen.

That was a relief. She flexed her hand, moved over to the cot and wiped the blood off on a blanket.

When she looked around, Mason stood by the door, which he'd opened a crack so that he could peek out. He summoned his wife and daughter with a jerk of his head. Bianca joined him, too, skirting around the hunched and panting Kemp.

Mason passed her his machine pistol. It was, Bianca saw at a glance, a Glock Model 18.

"You take point," he said.

26

It's all fun and games until the Glocks come out.

That was Bianca's thought as she moved rapidly along the hallway, sweeping the pistol from side to side in front of her in a series of defensive arcs. Warned to silence, Marin and Margery scuttled behind her, sandwiched in by Mason, who was performing the same exercise as Bianca only toward the rear.

Mason had taken a moment longer to exit the room they'd left behind than he should have. Bianca suspected that he'd spent that moment ending Kemp's life.

She didn't know. She would never ask. Instead she concentrated all her energy on doing what she could to get the four of them out of there.

Reaching the top of the stairwell, Bianca swiveled, aiming downward, clearing the steps visually before starting to descend.

The building was quiet. Too quiet. Not a sound to be heard.

No one upstairs. No one on the stairs. No one in the downstairs hall or by the east-facing outside door, where Bianca took a second to stomp her feet into boots and pull on a coat. Gloves were in the pocket. She pulled those on, too.

It was that pause that gave Bianca time to identify what was really bothering her.

"Wait," she said as Mason reached for the knob on the outside door. Solid metal, built to stop a tank. No way to see beyond it. "Groton never came upstairs."

"Groton?" Mason paused in the act of turning the knob. It was obvious he knew that name.

"He's here. Kemp spoke to him over the intercom, asked him to come upstairs. Groton never showed."

Mason's eyes narrowed.

"They know you're here. They know we're leaving. They're waiting outside." Bianca arrived at the only conclusion that made sense.

Mason's head dipped once in agreement. His hand fell away from the knob.

"What do you mean, they're waiting? What do we do?" Holding her daughter protectively close, Margery looked at Mason with open fear.

"It's going to be all right. You two are going to be all right," he told her. Wrapping an arm around her, he turned her and a now-sobbing Marin into his body for an embrace while he looked at Bianca over Margery's head. "It's me they're primarily after. I'm going to go first, create a diversion, get them coming after me. You take these two due east. There's an outbuilding about a hundred yards out. Beyond that is a stand of pines, and beyond that is a flat area where the chopper's due to land. Altogether, the distance is about three hundred and sixty yards."

Bianca nodded.

"No." Margery clutched his coat, looked up at him. "They'll kill you."

"They'll kill you, Daddy." Marin's eyes welled with tears.

"Trust me, I'm hard to kill. Go with Bianca." Mason kissed Marin, kissed Margery and stepped away from them. He looked at Bianca. "Take care of them."

She nodded. "You know I will."

He turned and let himself out the door.

"No," Margery moaned.

A burst of sustained gunfire from outside caused Marin to burst into tears.

Game on.

"Be quiet now," Bianca said to Marin. "It doesn't help to cry." Then, to Margery, "Hang on to her. When I open the door, run as fast as you can toward that outbuilding he was talking about. Take shelter behind it. I'll cover you."

The gunfire intensified. From where they stood, it sounded like fireworks on the Fourth of July.

Bianca reached for the knob, met Margery's fear-filled eyes.

"Go." Bianca pulled the door open, jumping out in front of the others into the blast of cold air as they spilled down the stairs and into the snow. The outbuilding was just where Mason had said it would be, a long, low pole barn hunkered close to the ground. She pointed toward it and they ran, leaping clumsily through the foot-deep snow. She stayed with them, positioning herself between them and the bursts of intense gunfire that rolled loud as thunder toward the front of the building, covering them with wide arcing movements of the Glock without firing a shot because she didn't want to draw attention until she had to, visually sweeping their surroundings as she ran because there was always the chance they might encounter a nasty surprise.

It was late afternoon, she could tell by the light, not quite twilight but close, and she could see the yellow flare from the muzzles of multiple weapons firing together.

From the direction of the gunfire, her father—Mason—must be heading in the exact opposite direction, due west.

It was classic misdirection. Playing hare to the hounds.

They reached the outbuilding without Bianca having to fire a shot.

"Good job. We can do this," she said to Margery and Marin as the three of them pressed up against the ice-encrusted wall of the outbuilding. It was, she saw as she peered carefully around it, a storage unit for snowmobiles, snowblowers and the like. The doors were open, and the thought of taking shelter inside was tempting.

The wind was cold, and there was no chopper in sight.

"Do you think they've killed him?" Margery asked in a high-pitched voice.

Bianca shook her head. "Hear the gunfire? As long as they're still shooting, he's fine."

"There he is. *Daddy*." Marin pointed back the way they had come. Bianca looked and saw a small dark figure running across the bottom of a slope maybe two hundred yards in front of the house. As she watched, he leaped nimbly over a snow-crusted mound, which he then proceeded to take shelter behind.

Chunks of snow blowing up around him told her how close the bullets were to finding their mark.

The sight set her teeth on edge. He wasn't her father, no blood relationship there. But feelings, she was discovering, weren't so easy to reassign.

"They shot him! They shot him!" Marin's voice took on a hysterical edge.

"*Shh*." Bianca and Margery hissed at the same time. Clapping her hand over the child's mouth and pulling her in tight against her side—if all that firepower got turned on them, they were toast—Bianca saw that Mason had, indeed, been hit. He was rolling on the ground in obvious pain, his hand clapped to his side as the snow beneath him turned dark.

"Oh, no," Margery moaned.

The bullets around Mason kept coming. He managed to return fire, edging onto his side and scooting up closer to the mound, his hand still pressed to the wound.

To Bianca, it was obvious he wasn't going to last long. As soon as the bad guys realized that he was wounded to the point of being unable to run, they would surround him and take him out.

She made a decision. Or rather, there was no decision to make.

"I need you to take your daughter and get to those trees," she said to Margery, pointing to the jagged line of tall pines slanting off down a slope about a hundred yards away. "Hide. Wait for the chopper. If it comes before I get back, get on it. Fly away."

"What are you going to do?"

"Go get him," Bianca said, and Margery nodded.

"Save my daddy." Marin looked up at Bianca, her eyes huge. Bianca nodded.

Margery grabbed Marin's hand and said, "Come on, baby, let's go."

Bianca didn't see them dart across the snow-covered field. She was already inside the outbuilding.

The nearest snowmobile had been ridden recently. No ice on the skis, traces of mud and grit on the running boards.

Hopping on, Bianca started it up and zoomed out of the building. The thing flew over the snow, bouncing over the moguls, sliding on patches of ice. Wind hit her in the face, smelling of snow, freezing her cheeks.

She reached the top of the slope, got a visual on Mason.

Guns were still going off like popcorn. That was a good sign. The noise of it might also help cover the roar of the snowmobile.

Yeah, no. Apparently not.

Ping ping ping ping.

She wasn't halfway down the slope when the bullets started slamming into the chassis.

Yowzers. She zigged. She zagged. She lay low over the handlebars. She juiced the throttle.

And she broke out the Glock 18 and started firing back.

Submachine-gun-style.

I am supersoldier, hear me roar.

Mason saw her coming and staggered to his feet, taking care to stay low against the snow-crusted mound he'd taken shelter behind. Yellow flashes from the trees to the left and from the top of the hill in front of the building told her the location of the enemy. There were a lot of them. Firing serious weapons.

She pulled up beside him in a fantail of snow.

"Get on," she cried.

No need. He was already hitching himself aboard. One arm slid tight around her waist. His weight was heavy against her back.

That told her how badly he was hit. That terrified her.

"Hang tight."

She took off, barreling back the way she had come. With his added weight, she needed both hands to steer. Mason picked up the slack, firing his weapon in intermittent bursts that nevertheless had the desired effect: it kept the pursuers back. Zigging and zagging for all she was worth, Bianca shot past the outbuilding just in time to watch a small red helicopter settle into the snow near the pines. The distinctive *whomp whomp* of the blades filled the air.

Margery and Marin were already running hand in hand toward it.

The snowmobile skidded to a stop a few feet away. Mason slid off, had to grab on to the seat to steady himself. Bianca slid off, too, to help him. He was bleeding badly, she saw, from a wound somewhere around his right hip. Blood had already soaked through the lower part of his coat. She slipped an arm around his waist. He draped an arm over her shoulders.

"Hurry," the pilot yelled.

They made it to the chopper. Marin and Margery were already on board.

"Shit." The pilot looked past them as Mason sank into the

front passenger's seat. Bianca glanced around in the direction the pilot was looking and caught her breath.

What looked like an army of pursuers advanced on them, weapons at the ready.

They were already at the far side of the outbuilding. For the moment they were holding fire.

"Mason Thayer, stay where you are," one of men in the lead yelled. "Surrender, and you won't be harmed."

Yeah, right. Liar, liar, camo pants on fire.

"They'll take us down," the pilot said.

"Go," Bianca told him and stepped back from the chopper. "I'll cover you."

Mason looked toward her. He had a hand pressed to his wound. His face was white and strained.

"Bianca—"

"You need to get them out of here. I got this," she told him.

His lips compressed. She saw acceptance in his eyes.

She made a gesture to the pilot, telling him to take off.

"Here." Mason reached down to pull something out of the foot well. He tossed it to her. It was a backpack, she saw as she caught it. "That's a SiuSiu Special, an E29."

Bianca nodded her understanding, grabbed it, pulled it on. The chopper was already starting to lift off when Mason threw her his MP5.

"Give 'em hell," he said.

She nodded, pivoted and jumped back on the snowmobile as the chopper peeled away into the sky.

The approaching army had just started to fire at the departing bird when she juiced the throttle, rocketed toward them and sprayed them with machine-gun fire.

They scattered. Machine gun rattling, she broke through the line. As she blasted past the outbuilding and down the slope, a quick glance over her shoulder told her that the chopper was safely away.

Minutes later she had a pack of snowmobiles in hot pursuit.

The snow-covered mountain was steep, craggy and dotted with outcroppings of black rock that perched like ravens in the snow. At the base of it, presumably, was the village Kemp had spoken of. But the day was growing dark, in the gloaming as the Scots called it, and Bianca increasingly doubted that she would make it safely down. She schussed to avoid crevasses, hung tight down sixty-degree chutes, skidded over patches of ice.

With a pack of—she counted—eight snowmobiles on her tail. She couldn't seem to lose them no matter how hard she tried.

Her biggest problem was, she was out of ammo.

Or at least that was what she decided when she careened down a slope, slid around a car-size rock—and found herself flying toward the edge of a cliff.

Skidding sideways, she managed to stop with feet to spare. All that separated her from disaster in the form of a black-walled fissure roughly the size of the Grand Canyon was a steep, icy slide about twenty feet long that fed right into it.

The pursuing snowmobiles surrounded her in a semicircle almost as soon as she stopped.

She didn't even bother trying to fake them out by pointing a weapon at them.

She was trapped, she knew it, and going down in a blaze of glory wasn't really her style.

They were wearing helmets. Her face was—she was surprised to discover—frozen. She hadn't noticed until now.

One of them got off his snowmobile and pulled off his helmet. He was an old man: tall, lean, gray hair.

"I'm Alex Groton," he introduced himself. "You must be Beth."

Bianca's eyes narrowed. She didn't reply.

"Unfortunate about Kemp," Groton continued. "I'm going to assume you didn't have anything to do with that."

So Kemp was dead. Well, she had expected it.

"What do you want?" she asked.

"You."

That answer was surprising enough that Bianca regarded him with wary interest.

"What do you mean?"

"I want you to come and work for us."

"Thanks, but no."

"It wasn't really a request."

"The answer's still no."

"Let me put this another way. Either you come to work for us, or—" He picked up the rifle that hung from his shoulder and pointed it at her. "I'm sure I don't have to spell it out."

"You'll kill me," Bianca said flatly.

"It doesn't have to come to that." The corners of Groton's eyes tightened impatiently. "You belong to us. We made you. Believe me, you really have no idea what you are."

Just like that, her decision was made.

"I know who I am," she said.

And she gunned the throttle, pointed her machine down the slope and flew off the icy lip into the crevasse.

A rifle blasted. The bullet passed so close to her ear she could hear it sing.

Behind her she heard someone shout, "No!" followed by the bang of another gun.

She knew that voice: Mickey.

As the snowmobile started its downward trajectory, nosing into the crevasse like a pelican homing in on a fish, she glanced over her shoulder.

He'd removed his helmet. She was too far away to see his features, but there was no mistaking his tall form or that black hair.

He was pointing a rifle at Groton, she was surprised to see.

Then she really couldn't spare any more time to think about it.

She was too busy falling to her death.

The snowmobile was showing an alarming tendency to want to cartwheel.

She flung herself free.

Mason had said it: the only way you ever get away from them is to die.

Only, she really didn't want to.

She was in free fall, plunging deep into the crevasse, when her snowmobile crashed into the far wall and exploded in a ball of fire. The *boom* echoed through the canyon. The shock of the explosion shook the air. It was the distraction she needed. Plummeting down through drifts of obscuring clouds into the enveloping darkness, she put all her faith in God. And SiuSiu.

Then pulled the rip cord on her backpack.

And watched the parachute mushroom overhead.

No way could anyone watching from above see her billowing ticket to freedom through the layers of mist.

As she floated down to earth, she smiled.

★ ★ ★ ★ ★

Acknowledgments

Writing a book is a solitary pursuit. Publishing a book requires a crackerjack team. I'm lucky enough to have one.

Many, many thanks to my agent, Robert Gottlieb, and everyone at Trident Media Group.

Many more thanks to my editor, Emily Ohanjanians, who is absolutely fabulous and did a great job on this book.

The same to Margaret Marbury and MIRA Books, for all your support and for believing.

And finally, heaping helpings of gratitude to my readers. You're the best!